MASTER
OF
SECRETS

SHANNON
McKENNA

OLIVERHEBERBOOKS

CHAPTER 1

Ethan

The elevator doors slid open near the reception desk, where a tall, stacked blonde with a headset was bent gracefully at the waist, poking at buttons on the phone console.

Regal posture. Endless legs. Amazing ass.

Wow.

I wrenched my attention back to Hugh Clemens, who was blocking the elevator door with his broad, bulky frame and shifted discreetly sideways for another glimpse of the blonde. Suddenly unable to focus on whatever Hugh was yapping about.

Hugh was easy to tune out, but I'd been more or less distracted ever since Shane's abduction, and my little sister, Freya's recent near-death experience hadn't helped matters. Lately, my brain had been stuck on the setting of constantly evaluating potential threats. Filtering out what was irrelevant to survival, or else obsessing over trivial things, like the fact that Hugh's deodorant was not working, and neither was his mouthwash.

I didn't know Hugh Clemens that well, hadn't seen him in years, but I bitterly regretted having agreed to this meeting. I vaguely remembered the guy had always talked too much, but today the verbal fire hose was unrelenting, and his eyes seemed to be bulging out of his head. It was only 9:28. Too early in the day for that much nervous tension. As if Hugh was scared about something. Or high, maybe. Odd.

"...opportunity to partner with such an innovative thinker! Everyone wants to be on your wavelength, you know what I mean?"

"Ah, yeah. Right," I said. "I look forward to meeting your team."

And to getting off the damn elevator. But Hugh was still blocking me.

"They want to grill you about the Masters Effect," Hugh rattled on. "One of my engineers read about you in *Wired* and he says to me, didn't you go to business school with that guy? Aren't you supposed to exploit those contacts? Call him! So, I say to him, hell yeah, you are so fucking right!" Hugh planted a meaty hand over the elevator door to keep it from closing.

I let out a silent sigh. My fight-or-flight system should relax. The only danger Hugh posed to me was the very real possibility of boring me to death. Which is why I'd left my security detail outside, until after this meeting. The last thing I wanted to do was explain my complicated corporate security issues to a bloviating gasbag like Hugh Clemens.

"...just need to make a quick stop here, so I can tell the girl to forward my messages down to the conference room on the eleventh floor," Hugh said. "And I need to run into my office to pick up the project specs. Why don't you just go on down to the eleventh floor right now? I'll tell Mitch and Follett to meet you when you get off the elevator and they can take you to the conference room and start showing you the plans."

Yes. Please. A moment alone. Beautiful idea. "Sure, no problem."

Hugh headed into the reception area, and a burbling sound hit my ears. It was a fake waterfall pattering into a mosaic tile pool, competing with the buzzy hum of the pump that cycled the water.

Then I caught the blonde's scent, wafting over to me. It wiped my brain as if I'd been tased.

I acted on raw impulse. Stuck out my hand, blocked the elevator door an instant before it closed, and followed Hugh back out into the reception area.

Hugh looked baffled, and alarmed. "Ethan? Hey. You were going on down to the conference room, right? I was just calling Mitch to meet you down there. Uh...Ethan?"

That scent. It pulled me. Sweet, but subtle. No perfume, just shower soap and shampoo and warm, nameless female pheromones that pumped primitive awareness through my body.

Whoa. Lust, mixed with my current whacked-out hyper-vigilance, was a wild combination. I was staring at her. Blatantly. Hungrily. Like a fucking caveman.

Stop that shit. Act civilized. Come on. Seize control, bonehead.

She was long and lithe and strong-looking. Crisp white blouse and snug wool skirt, cut to fit her fantastic curves. Thick, straight hair, chopped off jaggedly below the chin. Minimal makeup, which left her skin smooth and glowing. Full, soft pink mouth. Her blue-green eyes had long, sooty lashes. Straight, well-defined dark brows.

I shifted my briefcase to the other hand to discreetly mask the effect she was having on my body, and stood there at a loss. Belatedly remembering I'd agreed to go somewhere, do something. With Hugh, ahead of Hugh, what had I said I would do?

Fuck it. Not now.

Not yet.

CHAPTER 2

Kat

I'd had a strange feeling about this gig from the start. I'd pulled some really spectacular duds as an office temp in my time, but never one like this. From the moment the office manager got all sphincter-mouthed and tense when I asked about a closet for my coat and a fridge to stow my plastic tub of leftovers-for-lunch, I'd been uneasy.

No, the woman had said, all snippy-like, *"Keep your things under your desk."*

Hmph. Not a good sign.

As soon as I was left alone, I'd walked out of the reception area with its ridiculous, energy-sucking fountain, headed back to the office section, and found it empty. Monumentally empty. Unused desks. Empty cubicles. No computer equipment. Funereal silence. A quarter of the high-rise building's floor was deserted. Clemens & Associates did not exist, at least not here. And yet, a waterfall gurgled cheerfully in that lobby. I was manning phones for an army of ghosts.

Was C&A a front for a shady business of some kind? Some money-laundering operation? I *so* did not want to come to the attention of the law. Or even worse, the media. Not with that murdering son-of-a-bitch Tony Petruzzi scheduled to walk out of prison any time now. The idea of making the news, for any reason, made my guts cramp.

Maybe I should just walk right out of here. Right now, without a word to anyone.

The office manager hadn't even briefed me on my duties. She'd just bustled in, looking harassed, and told me to answer the phones. Nothing else. She'd signed the authorization form for the temp agency, and then scurried away. No instructions on fielding calls. No names to take messages for. No friendly chitchat. No hints or clues.

Fine, whatever. They paid me by the hour, and the form was already signed.

But still, it bugged me to just sit by a silent phone until my ass went numb. I'd gotten up early, put on mascara and heels and dragged myself in here on time, with brains and energy and good sense to trade for my hourly wage—and for what? I'd rather type, file, photocopy, even fetch coffee for somebody rather than just sit here idle.

No sense getting worked up about it. I needed to make rent for the martial arts school, and fix the latest water damage, since the landlord wouldn't. And get glasses for Charlotte, a fourth grader in my Stand Up For Yourself class. Charlotte was flunking out because she couldn't see the blackboard at school, or read without getting headaches.

Eyes on the prize, Banner. If some dumbass wanted to pay me to sit in front of a silent phone, sit I would. That was the price I continually had to pay for not getting a "real" job. Not that the martial arts school wasn't real. It just wasn't real in a financial sort of way. Not yet.

Thinking about the school made me restless, so I got up to pace the room. No one was here to see or care and just sitting there made me twitch and drum my fingers.

A minute later, the elevator door pinged. *Shit.* I lunged for the desk.

The door opened to reveal two men talking in the elevator. I leaned over and punched buttons on the phone console in a vain attempt to look as if I had something to do, then glanced up...

And kept on looking. No, not just looking. Gawking.

The object of my gawk gazed calmly back as he followed the other guy out of the elevator. I just stood there. His dark, penetrating gaze pinned me to the spot.

I couldn't move.

Panic stabbed through me. What the hell? This wasn't me. I never froze. That just didn't happen, not after that fateful day years ago, with Raffi and Gabri and Tony. That experience had wired me up to react instinctually. No time for thought. I always kept my cool, had fast reflexes, made rapid-fire choices.

That was why I was still breathing.

After years of intense martial arts study, I was highly sensitive to the quality of energy moving in a person's body, and the big guy vibrated with it. His body was broad, thickly muscled but still graceful and well-proportioned in his sleek tailored suit. The power of his sheer physical presence raised all my short hairs and made my toes tighten.

His face was rough-hewn. Long, narrow, with heavy brows and a strong, aquiline nose. Not pretty-boy at all. I liked that. And the sun wrinkles around those deep, dark eyes. Strong cheekbones, deep-carved seams around his mouth.

Which deepened as he smiled. I heard it almost as if he were saying it out loud. *Go ahead and stare. They all do.*

Someone was talking, but my brain was too occupied to decode the sound into words. This was ridiculous. I had to cough. Look up. Look down. Do anything.

The good-looking guy's gaze flicked to the shorter guy, and I belatedly realized the short guy was addressing his words to me.

"...even awake?" Short Guy was glaring, his puffy face red. "Hello? Are you connected?" He waved his hand sarcastically in front of my face. "Anybody home in there, blondie?"

Blondie? "Yes," I said coolly.

"Well, glad to hear it. As I was just saying, we'll be meeting in the conference room down on the eleventh floor with the engineering team, since the conference room on this floor is booked up, so forward all my calls down there. Got it?"

Conference room, *booked?* That conference room didn't even have a freaking table or chairs! Whatever weird shit was happening here today, I wanted no part of it.

The guy blathered on, his voice fake-hearty. "Okay, Ethan. We're done here. I'll see you downstairs."

Ethan. Hmmm. The sex god's name was Ethan. I liked the name Ethan.

"I'll head on down." The big guy's deep voice moved over my senses like warm, silky fur. He gave me a long, hungry look, and smiled.

I gathered my wits, and addressed Short Guy. "Excuse me, sir. Could I have your name?"

Short Guy froze, then turned to me slowly. His face had deepened to faint purplish red. "My name?" His voice was menacing.

"Yes," I said blankly. "So I know who to forward messages to."

He leaned over the desk, and his sour breath blasted in my face. I had to rock backward to avoid physical contact with him.

"Turn around," he said. "See that name? Gold letters? On the wall behind you?"

I ventured a quick glance. Clemens & Associates. "Um, yeah. And so?"

"Can you read?" Another blast of his hot, stale breath made me gag.

Seriously? Outrage stacked the vertebrae in my spine to absolute verticality. I lifted my chin and declined to reply, letting my eyes say it for me. *Asshole.*

"My name is Clemens. Not that you'll need it. Because you're fired." He turned to the door. "Julia!" he bawled. "Get out here right away!"

The office manager scurried out promptly. "Mr. Clemens? Is there a problem?"

Clemens waved his hand in my direction. "Get rid of this one immediately. There's no place in my organization for idiots."

"Idiot?" I leaped to my feet, sending the chair rolling back to hit the wall with a thud. "Mister, I just *met* you! What the hell is your problem?"

"Please get your things and leave, miss." The office manager's voice was shrill with tension. "We don't want any scenes. Just go, right now."

Clemens patted the shoulder of the tall guy, who was watching me with what appeared to be intense fascination. "Go on downstairs, Ethan," he said. "Sorry you had to see that. Just a little housecleaning."

"My ass!" I leaned to retrieve my coat and purse. "I am not the problem! This place is messed up!"

"Watch what you say," Clemens warned.

"Why should I?" I asked him. "What are you going to do? Fire me again?"

Clemens glared at me as I slung my shoulder-strap across my chest to secure my purse, as was my custom. Ready to run or fight at all times. Out came the athletic shoes, swathed in plastic and stowed in my big purse for the self-same reason.

The two men waited and watched in charged silence as I sat back down, tugged on my first shoe, and pulled the laces nice and tight. Not hurrying in the least, because fuck them. Let them sweat and fidget and wait for me to finish.

"You could do that outside, you know," Clemens growled.

"Maybe I could, but I won't," I said evenly, double knotting carefully. "I'll do it...right...here."

"Ethan, go on down," Clemens urged. "Mitch and Follett are waiting for you."

"And miss the floorshow?" he murmured. "Hell, no."

Floorshow? He thought this was *funny?* I knotted my second shoe with an angry jerk, looked up, and almost lost myself in those dark, gorgeous eyes again.

"I am not here for your entertainment, buddy," I told him.

"Of course not. Excuse me." He lifted his hand in salute to Clemens and Julia, and strolled out to the elevator banks.

I realized, to my utter chagrin, that I had to follow him, that being the only exit from this place, aside from twenty-seven flights of stairs. Right after being insulted, fired, and publicly humiliated right in front of him. Sweet. Just stellar.

I tossed my coat over my arm and marched out. The elevator door was opening right now, and no way was I waiting for the next one while those blithering jerks gave me the hairy eyeball.

Too bad I was too rattled to try flirting with him. Flirting was hard for me in the best of times. I was clumsy as hell at it. I wasn't likely to get lucky with it today, the way things were going so far.

"Hey! That elevator is for my associate! You wait for the next one!" Clemens lunged after me and grabbed me by the arm.

I wrested my arm out of his sweaty grip and pushed him, hard.

My shove sent him reeling backward, fighting for balance. I yanked one of my high-heeled shoes out of my bag. "Touch me again, and you get this heel right through your eye," I warned.

Clemens stumbled black, blinking frantically. "You crazy bitch! I'm calling security!"

Ethan held the elevator door open. "I'll share, Hugh." There was laughter in his voice. "In the interests of saving your eyesight. Or maybe your life."

He leaned out, and effortlessly scooped me into the elevator. I stayed right there, in the circle of his arms, astonished. For one...two...three seconds.

What the fuck had just happened? That was...unprecedented.

He'd touched me without warning, and I hadn't exploded into automatic defense mode. My few male friends had learned, to their cost, not to touch me without fair warning. I needed to clench my teeth, breathe deep, brace myself for the contact. Or else it turned into a bad scene, with bruises, torn ligaments, hurt feelings.

And this guy had just grabbed me and pulled me, out of nowhere. He had practically embraced me. And I hadn't slugged or elbowed or kicked or torqued or chopped or finger-stabbed him at all. Nothing.

The elevator doors began to close.

"Hey!" Clemens trotted forward, hands up. "No! Ethan! Wait—"

The doors shut in his face.

CHAPTER 3

Ethan

The gorgeous blonde edged away from me.

Fine, no problem. I was cool with whatever she wanted. In any case, hearing that stunning Amazon babe threaten Hugh Clemens with mayhem had already improved the quality of my day by a factor of ten.

I hit "L" on the panel for her. "That was interesting," I ventured.

She shrugged. "Nice way of putting it," she said. "Depends on your point of view, I guess. Are you sure you're safe in here? All alone in an elevator with the psycho receptionist from hell?"

I grinned at her, realizing it had been a while since my face muscles had performed that function for me. They were stiff and rusty at it. "I think I can survive for a couple minutes in the elevator with a disgruntled employee."

She let out a sharp laugh. "Disgruntled, my ass. Totally confused is more like it. I'm a temp, and it was my first day! My first few minutes, for God's sake. I hadn't even figured out how the phone system worked yet. I'd never seen that dickwad in my entire life, and he gets his panties in a twist because I don't automatically guess he's the boss? I'm supposed to intuit his name with no introduction? I really don't think it's me this time. I swear to God, I don't."

"No, certainly not," I murmured soothingly.

"Maybe I shouldn't have threatened him with violence," she conceded. "But he asked for it when he grabbed my arm. That was way out of line."

"By all means," I said blandly.

Her golden gaze raked me up and down. "I am in no mood to be condescended to, or made fun of."

"Got it. I'm not, absolutely. I want to keep both my eyes."

She waved her hand. "Oh, stop it," she muttered. "That bonehead had it coming." She fished a smartphone out of her big shoulder bag and peeked at it. "Text from the temp agency. I think I'll let that one cool off before I touch it."

"Good instinct," I agreed.

She crossed her arms over her chest, shaking her head. She looked baffled. "Wow," she murmured. "You know, I've been fired before, but I've never pissed off my boss to the point of no return that quickly. I mean, whoa. Five minutes. That's a personal best."

"Congratulations," I offered.

That earned me a glare, but I just grinned back, all innocence.

She smiled, a little reluctantly. "Sorry for babbling about it," she said. "It's not your problem. Or your business, for that matter."

"Don't apologize." I held out his hand. "Ethan Masters."

She hesitated for a second before putting out her hand. "Katrin Banner," she said. "I go by Kat."

My hand enveloped hers. Excitement pumped through me. Hers was warm and strong, and had callouses on it. Interesting.

The energy of the contact throbbed through me, straight to the party spot.

She actually blushed. She felt it, too. That was good.

In a normal universe, I'd get her number on the spot. Better yet, I'd pin her down for brunch, this very day. I knew for a fact she didn't have any plans today. So...maybe a luxury hotel, the most extravagant suite. Deluxe room service. I'd wine her, dine her, find out all about her—at least, whatever she was willing to tell me. I was willing to bet she wouldn't let anyone too close. She had a wild streak. That much was clear.

At the moment, she was ignoring me, watching the floor numbers go down swiftly on the digital screen. Another chance to admire her as my fantasy took form.

We'd share a good meal, and then I'd have her for dessert. For hours. The erotic images strobed wildly in my brain, full of intense sensory detail. Her thick, dark gold hair, crazy and mussed on the pillow, her long, strong legs wrapped around my back. Her face and lips and breasts damp and rosy, sobbing for breath as I rode her with my dick. Making her writhe and buck and come, wailing, against my mouth. And then again. And again. Every way we could think of.

My face was getting hot. Sweat pooled between my shoulder blades. I had to chill before I let my crew see me. A van full of Unredeemables were patiently circling the block, because I was on a lethal criminal's hit list, along with the rest of my family, who were all potential hostages.

Which meant that coming on to the smoking-hot fiery blonde temp was irresponsible, stupid, and selfish as fuck. I had to do the right thing, and stop this shit right now.

The elevator jolted, shuddered, and stopped. We shot each other wary glances in the sudden silence.

"Really?" she muttered. "Great. To make my joy complete."

Their cab was stuck between floors twenty-one and twenty.

"Don't worry," I said. "It's not really broken. I just willed it to stop with my mind."

Her mouth curved. "Why would you do a silly thing like that?"

"Because I don't want to get out." The words flew out, and already, I was kicking myself for flirting. But it was impossible to resist. I'd actually made her smile, and I sensed that winning a smile from this woman was a real triumph. It lit me up like a pinball machine, wheels twirling, lights flashing, bells going *ding-a-ding-ding.*

She gave me a considering look. "Your stop is seventeen, right?"

I nodded, reluctantly.

"So..." She bit her lip. "Here's a solution. Meet me for coffee, when you're done with what you're doing. The Hava Cuppa Joe two blocks south. My treat."

Aw, *fuck.* Kill me now. Just shove the knife in and give it a good three-sixty, why didn't she. Her cautious smile froze...and then faded.

"Or not," she said tightly.

"Shit," I muttered. "I'm sorry, but—"

"Don't be. Forget I said it. Please." Her face had gone red.

It had been a big deal for her to make that offer, which made me feel like shit. Mostly because I'd lured her into it myself. "My life is complicated right now—"

"Married?"

"No, I'm—"

"Otherwise engaged. Understood. Let it go. It would be madness to have a highly caffeinated beverage with the whacko receptionist from hell, even if your life weren't complicated. You barely escaped with your life. To say nothing of your eyes."

Keeping it light. Tough babe. But somehow, the brave face she put on hurt me even worse. I could've kicked in the elevator door, I was so frustrated. Having a mouthwatering treat dangled in front of my face, and then having it snatched away.

The elevator lurched, and started moving again.

She gave me a crooked little smile. "That was me," she said. "I did that. With my mind. Since we're all done here."

Fucked if we were. The elevator slid open on the twentieth floor. A herd of people waited to get on. And I was sulking so hard, I couldn't even smile at her joke.

The assholes crowding onto the elevator annoyed me. There were too damn many of them, and they were crowding unnecessarily into Kat's personal space. She shrank back into the corner, away from them. And me.

The last guy was talking into his smartphone as he got on. "...too bad," he was saying, in a low voice. "You had your chance to manage the situation. You didn't. We're moving forward, so get going on the damage control." The guy cut off the call, pocketed the phone, and checked out Kat's legs.

That appraising glance pissed me off. Who the fuck did he think he was?

One big guy had muscled his way between the two of us. A real bruiser. My neck prickled unpleasantly. I edged the interloper firmly out of the way, reclaiming my place near Kat and earning myself a dirty look in the process.

I abruptly decided to accompany her down to the lobby. Maybe even tell my crew to give her a ride home. Though she was sure to refuse.

My hands clenched angrily, closing on nothing.

CHAPTER 4

Kat

I ignored the crowd of guys in the elevator, my mind completely taken up with wondering what the hell had gotten into me. What the hell was that, anyway? Coming on to a complete stranger with half a mind to take him home for an afternoon's mindless physical enjoyment? Whoa. It was a crazy idea. Though it would definitely soothe my nerves after the shock of Hugh Clemens' humiliating rant.

Sex. Sure. Why not. Who could resist me, the seductive hellcat with all the hot, sexy moves?

Ethan Masters, that's who. Of course, he'd be married, engaged, whatever. At least he was principled and honest about it. I granted him three measly points for that, exactly three, and then immediately took away two of them for indiscriminate flirting. That bad, slutty bastard.

I was so busy stressing about Ethan, there was a short, distracted delay before I started to put my finger on the many things that were wrong with this picture. My attention was fragmented by his nearness. But the mechanism kicked in eventually.

When the elevator shuddered to a grinding stop once again, it hit me, all at once.

A cold, dark hole opened up inside me. Those guys. The other passengers. Too uniformly similar. All big and bulky, all about the same age, all men.

And after a first, cursory glance, none of them had looked at me at all.

No fucking way.

Men usually did. That was just how it was, which was why I usually went around in jeans and a hooded sweatshirt. But these guys weren't looking at me. Not a single one of them was. And a charge was building in the air. I felt that invisible pressure gauge right on my skin, nudging up, up, up.

That murdering slimebag Tony Petruzzi had found me at last. Or his father had, or his brothers, since he was still supposed to be in jail. Maybe some photos had slipped through onto social media after our last championship tournament, and made their way back to the Petruzzis somehow.

I should have been more careful not have the girls win so often. I should have made sure they didn't draw too much attention to themselves, and by reflex, to me.

Problem was, they rocked. And it was so good for their self-esteem.

Ego. It'll bite you in the ass every time. I scolded myself for it inwardly as I whipped off the shoulder strap of my purse, psyching myself up for what was coming.

Bring them on. I'd been training for over half my life for this, after all. It had to happen sometime. In some ways, it would be a relief to get it the fuck over with.

I'd go after those grunting bastards like a screaming harpy from hell, and either I'd win, or they'd kill me. And it would finally be over.

But I was truly sorry Ethan had gotten mixed up in my bad karma. That was a massive bummer. I would try like hell to protect him, but I was up against a flipping crap-ton of giant thugs, who probably had plenty of training of their own. I was good, yes. Very good. But nobody was that good.

I flexed my hands, softened my knees, breathed very deep, getting into that still place. Warrior zone. I tried to catch Ethan's eye to give him a heads-up, but he was frowning off into infinity, right over the other guys' heads. Being taller than all of them.

I let the coat and purse drop to the floor just as I caught the movement reflected in the shiny elevator wall. A black cylinder, slowly emerging from the sleeve of the guy next to Ethan. A shock baton. Seriously? Fuck them all.

I yelled as the baton flashed up, and exploded into violent movement.

A swift, mindless sequence; *chop*, at the arm with the baton, a punch to the face, a swerve to evade the other guy coming at me—

A blur, then a loud, wet *crunch*. Ethan had smashed the guy's head against the wall. A splotch of blood marked the big dent in the metal wall as he slid down. Then Ethan jerked back, seized the foot whipping up toward his face. Twist, flip, an elbow to the head, then a vicious kick to the side of the guy's knee. Wow.

I didn't have time to admire his form, since I was blocking the blackjack flashing down. Ethan's savage uppercut knocked the guy back, pinwheeling. I dodged a roundhouse swing from a big gorilla arm, but it still snapped across the end of my nose. I just barely blocked the knee to my gut. *Oof*, the man's bulk slammed me to the wall, knocking the breath right out of my lungs.

A heavy thud, a grunt, and the pressure abruptly eased. The guy gasped, clawing at his throat and gurgling as Ethan launched him into the onslaught of the other three men. Who knew. Ethan was a total ass-kicking berserker maniac. *Yes.*

Now we were fighting back-to-back, covering each other, as

if we'd trained together for years. When I caught his eye, every glance was loaded with wordless data that could only be decoded by a body in violent motion.

The other guys came on. I kicked and spun, blocked and whirled, grinning with fierce animal joy at the awesome rush of it. The synergy of joining forces with someone and feeling the power swell, bigger than the sum of the parts.

Ethan took a blow to the face, and hit the wall. His opponent bellowed as I smashed a kick into his thigh. Then the biggest guy locked his meaty arm across Ethan's throat for terrifying seconds until Ethan fought free, wrenching the guy's arm down. He whipped his leg up in a vicious front kick to the head of the thug coming at me, knocking him forward. I followed up with an elbow strike to the back of the asshole's skull, and down he went.

Then the choking sounds made my head whip around. Ethan, in a neck hold again. Same motherfucker.

I scooped up the fallen stun baton. Stabbed it into the neck of the guy holding Ethan. *Bzzzzzz.*

Ethan wrenched out of his grip as the stunned man staggered, and fell, writhing. He delivered a swift, businesslike blow to the guy's face for good measure.

Neutralized. All of them. Silence fell in the elevator.

Ethan hunched over, hands on his knees, panting. Then he looked up, and stared straight at me, his dark eyes glowing hot and fierce with fighting energy, as if seeing me for the first time.

There was a gun in his hand. What the *hell*? A SIG P226. I hadn't noticed it beneath his expensively tailored suit.

"Holy fuck," he said, still panting. "That was intense."

"Yeah," I said, still gazing at him in wonder. "Agreed."

"You are hell on wheels." His voice was admiring. "You blow my mind."

I looked at the tangle of unconscious, bleeding men on the floor. Bewildered. "Thanks, I guess." My voice was shaky.

Ethan's eyes sharpened as the elevator shuddered to life, and started descending again. He looked up at the lights, stabbing at the buttons. They did not respond.

The only button lit up was a sub-basement parking garage.

He hit something on his wrist, hidden beneath his cuff, and barked into it.

"Mick," he said. "I'm under attack. Heading down to elevator bank number three, second sub-basement, parking garage level. Move. And watch out." His arm dropped as he looked me over. "Your nose is bleeding," he said.

I reached up, felt sticky fluid on my lips. Tasted the salty tang. "Yours, too," I told him. I grabbed my dropped purse and ransacked it for the tissues I kept in there. "Want some?" I plucked out several and handed a wad to him.

He swiped at his bloody face with it, managing a split-lip smile before he tossed it. He kicked one guy away from the wall, shoving him out into the middle of the elevator. "Okay, Kat. We didn't select the parking garage. Someone's controlling these elevators externally, and that someone is not our friend. We're almost there. Get behind me and be ready to do whatever you need to do when the doors open. You ready?"

I got behind him, wobbling as I picked my way over the tangle of fallen fuckheads. I wasn't ready, of course, but who in life ever was? You just did stuff whenever you had to freaking do it.

I took a deep breath. "All set," I said to his back.

"That's my girl," he murmured.

"Don't call me girl," I told him crisply. "Don't call me yours, either."

Ethan's laughter cut off as the doors slid open.

CHAPTER 5

Ethan

Four men, heavily armed and dismayed to see me still on my feet.

Fuck them all. I opened fire, straight to center mass. The sound echoed endlessly against the parking garage's concrete walls and floors. Two of them staggered back but didn't go down. A third took one in the thigh and hit the ground, cursing.

Body armor. Kat and I didn't have that advantage.

I felt Kat duck and flinch as return fire pocked the smooth reflective metal of the back wall of the elevator. The goons scrambled for the cover of their van.

I leaned out and aimed for the driver. He fired, and a white starburst appeared in the window. Bulletproof glass. *Shit.* Ten shots left.

I aimed for the tires and jerked back as a bullet hit the back of the elevator, leaving another dimple. Their van surged, screeched around the corner, and shuddered to a halt behind a huge concrete column.

I punched the button on the handheld. "Mick! Where the fuck are you?"

"Trying to find you! We had to circle the whole complex and the traffic is fucking us up! Shoulda gone in with you, goddammit!"

"Just hurry," I snarled.

A gun barrel poked around the concrete column. I aimed for the spot. Fired.

The bullet gouged a hole in the concrete, ricocheted and smashed a nearby BMW's window. Glass shattered, tinkling. The guy who'd taken one in the leg was dragging himself, crawling on one knee, leaving a blood smear on the long slog to the concrete column where the others lurked. They hadn't waited for him. They weren't laying down any covering fire for him, either.

I edged out of the elevator, pulling Kat behind me, gesturing for her to bend double. A square of heavy concrete dividers separated the space in front of the elevators from the roadway. I pushed her down beside one, pressing her flat to the ground.

"Keep your head down," I told her. "And don't move from there!"

"Where the hell are you going?"

"To the guy crawling on the ground. I want to talk to him."

"About what? They'll fucking shoot you! Dude!"

I shook my head. "They could have done that in the elevator. They didn't. I'm no good to them dead."

"You? What the hell do they want with *you*?"

No time to explain SmokeScreen, or Shane, or the fucking hellscape my life had become since those assholes had kidnapped my younger brother.

Yeah, those pricks needed what was in my mind, so they wanted me alive. But by running out there with no body armor, I was betting my skin on it.

Still, knowing who had hired this particular pack of clowns, if it was Nicole, if it was someone else—that would be a fresh lead. And I was really fucking desperate for one of those.

A mechanical noise pulsed rhythmically behind me. I glanced back, and saw the elevator was opening, trying to close...opening, closing, again and again.

A foot protruded from the door, blocking it.

I crept out, away from the concrete barrier, bent low—

"Behind you!" Kat yelled.

I hit the ground. Kat lunged, exposing herself, and grabbed my arm, hauling me back to relative safety as bullets punched into the walls and shattered the car windows. She reached beneath the car we crouched behind, and held up a small dart.

"Tranq dart," she said. "Someone circled around behind us. I saw his feet under the cars. Stay here, Ethan, or they'll take you down."

I stared at her. How the hell did she recognize a tranq dart?

She held it out to me, and I slid it into my jacket, still speechless.

An engine roared. Someone was taking the spiraling ramp down into the underground garage at reckless speed. The van was armored, with gun ports on the sides and back. Take that, you pussy motherfuckers.

Mick squealed to a halt, the van angled to provide maximum cover. The door slid wide. "Come on!" Trey leaned out, beckoning to us, brandishing an M-15.

I pulled Kat to her feet. She squawked as I heaved her up inside the van and into Trey's grasp. "I'm grabbing that guy whose feet are sticking out of the elevator for questioning, so cover me—"

Another burst of machine gun fire punched volleys of bullets into the side of the van. I dropped to the ground while Shelby returned fire, then Trey reached down to haul me inside, too. Glass from shattered car windshields was glittering everywhere.

"We need to go," Mick said grimly. "The cops will cordon us in when they get here, and we'll be stuck down here with those sewer rats."

I cast a longing glance at the elevator, its door still patiently opening and closing on the unconscious guy's ankles. "Fuck," I hissed under my breath.

"Yeah." Mick's gaze raked Kat's disheveled figure with keen interest. "What's with the blonde?"

"Later." Another burst of bullets. Starburst scars suddenly marred the windshield. One, two...three bullet marks. *Bam.* Four.

I made my call, and barked the order. "*Go!*"

The van surged forward, bullets thudding into the armor plating.

Trey took his place at the other gun port, bracing himself as he peered through the sight. I sank down next to Katrin. She was on the floor, face smeared with dried blood, wide eyes darting from one man to another. She looked more frightened in here than she had outside. Or in the elevator.

"What in the hell is all this?" she demanded. "Who *are* these people?"

Now we were out of the garage, and careening out onto the street. "Are they coming after us?" I called up to Mick.

"Not that I can see," Mick replied. "You want the helipad, right?"

"Oh hell, yeah."

Mick's sudden acceleration into a turn shoved her back against me, and I put my arm around her to steady her. She pushed me away. There were bloody scrapes on her arms and legs. Drops of blood stained her white shoes. Her blouse was ripped open, buttons missing. She didn't seem to know it was open, revealing a white demi bra that cradled amazing tits.

I glanced around. All but Mick, who was driving, swiftly looked away.

Kat inhaled sharply and started fumbling with her shirt. She held it together, crossing the sides at her waist with shaky, bloodied fingers.

"What the hell just happened?" she forced out, through chattering teeth.

"It's complicated," I said.

"So...so those guys were after you, then? Not me?"

I puzzled over that for a second. "Huh? You? Why? What, is there a contract out on your life, or something?"

She stared at me blankly for a moment, eyes frozen wide, and then started to laugh. Tears started running down her face. She wiped them angrily away, smearing blood on her own cheek. "Oh, God," she muttered. "This is so fucked up."

"Agreed," I said. "An absolute shitshow. I'm so sorry. Try to calm down."

"Why should I? What the hell is going on? Why are those thugs after you, and what is...all this?" She gestured at the van, the men in it. "Your own personal army, complete with armored vehicles and gunports? Dude. What the *fuck* is your deal?"

"I'll explain it all when we get to my—"

"I'm not going anywhere with you!"

"Kat—"

"Let me out! Right here would be just fine. *Right. Here.*"

I took a deep breath, braced himself for who the fuck knew what. "No."

She jerked away from me, ignoring the staring men as she tried to stay upright and not slide wildly around in the speeding van. "What do you mean, no? Am I a prisoner now?"

"No, goddamn it," I said. "I'm assuming a lot of the guys we fought in the elevator are still alive. They all got a good long look at you. So did the building security cameras. They can run those feeds through facial recognition software, match your face to your driver's license. They'll know who you are, and they'll come for you."

"Why should they?" she yelled. "I have nothing to do with you! Nothing! I don't know you! I just got into a freaking elevator with you!"

"Yeah, but if you were one of them, and you saw us fighting together like we did, would you believe we had never met? That you had nothing to do with me? Would you think that for one single goddamn instant, if you had half a brain?"

Kat slapped me. Hard. I was so focused on her face, I barely flinched. Fuck, I barely noticed. I just kept staring.

Her eyes were wide and bright with the awful realization of the trap she had walked into. Her mouth worked. "But —but I—"

"You can't just get out," I said. "Not an option. Not anymore. Sorry."

Kat held up her hand. "You can't kidnap me. That's what this is, if you don't let me out."

Mick made another hard turn, and I slid right into her once again. I tried to brace myself with my legs, to hold myself in place and give her more space. "I don't see it that way," I said.

"I don't care how you see it!" She tried to wiggle away, but there was no place to go. "You can't do this!"

"I just did," I said.

The guys tried, elaborately, to look at anything but me and Kat as the van descended into relative dimness of the parking garage below the building and rumbled to a stop. Shelby unfastened the reinforced steel door and slid it open.

Kat struggled to her feet, batting away my helping hand, and leaped out of the van. "Thanks for the ride. I'll be on my way now."

I grabbed her from behind. "Wait," I said. "Just hold on. Let's talk about this."

"Let go of me, you son of a bitch!" She twisted wildly as I

tightened my grip, marching her out through the echoing parking garage and toward yet another elevator.

When the elevator doors slid closed on us, she exploded. It was all I could do to hold on to her without injuring her during the long ride up. The other guys shrank back and gave us as much space as possible, while pretending not to watch.

"Need any help there?" Mick asked finally, over her grunts and shrieks.

"Nope," I said, grimly patient. "I've got this."

"You've got nothing, you arrogant piece of shit!" Her legs jackknifed and Trey dodged back just in time to avoid getting kicked in the face.

The elevator opened into a room on the edge of the helipad. The chopper was ready and roaring, rotor blades churning air.

The other men ran out to it, but Kat planted her feet and shot me a horrified look, her eyes huge and betrayed. The chopper's wind coming through the open door made her hair swirl and snap around her face.

"I saved your sorry ass up there today, Ethan Masters," she yelled. "You'd be stone dead or duct-taped to a chair if it wasn't for me! And this is how you repay me?"

"Yeah, that's right. I won't let you get killed for your trouble. Call me selfish."

I pulled her toward the door again—and pain exploded in my jaw, rocking my head back.

She'd sucker punched me. A swift, vicious uppercut beneath the chin.

With that, we were at it again, full on. I was blocking blows that came thick and fast. Fuck. Bad conditions for fighting. The woman had just saved my life. I'd be damned if I'd hurt her, in any way. Not a fucking hair on her head.

But I wasn't letting her go, either. So it was tricky.

My guys were already strapped into the chopper and leaning forward to enjoy the show through the open door by the time I finally wrestled her down onto the cold concrete floor. I was using my body weight to pin her down, and blocking her arms. She was still arching and heaving under me. Damn, she was strong. My nose was streaming with blood from that punch.

I made a few adjustments and rolled us around, keeping her clamped between my legs, her back to my front, my legs wound tightly around hers, her arms wrapped around her waist, wrists immobilized by my hands.

I held her tense, straining body, tasting my own blood, and tried not to imagine how it would feel to have that lithe, graceful body writhing beneath me in bed. That was a sleazy thought to entertain while a woman was screaming obscenities at me.

I could have held her like that forever. Tired as I was, touching her made primitive show-her-who's-boss hormones flood my system. Some instinct that impelled me. Strength was imperative. Not to hurt or control her, but just to reassure her that she was safe inside the circle of my arms. That it was worth her while to stay there.

Shit, what was I thinking? Sexual fantasies, while swallowing blood and trying to keep my balls from getting crushed by the violently athletic warrior maiden.

I must have a secret kinky side that I'd never known about.

She was trembling violently. Maybe a panic attack. God knows, she was entitled to one, after what just happened. Or maybe she hated flying. My best guess was that she simply hated being pushed around. I got it. We had that in common.

Her blouse was gaping again. I tried not to peek as I situated my mouth right at her ear. "Relax, Kat."

That set her off again. We were both soaked with sweat. My heart was going at a pounding gallop and not just from the effort of immobilizing her. My post-combat hard-on was prodding her ass. Nothing I could do about that, under the circumstances.

"I hate doing this to you," I said into her ear. "But if you want to be treated like a human being and not an unbroken horse, then take a deep breath and *chill*."

A fresh, racking shudder went through her.

"Listen to me." I put my lips right against the glowing pink warmth of her ear again. "You saved my life and I'm grateful. I'm in awe of you. I worship at your goddamn shrine. I would never hurt you. Not in a million years. I'm taking you someplace safe. You have nothing to fear from me. I swear to God. Please, Kat."

Her head turned away, and I realized, alarmed, that the shuddering was tears.

She was crying. I was holding down a traumatized, crying girl. *Fuck.*

I pulled her closer into the strange, tense embrace, touching my lips to the salty, damp tang of her neck. Velvety soft. I wanted to taste more of it.

"This is why I said no to the coffee," I told her. "I'm not married or engaged. I just have some bad shit going down in my life right now and it was wrong to get a woman mixed up in it, so I tried to be good. It almost killed me to say no. And then you got mixed up in it anyway. Please don't cry. I can't deal with that right now."

"I'm not crying, you shitty bastard. Let go of me."

"That's better," I said, encouraged. "That's the spirit."

"Don't you dare talk down to me," she warned. "Arrogant prick."

I could breathe easier now that she was pissed at me again and not weeping.

In fact, her tension seemed to have eased, ever so slightly. I felt so minutely tuned to her, feeling every move, every breath, every heartbeat.

Her pulse had been frantic and stuttering before, but now it was just steady and quick and strong. She was breathing deeper and slower. Good.

"Please, go out to the helicopter with me," I said. Not that she had any choice.

She twisted, peeked up from under her lashes. Gestured with her chin for me to lower my ear, so she could speak into it over the huge noise of the helicopter. I did so.

Ouch! Fuck! She had nipped my earlobe, hard enough to make me yell.

Then she stayed still, her teeth laid against my flesh, her breath hot and moist against my ear. Her lips still touching me. Teeth still digging in, just hard enough to show me that she could have taken my earlobe off if she wanted to.

I didn't dare move, but a surge of hot lust went straight to my cock.

She let go of my earlobe, and murmured into my ear. "First chance I get, Ethan Masters? I am gonna kick your ass so hard."

Smiling was a kamikaze move, but a stupid grin still hijacked my face as I grabbed her hand and pulled her to her feet. My nose was swelling, and my chin was covered with blood and my earlobe stung and throbbed, but damn. I felt almost...high.

"I can hardly wait," I said.

We sprinted toward the waiting helicopter, holding hands.

CHAPTER 6

Kat

I was astonished at myself.

I couldn't believe I'd actually given in to him. Just like that.

I mean, practically speaking, there wasn't a whole lot else I could have done. He was much stronger than me, and had a whole armored van full of huge, flinty-eyed, combat-clad guys, armed to the teeth. The guy had his own fucking helicopter, after all. So yeah, he'd racked up all the points. He had won. Unarguably, definitively.

The strange thing was me. I had wired myself up to fight to the death, no matter what. Defeat was not an option. In my admittedly screwed-up world view, losing meant I was dead anyway, so fuck defeat. Better to die in battle than...well, no. I didn't let myself entertain those thoughts. I'd leave it at "fuck defeat," and go out on a high note.

But I did not feel dead right now. In fact, I had never felt so alive.

Masters was strapping me into the helicopter. As I looked down, I realized my blouse was torn open, which explained all

the side-eye and furtive grins. The vehicle would be full of
snickering and snorting, if those pricks could be heard over the
roar of the rotor blade. I attempted to rebutton it, without luck.
It was missing most of the buttons, at this point.

Great. I now got to flash my tits to the mercenary army from
hell on my mystery helicopter ride to who-the-fuck-knew-what.
Might as well render the whole thing a little more entertaining
for everybody while I was at it, I suppose.

Masters leaned closer, mouthing something at me,
inaudible in the huge noise. I shook my head, being no
lipreader, and he reached out and patted my cheek.

What the fuck? I was not some kittenish waif to cheek-pat!
What was going on in his head? What was he trying to say with
that gesture? *Awww. There, there, little one, it's going to be fine. Put
your life in my hands without fear! Trust the big strong filthy rich
guy who has his own personal army and deals death with noncha-
lance. No worries!*

Hardly. But trapped in the big vibrating chamber of death
with vast propeller blades madly spinning above me and a
bunch of mean motherfuckers watching us with intense interest, I judged that now was not the optimal time to freak out and
break the guy's very attractive, aquiline nose. Would be a real
shame to damage it, anyhow.

Now the bastard was smiling at me. Of all things. Blood
streamed from the earlobe where I'd bitten him. Amazingly, he
didn't seem to hold it against me.

That was a first. I was quite a handful for the unlucky
fellas who had dared to attempt physical intimacy with
me. None had lasted long. A couple days, and they beat a
hasty retreat, out of simple self-preservation. I didn't
blame them. I'd do the same in their shoes. At close
range, I was a freaking hot mess. Hell, I scared my own
self.

Ethan Masters would figure it out soon enough, just like

they had. He hadn't gotten the memo yet, but it was on its way to him, inevitable as the dawn.

My heart was trying to bang its way right out of my chest. I just sat there, frozen, letting myself be carted off to who the fuck knew where. Not fighting them.

I had drawn my conclusion long ago. Better to die quick, and hopefully have the satisfaction of taking a few bastards with me. Not a slow, ugly death, like Tony had promised me when I was fourteen years old.

I evaded that knife-stab of a thought, with the ease of long practice. This was not the same situation at all. Ethan Masters was some kind of huge boss, definitely, with a big-ass budget and some pissed-off enemies. But he just didn't have the same toxic, no-soul, dead-eyed vibe as the Petruzzi gang. This was a whole different scene.

I immediately started lecturing myself for trying to spin it. *Don't be a dumb bitch. He's just big and ripped and gorgeous, and you want some.*

Well, yeah. Maybe. But more than anything else, I had been enchanted by what happened when we'd fought those elevator goons, back-to-back. The way we came together, that subtle, magnetic *click,* like a well-machined instrument, and instantly, magically, he anticipated me, trusted me, read my mind. He was there for me when I needed him, and I was there for him. I had trusted him in battle. I'd never experienced that phenomenon before. I'd always seen combat as a solo endeavor. Or at the very least, me alone, fighting a big, snarling pack of bad guys. But never a team sport.

But with him, fighting had felt almost like…intimacy. Not that I was any sort of expert on that, God knows. On the contrary. I was intimacy-challenged.

It was all muddled in my head, my seesawing feelings as chaotic as the noise in the chopper, which made my whole head rattle and buzz. We were swooping heavily through the air, and as we banked a turn, I saw a glimpse of Seattle's burgeoning skyline. Then we turned again, and I saw mountains, clouds, mist. The water of the Puget Sound far below, steel-gray and rippled with whitecaps.

I tried not to stare hungrily at Ethan Masters, since he kept looking at me, and eye contact was just too damn much to deal with right now. The other guys kept sneaking peeks at me whenever Ethan was texting on his phone.

I could not project what was coming next. All I could do was to center myself to fight, as soon as I figured out what the hell was in store.

If it was the worst-case scenario, I still had a chance to go down fighting. Those guys had no clue how hard a cornered Kat could fight. I would punish the shit out of them, until I forced them to kill me. That had always been the plan.

But there was no need to jump the gun. I had to breathe, watch, wait for my moment. Be smart about it. Maximum damage, that was the goal.

Who *was* this guy? And that team that attacked us in the elevator...those guys were for him, and not for me? That went right in the face of all my expectations, which was a real brain-squeezer. I wasn't quite sure which scenario was worse. If those guys had been sent by Tony Sr. or Tony Jr., then at least I would know what course of action to take. Simple and obvious. Run like hell for as long as I could, or else turn and fight like hell, when running was no longer an option. To the death. End of story.

I'd known for fourteen years that I was destined to die young, so I'd spent my life learning to fight. When the day arrived that I finally engaged with the Petruzzis, the plan was to inflict memorable damage upon them before they took me down. I would extract as much revenge as possible for Raffi and Gabri. It wouldn't be anywhere near enough, but too fucking bad. All I could do was my best.

I was good with my hands and feet, not bad with knives, good with handguns, not bad with a rifle. And I had the added advantage of being blond, stacked, and relatively cute. I had half a chance to catch them off their guard. A girl could hope.

I had spent half my life gearing up for this confrontation. Of course, I was scared. I didn't like pain, or want to die. But nobody got to choose their moment. People died all the time. Even people whose lives were not as fucked up as mine.

Truth was, I was sick of waiting. That tight, suspended feeling, constantly waiting to breathe. I couldn't stand that tension any longer. I wanted it to be over. One way or another. If I was going to live, I needed more goddamn air to breathe.

If today's attackers were not the Petruzzis, then this was a whole different shitshow that I was letting into my life. I had to reconfigure my whole world, recalibrate my brain to deal with it. That took a crap-ton of energy which I was accustomed to conserving.

I kept things severely simple in my life. I never got attached. Not to homes, to things, to jobs. Or people, either. Sometimes people got attached to me, but there wasn't a lot I could do about that. I certainly didn't go out looking for friends. I wouldn't be doing them any favors if I did. If Petruzzi's goons found me while I was having a drink with my besties, I'd just get those poor women killed. So I never put out "friend" vibes.

My specialty was "cold bitch" vibes. That was a much better strategy if I wanted to keep the innocent off the firing line.

The same thing held true for men, for the most part. I had attempted to enjoy a man's sexual company a few times, when a likely opportunity presented itself, but it never worked out well for me. Mostly because I just couldn't relax in bed. I flinched or lashed out whenever anyone touched me unexpectedly, and I always ended up making the poor guy feel nervous and inadequate. That, added to the undeniable fact that I was endangering the poor dude's life just by getting near him, and the whole endeavor started to seem as selfish as hell. By the time I worked through all that conflict, the fun factor was drained completely out of it, leaving me bluer and more lonesome than before. It had been over a year since I'd tried it last.

Until this morning, when I'd basically invited Ethan Masters into my bed. Well, for coffee, but we had both known perfectly well it wasn't going to stop with coffee. I would have jumped aboard and ridden that train all the way to the end of the line. The very thought of it made my whole body clench and tingle and hum.

And he turned me down. Now, I would never in a million years have described myself as a vain person, but that snub had sent me reeling.

And then hell broke loose. But he said that those guys were after him, not me.

Why not be just glad? Relieved? Better him than me, right? What, was I jealous, or some twisted shit like that? I got all huffy because who the hell did he think he was, having problems that were bigger, more important and more dangerous than mine? I had my tragic backstory, and that was all I had. I should be able to win that pissing contest with my hands tied, right? Every time. Jeez, was I really that petty?

But speaking practically, if those bad guys were there for him, that also sucked for me. I'd been hiding under a rock for fourteen years, and that represented a lot of sacrifice. If Ethan Masters had real trouble, no matter who his antagonist was, and I got myself associated with it, then my profile would shoot up, the spotlights would flip on, and the Petruzzi clan would take notice. Their army of goons would come at me like a runaway train, to punish me for getting Tony Jr. put in jail. He was up for parole now, and still pissed. Looking to slice me open, from my chin down to my lady-bits.

Tony would want to do it himself. He was just that kind of guy. Real personal.

For God's sake, the problems I already had were more than enough to keep me occupied. I did not need anyone to pile on with more bad shit, no matter how handsome or rich or charismatic or intriguing Ethan was. No, thank you.

Tricky to get up on a high horse and hold that position while outnumbered by a mercenary army. I was ridiculously under-armed, too. I always was when I did office temp jobs. Many of the skyscrapers now had metal detectors. Rumors that I packed heat to my temporary jobs would get me blackballed at every employment agency in the city.

These were deals I made with the devil. Going to my temp jobs unarmed, so I could make the money I needed to keep my classes at the school going. And to repair that water damage. And to get Charlotte those glasses.

But it only worked if I stayed out of sight, at least until I managed to kill every last decision-making member of the Petruzzi family. Tony had gotten a reduced sentence because his lawyer had painted my murdered sister as a traitorous femme fatale, rather than the victim of vicious domestic abuse that she had been. And as for Gabri's death, and the bullet in my shoulder—they'd spun that as a tragic accident. Tony didn't mean to hurt us, the poor emotional guy. It was a crime of passion. Hah.

The helicopter banked, showing me a huge complex below with enormous terraces, and lots of glass, cantilevered out from the cliff, like some bad guy's lair in a superhero movie. The helipad was at the top of a luxury mountain fortress. In one swift glance, I took in the gardens, the pool, the hot tubs. Solar panels were everywhere, too. This place probably wasn't even on the grid.

I was on a mountaintop. Cripes. How the hell was I supposed to get away? I had things to do, bills to pay, promises to keep. Rent on the school was due in three days, and I had classes to teach, and an appointment scheduled to have Charlotte's eyes checked. It drove me nuts, that a kid as sweet and bright as she was flunking out of school because of a stupid mechanical problem. Plus, Charlotte reminded me of Gabri.

Aw, hell. They all reminded me of Gabri. Raffi, too. That was why I'd started the school for them in the first place. That was why I got out of bed in the morning at all. I was fortunate to have something to do that made this much emotional sense to me.

Otherwise, I might as well just lie down in front of traffic.

Masters helped me out of the helicopter. The wind from the blades whipped wildly at my blouse, blowing it almost off my body, so many buttons were gone.

He led me down a wide stone staircase and onto a terrace paved with big, granite paving stones. We descended into an area that was sheltered from the wind, with a breezeway between two buildings. I glimpsed outdoor furniture, a firepit, a huge barbecue, a wood-burning oven. My backyard consisted of a single lawn chair, a chain-link fence with a big hole in it, and an assortment of turds continually provided and replenished by the neighborhood dogs. Who were all my good buddies, even so.

Money. This place was huge, huge money. Which meant one of two things.

One, Ethan was the pampered heir to an obscenely large fortune, and fate had seen fit to shower him with looks and charm on top of it, and he got into trouble because he was restless and bored. For the entertainment value. In which case, fuck that guy.

Conversely, he was a career criminal. An insanely successful one. In which case, fuck that guy sideways, frontways, backward, and upside down. I'd already had my life destroyed by heartless, soulless dickheads like that. No more.

I pulled my arm from his grasp, and he let go without protest. Which surprised me. In my experience, those types always had something to prove, when it came to maintaining their grip.

I would have run if there had been anyplace to go to. As it was, I just followed him, feeling scared and hating the feeling. The corridor was as deluxe as the terrace. Towering ceilings, huge wooden beams, beautiful wood paneling. He gestured at a big carved door. "This is my library, if you should need it," he said. "Feel free."

Library? Library didn't really say career criminal to me. Those guys weren't big on cultural acquisition, as a general rule. Which tilted the scale back toward the pampered-heir scenario. "What is this place, anyway?" I asked.

"My house," Ethan said. "Or one of them."

"One of them," I repeated, incredulous.

"Yes, that's right."

"How many do you have?" I demanded.

"Let me think about it for a second."

I laughed at him. "You're joking, right?"

"No. I have townhouse in Seattle, a loft in Portland, a condo in San Francisco, a penthouse in New York, a beach place in Miami, a ski lodge in Montana, an apartment in London. I think that's it."

"Are you showing off?"

"I have nothing to prove. But as far as houses go, this one is my favorite. It's the one where I feel the safest. Safe being a relative term."

"Because it is so remote, you mean?"

"Yes, and fortified, and heavily guarded by a robust security staff."

"Which brings me to the question I asked before," I said. "Who are you?"

"I'll give you the same answer I gave you before. I'm Ethan Masters. I am the owner and CEO of MasterTech. Among other companies."

"Oh, my God," I said blankly. "MasterTech? I use some of your products myself. Holy shit."

There was a gleam of humor in his eyes. "Excellent," he said. "That shows good judgment and taste on your part."

"You mean, the MasterTech that does cybersecurity and encryption products, right?"

"Exactly."

"Well, that explains you being so rich. But it doesn't explain why people were shooting at you, or why you insisted on dragging me into a fucking helicopter."

"There will be time to discuss all that later," he said. "Tear me to shreds over lunch. But first, come in here." He opened a door, and ushered me into an enormous bedroom. A wall of glass showed yet another stunning view. A king-sized bed held a stack of fluffy silver towels, and a pile of neatly folded clothing.

"What is this?" I demanded. "Is this your bedroom?

"God, no. I asked my housekeeper to prepare this room for you. It has an attached bath, so you can freshen up at your leisure. There are first-aid supplies in the cabinet." He paused. "Unless you'd prefer some help with that."

I imagined Ethan Masters ministering to my bumps and bruises and it made my heart skip a beat. "Um. No. Thanks."

A smile flicked across his lips. "I didn't mean me," he said. "My housekeeper, Angela, would be happy to help. She's very competent."

"I'm fine," I assumed him. "I can handle it alone."

"Good. I just thought you might like to clean up and change. Your blouse is missing a couple of buttons."

I looked down at it, suddenly remembering that my cleavage was on full display. I was not a prudish person, but it took all my self-control not to clutch the flapping sides of my blouse closed with a squeal, like an outraged heroine in a melodrama.

"Take your time. Get a shower, or lie down. I've asked for lunch to be served at twelve, which gives you an hour. Any dietary issues my chef should be aware of?"

"Chef?" I echoed.

"Yes. My housekeeper, Angela, is also an extremely talented chef. Anything she should know? Allergies, intolerances? Are you vegetarian, vegan, anything like that? Angela's very flex."

"I eat whatever," I said faintly.

"Great. Then take your time. The door locks from the inside, so you'll have all the privacy you want. When you're ready, come out, go to the left, go down to the living room, and I'll make you a drink. After everything that happened today, I could really use one."

"Got it," I echoed. "Turn left. Living room. Drinks. Great."

I wasn't much of a drinker, but it wasn't a moral position, more an economic one. Drinking was expensive, and I had house and school rent to pay, girls to train. If somebody poured me a glass of champagne or mixed me a mojito, I did not complain.

But alcohol offered by Ethan Masters, with that gorgeous, come-hither smile? Hoo, boy. That was uncharted ground.

I just had to focus on my fact-finding mission. Figure out the dirt about Ethan Masters, and who wanted him dead, while at the same time figuring out how to get out of this place and back home. Aside from all my responsibilities at the school, there were several feral cats who had come to expect the water and kitty crunchies I left under the shelter I had built for them outside my back door. Plus, Ambrose, my friend Joanna's cat, came to visit me every day. I didn't want to let them down.

I looked over the clothes the housekeeper had left. Stretchy, comfy lounge wear, meant to keep me warm and relaxed. I wondered what this stuff was doing in Ethan Masters' place. I would understand if he had a stash of silky unmentionables from his past conquests, but athletic pants and thigh-length cashmere sweaters? Odd.

I took advantage of the shower, since I was sticky from blood and stress sweat. It was stocked with luxurious perfumed soaps and shampoos and conditioners. The pounding water felt wonderful on my sore spots. My scrapes didn't really need any bandages. Most of the blood had been from my nose, and that had stopped during the helicopter ride. I hoped I wouldn't get two black eyes. I'd had many, in my martial arts career, but right now was absolutely not the time.

I pulled on the fresh clothes, since my blouse was trashed and had bloodstains, but I stayed with my own underwear and shoes. I combed my wet hair back behind my ears, like always. It was just long enough for a stubby, blunt ponytail, so I created one with a covered rubber band from my purse. I was going for severe, sexless. The peeled-onion look. The frowning schoolmarm.

I laced up my shoes, and studied myself in the full-length mirror.

I looked excited. Face pink, eyes bright. And the cashmere I wore felt soft, warm. Touchable.

Damn it. This guy was dangerous to my peace of mind, and I had a limited supply of that.

I just had to keep my eyes straight ahead, my lips pursed, and my panties on.

CHAPTER 7

Ethan

"Pasta? Are you sure?"

"*Penne alla vodka*," Angela said firmly. "She didn't say she was gluten or lactose intolerant, right? Everybody loves my *penne alla vodka*, Ethan. Relax."

"I am relaxed," I barked, and immediately felt guilty. Angela was an awesome chef, and enjoyed living out at the Mountain House whenever we were in residence here. She was bonded with Freya, too, and she loved my nine-year-old niece, Holly. We didn't have any other mature grandmotherly vibes in our family, orphaned as we were, with nothing but estranged toxic assholes for relatives. Angela was a treasure to be treated with kid gloves.

"What about the steak you were talking about?" I asked.

"That's for the second course. We'll start with a plate of red olives and grilled artichokes, with crusty ciabatta rolls, then *penne alla vodka*, then the *tagliata*, sliced and dressed with cherry tomatoes, arugula, and flakes of Grana Padano. For dessert, lemon profiterole."

"Lemon? You think that's a better choice than chocolate?"

Angela was trying not to smile. "Yes," she said, patting my hand. "Lighter."

Aw, shit. I was making an ass of myself, acting all jittery. "Fine," I snapped. "She said she was flexible, so I'll take her at her word. Whatever you do is fine."

"It'll be good, don't you worry."

I swallowed back the profanity that was pressing to get out. "I'll go pick out some wine."

"Done," Angela said. "I picked out a Salice Salentino for the meal. And a Prosecco rosato. Polvanera. Very romantic. Delicately pink."

"It's not like that," I told her. "I barely know the woman, but she got in the middle of a gun battle this morning just because she happened to be standing next to me, so the least I can offer her is a nice lunch."

"Of course," Angela soothed. "Now go get yourself cleaned up while I get to work. You look disheveled."

I looked down at my grit-stained, bloodied shirt, and turned without another word, heading to my room. Each of us—my brother Shane, my sister Freya, and me—had our own comfortable apartment in this complex, on different floors. Each apartment had three bedrooms, two and a half baths, and a full kitchen. I had wanted to have my family near me, but not to be in each other's faces all the time.

I hurried through my shower, wanting to be ready to greet her when she emerged. I felt like I was jazzed on coffee, I was so excited about lunch with the lethal receptionist.

I was probably cruising for a bruising, as my dad used to say. My earlobe still stung. Some of the bruises on my shins were from her. She might just kick my ass.

But she'd made the first move, in the elevator. So, aside from the bullets and the darts and the stun gun and dragging her into a windowless van and then a helicopter against her will, at least I could be sure she had been genuinely interested. At one time.

And holy shit, what was I thinking? I had no business lusting after this woman. She might be right where her bosses wanted her to be. Well-positioned to seduce me. She certainly wouldn't have to try very hard. I was easy, when it came to blonde hellcat warrior maidens.

How was it even possible, that a girl with that level of combat training had just happened to be there, at the right place and the right time, to save me from Nicole Volange's goons? She'd probably severely injured or even killed a couple of them.

That wouldn't have happened if she had been on their team. No way. And besides, she seemed so clear, so straightforward. The personality equivalent of a knife blade. I just didn't see her as a spy, an assassin, a honeypot. She seemed so direct, honest to the point of brutality. She'd practically put a spike heel right through Hugh Clemens' eye.

She had a fire in her belly. And in her gorgeous golden eyes. Maybe they had sent her to gather information about my movements, not to kill me. They wanted the data locked in my brain first. Could be they had sent her to bone my brains out and then fuck me up for good?

I could think of worse ways to go.

But no, this wasn't about killing me, at least, not yet. First, they wanted what they wanted, and my brain had to be intact, for that. If Kat was a blameless, innocent bystander, all unsuspecting, then it would be a dick move to come on to her. But from the look in her eyes, her lethal instincts, her peppery temper, she was anything but unsuspecting. She might be the most suspecting woman I'd ever met, up to and including my own little sister. Freya was a prickly, iron-clad piece of work. Or, rather, she had been, before she fell in love with Jed Clearwater.

But I did not have the energy to contemplate that cluster-fuck, which had almost gotten Freya gruesomely killed. It was bad enough to be uncomfortably aware that my baby sister was rolling around in bed with one of my comrades-at-arms.

On the plus side, Jed was suspicious, too. A boot-leather tough sonofabitch with lightning-fast reflexes. He'd saved Freya many times over, and each time had earned him a few grudging points. It was comforting to know that someone else out there was as ferociously motivated as I was to keep Freya safe, with Shane still missing in action.

Who the hell could have sent Kat to protect me? That bloodthirsty, murdering bitch Nicole Volarge was still on the loose, still slavering for a Masters sibling so she could torture the access codes for SmokeScreen out of us. But where did the warrior maiden fit in? If not for Kat, Nicole Volange would have had my sorry ass for sure.

Other forces were at play. I was getting to the bottom of this. Things were still too weird to let down my guard. Or let out my dick, either, for that matter. I wasn't taking my eyes off that woman until I was absolutely sure of her agenda.

Of course, I couldn't seem to take my eyes off her in any case. Problem solved.

If I hadn't seen her fight, I would never have believed it. No temp receptionist had combat reflexes like that, or was so lucid in the face of heavy gunfire. She was a career fighter of some kind. I just had to figure out who she fought for. And if she was a danger to my family.

It was good that Holly was off at Freya's place in Seattle, with Jed and a cohort of Unredeemables. Amos, Remy, and Darius Drake were with them, keeping them safe.

I pulled on some jeans, and a warm navy sweatshirt. Splashed on some aftershave, sprayed on some deodorant. Brushed my teeth, as if I were hoping to get close enough for her to smell my breath. A guy could hope. Whether or not he should.

When I got to the dining room, the smells were mouthwatering. The Polvanera was chilling in a bucket of ice. Trays of grilled peppers, artichokes, eggplant, and zucchini were dressed with olive oil and chopped parsley. Plump olives were sprinkled with red pepper flakes. There was sliced bread, chunks of seasoned cheese. Little mozzarella knots.

Angela had outdone herself. As always.

She appeared, at the entrance of the kitchen. "I went all out," she said smugly. "I mean, a gun battle, and then being dragged off into a helicopter? The poor girl. That kind of stress calls for some serious overcompensation."

"This is not a joke, Angela," I said.

She waved her hand dismissively. "Of course not."

"It does look awesome, though," I conceded.

"I have the pasta all ready to boil whenever your lady friend comes out."

I winced. "She's not my lady friend, Angela."

"Well, that's for damn sure."

We spun around at the crisp, low voice from the dining room entrance.

Kat looked great in my sister's loungewear. The blue thing clung lovingly to her stunning figure. Her gaze was bold, unflinching. That stark hairstyle showed off all her perfect bone structure. I wondered if she'd done it on purpose.

"Welcome," I said, nonplussed. "I hope you're hungry."

"I am, thanks. And I appreciate the fresh clothes. Whose are they? Your exes?"

"They belong to my sister," I said.

She grunted thoughtfully. "I hope she won't mind."

"She won't," I said. "I guarantee it."

"I'll go dump the pasta." Angela turned to go to the kitchen, and winked at me.

"Ah, yeah," I said, flustered. "Kat, this is my chef and house-keeper, Angela."

Angela shook hands with Kat. "I hope you like Italian food," she said.

"I love Italian," Kat said. "Great to meet you."

"Pour out some of the Polvanera for Kat, Ethan," Angela reminded me.

Of course. The Prosecco. My duty as host. I'd gotten hypno-tized by the shape of her collarbone, that mysterious little hollow at the base of her throat.

A diamond and sapphire pendant would look really good nestled in there.

I got the wineglasses, just to give my hands something to do. I was feeling the urge to shove them into my pockets. For fuck's sake, we had fended off death together. Now here I was, sweaty-palmed like a teenager. Nervous about talking to a girl.

She was giving me that what-planet-are-you-from stare. "The hell, Masters?" she said. "Are you trying to impress me? The fortress, the helipad, the private chef?"

"No, not really," I admitted. "That's just how my life looks."

"That's good, because I don't get impressed," she said sternly. "I don't give a shit how rich you are. Swear to God. From the bottom of my heart. So don't try to dazzle me. I just do not care."

"I hope it doesn't bother you, or piss you off," I said.

"That depends on you." Her voice was crisp.

I did not run into women very often who could convinc-ingly say that. Nor did I blame them. After all, I liked money, too. I had sought it with great energy. I would never judge a person for being attracted to luxury. Hell, what wasn't to like about it?

But Kat was a whole different breed.

"Message received. You don't approve of money. What do you approve of?"

Kat thought about that for a moment. "Respect," she said. "Not muscling people around. Not throwing them into vans or helicopters. I favor people who refrain from that kind of activity."

"I told you," I said. "I was just trying to—"

"Yeah, said every man ever when throwing his weight around," she said. "It's always the same song."

"If I had left you outside that building, you would be dead. Or worse."

"Worse?" she let out a sharp laugh. "Tell me about worse."

I hesitated for a moment, and then decided she was tough enough to deal with the truth. "The people gunning for me like to inflict pain," I told her. "I couldn't let you fall into their hands. At the risk of throwing my weight around and pissing you off, and offending you with my gratuitous wealth. I'm sorry. But I wanted you to live. So sue me. Call me a bully if you want. God knows, my sister does."

"Tell me about this sister. Does she live here?"

"Sometimes she stays in her own private apartment here," I said. "All of us do."

"All? How many of you are there?"

"Just the three of us. My brother, Shane, and my sister, Freya. She's in Seattle, right now, with her husband."

"How about your brother? What's his story?" Her voice had a challenging tone, like an interrogation, so I ignored her question. That was no way to talk about Shane.

Later for that.

I poured her a flute of the sparkly, pale pink Polvanera. "Shall we get to know each other over lunch?"

"Lunch," she said. "Check us out. We've run full gamut. From blood and bullets and forcible abduction and imprisonment—to lunch."

"This is not abduction and imprisonment," I said patiently. "This is a disagreement, to be negotiated and discussed. And it is an excellent lunch. The food's ready, you're here, you have questions, and I want to learn about you, too. We might as well do it over grilled antipasti, *penne alla vodka*, and Angela's perfectly grilled *tagliata*. And lemon profiterole, of course."

"Lemon?" Her eyes lit up. "Lemon profiterole? Really?"

"You like lemon?"

Her mouth tightened, as if I had caught her in some kind of sneaky trap. "Sure," she said. "I just don't like talking about myself."

"We can sit and eat in tense, uncomfortable silence, if you prefer," I offered.

"Just the clinkety-clink of forks against plates. Chewing sounds."

That got me a crack of stifled laughter, which I took as a huge win. I proffered the flute of Polvanera to her once again.

"Have a glass," I coaxed. "It's not a trap. It's been a hell of a morning. You must be hungry." I gazed into her haunted eyes, trying to project good vibes. Righteous dude, trustworthiness, honesty, respect. Dudley Do-Right in the flesh. "Please, Kat."

She let out a sharp sigh. "Well, hell. I still have a container of leftovers in my purse for lunch. But I will not lie to you—Angela's lunch smells better."

My spirits soared as she accepted the glass. I picked up the other one, and held it up. "To unexpected encounters," I said. "Thank you for saving my life today."

She sipped the wine with a sigh of pleasure. "Ah, nice," she said. "You saved mine, too, so we're even. You can forget about it right now, okay?"

"No," I said. "It was one of the most memorable experiences in my entire life."

"Getting rolled in an elevator? Dude. Please. You need to get out more."

I choked on my Prosecco, and clapped a napkin over my

face, lowering it only when I trusted my face to behave. "I was talking about that combat synch, with you."

Her eyes slid away, but I was certain her gorgeous lips twitched.

"Yeah, that was pretty special," she agreed.

"How did you learn to fight like that?" I asked. "Were you in the military?"

"I'd like to know why those guys were trying to kill you."

"Not kill me," I said. "Kidnap me." But the less I talked about my problems, the better, in case she really was on somebody's payroll, and infiltrating any life. "Why did you think they were after you?" I asked. "Do you have enemies?"

Her face hardened. "If I had dragged you to my home by force, and sequestered you in my kitchen, you might be justified in demanding explanations from me. As it is? Not so much."

Ooh, burn. The woman had a valid point. Time for some distraction.

"Come this way," I said, gesturing toward the sun room. "Lunch awaits."

The sunroom was a glassed-in section of the terrace, for when I wanted to eat outside but didn't want the mountain breeze to blow the candles out. It was filled with plants, had a big wooden table, set for two at the end. Angela's antipasti spread looked extremely appetizing.

Kat stared out at the view for a couple of minutes. "It's incredible," she said finally. "You must feel like the king of the world up here."

"Yeah, I like the way this place makes me feel. But it's not a power thing. It's more a safety thing, like being high up in a watchtower. Being able to see them coming." I thought about Shane, and added, "Theoretically, anyhow. These days, there's no place to be safe."

"That's bleak, coming from a guy who made his fortune in cybersecurity."

I poured us both more Prosecco. "I guess it is," I said. "You're as suspicious and paranoid as me, if not more so. But you're safe up here, in my watchtower."

She nibbled an olive, frowning. "I don't feel safe," she said. "I feel like a cat up a tree."

I passed her the cheese plate. "Some *pecorino sardo*, or *mozzarella di bufala*?"

She let out a sharp laugh. "See, Masters? This was the part where you were supposed to say, 'oh, no, Kat! You're not trapped! Not at all!' But you don't say it."

I put the cheese platter down, with a slow sigh. "It's complicated," I said.

"Well, your complications are not my business," she said. "I want to be taken back to the city after lunch. If you don't agree, I'm going to make life extremely difficult and unpleasant for you. I won't enjoy it, but it's a matter of principle."

I considered and abandoned a bunch of different entry points into the case I had to make to her. "Let me explain," I said. "I'll give you the short version."

"I don't care how long it is, as long as it is true, complete, and convincing."

Angela bustled in, with a platter of *penne alla vodka*, and I had a couple of free minutes to decide what I could tell her that would not compromise my family's security, while still being true. In the meantime, we loaded our plates with creamy, pink-tinted pasta, and anointed it with grated pecorino cheese, and lots of it.

"You know I design software," I said, as we dug in.

"I'd have to live at the bottom of the ocean not to be familiar with MasterTech products," she said, dabbing her mouth with a napkin. "God, that tastes good."

"That's gratifying," I said. "Anyhow, over the past several

years, I've been developing a security-penetrating algorithm that has some very extreme capabilities. I started realizing along the way that it was too potentially dangerous to ever be a commercial product. Then, I concluded it was too dangerous to be used at all, ever. Too much potential for abuse. But my brother, Shane—"

"The one who also has an apartment here?"

"Yes. Shane, who ran his own executive protection and security company, urgently needed to use it, to do some job somewhere, to protect his client, to prevent a war, I wasn't sure of the details. But I trusted my brother. So I let him use it."

"Ah." She nodded slowly. "I see. So I'm guessing that someone got wind of it. Someone who shouldn't have ever known it existed."

"You got it," I said grimly. "My brother and I were the only ones who knew the code to open it, and how to use it. So, when it was stolen, Shane was stolen, too."

Her eyes widened. "Oh, no," she said. "When did that happen?"

"It happened eight months ago. Three other men died that day. Colleagues of Shane. Friends of mine." It still made my gut ache and my throat clench, talking about it. "Since then, other bad things have happened. Disasters, very nearly averted. My sister and her husband almost died, too. SmokeScreen is out there on the dark web, but it's locked up tight. Frey and I are the only ones who can open it, now that Shane's gone. Which is how we want it to stay. But because of that, we're targets now."

"I see," she said.

"That's why I'm doing this to you," I said. "That's also why I turned down your offer to have coffee. You will never know what that cost me."

"I'm sorry about your brother," she offered.

I nodded in acknowledgement. "So that's it," I said. "That's my explanation. Some really powerful and well-funded assholes want to pry open my brain by any means necessary and get the key to SmokeScreen. They almost killed my sister and Jed to do it. The two of them stayed alive by the skin of their teeth."

"And your sister and her husband are in Seattle, you said?"

"Yes, with Holly, our niece. Shane's daughter. She divides her time between Freya and me. She's nine. The best kid who ever existed. She's a target, too. And it makes me crazy with anxiety."

Kat nodded. "I see. Your protective instincts were activated, on my behalf. That is very nice of you. I appreciate that you give a shit. But this is the thing. I don't know if you noticed, but I have invested a great deal of time and energy in learning to defend myself. In fact, it's kind of a thing, with me."

"I noticed," I assured her.

"I run a martial arts school for women and girls," she said. "I'm due there tomorrow evening. I have three classes to teach. The beginners, the intermediates, and the adults. They paid me to teach them, and I will not let them down."

"Excuse me, people!" Angela marched in with a sizzling platter of fragrant *tagliata*. "I just wanted to leave this with you. The fruit plate and lemon profiterole are on the counter. I'll just get myself out of the way, and go back to the service floor. I hope medium rare works for you. I didn't want to interrupt your conversation to ask."

"It's great," Kat said warmly. "Thanks so much." She waited for Angela to leave. "Sheesh," she murmured. "The service floor? What is this, Downton Abbey?"

"That's what she calls it," I said. "That's where I have quarters for all my staff."

She prodded at the steak, letting out a murmur of approval at how juicy it was. "You should have warned me. I would have left more room," she complained.

"Knowing Angela, it's worth overeating," I said. "Do you like to cook?"

She shook her head. "I can make a decent sandwich," she said. "I try to sometimes consume a vegetable. That's about it. After my usual diet of cold cereal and toast, something like this is extremely nice. Almost worth getting shot at by evil goons."

I winced. "About that. What I said, about them knowing your name by now—"

"Not. Your. Problem." She looked me in the eye, a stony, uncompromising gaze. "You can't protect me by locking me up. I'd have to kill you. Please, don't make me."

Wow. The woman did not hold back. "Let's hold off on the death threats until after dessert, okay?"

That earned me a furtive smile, quickly squelched. Small conquests like that made my spirits soar, in spite of Kat's promise of violence.

Progress.

CHAPTER 8

Kat

H e was so handsome, it was ridiculous. I was in a state of total sensory overload. Perched on top of the world in his luxury lair, eating kickass Italian food, and I still remembered the way my mother used to make it, just as her own mother back in the old country. The mozzarella had to be just so, the tomatoes had to be fragrant and sweet and salty, and the oil had to be extra-extra-extra virgin, so new and peppery fresh, it burned your throat. She died before I could pick up the knack, and Raffi and Gabri and I were all so sad for so long afterward, we hardly ate at all. We forgot all about food. It was canned soup or toast, if we ate at all.

But this stuff was the real deal. The *penne alla vodka* was tangy and amazing, with real melt-in-your-mouth fresh grated pecorino. The *tagliata* melted in my mouth. I would never have described myself as a foodie, since I could never afford to be. I cared more about getting Charlotte a pair of glasses than I did about real Parma ham from Italy, or balsamic vinegar from Modena. But serve me a meal like this, and I was converted instantly into the hopeless food snob I was born to be.

I ate more than I had ever dreamed I could, but I didn't feel stuffed. It felt more like I was shoveling coal into a raging furnace. I just couldn't shovel fast enough.

I guess I had been hungry for a while, but too nervous to know it or feel it. I was also not used to eating in company, but I was enjoying the food too much to feel self-conscious. Ethan went into the adjacent kitchen and brought back a tray of fruit, and a dish heaped with plump profiterole drowning in creamy lemon goop.

He served some to me, on the dessert plates that been left on the table. "Angela's desserts are amazing," he said. "With her profiterole to bargain with, I even dare to ask you a slightly more personal question."

I braced myself. "Let's hear the question first," I hedged. "I don't buy a pig in a poke." No way was I going to fawn on him like his other women did. No matter how gorgeous he was. I would not be so cheaply bought. Lemon profiterole, my ass.

But he just looked amused. "I want to know how you learned to fight like that."

Fair question, but I was having a hard time answering. The effect he had on me was just hormones, I reminded myself. I couldn't even blame myself for it. But it still made me angry, as if I'd been infiltrated. Some traitorous part of me wanted to simper at him and bat my eyes. Cross and uncross my legs. Curl my toes and giggle.

I scooped up another profiterole, grabbed a cluster of red grapes, a few slices of kiwi, and organized my unruly mind. I didn't often let myself get so close to people that this question came up, so I wasn't all that smooth in the telling anymore.

"I'm from San Diego, originally," I told him. "I started studying martial arts in college. I had a knack for it."

"What discipline?"

"The gym I attended had a lot of different disciplines, including plain old street fighting. I tried everything, but after, I specialized in karate and kung fu. Now I run my own martial arts school for women and girls. I believe in empowering girls."

"That's great," he said.

"In some ways it is," I said. "But it's in a neighborhood where nobody has much money, so it's not terribly profitable. That's why you found me temping."

"You're a crusader and protector," he said.

I shrugged. "Oh, I don't know. I just like teaching."

"So, San Diego," he said. "Parents? Brothers, sisters?"

"None. My mother was single, my dad out of the picture. She knew better than to make that mistake again, so no brothers or sisters for me." I felt the shades of Raffi and Gabri in my mind, a streak of pain and loss, like the trail left by a falling star. Blessedly quick, as I was adept at moving on quickly.

"So you're all alone in the world?"

I glared at him. "Maybe, but don't get any dumb ideas."

"Such as?"

"Oh, I don't know. Feeling sorry for me? Don't. I'm fine on my own. Until I get dragged into somebody's goddamn helicopter. Then things get questionable."

"Please don't start," he said. "I brought you with me because I am sure you would be killed if didn't. I still am convinced of that."

"I appreciate your concern, but it does not translate into authority," I said. "If I find myself in danger, I'll deal with it. Those motherfuckers would get a rude surprise."

"Not anymore," he said. "You've lost the element of surprise, Kat. They know what you're capable of. They have good reason not to shoot me in the head, because they need what's in it. But they would blow yours right off your shoulders."

I let out a long sigh, my mind reshuffling plans, goals. "Well, shit," I said grimly. "Maybe it's time to disappear."

His eyes narrowed. "You say that as if it's no big deal. You've done it before?"

Damn, the guy was laser-sharp. "Not at all," I said crisply. "I just have a practical nature. I see no reason to whine."

"And your martial arts school?"

That did hurt. "I would hate to leave them," I admitted. "With no warning, no explanation. It feels like a betrayal. But I tell you what, Masters—how is it any different for them, if those assholes kill me, or if you trap me up here like a cat in a tree?"

"It is not the same," he said, through his teeth. "You would be safe."

"I beg to differ. Anyhow. Now that we've cleaned up, chilled out, had some lunch, let's just call your helicopter, or car, or teleporter, or whatever the hell you've got in your space-age garage, and have someone drive me straight back to Seattle, to my house. Where I live. Like a goddamn normal person. Okay?"

"To certain fucking death," he said harshly.

"Just please, leave me to my fate," I said, through my teeth. "My certain death is my own business, thank you very much."

"Let me make a counter-offer," he coaxed. "Let me send my people to monitor your home and your martial arts school while you stay here tonight. Let's find out if our mutual enemies have put a name to you, hunted down your address, possibly even put your students in danger. That would be solid, useful, actionable data for you, right? And it costs you nothing."

"And what would I owe you for that?"

"Nothing," he said. "It would be sleazy and opportunistic to expect anything of you, since I muscled you into this. I give you the info you need, you stay safe. If they make a move on you, then I have a fresh opening, which I badly need. In the meantime, you can kick back, have a glass of wine, enjoy the view. Let yourself be pampered."

His expression revealed nothing, but I felt the energy,

roaring off him. The heat, the need, the intense curiosity.

Curiosity was the most dangerous thing of all.

"Maybe you haven't gotten my vibe," I said. "I don't do pampered. I'm not the type to lounge around sipping a drink and enjoying the view."

"Don't knock it until you've tried it. I would go to incredible lengths to make you feel welcome, if you'll just stay safe in my fortress while my team does its thing."

I crossed my arms over my chest. "Anything?"

As soon as it came out of my mouth, I regretted it. It sounded so suggestive, so flirtatious. And how could I risk that, isolated with a guy so accustomed to having the upper hand? It was too late, though. The smolder in his eyes was a hot blaze.

"Anything," he said softly.

I licked my lips. "Um. Maybe I gave you the wrong idea, back in the elevator, when I invited you to coffee." My voice sounded nervous and prim to my own ears.

"Did you?" he said. "And then saving my ass in that elevator, like the warrior goddess that you are? I have never had such a powerful idea. Right or wrong."

"Ah..." My voice trailed off.

Okay. This was the part where I put him in his place. Made him feel like a fool for suggesting it. Bitch-slapped him into gibbering submission. That was my usual playbook, when men came on to me.

It was the kindest thing I could do for them, after all. I was trying to protect them from my shitty life, from my fucked-up destiny, and my numerous personality disorders.

But Ethan Masters was the kind of man who didn't need to be protected. I could even consider indulging—until he figured out for himself how bad an idea this was.

Maybe, if we imposed clear limits from the very start, it wouldn't even come to that. Maybe this could be a brief parenthetical statement in the more or less arid shitshow that was my life. A moment of sensual luxury to treasure in the years to come.

Holy freaking crap, look at me. I was actually considering it.

And he knew it. He could read it, in my aura. Damn the man.

"It would be really stupid," I said.

"Oh, probably," he agreed. "But it would be a lot of fun. I would make very sure it was worth your while."

I could feel my face heating up. Jeez, was I actually blushing? I licked my lips again, then wished I hadn't when he stared at them as if he was hypnotized.

"I am not interested in having a boyfriend," I told him. "Particularly not a boyfriend that a whole bunch of assholes are trying to kill. That sounds stressful."

"That actually works for me, too," he said. "I love sex, but I don't do romance, or commitment, for all the reasons you saw today. My life is nuts, it's too fucking dangerous, and my priorities are elsewhere. But here we are, together. If you were into it, today is the perfect moment to indulge. No strings, no obligations. No expectations, other than pleasure. I will make it good for you. I swear it."

I let out a nervous, jerky laugh. "Wow. That is, ah...quite the claim."

"I'm good for it." His voice was deep and resonant, a caress of my nerve endings. It made shivers rush over the surface of my overheated skin.

I got up, and walked out onto the terrace. It was cool out there, a breeze ruffling my hair. I leaned on the wrought-iron railing, clutching it with both hands, until my knuckles were white. Staring out at that vast array of peaks and shadowy valleys.

Ethan joined me, leaning on the railing next to me. "I didn't mean to upset you," he said. "I shouldn't have made a move on you after what happened today."

"Oh, God, no," I said. "That has nothing to do with it."

"Was it something else that I said?"

I shook my head, angrily. "No," I said. "It's me."

"What do you mean?" he prompted.

"I mean that I'm the problem," I said, my voice tight. "Not you, not the whole forced-abduction-to-your-deluxe-bat-cave schtick, none of that. Me."

"I fail to see any problem," he said. "On the contrary."

I let out a harsh laugh. "Oh, but you will. I promise, you will."

He waited, a long, careful pause. "Tell me about that," he said evenly.

I shook my head. "It's just that I'm bad at it."

He gave me a blank look. "Bad at...you mean—"

"Yes. Yes, that is exactly what I mean. Bad at sex. It's not like I'm asexual, or anything. I am definitely not asexual. Things would be easier if I were. But I just...it just does not work for me."

"Why not?" he asked gently.

I threw up my hands, then grabbed the railing again. "I'm too tense," I said. "Too anxious. If anyone tries to touch me, I slap his hand away. And after a while, that puts a real damper on the sexytime, let me tell you. Remember when I practically drove my high heel through that asshole Clemens' eye this morning? It's like that with all the guys. Even if they aren't assholes."

"Are you a virgin?" He sounded curious, fascinated. Not put off.

"No," I admitted, embarrassed. "I've done the deed, in a matter of speaking, but it was never an event that I or any of my lovers wanted to repeat. I'm too guarded, too tightly wound. As far as I can tell, you have to let down your guard to make sex work, and I just can't. So it always goes to shit." I looked away, hoping he couldn't hear the quiver in my throat.

But he just shifted, until he was standing next to me. Almost making contact.

"I touched you, today," he said. "Several times. I lived to tell the tale."

"Yeah? I hope you put some antibiotic ointment on that ear. I'd really hate to see it fester. Human bites are nasty that way."

He laughed, putting his hand to his ear. "I disinfected it. No worries."

"It's a bad idea, Ethan. I would disappoint you. And I would probably make you feel bad about your sex game, which would be unfair, since I am sure it is perfectly amazing. True thing. I am not the girl you think I am. Too much baggage."

Now he was even closer. Usually, I would be cringing away from that much closeness, but I was almost tempted to lean in to his warmth.

"Tell me about your baggage," he urged. "I'm curious."

I let out a crack of bitter laughter. "Hell, no. Talk about unsexy."

"Everything you do is sexy. You won't disappoint me."

"Hah. Just give me time."

"All the time you need," he said smoothly. He laid his hand on mine.

Instead of the usual knee-jerk flinch, I just felt a whole-body shiver. A shuddering, knee-weakening rush of sweet, startling heat—and anticipation.

This was unprecedented. This yearning. To know him, to be known. His hand was so warm on mine. He leaned closer, those gorgeous dark eyes looking right into the fathomless black hole that was my life, and not flinching from it.

Abruptly, my paranoia shifted from being afraid of the sad non-event that sex would inevitably be if I couldn't let down my guard.

Suddenly, I was terrified of where I might end up if I found that I could.

CHAPTER 9

Ethan

I could have stayed in that state for hours. Teetering on the verge of that first kiss. The precious, perfect first time that our lips touched. I couldn't rush this. I had to get it right, because there would be no do-overs if I got it wrong. Not with this woman.

She was a mass of contradictions. Immensely powerful and immensely fragile, in the same moment. And she shone like a goddamn star. I had never seen anything so beautiful. Those bright topaz eyes, so wary, so hopeful. Full of wonder and curiosity as she swayed, infinitesimally, toward me. Fuck, yes. Please.

We danced with the closeness for a while, enjoying the humming charge of the energy between us, connected us even without touching. Her sweet heat buzzed against my skin. I had never been so turned on. I shook with it. This the trembling brink-of-a-fucking-miracle moment. Waiting for something, some signal, some certainty. I was following instinct, helplessly advancing, retreating, our lips never making contact. Sensing her heat, her scent, the smudge of dark shadows under her gorgeous eyes, the hot blush of her cheeks and her slightly parted lips. I wanted to inhale her, devour her.

But if I put so much as a pinkie finger wrong, she would freak out and kick my ass to hell and gone.

I was waiting for a sign. That tiny move from her that would unleash me. I didn't care how long it took. I could do this forever. I could just stay out here with her, let the seasons change around us. Let the wind howl, let the snow fall, let the moon change its phases. I wouldn't notice. Not with her to look at.

She let out a breathless laugh, and laid her hand on my chest. She lifted her chin, and gave me a teasing look, through long, gold-tipped eyelashes. "So, Masters? What's your deal? Have you lost your nerve? I wouldn't blame you if you had."

Ahhhh, yes. All the invitation I needed. I pulled her close.

The contact unleashed a shockwave of emotion. More than my system could handle. I was in overload, losing control, and I couldn't lose control, not after all my bold words about driving her crazy with pleasure. That required technique, relentless self-command. Not some snorting, grunting caveman.

We tasted each other hungrily, her fingers digging into my chest. She didn't have long fingernails, martial artists never did, but her fingers were strong, and her grip felt good. Sexy.

She was shapely, sinuous, in my arms. My hands could not get enough of her. Every detail pleased me. The shape of her spine, the dip of her waist, the beautiful rounded swell of her ass, those long, strong legs. The fine texture of her skin, the calluses on her hands, the satiny luster of her hair. Subtle, delicate details, the rosy, well-shaped ears, her white teeth. High, pointed breasts, pressed against my chest. I was so hyperconscious of every point of contact, as if it burned me.

I leaned back, gasping for air. She looked dazed, licking her lips. Panting.

"Hey," was all my muddled brain could articulate. "You, ah...okay?"

She laughed, a soft, whispery sound. "Is this all part of your technique? Feign vulnerability, so that I feel charmed and disarmed? Is that your move, Masters?"

"No moves," I said. "I'm not capable of feigning anything right now."

She narrowed her eyes. "Okay, then," she said slowly. "Then let me turn that around on you. Are you okay?"

"I'm overwhelmed," I said.

A frown appeared between her brows. "Ah," she said. "I'm too much, huh? I get that a lot."

"No!" I said, horrified. "Oh God, no! You're not too much. You're fucking amazing. I'm just so excited, my self-control slipped, and that freaked me out."

"You're not scared of me, then?"

I lifted her hands to my lips, kissing them. "Not in any bad way," I said. "I'm just nervous. Hoping I'll prove worthy of the mysterious warrior maiden."

"Warrior maiden," she repeated with a tiny smile. "That's a new one for me. Worthy, huh? From the pampered billionaire with the helipad?"

"That's irrelevant, and you know it," I said. "You already told me you didn't care about that, and I took you at your word."

She nodded. "I meant it."

"So, you're staying here tonight," I said. "You agreed."

She gave me a sharp look. "I'm guessing that wouldn't change anything if I didn't agree," she told me. "Your mind was made up. You're just sweetening the pot by offering to fuck my brains out in the meantime. Very hospitable of you, Masters."

I studied her face, wondering where I had made a false step. "Put that way, it sounds really self-serving," I said. "Try looking at it this way. I am placing all my resources at your service. Including my body. All for you. I lay it at your feet."

"Hmmm," she murmured. The sound was almost like a purr.

It was one of those moments when the fate of the world hung on the flicker of an eyelash. Emotions burned in her eyes. This was dangerous for both of us, not just to her.

I took a step back, so she wouldn't feel pushed, or smothered, or pressured, and watched the wind play with her hair, blowing strands across her flushed face.

"You're not one of those guys, who's going to start acting like the big boss as soon as we have sex, are you?" she demanded. "Because I find that really tedious."

I let out a short laugh. "Full disclosure? I'm the kind of guy who will act like the big boss whether we have sex or not," I said. "My sister says I have a character disorder when it comes to that. I piss her off regularly. I'm sure she'll tell you all about it."

Her eyebrows shot up. "Dude," she said sternly. "I won't be meeting your sister. This is a total one-and-done. If we do it at all. Which is by no means certain."

I lifted my hands. "I bow to your will," I said.

"Bullshit you do," she said, studying me keenly. "You don't bow to anyone's will. You just manage people, expertly. Because you're smart. But it's always your will being done, in the end. Am I right?"

I considered my words carefully. "Maybe," I said. "But I don't think that's necessarily a bad thing, if our interests align. And they do. What I want right now is to give you unbelievable pleasure. Hours of it. Until you're exhausted from it."

She harrumphed. "That might be harder than you anticipate," she informed me. "I'm a tough nut to crack. Or so I have been told. I have a hard time letting go, relaxing. So really. Don't get your hopes up."

"Great," I said promptly. "And this is where my character disorder comes in handy. The positive flip side of thinking I'm the big boss is not being afraid of a challenge, or strategy. Being willing to play a really long game. As long as it takes."

Her eyes dilated. She licked her lips. My cock swelled against my jeans.

Whoa. So, the name of the game with Kat was slow. That was the key.

I held out my hand, and the gesture had the feel of a ritual. A point of no return, for both of us. Relief and elation flooded through me as she took it. Gratitude, too, because I was desperate for this, after all the flirtatious foreplay of that meal, that conversation. If she had turned me down, I would have needed to be hospitalized.

I bent over her hand, and started kissing it. Slowly, thoroughly, figuring I'd begin as I meant to go on. Worshipful. She was skittish, shy, so I had to get her to the point where she was half-mad with frustration.

I felt the shiver go through her. Goosebumps, the nipple jut.

"Shall we go back inside?" I asked.

"Sure." I kept hold of the hand she had given me, resisting her first, instinctive tug to free herself. I wasn't giving any ground right now. Not right after winning it.

Back in the sunroom, she turned to face me. "So, how's this going to work?"

I just smiled. "I'll follow your cues."

"You mean...here?"

I looked around, assessing the erotic possibilities of the sunroom. It had strong points. The heater made it warm enough, the afternoon sunshine filled it with light, and there were lemon profiteroles to play with.

But it wasn't the right vibe. Not yet.

"Let's go to my room," I said. "I think this should start on a bed."

She laughed. "Ah, okay. Traditional much?"

"I just like my soft mattress," I said. "Later on, I can impress you with how adventurous I am." I tugged her hand, to get her moving, and led her through the place.

Through the huge corner living room with the glass wall on two sides, one opening on to the terrace, the other out over a cliff. There was a little sunshine slanting through the jumble of heavy clouds. She glanced at the photo gallery.

"This is your family?" she asked.

"Family and friends," I said. "Only the closest ones. You'd like them."

She harrumphed. "That's not in the scope of our night," she said. "So don't plan on introducing me to your parents."

"My parents are long gone," I told her. "When I was sixteen."

"Oh. Like me, then. So, you didn't inherit all this?"

"No," I said. "My folks didn't have a dime."

"Ah. This is all you, then. Self-made man. Very admirable. Yay for the American dream."

I paused, carefully. Money always tended to be an emotional minefield. "I had this house built about eight years ago, after things really took off with MasterTech. I wanted to create a place where we could all be together and feel safe."

"You're a very family-first kind of guy," she said.

"Absolutely," I told her. "Even though it's just me here right now. Freya's back in Seattle with Jed, her new husband, and my little niece, Holly. I personally think they should all be living here, just to make it easier to secure them. But Jed is protecting her. He's been my friend for years. We were in the Army Rangers together."

"Ah. The Rangers. No wonder you can fight. And those other guys, in the van? Were they Rangers, too?"

"Yes," I said. "We formed a very tight group. After Shane was kidnapped, we've all been working together to find him. We called ourselves the Unredeemables, back in the day, and it stuck. Guess we thought it sounded cool and tough, at the time." I paused, shook my head grimly. "Funny how the years layer new meanings onto things."

"You want to redeem Shane," Kat said thoughtfully. "And you think the Unredeemables name jinxed him?"

I winced. Put that way, it stung me. "I guess. Maybe. It's silly, but maybe."

"Don't worry," she said. "A name can't jinx you. He's lucky he has a brother who's moving heaven and earth to find him."

"A sister, too," I said, since I had to give credit where credit was due. "Freya almost got herself killed, trying to get information about what happened to him."

"You think he's still alive?"

I stopped breathing for a second, with the clutch of pain that question gave me.

"I have no idea," I said grimly, although I did. God help me, I did.

There was no reason to think that Shane was still alive. There were plenty of reasons to conclude that he was dead. But until I saw his body with my eyes, I would choose to have hope. It made it easier to breathe.

"You said you thought the guys in the elevator were coming for you," I said again, just to change the subject. "Who are you fighting with?"

She was silent for a moment. "You don't get access to all my secrets just because I let you touch me, Masters," she said coolly. "And with Shane, and your bad guys, you've got enough on your plate. Don't even ask about my problems."

"At the risk of pissing you off, I have to remind you that my enemies saw you fight at my side," I said. "Now they will identify you as their enemy. Please factor this into your decision-making processes. Don't ignore it because it irritates you."

She grunted. "I promise to factor it in if you promise to shut up about it."

I laughed, and stopped in front of the big, carved door.

"What's this?" she asked. "Your bedroom? Should I prepare myself? Will the angels sing when the door opens?"

I punched the security code into the pad, trying not to smile. Hah. Tough babe. The more nervous she felt, the snarkier she became. But she would never admit to fear.

My curiosity was sharp, but now was not the time to press her. "Time will tell," I said. "I'll do my utmost to make the angels sing for you until their throats crack."

"Brave words," she murmured.

"Would you be interested in any other kind?"

She snorted. "Come on, let's get this angelic concert started. Open the door."

The room had two towering walls of glass looking out over the mountain range and a glowing sunset. I liked my big open spaces, so the room was huge, with very little furniture. Wood paneling, heavy beams, gleaming plank flooring. A huge bed with a silver-gray patterned spread. A simple sand-colored rug next to it. A soft easy chair facing the window, a floor lamp. A bedside table. A deep-colored Persian rug in the open, empty side of the room. No other furniture. My clothes were in an adjoining room.

She looked around with a nod of approval. "I might have known you'd be a minimalist."

"I like to keep it simple," I said. "It's soothing."

Her lips curved, as she spun around, admiring the room, the view. "Soothing, huh?" she murmured. "Simple? I sure hope you don't expect that from me. I am not a soothing or simple person."

I opened my mouth to tell her that I didn't expect anything from her, but the words froze in my throat as she whipped off the loose blue cashmere sweater and tossed it away, tousling her hair over her face. Her eyes were glowing, a topaz gold so bright they seemed backlit by the sunlight. She was wearing a simple white bra.

"Not soothed," I croaked out. "Don't want to be."

"That's fortunate," she said, reaching back with that twist and arch that showed how strong and flexible she was. She undid the bra, and tossed it at the sweater.

A breath hissed audibly out of my mouth. Holy fuck, she was beautiful. Her breasts were high and tight and beautiful. Dark pink, puckered nipples. Shoulders proudly back. Gorgeously strong, lithe, and graceful. The body of a pro athlete, except for one puckered scar near her collarbone. He'd seen too many of those to mistake it.

That was a scar from a bullet.

"You're really going for it," I commented. "Maybe slow down a tiny bit?"

A smile flitted across her face. "Nope," she said. "I could lose my nerve."

She leaned down to loosen the laces of her athletic shoes, then pried them off, along with the socks. Tossed then in the direction of the other garments. Leaving her clad in only the soft black trousers that Freya left at every dwelling she frequented. Her favorites. They were as soft as yoga pants, but as classy as business pants. They looked great on Kat. Looser than they were on Frey, so they hung a little lower, showing off the sexy curves at her belly, the dip of her waist, the jut of her hipbone.

Then she yanked them down too, along with her underwear.

Her naked body was so perfect, it was an assault on my eyes. Standing there, chin up, eyes brilliant with defiance. As if she were challenging me to a duel, not seducing me.

She made an impatient gesture. "So? Let's see what you've got, pretty boy."

Pretty boy? I swallowed a bark of laughter that I strongly sensed would not help my cause, pried off my shoes, and whipped off my sweatshirt. "Is that better?"

"Almost. If you keep at it, we'll get there eventually."

I undid my belt. Shoved down my jeans, and kicked them away. My cock jutted out, hard and heavy and urgent-looking. It was a little too soon in this seduction to be waving my dick at her, but she'd forced my hand. I could see her gaze linger on my scars, just as mine had landed on hers. The gut shot that had ended my Amy Rangers career. But I hadn't commented, and she didn't either.

Her blatant appreciation looked absolutely unfeigned. "Well, look at that," she said. "I am completely unsurprised. Both that you've got a killer body, and that you've got a big, gorgeous dick. Hey, you do have latex, don't you?"

"Of course, but we can slow down a little," I told her.

"I don't want to slow down," she said. "You look like you're up for it."

"God, yes. Of course I am. But what's the rush?"

"What's the hold-up?" she countered. She grabbed my cock, squeezing it appreciatively. "Mmm. Nice and hot. Stone hard. Why wait?"

"This erection is not going anywhere," I said, my voice strangled.

Her clever hand twisted, swiveling along my shaft. "I can feel your heartbeat against my hand. Mmm, hot. Shall we go to the bed?"

I grabbed her hand. I was on a hair trigger. Her bold caresses put me on overload. "Hold on."

"I'm trying to," she purred, her hand tightening around me.

"We're going too fast," I told her. "Let's put the brakes on." If I didn't know how tough she was, I would have read the look in her eyes as fear.

"I'm ready now," she said.

"But I haven't even touched you yet," I said,

"What's stopping you?" She grabbed my hand, pressing it against her breast. The contact made me gasp. She was perfect.

Her skin so hot and baby smooth, her breast so springy soft, her nipple so tight, tickling my palm. I was going to explode.

"You're scared," I said.

"The hell I am." Her voice was sharp. "Why are you being so coy?"

I shook my head. "I just want it to be good for you."

"So? Come and get it. It's already good for me. I can hardly breathe. That never happens. Let me capitalize on it while I can."

I put both hands on her slender waist, and pulled her close, wrapping my arms around her. She stiffened, arching back away from me. She was not ready at all.

"You're tense," I said softly. "You have to relax first."

She laughed. "Aw, crap. Here we go. Have you not been listening, Masters? I don't do relaxed. It's not on the menu."

"Just try," I coaxed. "Let's slow way down, and—"

"No," she blurted. "I can't. I have to get out ahead of it, if I want to do this."

"Ahead of what?" I asked, mystified.

She pushed me away, frustrated. "If you have to ask, it is not going work."

"No, no, no." I grabbed her hand, kissing it. "I just need for you to trust me."

"Yeah, right," she said. "You're asking for the moon." But she shivered, lips parted, as I kissed her knuckles. Her fingers. Every joint. "I wouldn't even know where to begin."

"I'll show you," I said gently. "Close your eyes."

"You're joking, right?"

"Not at all," I said, my voice low and coaxing. "Just follow my lead, Kat. You're going to love giving me the moon."

CHAPTER 10

Kat

Goddamn him. Why did he have to be so difficult? Why make this impossible for me when I wanted it so much?

Usually, with sex, I could take it or leave it. So if I crashed and burned, whatever. No biggie.

But with Ethan, it was huge. He'd snatched me up out of my normal life like a rapacious bird. Carried me off to his mountain stronghold. I cared, this time. I cared desperately. I wanted this to work. I deserved this. One night that somehow wasn't ruined by what had happened that long-ago night, and what it had done to my life.

I'd had so much taken away. My mother, my sisters, my cat. My life, my town, my name, my identity. The trappings of a normal life. Parents to bitch about. Skinny dipping in the moonlight. A trip to Vegas with the girls, a first kiss, a first boyfriend. Romance. A family of my own. None of that stuff was in the cards for me, ever.

Besides, I wasn't the kind of person who could be a mother,

after what had happened to me. All my soft bits were burned away, leaving just the hard metal frame beneath.

The Petruzzis were going to find me eventually. When they did, I would die. But I was by God going to take my golden chance to get nailed properly by a big gorgeous guy who set my hormones ablaze before the inevitable happened.

Problem was, I couldn't keep myself safe behind my shield. Ethan was smart, and hungry, and he craved surrender, yielding, opening. And I had no freaking clue how to give it to him. I didn't even know where to begin.

I shook my head, helplessly. "I don't know how."

The truth sounded so stupid. Something that was so easy for other people, just relaxing and enjoying a good afternoon lay, letting someone else take the lead...for me that scenario was fraught with peril and confusion. I felt ignorant and clouded.

"You actually do," he said. "Just remember what your body already knows."

I gulped back my laughter. Such conviction in his voice. Hah. "You just met me a few hours ago," I told him. "And I've already made you bleed twice. That's an awfully confident statement for a guy who almost lost an earlobe."

"I'm willing to risk it," he said. "I want to make you come, and I want it to be deep. I want you floating on air. Soft, like your bones are made of rubber. Ready to have lemon profiteroles hand-fed to you, to give you the strength to do it all again."

Wow. The guy had more self-confidence than I'd ever seen in one place before.

"Um." I swallowed. "That sounds nice. But I've got this wall-of-thorns thing happening, and I don't know the spell to let you through it. So you might just have to make do with me just like this. Tense, bitchy, and combative."

"You've been that way from the moment I met you," he said.

"And my hard-on has not relented for one fucking instant. Don't worry about me. I'm very tough. I have thick skin, and lots of stamina, and I want this. How about you just try trusting me?"

Goddammit. I wanted him. I would never get another opportunity like this. Sex with a guy who fascinated me, who wasn't afraid of me. A guy I both respected and lusted for. Men like that were not thick on the ground. I certainly had never found one in the wild before.

I slowly exhaled. "How?" I whispered. "How do you do that? Trust can't be chosen. You feel it, or you don't. It's not up to me."

He considered that, his eyes thoughtful. "Maybe we can change that," he said. "It's not set in stone. I think the rules are different between us."

"Why, because of your magic dick?" I scoffed, immediately regretting my sarcastic tone. God, was I actually trying to scare him away?

But Ethan didn't look scared or angry, just amused. "It's a little premature to call my dick magic," he said mildly. "I'm talking about what happened between us when we fought those guys in the elevator."

"How so?" I demanded. "What of it? I fight when I have to."

"You saved my life," he said. "You were there for me. A complete stranger. You covered for me, blocked for me, watched out for me. You had my back."

"Well, duh," I said. "Of course. And you did the same for me. So?"

"They would have had me," he said. "There were too many of them. But you were there. You were brave, fast, smart. You made the difference. That inspires trust. Not just relaxing enough to come. I'm talking the real thing. Real trust. Real intimacy."

"Ah…" I realized that my mouth was open, and closed it. "You might be getting ahead of yourself. I told you that I intend to bug out of here and go back to my life. Not explore the outer limits of sexual intimacy as a trapped concubine in your gilded cage."

He laughed at me. "That has real possibilities as a hot sexual fantasy."

"I'm serious, Ethan."

"So am I. You can trust me. You already have trusted me. With your life. I came through for you, just like you came through for me. Let's start there. Build on that."

I grunted. "Combat...sex...same thing. Really, Masters? There'll be slightly less blood and bruising, I hope."

He rolled his eyes. "Don't pretend to misunderstand me."

"I don't see the parallel," I said. "That fight went by really fast. Badda-bing-badda-boom, and we were down in the garage in the middle of a gunfight. I don't see how that relates to my sex life."

He sighed. "All I'm saying is, trusting me might not be so hard if you remember that you've already done it, and it turned out okay. I didn't let you down."

Ah. For the first time, what he was saying made sense to me. Like a little ray of light. Fleeting, but nice.

Yes, it was true. I had trusted him. And I had lived to tell the tale. Of course, he had promptly fucked it up afterward by muscling me into his helicopter, but hey. I was getting over that remarkably fast. A bottle of Prosecco, a fabulous hearty meal, some good wine, and his naked body right in my face? Damn. I was more flexible than I'd ever dreamed. Disposed to let bygones be bygones.

"Okay, you have a point," I said. "I trusted you, and we lived. Now what?"

He reached out, so slowly that I had all the time in the world to prepare, to brace myself. No need to flinch as he traced the angle of my cheekbone, the point of my jaw.

"Close your eyes," he said.

I swallowed back my knee-jerk *hell, no*, and examined it. That was just my alarm system, functioning exactly how I had wired it up to function. I would never get what I wanted from this guy unless I reprogrammed the damn thing.

I gave him a jerky nod, and closed my eyes. "Don't make me stay this way too long," I said. "It's a big waste. You're hot, and I like to admire your assets."

That made him laugh, but then he moved around behind me, the heat coming off him surrounding me. And my body reached for it, pined for it, ached for contact with his skin, but he was not touching me yet. That tease.

"So?" I asked, impatiently. "What are you waiting for?"

"The right moment." There was a hint of humor in that deep, rumbling voice that was like the stroke of something silken, something furry, making the nerves in my skin shiver and thrill.

"News flash, buddy," I told him. "The moment has arrived."

"I'll be the judge of that," he said.

My body shook with a burst of sharp laughter. "Oh, will you? Who died and made you king?"

"Nobody. I am not being arrogant. I'm just paying attention. Slow down. Breathe. You'll feel it. You'll see what I mean. We need to get in synch. In tune."

His voice was so soft, so patient. Usually by this time, my would-be lovers were evaluating their poor life choices, and deciding that an erotic tumble with the razor-tongued Amazon blonde was not worth the cuts and bruises.

And I didn't blame them. I hurt guys' feelings, always. I put them on the defensive, and made them feel emasculated, all of it. I was a hot mess as a sex partner.

So, there it was. The awful truth. This admittedly fabulous specimen was going to come to the same conclusion about me as the other guys had, sooner or later, and probably sooner. The only question was, could I get lucky before that happened?

Anybody's guess. I did not have any control over what came out of my mouth when I felt this vulnerable. I'd been swept up into the mountain aerie of a mysterious gazillionaire, for fuck's sake. And he wanted me to relax. Hah.

"You're a huge tease, Masters," I told him.

"Call me Ethan. And I'm not teasing. I'm just not going to let you rush this."

I opened my eyes wide, laughing at him. "Oh really? Aren't you masterful! No pun intended."

"Pun completely ignored. Can I make an outrageous suggestion?"

A million wild, erotic possibilities exploded in my mind, making my thighs clench and my toes contract. "Let us hear it," I said.

He reached out, and stroked me. A touch so light, I could barely feel it, yet it felt like wind rustling grass, all over my body. "Let me lead," he said.

I blinked at him. "Excuse me?"

"Give me this one," he said. "Let me make the decisions. You can just—"

"Lay back and let you control me?" My voice was uneven, and I didn't like that. It showed weakness.

"Let me please you," he corrected.

"You're asking me to do something I can't do," I said. "Asking me to be someone I'm not. Maybe we should just forget this."

"Hear me out," he coaxed. "I'm not asking you to be someone you're not. I love the way you are. You're hotter than hell, just like this. My fiery warrior maiden."

"I'm not your anything, Masters," I told him. "And don't you forget it."

He grinned. "That's my girl. Please call me Ethan."

"Dude, you are a slow learner," I said.

"No, just stubborn," he said, "I don't want you to change who you are. Just play a little game with me."

"I'm not the playful type, in case you haven't noticed."

"It's no big deal. Just try, really try, to give me this one. Let me lead. I swear to God, we can take turns. The next time, you dictate the rules, you run the game. I'll do anything you want. Knock me around, whip me into shape, break me to the saddle and gallop off into the sunset with me."

"Well, uh, yeah," I said. "That sounds more dynamic and fun than me lying around being passive like a shivering virgin."

"The shivering virgin scenario might have possibilities you haven't explored yet," he said.

"I don't know," I said simply. "Truth is, I don't even know if I can. My stress levels are too high. I'm like a feral cat. I can't just relax and purr. I'm always on my guard. It's my default mode."

"Could you just try?" he coaxed. His hands had moved around to my back, and stroked tenderly down over my shoulder blades, down to the small of my back...stopping short at my ass and moving gently back up again.

The guy meant exactly what he said about taking it slow. The suspense was going to kill me.

"I can try," I said, in a small voice. Try. I could try to walk on air or fly to the moon, too. But all the trying in the world wouldn't turn the impossible into the possible. "I just let you control... everything?" I repeated, to make sure I got the rules straight.

Ethan laughed. "It's more like letting me lead in a dance. I'm not proposing anything dangerous. More like a fun, sexy game, and just this time. Next time, I can spend the whole time on my knees, paying homage to your gorgeous pussy with my tongue, if you let me. Or whatever else you mandate. Or all of it. We can try all kinds of things, whatever we want, down the line."

"There is no down the line," I told him. "Remember? This is a one-off."

"Right, right," he soothed. "Whatever you say."

"Okay, you sweet talker, you," I said briskly. "Clue me in. How is this supposed to look? Me, letting you lead, I mean? I can't even see it in my mind's eye."

He reached up to my face, freezing as I flinched away. "First, take a deep breath, and let it out slowly," he said. "Then, do it again."

I swallowed back my knee-jerk smart remark, and just did it.

I was surprised at myself. I never followed anyone's orders. I'd built my whole life around that principle. But in his mouth, it sounded like a sexy invitation. One I wanted desperately to accept.

I wished I could be a different woman, just for tonight. But I was what my childhood trauma had forged me into. I couldn't mold myself into some new shape to suit him. I just looked at him, and mouthed the word. *How?*

He clasped my hands, winding his fingers through mine, and pulled me over toward the big easy chair, upholstered in battered dark brown leather. He sat, facing the window, and pulled on my hand. "Sit on my lap."

I stared down at him. "What, like you're some naked sexy Santa?"

He exploded with muffled laughter. "Goddammit, Kat. Stop making me laugh. It was supposed to sound a whole lot more innocent and less threatening than that."

"Sorry, but with that body, stark naked? Innocent is not the word that comes to mind. And a dick of those dimensions definitely falls under the category of a threat. Not that I'm complaining, of course. I have invited you in every way I know how to threaten me with your gorgeous dick. Bring on the danger, buddy. Menace me."

"I'd rather seduce and coax and persuade than threaten

you," he said. "It's a vibe thing. I want the vibe softer. But you have to allow it. I can't make you."

"Humph," I grunted, still resisting the pull of his hand, clamped on mine. "And you think sitting on your lap will make that happen?"

"We won't know until you try it, right? Neither will I. I'm just feeling my way."

"Ah." I swayed, barely, in his direction. "The lap thing seems kinky."

He grinned. "Sure, maybe. In a good way. I figured, if you're sitting on my lap, you won't feel trapped or crowded by me. Any time you wanted to get up, you could."

I swayed closer. "I don't know," I whispered. "I think it is a trap."

"Maybe," he whispered back. "But the bait is sweet. And there's plenty of it. As much as you can take."

Oooh. I was getting those naughty bad-boy vibes again. Easier for me to process than tenderness, solicitude. Tenderness terrified me, and I did not like being terrified.

I took a step toward him, then another, then another...and carefully, gingerly, perched myself on his lap. But something happened as our bodies touched. The heat, the sudden shock of contact, pulsed a throb of sensation through me that just unraveled me.

It took the starch right out of me. If I hadn't been sitting, I would have fallen. I had jelly-legs, a soft, liquid throat. Wet eyes, gazing into his with shocked awareness.

His arms slid around me, and I didn't slap them away. He looked up into my face, with that look on it. He didn't look uncomfortable. Just looked intensely interested. Wide awake. Not going anywhere.

"You okay?" he asked softly.

I shook my head. "Okay" was so absolutely not the word for whatever this was.

"Did I do something wrong?

I shook my head again. "Good, then," he whispered. "Come closer."

"I can't," I said shakily. "I'm sitting right on you. How much closer could I be?"

"Let's find out," he said.

I melted into him. Found myself with my forehead touching his forehead. His arms, going up around my shoulders. The contact was deeper than any kiss I'd ever known. It was like the glow of a like a star in my mind. Something was happening to me. As if he'd put a spell on me and it was dismantling all my defenses, they were melting before my eyes, and I couldn't make it stop. I couldn't ramp up my snotty hag routine again.

I was speechless, trembling. He was hugging me, and shudders of astonished release kept going through me, almost like I was coming, except that it was far deeper than any orgasm I'd ever given myself. Those were the only ones I'd ever had. Sex was fun sometime, but it had never yielded orgasms, at least not for me.

Then he kissed me.

I wrapped my arms around his neck and let myself be swept into the vortex.

CHAPTER 11

Ethan

Control. *Control.* That was the drumbeat throbbing in my mind as I kissed her. She was letting herself be vulnerable, and it was fucking miraculous. So courageous on her part. Heroic, even. And now, somehow, I had to live up to my bullshit hype, and be worthy of her. I had to lead.

Fuck. It scared me out of my wits. This was a huge responsibility. Put alongside the fact that I'd never been this turned on in my entire life. I'd had a whole lot of sex, with many women, but I'd never interacted on this level with them. Live wires, twined, sparking wildly. Naked souls, touching. Charged with emotion, bright with potential.

God, she was beautiful. Slim, but muscular, so strong and sexy, my greedy hands wanted to wander over every inch of her. But it was too soon. I had to keep it exquisitely delicate. A first-kiss-after Sunday-school kind of vibe, to start with. Tough to pull off, when we were both stark naked. But it was too soon for hot carnal lust.

I fought for control as I savored the flower-petal texture of her lips against mine, not groping for anything more than that.

And reality shifted, perceptions upended, and suddenly her lips were my whole world. Her lips were my whole universe. I could have kissed her forever and died satisfied. I stroked her back, let my fingers slide through her satiny hair, losing myself utterly in that kiss, as if I were Sleeping Beauty, and she had come to wake me up. And once my eyes had opened, nothing would ever be the same.

I had done this to myself. By getting her to let her guard down, I had dismantled my own, and I was startled by how naked I felt. How armored I had been. Who knew.

Ironically, it was Kat who made the move that pushed our kiss from the chaste and reverent to the erotic. She cupped my head in her hands, slid her tongue into my mouth, and suddenly we were making love with our mouths, tongues dancing. I drew energy and heat and wild sweetness from that miraculous fountain of her lips.

She shifted in my arms, clambering over me so that she faced me, straddling me. The chair was more than wide enough. My dick throbbed with eagerness, in contact with her beautiful ass, but she rose up, a secret little smile on her lips, so that her plump tits were at mouth level. She leaned forward. "Taste me," she whispered.

I seized her and buried my face in her breasts. Fucking perfect. Springy, soft, velvety smooth, the tight little nub of her nipple teasing my lips. I rubbed my face over it, cupping and caressing, sucking her breast into my mouth, swirling with my tongue, holding her steady as she arched and moaned, head flung back.

My hand slid lower as I suckled her, and I let myself go, letting instinct guide me as I stroked between her legs, petting that little triangle of hair, and then below it, oh yeah. Slick, sticky, tender. She was so wet, so hot, so heightened. She moved eagerly over my hand, and I let her body tell me where she wanted the touch, how much, how deep. My thumb, circling her clit, my two fingers slowly thrusting into her pussy, petting and dragging and stroking. So tight, so hot. It scalded me, clutching my fingers.

She moved as if she were on my dick, and I practically came right there. That sexy, wanton, undulating dance. The miraculous trust. She was allowing me to please her. This was my job description now. Kat Banner's sex toy. I needed no more self-definition than that.

She was moving faster now, and my fingers loved fucking her so much, they were about to come, too. They were slippery and hot, and I wanted to suck them clean, I couldn't wait to taste her lube. The aroma made me crazy. Hot, rich, flowers, sea. Woman. Strong, earthy, life. I grabbed her with my other arm, holding her tight as she came. Crying out, clenching, milking my fingers.

I don't know how I managed not to explode under her. I savored those endless little pulsing clenches around my fingers that just went on and on.

Finally, she sank down, and hid her face against my shoulder, panting.

No rush. I promised I'd be in control. I had this. After a timeless moment of just holding her, breathing with her, she lifted her head, and stared into my eyes.

"You ready?" she asked.

I didn't trust my voice, but I nodded.

"Good," she whispered, reaching down to grab my cock. I jerked, gasping.

"Did I hurt you?" she asked. "Did I squeeze too hard?"

"God, no. I'm just...really turned on."

"Good," she murmured. "Then I've got you right where I want you."

I reached down to the side of the cushion, where I had sneakily stashed a condom, just in case. I presented it to her. She gave me an approving smile and ripped it open with aplomb, rolling it over me with a bold, tight, caressing swirl of her hand.

She gripped me, swaying over me. Anointing my cockhead with her slick balm. Kissing me with her tight, juicy pussy...and then nudging me deeper.

She took me slowly inside her clinging depths, swaying forward to kiss me.

"Shall we dance?" she whispered.

CHAPTER 12

Kat

I t was the look in his eyes that did it. It went right through me. He saw the real me, the one I barely saw myself, I'd buried it so deep behind the sandbags and barricades and coils of razor wire. It felt strange to be seen. A spotlight on me, when I was used to darkness. Used to staring out an artillery slit in an armored tank.

Now here I was, not just seen, not just naked, but riding his gorgeous dick, with wild, wanton abandon. He clutched my ass, lifting me, pumping his thick, hard cock up deeply as he gave me that look...as if he was afraid to be seen, too, but he had no choice but to reveal himself to me.

There was nothing more exciting than that. My pussy clenched greedily around him, squeezing, fluttering with wave after wave of shimmering sensation, already like an orgasm. My whole body welcomed him, the field beyond my body as well. I was conscious of whole new realms of existence where he and I were linked, where there was no time, where I had no limits, where no roles were imposed on us. What had happened to me, to my family—it had not broken me. It did not limit me, it had not damaged my core self, and that was the person he was making love to. She was a creature I barely recognized. Free, wild, powerful. Unashamed and unafraid. Exploding with power, and wild joy.

It was an explosion of light in my deepest foundation, and it blew everything into vapor and dust, leaving me floating. Glowing. Exquisitely soft.

I stayed out there, in that soft, weightless place for a long time. It was the throb of his heart against my fingers that brought me back to our bodies.

I had splayed my hand against his sinewy neck, and I was feeling his pulse against my fingertips. Strong, steady, galloping. We were glued together with sweat.

He stirred, lifting his head. "You must be cold," he said.

I realized, startled, that I was smiling at him like an idiot. "I am so far from cold right now," I said.

"It was good for you?"

I laughed at him. "Aren't you a suave billionaire playboy?" I teased. "Asking for reassurance is not in the script."

"You're not in the script, either," he said. "And you are no plaything."

I threaded my fingers into his chest hair, gently digging my short nails into that thick, cut wall of muscle. "You got that right," I agreed. "But in answer to your question, it was incredible. Like nothing else I've ever felt. Don't get cocky, though."

"I won't get cocky, trust me," he said. "I certainly don't take any credit for what just happened. It was like...I don't know. Like being carried away by a flash flood."

"Did I hurt you? Did I leave bruises?" I asked.

His eyes narrowed. "Are you fucking with me?"

I put up my fingers, thumb and forefinger touching, smiling. "Maybe just a *leetle* tiny bit," I admitted. "But you can take it. If you can survive the cataclysmic tsunami of my lovemaking."

"Oh, hush up. You're shivering. Let's get into bed."

"I am in a state of perfect bliss. Don't mess with me. I don't want to move. I don't want a thing to change."

"Fine, don't move. I'll do everything." He picked me up, with shocking ease.

"Whoa!" I stiffened in alarm. "Don't do that!"

"Relax," he soothed, toting me across the room as if I weighed nothing at all. "Remember how you were going to trust me, and let me lead? Did I let you down?"

I slowly wound my arms around his neck, clasping his ass with my legs, and squeezed my pussy appreciatively around his already freshly hardening dick.

"No," I admitted. "But how long is the statute of limitations on this 'you take the lead' vibe? I should have defined the terms more carefully, you sneaky bastard. Goddamn billionaires. Can't trust 'em as far as you can throw 'em."

He laughed, as he strode across the large room, now full of shadows in shades of gray and blue. He slid me off his gorgeous prong with a shuddering sigh, and then set me onto my feet long enough to fling back the covers. "Lie down," he said. "Let me just get rid of this condom, and I'll be right with you."

He disappeared into an adjoining room, and in those few seconds alone, I felt my usual stupid anxiety start to rise again. Goddamn it. It made me angry at myself.

When he came back, he lifted the covers, an inviting gesture. "Join me?"

"You know, I'm not really the hang-around-and-cuddle type," I told him. "I'm more the 'wham-bam-thank-you-Sam' type. I'm nervous and twitchy. I run off my mouth, hurt people's feelings. And I don't want to ruin this. It was too perfect. Maybe it's better if we say goodnight now. And I go crash in that room you gave me before. We can leave this thing just as it is. Still perfect."

"No," he said. "We're not done. Not even close."

I just flapped my mouth, at a total loss. "But this is not me," I said. "This isn't my playbook."

"I'm not in your playbook," he said. "But I'm not going to waste one single fucking instant that I could spend with you. You're nervous? Tough shit. So am I. You're terrifying. But you're also incredible. And we've now solved that mystery that was tormenting us."

"And what mystery was that?"

He sat on the bed, slid between the covers, pulled me close. "We were wondering if the sex could be as intimate as the combat. I say yes, definitely. Maybe even more, because, you know. Orgasms. What do you say?"

He deserved for me to bat him around and give him shit, but I just opened my mouth and told him the naked truth. "Better," I said.

We lay there, facing each other. My face was hot, and pressure was building up in my chest. Too much feeling. I just didn't have the voltage to handle it anymore.

Ethan rolled over, snapped his fingers, and a rosy light turned on next to the bed.

"I prefer the dark," I said.

"But you're so beautiful," he said.

"You're throwing your weight around," I told him.

He looked over at me. "Sorry," he said, clicking the light off.

I immediately regretted that I could no longer see his gorgeous face. "I'm sorry I'm such a basket case," I said. "I know I'm not easy to deal with."

"No, not easy, definitely. But oh God, so worth it."

That made tears spring into my eyes, and I was desperately grateful that he had turned off the light. "Thanks." My voice sounded soggy.

Ethan reached out, and brushed away my tears with his finger, as if he could see in the dark. "I'm not easy, either," he admitted.

I laughed, under my breath. "Well, duh! Hot billionaires aren't expected to be easy. They're expected to be arrogant and spoiled and self-involved. And eccentric."

"And am I?"

"Arrogant, yes," I said.

"My sister gives me no end of shit about how controlling I am," he said.

"Yes, controlling, too," she said. "But people expect it of you, I bet. They don't expect it from blondes, whose job it is to be sweet and nice and accommodating. But somehow, I never got that memo. So I end up, well. Surprising people."

"You were exactly the person to be with me in that elevator, or I'd be dead."

"You might have taken them," I said.

I sensed his shrug in the darkness. "Maybe, but they would have gotten in a whole lot more licks. It's unlikely I would have gotten through that without you."

I felt absurdly pleased. "Well. Then I'm glad I was there. I guess that's why you're putting up with how weirdly defensive I am. My encounters usually don't last long enough for conversations like these. I make sure of that."

"I get it," he said. "You're that way because you have to be. It can't be undone by flipping a switch."

I went tense. "You don't know the first thing about me," I told him.

"Not the details," he said. "But the size of the scar, that can be measured."

"Don't lay any pop psychology bullshit on me," I warned him. "It bugs me."

He reached out, but I jerked away. "I'm not," he assured me. "And it's not pop psychology. It's just personal experience. Of a kind I wish I didn't have."

I gazed into the shadow that hid his eyes, suspicious. "What experience?"

"Long story," he said.

"You started it," I reminded him. "Let's hear it."

Ethan rolled onto his back again, stretching his arms behind his head. "It's actually more a story of what happened to Frey, my sister," he said.

"Yeah? What happened?"

He let out a sigh I could barely hear. "Okay, some background. My parents died in a car crash when I was sixteen. Drunk driver T-boned them on a country road at night."

"I am so sorry to hear that," I told him. "I know how that feels."

"Yeah, I know you do. Shane, my brother, was fourteen, and Frey was only seven. They sent us to stay with my mom's older sister, Jean, and her husband, Orren. They were super-religious, but of the toxic, doomsday variety. And they hated us. They were also afraid of Shane and me. We were already big, and Orren knew he couldn't physically control us. He was friends with one of the sheriff's deputies who went to his church. He got us accused of assault, and locked up in the juvenile detention center."

"Oh shit," I said. "Leaving your little sister all alone with them."

"Right." The silence that followed his words was awful for all the sinister possibilities it contained.

"So, uh...how bad was it?" I asked, cautiously.

"I'll probably never know," Ethan said. "I know they beat her. They locked her up in the basement. In the dark, for weeks at a time, with no clothes. Just a bucket. She was skin and bones when we finally got her out."

"Oh, my God," I whispered.

"I don't know what else he did to her," Ethan said. "Maybe even my sister doesn't even know. But she wasn't right for years. She still sleeps with the light on."

"You said she's married now, right?"

"Yeah. To a guy I served with in the Ranger Regiment. Jed. She seems happy."

"Good," I said fiercely. "Then they didn't take that from her."

"Yeah. At least that. Shane and I finally broke out, and came to save her, but it took us months to pull it off. She was in that hellhole for fucking *months*." His voice was harsh with suppressed violence.

"What about the uncle and aunt?" I asked. "Did you do any payback?"

Ethan didn't answer for a long time. "We wanted to. So bad. We were burning for it. But Shane and I sat down one night and thought it through. If we punished them, our status as outlaws would upgrade. They would have come after us harder, and tried us as adults if they caught us. And Freya would have gotten tossed into the foster care system alone. We decided not to risk it. Being there for Frey was more important than revenge."

"Good choice," I said. "I approve of that choice. Where are they now?"

"You mean, my uncle and aunt? What makes you think I monitor then?"

"Of course you monitor them," I scoffed. "Duh. What's up with them now?"

He made an irritated sound. "They're both still alive," he admitted. "He has Parkinson's. She has arthritis. They still go to church every Sunday. Fuck them both."

"Hmmph. You did the right thing by putting your little sister first."

He hesitated. "Thanks. How about you? Have you gotten revenge, for your thing?"

I shrank back, zinging with fresh tension. "We are not having this conversation. I told you. We don't talk about my private business."

"I told you mine," he said. "It's only fair."

"That was your free choice. Don't give me that 'it's only fair' crap, Masters."

He sighed. "You always call me that when you're pissed at me. And you're always pissed at me."

"Yes, I am! You keep on reaching in for more, and more, and more!"

"You fascinate me," he said. "I can't help it. I'm so curious."

"Bully for you," I told him. "Be as curious as you want. I'm not telling you about my shit. I don't do that. Ever. With anyone. End of story."

"Okay," he said meekly.

I was suspicious at his sudden agreement. Then he rolled over, covering my mouth with his, in an ardent, ravenous kiss.

CHAPTER 13

Ethan

Maybe the dark was better after all. I was overstimulated, but taking away one sense just made all the others get sharper. Her scent, her delicious taste and texture, the vibrant, perfect shape of her. And after that first panicky gasp, she responded passionately, kissing me back. She pulled me toward her, and I rolled on top of her.

Her muscles went rigid, and I stopped. "Is this okay?" I asked.

"I don't know," she said. "I usually, ah…"

"You could get on top, if you want," I suggested. "I'd love that too. I know it would be great. But you've trusted me so far, and it's been good. More than good."

She thought about it for a second, and I felt her shrug. "Oh, go ahead," she said tartly. "Do it, do it. Quick. Before I have time to make a big thing of it in my head."

I laughed, under my breath, nudging her into position. "I will not rush this, no matter what you say," I told her. "I'd rather sneak up on it slowly, even if it takes hours. Not try to get out in front of it. I don't want to fuck it up. Break things."

"Damn it, Masters," she grumbled. "Don't try to fix me."

"No way. I like the way you are. I think you're fucking perfect."

"Then you're pretty twisted, buddy, but it was still a very sweet thing to say. Stupid, wrong-headed, possibly pathological, but sweet."

Damn, the super-erotic vibe was weird, mixed with giggling and snorting. But laughter was another defense mechanism. I was on to her, and it didn't dent my appetite one goddamn bit. I groped for another condom in the drawer of the bedside table, ripped it open one handed and rolled it over myself in one swift move. Then I shifted, tilting her hips, and her beautiful, strong legs wrapped around me, hugging me jealously tight as I slowly slid my cock into her clinging pussy. She was still drenched from the last time, and that was very fortunate, as tight as she was.

"Perfect," I said again, but my voice shook.

She started to speak, but her voice choked off as I surged inside again. "Oh God."

"I know," I said, breathless. "You feel so good. It's different with you."

She kissed me, and the kiss unleashed me. We were off and at it, wild and fierce. I'd never been with a woman so lithe and physically strong. She wrapped herself around me, put me right where she needed me, those powerful thighs locked around my ass, pulling me in, bracing me. We were one thing, heaving and gasping together.

I barely held back my orgasm when she exploded, her pussy squeezing me rhythmically. I held my breath, motionless, teetering on the edge of my self-control.

Our hearts slowed, after a few panting minutes. "You didn't come?" she asked.

"Not yet," I said. "I want to make you come again. At least a few more times."

"You are one hardcore macho control freak, Masters. Is that a billionaire thing?"

"Couldn't tell you. I think it's just me, but I can't be sure. I haven't fucked any other billionaires, at least to my knowledge, so I can't really say."

She laughed softly. "Smartass."

"It was the answer you deserved." I kissed her again, still wedged deep inside her, and tossed back the covers, rising up onto to my knees. I folded her legs up, and began again. Slow, gliding strokes, tenderly caressing her clit with the pad of my thumb.

I was following a path toward her pleasure that was mapped out for me by raw instinct. All I had to do was silence the yapping voice in my mind and pay attention to it. I had never been so motivated to get this right. She deserved for this to work, explosively. Repeatedly.

She slid her fingers into my chest hair, digging in her nails. "Come. Right now," she urged. "I want to feel you come. I need it."

Her whispered command took me by surprise, and shoved me right off that tightrope of self-control. I lost it completely, and let go. Arching over her, hips driving. Feeling the delicious bite of those nails as intense pleasure, her low voice inciting me.

Then, that huge crashing, falling. That obliterating rush. It carried me away.

When I finally opened my eyes, I was collapsed over Kat's body.

"Damn. I think I lost consciousness," I mumbled. "Sorry. Am I squishing you?"

"I can breathe," she said, a hint of humor in her voice. "But only because I'm very strong. I can make my ribs expand, even with—what are you? Two-forty?"

"Bite your tongue." I said lazily. "Not an ounce more than two-thirty." But I rolled off and out of her. We shivered as the air hit our sweat-drenched bodies.

"You kept me warm, at least," she commented.

I grabbed the cover and pulled it up over us both, and shifted closer. No grabbing, or she'd stiffen up. I was starting to get the Kat choreography down. She needed extra time, she needed breathing room, and she needed for her prickly bull-shit to roll right off my back, and not be taken personally. I was getting the hang of it.

But if I tried to lay down the law, she would tear me to pieces. Hmm.

It was a thorny dilemma, since I wanted to keep her safe. And in my bed.

I heard a grumbling sound from her belly. My own, always suggestible, responded, and we both laughed. "Are you hungry?" I asked.

"I could eat," she admitted "Have we got some leftovers from that amazing lunch in a fridge somewhere?"

"I'm sure we do, but I'll do you one better," I said. "I can make kickass buttermilk blueberry pancakes. Like you would not believe."

She let out an involuntary whimper. "Oh, my God, really? Lay it on me, Masters. What kind of eccentric billionaire makes his own pancakes?"

"From scratch, I take pains to point out, and enough with the billionaire cracks. I had a little sister to feed, okay? I could even make you a pancake mouse, or a pancake man, or a pancake flower if you want, with decorative chocolate chips or blueberries. I have got game, when it comes to pancakes. My French toast isn't bad, either."

"I think I hit a nerve," she teased.

"Well then?" I slid out of the bed and snapped to turn on the light. "Let me show off."

"I can't wait to check out your pancake game, but I cannot walk around your apartment in the condition you have reduced me to," she said. "I need a shower."

"Fine. Right through that far door. On the other side of the bathroom is the wardrobe. Use anything. One of my robes, or shirts, whatever else you find. Feel free."

"Sounds good," she said.

"You remember how to get to the kitchen? I'll turn on the lights as I go."

Her smile was more relaxed than any look I had seen on her face thus far. "I'm sure I can blunder my way back to the kitchen," she said. "Particularly with the smell of pancakes to guide me. Go on, Ethan. Get to work. I want my pancakes."

"I'm afraid to turn my back," I blurted, out of nowhere. "I'm afraid you'll disappear."

"Not without my pancakes, I won't," she assured me.

But I just kept on standing there, mind wiped blank, smiling like an idiot. Amazed at how freaking beautiful she was.

"You're just going to have to trust me," she said. "It's your turn for that."

I turned and marched out to the sound of her soft laughter.

CHAPTER 14

Kat

I took longer in the shower than I had to. It was just too much, all that pleasure and excitement and revelation. I had to back off.

I couldn't believe I had found myself actually wanting to tell him my awful, dangerous secrets. The disaster that had befallen my lost sisters and me.

I'd stopped myself just barely in time. That way lay a whole world of hurt. I wasn't going to do that to him. He didn't deserve it. No one did, but particularly not this guy. This delicious, attractive, charismatic, yummy, problematic guy. He'd been through plenty of hell of his own, just like me. Which somehow made the barriers between us thinner.

He was sneaky as hell, though. Like an expert cat burglar, delicately picking all my locks, and hey presto, my legs fell open.

And now he'd decided it was his moral responsibility to keep me safe, which was sweet of him, very gallant, but a huge pain in the ass. That triggered all kinds of territorial animal behaviors in men, which were extremely difficult to manage. It was up to me to keep my head on straight. Too late to keep my panties on, though. Oh, well.

God, the man was magic. He could actually touch me at will without triggering my defensive reflexes and getting clobbered. I couldn't imagine how he pulled it off.

I went into Ethan Masters' wardrobe, and laughed out loud. That room alone was the size of my living room and kitchen combined. Closets with racks of suits, coats, pants, shirts. Shelves full of gleaming shoes. Drawers full of silk ties. For fuck's sake.

I found a drawer filled with exquisitely ironed and folded T-shirts, and picked one out. It was wine-red, and very soft. I tossed it on, and the neck slid off my shoulder, and the hem hung down below my butt, but it was perfectly fine for midnight pancakes.

My mouth watered, but who knew if it was hunger or lust? I'd never been so fascinated by a man. I wanted to know him, for real. Even more dangerous, I wanted to be known by him. But this guy could take me apart from the inside out.

It was a disaster waiting to happen. But I couldn't walk away. Not without some more of this. He'd stimulated my appetite.

I wandered through the apartment, following the tantalizing scent of pancake batter browning in butter. I leaned in the kitchen entryway, enjoying the spectacle of a stunning, muscular guy, naked to the waist, wearing only loose athletic pants, standing at the stovetop griddle, spatula in hand.

"Aren't you worried about getting burned?" I asked.

He smiled over his shoulder. "I wouldn't fry bacon like this," he admitted. "But pancakes don't scare me." He waved me over to a stool at the bar that was an extension of the kitchen island, and piled four fluffy, golden pancakes with perfect, crispy borders onto a plate, sliding it toward me. "There you have butter, syrup, whipped cream, jam, and Nutella, and sliced strawberries, too," he said. "Dig in."

I pulled the plate to myself, inhaling the aroma. "I'm a real basic bitch when it comes to pancakes," I confessed. "I'm a butter and real maple syrup kind of girl."

He gave me an approving look. "A woman after my own heart."

I smeared a little butter on top, and drenched them with maple syrup. The first dripping, fluffy, steaming bite made me practically moan with pleasure.

"Oh Lord, have mercy," I mumbled. "These are insane."

And they were. High, tender, fluffy, with a delicate golden crust, and that tender buttermilk zingieness. It was an oral orgasm.

"You like?"

"Oh, my God," I muttered, around a mouthful of food. "So good."

"I had harsh critics, and frequent practice," he said, dropping another knob of butter to sizzle on the grill. He expertly ladled another batch onto the griddle.

"Your little sister?" I asked.

He nodded. "She was a pancake freak. Very fussy eater. We had them a lot."

"Can I ask you something?" I asked.

His eyes lit up. "Can I have one question for every answer that I give?"

"No," I said flatly. "Never mind. Forget I asked."

He let out a sharp sigh. "Okay, fine. No bargains. Ask whatever you want."

"You said you and your brother broke out of juvie and rescued your sister from the basement," I said. "So, what then? Since you didn't hurt the evil uncle and aunt, what did you do? Where did you keep your sister? How did you feed her?"

Ethan flipped his pancakes, and stared at them as they sizzled on the grill.

"I got lucky," he said. "I met a guy in juvie. He put me in touch with this guy in Portland. Renzo was his name. He was a hacker, and he needed crackerjack hackers for his crew. I was good, and Shane wasn't half bad, either. So when we got Freya away from my aunt and uncle, the three of us shoplifted and grifted our way to Portland. We worked for Renzo for a couple of years, until we found our feet."

"No school for you, then?"

"Nah. I made Shane go, and Freya. I figured I'd be the only freak. Then Renzo got busted, and that was the end of that. I got myself a GED and once Shane was big enough to look after Frey for me, I joined the Army."

"So, you hacked for criminals by night, and made pancakes and helped little sis with her homework by day," I said.

"More or less, but she didn't need much help." He flipped the cakes onto a plate. "She's the genius of the family."

I shook my head. "The bar must be high for you Masters types."

He grinned at me. "You want more pancakes?"

"Oh, no, this is fine. I'm stuffed."

He made short work of his own plate of pancakes. I watched, imagining his teenage self, on the lam, figuring out how to provide for his family at sixteen. Not a whole lot different than how it had been for Raffi, back in the day, with Gabri and me on her back.

Not that I could say anything to him about that. I blew out a sigh, and then nibbled a meltingly sweet strawberry. "We should get some sleep," I said. "I think tomorrow will be busy. We need to figure out what the hell was going on at the Fletchley Building."

He murmured at me noncommittally, around a big bite of pancake.

"You want to know something weird about today's job, at Clemens & Associates?" I asked.

He swallowed his bite of food, eyebrows going up. "Of course."

"I was freaked out by that job before you even got there," I said. "Who is Clemens, anyway? He was talking about you as if he knew you from way back."

"I met him when I was getting a master's degree in business," he said. "He contacted me about his start-up. He wanted me to partner with him on his new cryptocurrency. It seemed interesting from the prospectus, but I had the sense it was shakier than he was saying. Then I met you. And all hell broke loose."

"That's odd," she said. "Because the whole place was just a front."

"In what sense?" he asked, frowning.

"In a literal sense. There was nothing there. They called me from the temp agency, and sent me there to work the front desk, but there was nobody in the back. I peeked. The place was empty. Empty cubicles, a phone that never rang. The office manager, Julia, was as nervous as a wet cat. I asked about the bathroom, to put my lunch in the fridge, and she bit my head off."

"That is weird," he agreed.

"Yeah, considering what happened in that elevator. When I saw the empty desks, I thought, oh shit. They're running a con, and I'm just window dressing. That guy's name on the wall, and behind it, nothing."

"I tried calling Hugh, while you were in the shower," he said.

I grunted. "He's not going to talk to you. They've got him by the balls. Something big. Gambling debts, embezzlement, selling financial secrets to foreign nationals, kiddie porn. Something awful."

"You have a devious mind," he said.

"It was his vibe," I said. "The stench of sleaze cannot be mistaken. He was also a dickhead. I'm not sorry for him, even if they're squeezing his balls in a vise."

Ethan's phone, which lay on the bar, began to buzz. I glanced at the clock on the wall. Midnight-thirty. No rest for the wicked. Unless this was a girlfriend, doing a booty call, of course. Always a possibility.

He glanced at the display, cursing under his breath. "I should have buried this thing," he said," Will you excuse me for a second?"

"Of course," I said. "Go right ahead."

He hit the screen and put it to his ear. "Jenn, why are you calling at this hour?...yes, I know, but I was busy..."

I heard a burst of high-pitched yapping on the other end of the line.

Ethan rubbed his brow as if his head was hurting. "Oh, fuck. That lunch with the senator is tomorrow? You're kidding me. What time?"

Another vociferous burst from the phone.

Ethan rolled his eyes. "No. I'll do the press conference tomorrow morning, but you need to call the Emory Summit people and tell them I can't make it for the opening address...I don't know, Jenn! Tell then whatever you want. Get creative. Tell them I broke my leg...no, I'm not mad at you. I got attacked in an elevator this morning by eight goons, so I'm on high security alert...yeah. I'm fine, but it killed my appetite for public appearances. I want to lie low while I figure out who the fuck was trying to kill me...no, that won't work. Don't guilt me, okay? Not tonight. I'm not in the mood. Ten-thirty tomorrow. Got it."

As I watched, it dawned on me, what an incredibly public figure this man was. His money, MasterTech, press conferences, lunch with the senator. He owned at least six different companies under the parent company MasterTech, and they were launching a hotly anticipated new product, FireGlass, one that even I had heard of. Pictures and videos were taken of him constantly, microphones were shoved in his face, questions shouted by eager journalists, everyone hanging on his every word.

Women fawned all over him. The hot, charming, genius billionaire.

Getting involved with this man was like sending an embossed invitation to the Petruzzi family to find me, and end me. Which, incidentally, put Ethan in danger too. Just being near me could hurt people. The kindest thing I could do for any guy that I really liked was to disappear.

And oh God, how fucking depressing that was. It had always been a fact of life, but it had never stung me like it did tonight.

His eyes narrowed as he studied me. "What?" he demanded.

"Meaning?"

"Your face," he said. "You were looking happy and relaxed. Suddenly, you weren't. It was like a light switching off. Was it something that I said, or did? What happened?"

Shit. The guy was as sharp as a tack. Which sucked for me right now.

"Nothing," I said. "It's just late, and it's been a hell of a day."

"Yeah. Which was ending well. Orgasms and pancakes. What was it? Was it because I answered that fucking phone when my assistant called? I'm sorry, but I saw ten missed calls from her. I had to throw her a bone, or she would've had a meltdown."

"No, no, no," I said. "That didn't bother me. It's fine."

"Bullshit." His voice was hard. "We fought back-to-back together, and we just had the best sex of our lives. You can't lie to me now."

"I'm not lying," I said, through my teeth. "It's just my own private stuff, Masters, and I do not have to share it with you if I don't feel like it. Understand?"

He just sat there and waited, the bastard. The clock in the kitchen was loud, and the tick-tick-tick banged on my eardrums, driving me nuts. "Goddamn it, Masters!"

"Call me Ethan," he said stubbornly.

I let out a sigh, and gave in. The guy was chipping away at me like nobody's business. "Okay, fine," I snarled. "I realized, while shamelessly eavesdropping on your phone conversation, that you lead an extremely public and outward-facing life. And for various private but extremely compelling reasons, I do not. I stay off the radar. It's necessary for my health and safety. And this makes me sad, okay? Are you happy now that you know the terrible truth? I had an incredible time with you, and it's very hard not to glom onto that and want more. But there it is. We cannot hang out."

"You're in hiding?" he asked.

I rolled my eyes. "For a guy as bright as they say you are, you sure do make me repeat myself a lot."

"Tell me what your problem is," he said. "And I'll fix it."

Oh crap. Now I was in for the fight of my life. "You can't," I said flatly. "It's not safe. And clearly, you have enough problems without piling mine on top of them. I certainly have enough without yours. The whole would end up being more than the sum of the parts, and we'd both end up dead. So, no. Forget it."

"At least tell me. I won't make your problems worse just by knowing what they are," he urged.

"Oh, hell, no," I said. "I know you, buddy. You'd get all overbearing and start thinking Master Knows Best for the little lady. Be real with me. You know you would."

"Goddam it, Kat." He slapped the countertop. "Let me help! This thing, with you...it's special. It's not the kind of thing you find every day. It's the kind of thing almost nobody finds, ever. And I fucking want it!"

"Well. That is gratifying. I want it too. But my secret problems suck, Ethan. If you knew them, then suddenly you'd feel like it was your job to solve them, but they are life-ruining problems. And you know what? I like your life. I want it to continue, unchecked. I like the whole package. The great, brilliant, tough, benevolent Ethan Masters. Yum, love that guy. May he live forever. The world is more interesting with you in it, Ethan. Give my problems a pass. Really."

"I want your life to continue, too," he said forcefully. "I want to be part of it!"

I shook my head. This was awful. "I'm sorry," I said, my voice strangled. "I swear, though, and I mean this from the heart, even though it's a dumb cliché. But it's not you, it's me. You're awesome. Aside from the bossiness and the forced abduction thing, of course, but nobody's perfect."

"Kat, listen." He shoved his empty plate to the side. "I'm sure your problems suck, but you know a thing I have a lot of? Solutions."

"Ethan, I can't let you—"

"If your problems can be solved with money, I have a fuckton of it, more than I will ever need."

"It is not that," I said. "Please, don't push me."

But of course, he kept pushing me. "If your problems are with the law, I have great connections. I'm owed a ton of favors. Is your problem with the criminal underworld? Guess what...I have connections there, too, what with my checkered past, and all."

"Ethan—"

"Are your problems something that can be solved with brute physical force? Commando soldiers, explosives, firepower? Guess what...I'm your guy. I have those things, too. As long as I'm not hurting any innocents."

"I would never," I said haughtily. "As if."

"Of course not, but I had to say it. The bottom line here is that I have whatever resources you might need to solve your problem. For fuck's sake, Kat. Use me."

I crossed my arms over my chest, shivering. "In exchange for what, Masters?"

His mouth tightened. "That's not fair."

"Nope, it sure isn't, but too bad," I said. "I have no way to pay you back for a favor that big. Beyond the crass, obvious ones."

"That is not an issue for us. We're past that."

"Yeah? Seriously? You've known me for what, twelve hours? And now you're laying your fortunes and armies at my feet? Come on. You're busy, you're stressed, you're overextended with your own problems, and our thing is just too new for this. You're not thinking straight, so I have to think straight for you. Let it go, Ethan. We are not having this conversation right now."

"I can't," he said.

"Well, that's not up to you," I said. "However..."

"However, what?" His eyes brightened.

"The night's still young," I said. "And we are all fueled up with your incredible pancakes. Do you want to spend this precious night arguing with me, and trying to manipulate and control me? Or would you rather spend it blowing my mind with your magic dick?"

I strolled around the bar, and laid my hands on his shoulders, then slid them down his chest. Then still lower, down that tangle of chest hair that narrowed to a treasure trail over his gorgeous, taut abs. His cock tented his sweatpants out, fully erect, hot and eager. I pulled it loose, caressing the big, blunt, heart-shaped head, sliding my fingers around, making them slick with pre-come. Swirling my fingers in tender little teasing circles on his velvety cockhead.

"Well, damn," he said, unevenly. "When you put it that way..."

His arms went around me, our lips touched, and something

inside me just threw up its hands. It was stupid, ill-considered, risky, self-indulgent. And more fabulous sex was not going to make this man's protective instincts any easier to manage, that was for damn sure.

But I wanted this. I wanted more. As much as I could get.

And I was by God taking it.

CHAPTER 15

Vincent

He looked up from the video he was watching on his tablet as the door opened.

Ah. His sister, Nicole. Back home to be punished for her latest fuckup.

He looked back down, letting Nicole stand there and wait as he finished an inspiring YouTube video that had just been posted by Mia Wilkes, an attractive female neuroscientist. She was a popular viral sensation, having released a series of documentaries and a very well-received TED talk, which already had millions of views.

She'd released a bi-weekly flurry of YouTube videos since then. Mia focused on motivation, not that Vincent lacked it. She promised life-transforming results from following her recommended routines. He liked her low, velvety voice, the way he felt when she demonstrated the explosive energy in her thigh muscles in her burpees and squat jumps. Exercise was an important component of Mia's secret sauce for success.

He spared a quick glance at Nicole. The controlled anger in her face. Their father had made him team leader after Nicole's shocking fuckups, and had given Vincent full control of this operation. About fucking time, after being under that snotty bitch for years. Vincent could finally get back at her for her many cruelties and humiliations, small and large, over the years. Ever since they were kids.

The video ended, and he sighed, contemplating how he might gain access to the dick-tingling Mia Wilkes. Large sums of money were an unbeatable strategy. And he felt oh, so motivated by her exquisitely defined ass.

Once they got SmokeScreen, after the Event happened, he'd be able to summon any woman he pleased. Any woman on earth would open her legs or her mouth for him, on command. That was how it was for Vincent's father, Owen Halliwell, with his almost inconceivable wealth.

Not that Vincent had ever benefited from his father's wealth. Vincent was just one of Halliwell's illegitimate brood, just like Nicole. Halliwell had groomed and molded them all into tools to serve his empire. Disposable tools. Because if one of them failed, he or she was disposed of, usually in front of the rest of them. Owen Halliwell considered it very important that they all fully internalize the price of failure.

This was Nicole's last chance...and it would take place squarely under Vincent's grinding thumb. Sweet.

He wanted to punish his father and Nicole both. Vincent would show that arrogant old goat Halliwell what he was made of. Nicole would regret having bullied and tortured him. His father would regret not recognizing his true potential. After the Event, Vincent would be exponentially wealthier than Halliwell ever had been. Not that his father would live to see it, of course. But he could watch from the fiery pits of hell.

Thinking of the pits of hell reminded him of Nicole, still waiting for his attention. She resented being placed beneath him? Good. Let her squirm. She deserved it, after her mistakes. And when he'd used her up, she'd join their father in hell...and both of them could watch Vincent rule. While they writhed and shrieked in the flames.

Vincent had been a member of her team last year, when she'd been tasked to get SmokeScreen for Halliwell, and to secure one of the Masters brothers to unlock it. She'd almost pulled it off...until she didn't. She'd captured Shane Masters, but she had let their fall guy, Jed Clearwater, get away clean, which meant that all their complicated, expensive, exhaustive months of prep work had been for nothing. She'd let the meathead she'd partnered with, Wex Boer and his band of idiot mercenaries, fuck everything up.

Halliwell had been so furious, he'd taken Shane Masters for himself, since Nicole clearly could not be trusted with him. Not that the man was of any use, to him or anyone. Then Nicole failed again, in Oregon. She'd had Freya Masters and Jed Clearwater right in her grasp...and she'd lost them. Again.

The incompetence boggled his mind. She'd barely stayed ahead of Jed Clearwater and the other Unredeemables' relentless hunt ever since. Vincent had expected Halliwell to have her shot on sight, but oh no. Little Nicky had gotten yet another chance to win back her status as Daddy's fucking favorite.

The only way Nicole could get out of the doghouse now was to get her hands on another Masters brother, and once again this morning, she had failed. The debacle at the Fletchley Building was another expensive preparation, wasted. A huge, embarrassing clusterfuck.

Therefore, Vincent was swooping down to take the situation in hand. Halliwell had explained Vincent's new role; to control and manage Nicole's excesses while continuing to make use of her remarkable abilities. In a nutshell, to make that naughty bitch behave, by any means necessary...even if he had to punish her severely. He'd gotten explicit permission from Halliwell to take that punishment as far as he liked.

And oh...he liked. He liked, very much.

When he finally had Ethan Masters in his grasp, he would have not only the key to using that algorithm, but also the mind that had dreamed it up. Vincent would keep that mind for himself. If he controlled it, it was almost like being as brilliant as Masters himself. Ethan Masters, his own personal possession. Like a gerbil in a cage.

And speaking of personal possessions...he turned with leisurely slowness to study his latest toy. Nicole, still standing by the door. She wore black silk pants and a white silk blouse, and her hair was swept into a low bun. Her face was unrepentant.

"I'm surprised you have the nerve to show your face," he said. "You wasted still more of our money and precious time this morning. You put us out there, in danger of discovery. Three men died. Five more are so injured, they're now useless. And we have nothing to show for it, other than putting Ethan Masters even more on his guard. I'm team leader now. I have the final say. You're done costing us money, time, and lives. You've outlived your usefulness, Nicole. Congratulations. You've been retired."

Nicole's face had turned a dull, ashy color. She knew what "retired" meant, in the context of their lives as Owen Halliwell's unlucky bastard spawn.

"Let me fix this," she said. "I'm already working on an even better plan. Our plan, Vincent. Not Halliwell's plan. You can't execute the Event without me."

"You think not? I've been doing this for years, Nicole. Just like you. You're not so fucking special."

"I came up with the Event. I put everything into place. I'm the only one who can troubleshoot for you in real time. I know every moving part of it intimately."

He considered that for a moment. What she said was literally true, not that he would ever admit it to her. But she still needed to be put in her place.

"What do you know about the blonde woman who fought beside Masters in the parking garage?" he demanded.

Her eyes flashed. "Everything," she said. "I got her name, address, and social security number from the temp agency who sent her to Clemens' office. She lives in Rainier Beach. Her name is Katrin Banner. My men have been to her house, and the dump of a martial arts school she runs for neighborhood kids. She's a wild card that we don't understand yet, but we will, if you let me do my work. If you retire me, I won't be able to tell you if her identity is real. No one gets the dirt on people like me, Vin."

"Don't call me Vin," he said. "Call me 'sir.'"

Her face twisted. "You've got to be fucking kidding me. *You?*"

"Have them bring in the portal," he told Maynard and Lopez, two of his men, both of whom had been present at the Fletchley disaster this morning, and had lived to tell the tale. Both of whom had reason to be disgusted with Nicole's leadership. They had disposed of three of their colleagues' bodies in the incinerator this morning.

They moved quickly, and soon they and two more men, the guards who had been stationed outside the room, wheeled the big machine inside. It was one of Owen Halliwell's own security designs, made to protect himself from his many enemies. Its battery of intensely sensitive sensors would sense any electronic device, explosive, or poison present on or inside a human body.

Vincent gave Nicole a thin smile. "Strip," he commanded.

She hesitated. "But I—why would I need to demonstrate—"

"I don't trust you, Nicole. You have proven yourself unreliable. I can't let you near me unless I am sure you are clean, and as you know, the device gets a more reliable reading when the subject is naked. Not that I need to explain myself to you."

"No, you don't," she said. "But I would never—"

"No, 'sir,'" he corrected.

Nicole stopped, swallowed. "No, sir," she forced out. "But…" She glanced around at the four men in the room, who were paying very close attention. Their eyes gleamed with hot anticipation, despite their blank expressions.

"The men are here to protect me from you, Nicole." Vincent kept his voice soft and mocking. "And you have no one to blame for that but yourself. Now strip. Do not make me tell you a third time. You won't like what happens then."

"Yes, sir." Her voice had taken on a robotic tone.

She quickly and mechanically removed her shoes and then clothing, carefully draping each piece over the back of one of the desk chairs.

The portal looked like something straight out of a science fiction tale. A gleaming chrome door, the inner frame winking and blinking with colored lights. A magic door, leading to nowhere and everywhere.

"Take your hair down," Vincent instructed. "You know that already, Nicole. No hairpins or jewelry or any foreign objects can go through."

Nicole lifted her arms, unfastened her hair, and shook it down, holding herself very straight, jaw clenched, gaze straight ahead. He enjoyed watching her struggle.

"Turn, slowly," he ordered.

"Yes, sir." That robotic voice was beginning to annoy him, but he was distracted from it by the spectacle of her spinning around.

He'd seen her naked before, of course, during their training modules over the years. He always enjoyed the spectacle of a naked girl, whether she was one of his half-sisters or not. Nicole's body was fit and beautiful, as was her perfectly made-up face. But he was disturbed by the unsightly raised scarring on her cheekbone that makeup did not entirely hide, ruining the smooth texture. And that ugly red, puckered scar in her shoulder, too. Relics from her adventure with Freya Masters and Clearwater. Flaws that urgently needed to be dealt with.

"After the Event, organize cosmetic surgery immediately to correct those disgusting scars," he said. "They're repellent. They lower your value."

"Yes, sir," she said.

"Well?" he said sharply. "What are you waiting for? Go through the portal!"

She moved very slowly through the portal. Maynard stepped forward to study the readout on the screen embedded on the outside surface. It took him a few minutes.

"The portal did not recognize any frequency, toxin, or other substance that is in its database," Maynard announced. "Shall I integrate with a physical cavity search?"

Vincent was taken aback by Maynard's bold question, but it was understandable. Maynard was angry, and eager to intensify Nicole's humiliation. Vincent was tempted to agree. And Maynard had an erection. All the men in the room but himself had one.

He could order Nicole to put her sexual skills to work to service his men. That was clearly what they were hoping. She'd done worse to him in the past, when she was team leader. But it would make it more difficult for her to exercise authority with those men thereafter. Nicole was flawed, but still quite useful, he mused regretfully. It was difficult to effectively give orders with a dick shoved up one's throat.

"Bring in Dr. Silvano," he said. "And the chair."

Nicole betrayed herself by turning to stare at him, wide-eyed. "What? Who?"

"I require a demonstration of loyalty," he told her. "I decided Halliwell's system was a good one. Streamlined. You'll get a loyalty tooth today...keyed to me."

She stared at him in stark horror. Dr. Silvano was the oral

surgeon Halliwell had used to implant the loyalty teeth. He was also an icy-blooded sadist.

If one of Halliwell's bastard children failed him in some significant way, he or she was compelled to get a loyalty tooth, as a final trial before execution. A molar was pulled, and a fake one implanted that had three components inside it; an electronic receiver, a tiny charge of explosives, and a fast-acting poison. Halliwell had an implant that monitored his vitals. If he died, a signal was sent to all of those implants. They would burst open and release the poison. His erring children would die instantly.

So, of course, would all the others with a poison tooth that was keyed to his vitals, those who had not erred. But no system was perfect.

Halliwell had given Vincent permission to implant a loyalty tooth keyed to her brother. It was fortunate neither of them had one that was keyed to Halliwell...at least, not yet. But it could always happen.

Yet another reason to be sure the Event took place as soon as possible.

"No, Vincent," she said. "Please. You don't have to—"

"Call me 'sir.' This will keep you honest. Now our fortunes are forever linked, Nicole. You know the drill. Anesthesia won't be necessary. Neither will painkillers afterward. Halliwell even shipped me the special chair, the one he always uses for the loyalty teeth. I'm supposed to send it right back, because the old pervert is attached to it. Fond memories, and all. Try not to piss yourself, Nicky. But you know they always do."

Dr. Silvano walked in. A tall, cadaverous man with sunken cheeks, dead eyes. Dyed black hair in a strangely lacquered comb-over. He looked at Nicole's naked body with casual appreciation, but Nicole looked far less beautiful now, having gone a gray color, which made her heavy make-up stand out grotesquely vivid.

They wheeled in the chair, which was an old dentist's chair with a few extra leather buckled straps attached. Wrists, ankles, throat, waist, forehead. Dr. Silvano had insisted on it. Dental work was difficult to perform when the patient was writhing.

"Maynard, strap her in," Vincent ordered. "You can all stay to watch."

CHAPTER 16

Ethan

My mind kept looping and spinning in wild circles as I lay in bed, dazed and confused, with that stunning, enigmatic girl in my arms. The contact with her skin was thrilling. I kept pulling her close to feel the rush again, all along my side, my arm around her shoulder, her silky hair coiled up against my neck, tickling my nose.

It didn't matter how many times we'd had sex. One fresh squeeze or stroke or caress, and my dick just sprang up for more, more, more.

Like it was doing now, but I ignored the impulse so I could think. Something at which I usually excelled. But it was hard to think straight around Kat Banner, woman of mystery, object of extreme desire, because I kept getting derailed by feelings about her. And that fucked up everything.

I was ninety-nine percent convinced that she was not a honeypot spy. If she'd wanted to hurt me, she'd had many opportunities, with me naked and dozing.

She hadn't. She'd cuddled me, and dozed herself. Boneless, relaxed. She would have to be skilled sociopathic liar to put on a show like that, and I was dead sure she wasn't. She was passionate, intense. On fire with fierce integrity.

I was inclined to trust her. To believe what she told me. Maybe I was a dickhead idiot, but fuck it. I still had to figure out what her problem was, and how I could help her solve it. Letting her walk away wasn't an option. Nicole's people would kill her.

I wasn't going to let that happen.

If that involved throwing my weight around and making her hate me, then so be it. If I had to violate her precious privacy to figure out who the fuck was gunning for her, so be it. In any case, I would lose her. That part was inevitable. But me, taking care of business? That gave her a fighting chance to survive. That was all that mattered.

That was how my reasoning went. No point in sharing it with her because she didn't know how to lean on anyone. Still. Making her hate me was going to suck.

This past night had been like nothing I'd ever imagined. There had been a completely different woman in my bed than the one I had expected. I thought I'd be in for a hot, stimulating romp with a confident, athletic woman who knew exactly what she wanted. But once I sneaked past her enormous defenses, I had found the opposite.

Kat had been so open to me. So vulnerable, astonished by pleasure, overwhelmed by emotion. Touching her was like hanging on to raw electricity. I'd spent the whole time doing a balancing act on the extreme far edge of my self-control, terrified of hurting her, scaring her, or triggering her defense system.

And now, as dawn slowly lightened the sky, I was becoming fully aware of what I held in my arms. She was precious, rare. She'd forged herself into a magnificent weapon, at the expense of everything else that life could give her, and she had never complained, because complaining was for losers.

I was as vulnerable to her now as she was to me, which was inconvenient and dangerous. But whatever wrenching emotions I was going through, it didn't change the plan. I just had to grit my teeth and fucking do it, already.

Just then, she shifted with a murmur, and turned onto her side, snuggling back so that her ass pressed against me. The effect was just about what one would expect. A frantic hunger to fuck her once again.

I figured I might as well. It was the last chance I was going to get, before the inevitable storm hit. The little voice in my head was self-serving and cynical, but true.

I stretched out my arm and groped for another condom, and swiftly suited up. Then I rolled onto my side, guiding my stiff, aching dick up into the juicy cleft between her thighs. We had drifted off to sleep together right after the last time, and lucky for me, because she was wet enough to take me inside with no elaborate preliminaries.

I slid my hand around, caressing her clit, and she woke up with a gasp, stiffening. "Oh, my God."

I didn't answer, just kept petting her. She trembled in my grip, but after just a few minutes, she was moving against me, opening to me.

I rolled her over so she was flat on her belly, me on top, writhing and gasping and eased inside her. Slow, sensual pumping thrusts. She tried to speak, but the sound kept breaking off into tiny, whimpering pants as I moved inside her, sliding my hand around to work her juicy little clit, and tease it. Petting, circling, two fingers, whole hand...I made her melt around me, releasing more lube. So slick, so hot.

I brought her off twice, freezing in place and doing that breathless balancing act so I wouldn't climax too soon, not even while her hot little hole squeezed and clenched around my dick, not even while she sobbed her pleasure into the pillow.

And as soon as she caught her breath, I lifted myself,

gripped her hips, and tugged them until her legs folded and she was on her knees. Then I sank my cock into her again, with a wrenching groan. It was so fucking good, those hot sliding strokes, feeling her gasp, seeing her brace herself, jolt down to her elbows, ass in the air.

I cradled her clit between my fingers, squeezing gently around it. "I'm going to come," I said. "Come with me."

She laughed, her mouth muffled against the pillow. "This may come as news to you, Masters, but there are some things you can't command."

"Yes, I can," I said, lifting up the hood of her clit and squeezing it tenderly as I swiveled my cock inside her. "This, I can. You're right on the edge, and I want to fly with you. I'll just keep on fucking until you give me what I need. One last time. I go for that."

"Damn it," she muttered, trembling violently with excitement. Fighting it.

"I want it," I repeated. "Give it to me." I was abandoned to instinct, no more thought, no more strategy. Just my naked soul, demanding that intimacy with my body. Pleading, devouring, desperate to have it.

When she gave in, it was the deepest, most wrenching orgasm yet. She cried out, pulling me with her into an explosive joining outside of time and space, where we were our essential selves. No lies. Just light.

But we came back to earth soon enough. I opened my eyes and felt her beneath me, still shaking.

I slid my cock out of her, rolling onto my side.

She pulled away and sat up. "What the hell was that all about, Masters?"

"That was amazing," I told her. "You came like a supernova."

"That was master-and-commander sex," she said. "It was weird. Controlling."

"Maybe, sort of," I conceded. "Worked for you, though."

"That is not the point," she hissed.

"No? Oh. My bad. Sorry."

"Screw you! You cannot be flip about this!"

I just shook my head. I had no excuse. I had nothing to say for myself.

She made a growling sound under her breath and slid out of bed. "This is the catch," she said. "I was wondering when it would show up."

"What do you mean? What catch?"

"You," she said. "You're all sweet and charming all night long, and then in the morning, the truth comes out. You're actually an asshole. I don't know why I'm surprised. Just stupid, I guess."

Here it came. Better sooner than later. "I just wanted to make you come again," I said. "You're just angry because you liked it. Get over it."

"Fuck you, Masters." She stalked into the bathroom, set the shower running.

I got my clothes, the shirt, suit, and tie. Had to look the part for the lunch with Senator Brickell. I grabbed socks and shoes, and took them to the next bathroom down the hall to shower. The least I could do was to give her some privacy.

I got ready, swiftly and methodically. Shower. Shave. Clothes. Thinking of when I broke it to her that she was going nowhere today made me tense. I'd lied about that. Which was bad. Betraying her trust was a deeply shitty thing to do.

But it might keep her alive for another day, so I was unrepentantly doing it.

Angela had prepared an extensive breakfast buffet. Grilled sausage links, fresh eggs Benedict, lemon walnut blueberry muffins right out of the oven, fresh squeezed orange juice. Despite my funk, I was hungry, and I did full justice to it. Mick walked in, a file in his hand. "I did that background check you asked for yesterday," he said.

"Let me see it," I held out my hand.

He slapped the file into it.

"Did anyone come to her home, or to the martial arts school over the night?"

"Not that we could see, but they might have gotten there before we did, or opted for electronic surveillance," Mick said. "She never showed, so why expose themselves? I wouldn't. I'd stick a camera in a tree. They know she's with you. They won't make it easy for us. I bet they'll move in a hurry if she comes back, though."

I frowned. "Jesus, Mick. I hope you're not suggesting I use an innocent young woman as bait."

Mick laughed under his breath. "A woman who fights like that? How innocent can she be?"

I thought about last night, in bed. The pure flame she burned with in my arms. Innocent as the dawn. Like nothing I'd ever felt.

But that was none of Mick's damn business. "Keep digging," I said.

Mick's gaze slid to the door. I looked behind me, and saw Kat in the doorway. Her wet hair was combed back, her color high, lips a gorgeous hot pink, eyes blazing.

Fuck, she was beautiful. Mick was dumbstruck. There were a few silent seconds.

"Good morning," I offered. "Want some breakfast? Angela outdid herself."

Kat's gaze snapped onto the file in his hand. "Is that about me? Let me see it."

"This doesn't concern you," I said. "Coffee?"

"No, I do not want your fucking coffee."

Mick gave me a nervous look. "Should I, uh, go?"

"No," I said. "Stay right here. I have to take off in a few minutes if I want to get to that press conference.

"Good. I'll go get my coat and bag," Kat said.

"Not you," I said. "You're not going anywhere. Just get some breakfast."

She sucked in air, eyes widening with outrage. "What? You asshole! All that stuff you said last night was bullshit?"

"Only the part about you leaving today," I told her. "The rest of it was as non-bullshit as I have ever been in my entire life."

"You can't keep me here!"

"The same thing I told you yesterday holds true today," I said. "If I let you loose on the streets of Seattle, anywhere at all, you'll be dead in a day, and I am not okay with that. Therefore, for now, you stay right here. I'm sorry it upsets you."

Kat crossed her arms over her chest. "That's how you get off? I should have known. The captive sex slave vibe? That's your kink? Because I won't play."

I took the final swallow of my coffee, and slammed down my cup hard enough to make both her and Mick flinch. "We'll discuss the captive sex slave issue at great length when I get back," I told her.

"The hell we will, dickhead!"

Mick made a desperate sound under his breath. "Ethan, I don't want to hear this. Can I go?"

I ignored his pleading. "Mick here, plus three more extremely competent ex- special Forces soldiers, will guard you while I'm gone. I'll be back in the evening."

"Sweet Jesus," Mick murmured.

"I will leave," she said. "You can't keep me here."

"Yes, we can, and no, you will not be allowed to leave. You can go wherever you want inside the complex. You'll have every comfort."

"What I need is to order a car and disappear!"

"That option is not on the menu. Use my library, watch TV,

use any computer. Just click on the guest account icon, and use the words 'trusted visitor' plus today's date as the password. Full disclosure, though. Everything you write or click on will be monitored in real time."

"I'll call the police," she said.

I smiled. "No, you won't."

Her lips tightened, and I knew I'd called it. Whatever her secret problems were, they weren't problems she could share with the cops. Which suggested many interesting possibilities, but no time for that now.

I walked past her on my way outside. "It's just a few hours," I said. "Please don't hurt my staff while I'm gone. It would be unfair. Save it all for me."

"No promises," she said.

I didn't look back as I beckoned to Mick. "Walk me out to the car."

I waited until we were outside before waving the file. "So? What did you find?"

"Not much," he said. "All the stuff she told you about San Diego, the mom, the dojo, it checks out. But it's thin. Thinner than a real girl living a normal California life. It's thin here in Seattle, too, in my opinion. I mean, she's here, she's on record as having a degree from UCSD, there are records of her living and working in San Francisco, Portland, Seattle, various jobs. Six years ago, she settled here, rented this dumpy little place in Rainier Beach, and started teaching martial arts to women and girls. She temps occasionally, as a secretary, a paralegal, a receptionist. Won a few championship titles for karate, judo, aikido. But there are no pictures of her. Not on the dojo website, not on any social media platforms. She's like a ghost."

I took the file. "Keep digging," I said. "And watch out for her. She's extremely dangerous if she wants to be.

"Yeah, I heard." Mick looked pained. "Wrangling this girl is your job, Ethan, so get your ass back here as soon as possible to attend to it."

"Absolutely,"' I promised.

Trey and Cade were waiting for me in the helicopter, which was ready to go. I got in, strapped in. Trying to justify and re-justify my decisions to myself.

So fucking ironic, to find a woman who blew my mind, and then be forced by circumstance to make her hate my guts. The last thing I wanted was to betray her.

No, that was the second to last thing.

The last thing was to find out my enemies had slaughtered her.

CHAPTER 17

Kat

That two-faced, lying bastard. After the amazing, scorching intimacy of last night, his behavior this morning felt like a rank betrayal. He was just leaving me here, under heavy guard? What had I done to deserve this? I should have let those guys in the elevator flatten his ungrateful ass, for all the points it had earned me.

But the intense and revelatory night I had spent with Ethan made it harder than usual to lie to myself, or resort to anger. I walked out onto the terrace, and watched the car Ethan was driving come into view for the briefest moment on a curve of the road below on the mountain. I was furious at him for insisting that I stay under his staff's watchful eye, as if I were a helpless child who required babysitting.

But that bit was actually secondary. Mostly I was angry at him for shutting me out during the sex this morning. While still somehow managing to make me come, whenever and however he wanted, as if he had all the keys to the kingdom. He had power over me. He had demanded my complete, shuddering, sobbing sexual surrender...and yet, he held himself apart. He had been cold and distant and dismissive. He had left me feeling abandoned, alone...and fucking furious.

And then, he'd locked me up.

Decisions were being made for me. I was being kept, but for what? For his sexual convenience? Well, crap. I was in a girlish tizzy because of a guy's morning-after bad behavior, and now I was being shoved around. Aw, poor me.

So? Tough shit, Banner. It was up to me to find a solution, like it always was. My hair was wet, and the morning wind was cold on my neck. In the back of my distant memories, I heard my mom's voice, scolding me about catching a draft when I had wet hair. How I would catch my death from a *"colpo d'aria."*

It had been a while since I heard her voice in my mind.

I went back to the dining room, and was struck by the amazing breakfast buffet. I grabbed a muffin, crunchy on the golden outside, and fluffy and warm and full of gooey hot blueberries on the inside. My stomach yawned open with a tiger-like roar.

I might as well find the solutions to life's problems with a belly full of good food, so I grabbed a plate, one of the big ones, and loaded up. Mmm, eggs Benedict, one of my long-time faves, and there was even a jug with extra Hollandaise sauce. I slopped a few more lashings of it over my two eggs, got myself a pile of fruit, another muffin, some coffee. Then I sat down and tucked in, with appetite.

Damn, that was good. Particularly compared to my usual morning meal, which was peanut butter on toast, or else corn flakes. I wasn't much of a cook.

I was well and truly stuffed, and all coffeed up and jittery when Angela bustled in to monitor the situation. She beamed when she saw that I'd done justice to her breakfast. "Oh, good! I'm so glad you found something you liked!"

I took another bite of muffin, and washed it down with

coffee. "You know I'm being kept here against my will, right?" I demanded.

Angela's lips tightened. "Well, that depends on how you're looking at it."

"How else can I look at it? He won't let me freaking leave!"

"Mick did tell me that you were, ah, upset. About Ethan insisting you stay here, where you're safe."

"That's a delicate way to put it," I said sourly.

"Mick also told me what happened yesterday morning, in the elevator of the Fletchley Building. What you did for Ethan there."

"Um, okay? And?"

"Well, obviously, I am so grateful you were there to help him," Angela said. "Mick says, you saved Ethan's life. That it was two against eight. Dear God."

"Yeah, I guess?" I said, dubious. "But I don't think it counts, if he saved my life, too. We're even. So no worries."

"You most certainly are not even," she said sternly. "He is forever in your debt. We all are. It was a miracle. So thank you."

I gazed at her, utterly perplexed. "Ah...you're welcome, but why? Would you be out of a job, if something happened to him?"

She harrumphed. "I doubt very much I would be out of a job, but I would certainly be out of a friend, and one I care for dearly and think of as family. It would break my heart to lose him. For that reason, I'm inclined to think well of you, Miss Banner. You're brave, and tough, and you don't flinch from trouble. I respect that."

"Thanks," I said, bemused. "Call me Kat."

"Very well, Kat. I always speak my mind freely to Ethan and Shane and Freya, too, so by now, I'm in the habit. And I'll offer you the same courtesy."

"Thanks. Should I brace myself?"

"If you like," she said briskly. "Mick said you've come to the attention of Ethan's enemies. That they'll assume you're on Ethan's team."

"That may be the case," I said. "But it's my problem. No one else's."

"Ethan is a natural leader," Angela went on. "He can't stop himself from taking responsibility for your safety, particularly since he was the one who put you in harm's way. You wouldn't be in danger at all, if it weren't for him, am I right?"

I shrugged. That wasn't strictly true, but it was better not to open that particular can of worms, for her or anyone. "Even so, I have things to do. Promises to keep."

"They can wait," Angela said sternly. "The way they'd wait if you were ill, or if you had hurt yourself. And Ethan wants to make sure your life goes on."

"Angela—"

"Your safety is of paramount importance," she told me, in ringing tones.

Aw. Her zeal was actually kind of touching. "I can take care of myself."

"Clearly, you can. But safety is more important than your duties, or your convenience, or your pride."

"Or my freedom?"

"Or your freedom. Ethan is trying to help you, and...well, honey, I hate to be rude, but I think, in modern parlance, that you are being a whiny little bitch."

I was so startled by her choice of words, I almost laughed out loud. I stopped myself just in time. My mama taught me better than to be rude to a grandma-figure, even if she was lambasting me. Here I spent all this time and energy at the martial arts school, teaching girls and women to speak their truth, to not be hogtied by having to always be nice, at all costs. I'd be a real hypocrite if I didn't accord Angela the same privilege. I respected a woman who just let it all hang out.

Angela's chin was up, arms wrapped across her considerable bosom, braced for a rude retort, but I just nodded. "I guess I may have been guilty of that, a time or two," I conceded. "Thank you for sharing your honest opinion. I'll search my conscience."

She let out a small huffing sound, mollified. "Well, in any case. I am very grateful for what you did."

"Anytime, ma'am."

"Angela, please." she said.

"Okay, Angela. By the way, your breakfast was absolutely divine."

"Yeah, not too bad for prison fare, hmm?"

That made me snort coffee out of my nose, which spattered all over Freya's baby blue cashmere sweater. "Oh, crap," I said. "Sorry, but you made me do it."

"Looks as if you'll need to change. Just leave it in the bathroom. Which reminds me, I got a few more things from Freya's closet, and put them in the bedroom I assigned you yesterday." *The one you didn't sleep in* was the silent subtext.

"You're sure she won't mind?"

"Once I get them cleaned, she probably won't even know," Angela said. "So, you have the run of the place. Take a tour. Poke around. Freya's and Shane's apartments are locked, but you can wander around anywhere else, in Ethan's place or any of the common areas. Use the TV in the den, use the computers, and Ethan's library is full of books. There are gardens, a pool, a hot tub. I serve lunch at one, but there's always coffee, tea, juice, and snacks in the kitchen. Make yourself entirely at home."

"Thanks. I'll keep your generous hospitality in mind when I start feeling sorry for myself."

That earned me a smile. I refilled my coffee mug, and took off to follow her advice, and tour Ethan's luxury lair. Or else do recon of enemy territory, depending on my mood. After being subjected to Angela's cooking, I was inclined to be a tiny bit more positive about my plight. A full stomach could have that effect.

I started with Ethan's apartment. First, I peeked into what turned out to be a little girl's room, and felt a sharp pang, thinking of my sister Gabri. How she would have loved a room like this. The fanciful wood molding, the big, long windows with a view of mountain peaks, the shelf upon shelf of books, the dresser covered with dolls. One shelf had a big headshot portrait of her dad, like a shrine. That made my throat catch.

The next spot I lingered was the corridor and the living room, to study all the photo galleries. I could tell who the Masters siblings were from family resemblance. The sister was a beauty, but she looked like trouble. It took one to know one.

Shane, the middle brother, was likewise a top-of-the-line hottie. Tall, dark, and handsome, as muscular as Ethan, cheekbones that would cut glass, sexy lips, smoldering dark eyes. The good fairies definitely got invited to the Masters' christenings.

Though come to think of it, considering current events, and the stories Ethan had told me, the mom and dad killed by the drunk driver, the evil aunt and uncle, the reformatory, the time spent running, poor and desperate...well. Maybe it wasn't just the good fairies that came to their christenings. The Masters kids had rated a few nasty-hell-bitch fairies, too. We had that in common.

It felt odd, feeling sorry for someone so stinking rich, but I genuinely did. Money wasn't everything. In fact, money wasn't really much of anything. That prick Tony had piles of it, and it hadn't done him any good. I was sorry about them getting targeted by these bloodsucking assholes, whoever they were. Sorry that Shane had been taken from them. I knew exactly how that felt, God knows.

I was so glad the sister had survived, and even found love. Good for her. There were lots of wedding photos. Freya and her guy, also four-alarm-fire handsome. Them in a clinch, kissing passionately, dancing. Very romantic. Her, with her head thrown back. Him, laughing. Bright moments, in the midst of the darkness. Very nice.

Then I saw pictures of the little girl, and I froze, my throat clutching painfully. Oh, God, Ethan's niece looked so much like Gabri. She had that wide-open, bright-as-the-headlights-of-a-car kind of eyes. So pretty, with all the long blonde hair. Gabri's had been lighter.

My throat tightened until it felt as if something in there was going to snap.

My anger was gone. Most of it, anyway. Not all, because he had behaved like a real prick to me this morning in bed, and that bit was inexcusable. But for the rest of it, I could sense how desperately this guy was trying to keep his family safe. Somehow, he had started lumping me into that category of people he was responsible for. Most likely because of the elevator escapade. He couldn't help it. It was hardwired into him.

That, however, did not help me in my quest to come up with a plan of action. Sadly, empathy never did. The minute you let yourself see from someone else's point of view, you were in serious danger of losing a firm grip on your own.

I sat at one of the computers, typing in the password "trusted visitor" with grim irony. Trusted, my ass. I was anything but. I sent emails to my student volunteers who helped teach classes, telling them I was stuck out of town for the next couple of days, that I'd explain when I got back. Best I could do. I drained my coffee, left the mug in the kitchen sink, and went to change that coffee-spattered sweater.

It was as embarrassing as hell, but even as pissed as I was, I still wanted to look nice when he got back.

CHAPTER 18

Ethan

"What are we doing way down in south Seattle?" my assistant Jenn complained. "You already bailed on the morning appointments. Which, by the way, makes me look like a total flake. But we can't bail on lunch with Senator Brickell! Canlis is way up there in East Queen Anne, so let's move! No time to waste!"

"Not yet. There's a thing I need to do here." Trey was driving, and I was watching the Rainier Beach neighborhood roll by. I'd canceled all my morning engagements, to Jenn's intense dismay. I had decided that a visit to the Fletchley Building to get some answers from the security staff was more urgent, but Jenn hadn't quite comprehended my shift in priorities yet. The process took some time.

Not that we'd gotten much info at Fletchley. Their whole roster had been wiped out by a violent stomach bug the day before, a pathogen so severe, some of them had ended up in the hospital, including the guy responsible for staffing. He hadn't even been discharged yet, and some of the ones back at work were still a little green. Not a one of them had the slightest clue what had happened to us yesterday.

Not surprisingly, the security footage had also vanished. And no one in the building had called the police, except for a few complaints that had trickled in this morning about property damage to the cars.

The trap had been laid with extreme care and forethought. They had thought of everything, except for Kat, and left almost no trace. I was grateful that I'd left my guys circling outside in the van. We would have suffered heavy losses if they had come into the garage to wait for me, and gotten trapped in there.

"If we really floor it and get lucky with the lights, we might get to Canlis on time for lunch with the senator." Jenn's voice was tight. "You're acting almost as if you want to be late! What is up with you? I can't work like this!"

I thought of several sharp replies, abandoned them, and shook my head. "Back off, Jenn."

Her mouth fell open. "But I—"

"I appreciate your dedication to organizing my professional life. That's why I pay you an excellent salary and bonus. I'll be back out soon. This won't take long."

I ignored her muttering as I got out of the car and looked at the tiny, rundown house Kat rented in Rainier Beach. It was on a shabby, raggedy-edged, pot-holed street with no sidewalk. There was a chain-link fence in front and back. The exterior had not been painted in many long years, but it probably used to be gray. I wasn't sure what I was looking for here, but I had to start somewhere.

The door lock was a joke. I didn't even need my pick. My credit card got me inside in just a few seconds. She clearly didn't prioritize security.

Then again, her hands could probably be registered as lethal weapons.

I stepped into the foyer, looked into the tiny living room. It smelled fresh, like lavender and pine. The ancient wooden flooring was battered and scarred, but it shone. The place had been painted recently. The Venetian blinds showed not a speck of dust. There was a wingback chair in the living room, positioned in front of a thrift shop coffee table with a small, old laptop on it. A single simple floor lamp. No pictures on the walls, no shelves, no books or knickknacks. No decorative bowl to drop her keys, no hook for her coat or scarf. There were envelopes on the floor under the mail slot, but no other signs of paper clutter. No receipts, coupons, brochures, take-out menus. The only thing that indicated the place was hers was rigorous cleanliness, which was very much in character.

Wow. Forget minimalism. This was more like nothing-ism.

I strolled through the place. The bedroom had a single twin bed, made up as tight as a drum with a fuzzy blue fleece blanket, a rare note of whimsy. Workout clothes hung on the bathroom hook. No jewelry box. No concert tickets, or postcards, or photos, or metro tickets tacked to the walls or tucked in the mirror. No carpet, just a rolled up rubberized exercise mat. An absolute minimum of toiletries in the bathroom. A stack of gray towels. Soap and shampoo in the shower. The cabinet over the sink was close to empty. Just toothpaste, floss, deodorant, nail clippers, a comb, Advil. It was monastic. Starker than a hotel room. Hotels at least tried, in their tired way, to simulate a decor. This place had anti-décor, which was a statement in itself.

The kitchen was more of the same. The cupboards had two of each type of dish or plate. A single pot, a single frying pan. The fridge was nearly bare. Some yogurt, some sliced turkey. A loaf of bread. A carton of milk.

She had tried to give no clues about who lived here, but the intensity of her effort had created the opposite effect. This place said so much about who she was.

Then again, perhaps only someone as fascinated by her as I was could decipher it.

I looked at the tiny table, the mismatched chairs. Anger grew hot inside me at whoever had reduced her to this. The house demonstrated everything that had been taken from her, everything she'd trained herself to uncomplainingly live without. It also showed her toughness, which could not be taken away. It was an intrinsic part of her.

It wasn't right that she had to live such a stripped-down life. She deserved more.

I heard a soft sound, and looked around several times before I directed my gaze downward. A fat gray cat had slithered in through the cat door. He looked up, clearly taken aback to find me there.

"I come in peace," I told him.

He made a disapproving *prrt*, and then stalked haughtily, tail high, to a small pantry, which had probably been left open on purpose for him. I heard subsequent crunching sounds. She had a cat. That was interesting.

I was jolted again when I heard a key rattling in the back door. It opened, and a young woman stepped inside. "Ambrose, you have food at home, you miserable beast! The kind I can barely afford. So don't you even try to—oh *shit!* Who...?"

I held up my hands. "I'm harmless, I swear. Don't be scared."

A young woman stood there, frozen. She wore workout clothes, her long dark hair was twisted into an explosive messy bun. She looked frightened. "Who the hell are you?" Her voice was sharp and tight with nerves. "Why are you in Kat's house?"

"I just dropped by to pick up some things for her," I improvised. "She's fine.'"

"Yeah? She never came home from work! And her phone keeps going to voicemail! How fine can she be? Where the hell is she?"

"I'll tell her to call you. What's your name?"

"Joanna." The girl crossed her arms, studying me with growing fascination. "You sure don't look like a housebreaker, in that fancy suit. What's your name?"

"I'm Ethan," I hedged, since my surname was often recognized "Are you a neighbor? Is that your cat?"

"Yes. Her neighbor, her student, and her friend. This is Ambrose. He's also her friend. He's mine, but he's adopted Kat, ever since she rescued him."

"Rescued him? From what?"

"She saved him from my butthead ex-boyfriend," Joanna confided. "We broke up, and he was holding Ambrose hostage to spite me, even though he hates cats, and kicked Ambrose when he was drunk. That was actually why we broke up, the dickface. So, anyhow, Kat shows up at my mom's house—my mom lives across the street—and she's got Ambrose in her arms, and she's all scratched up and bleeding from Ambrose freaking out. And she told me she didn't actually do anything bad to Ricky, but I don't believe it, because he's avoided me ever since. Then I heard he went up to Alaska to work the fish canneries, or some shit. Good riddance."

I drank it all in, fascinated. "Wow, that's some story."

"Yeah, I know. Probably shouldn't have told it. Kat says I gotta learn to keep my mouth shut. So I study martial arts with her. To calm down, see?"

"Yeah, martial arts can chill you," I agreed. "I have found that to be true."

Worry still shadowed Joanna's eyes, in spite of her nervous babbling. "Kat's a badass," she said, in a low, warning tone. "You better not mess with her."

"I absolutely am not messing with her," I assured her. "I have nothing but the deepest respect and admiration for her."

"Yeah?" Joanna narrowed her eyes. "Well, good, then. Have her call me."

Ambrose stalked out of the pantry, sat, and meowed, as if placing his own emphasis on Joanna's command. She scooped him up into her arms. "Let's go, you greedy chunk, you. You weigh a ton." She glanced at me. "So...Kat gave you a key?"

Yikes. "No, actually," I admitted. "I got in here with my credit card. But I'm not a burglar. I'm just picking up some stuff up for her."

Joanna looked unconvinced. "There's not much stuff to pick up," she observed. "Kat has less stuff than anyone I know. She says it's easier to clean that way."

"True thing," I agreed.

"What's your last name? You know. In case I need to tell the cops."

I let out a sigh, and gave in to the inevitable. "Ethan Masters."

Her brows came together. "Sounds familiar. Are you, like, a movie star?"

"Nah. I work in tech."

"Hmph." She held up her phone and snapped a photo of me. "There," she said. "That's for the police, if she doesn't call me right away. Got me?"

I almost laughed, but it would be disrespectful of the girl's uncompromising instinct to protect her friend. "I will tell her to contact you, I promise."

She jerked her chin at the door. "How about you leave first? Then I'll lock up."

My phone pinged with a text. I glanced at it. From Jenn.

for the love of God please hurry

"I'll head out," I told her. "It was good to meet you, Joanna."

"I can't really say the same," she said, as I went out the door. "Not until I'm sure you're not a serial killer." She leaned out the door and studied the car waiting for me at the end of the walkway, Trey in the front, Jenn glaring from the back. Ambrose writhed in wild protest in her arms. "I don't think serial killers drive cars like that," she added, a note of grudging admiration in her voice. "Or get driven in them, as the case may be. Mobsters do, though. Are you a mobster?"

"No. Like I told you, I'm in tech. Just your average computer geek."

"If you say so. But if she doesn't call me, I'm rolling over on you, buddy."

I got into the car laughing, in spite of Jenn's reproachful frown. Kat's power and moxie had rubbed off on Joanna. I could feel its effects, and it was energizing.

I looked over at Jenn, who was texting furiously into her phone. "How are we doing on that lunch date?" I asked, to mollify her.

"You mean, besides being egregiously late?" she said snippily. "I'm in touch with Canlis, and the Senator's staff. They'll wait. Just to get our stories straight, you've been stuck on the highway five hundred feet from the exit behind an accident. A real, documented accident. If we don't hit any actual accidents or traffic jams, we should make the new time, by a hair." She shot me a warning glare. "With no more stops."

"I'll save the next one for after lunch," I assured her, and then tried calling Hugh Clemens, for the fourth time. Like all the other times, it went to voicemail.

"Hey, Clemens," I said into the phone. "Ethan Masters again. We need to talk about what happened in the Fletchley Building. I'm guessing that someone very hardcore is breathing down your neck, but you need to find your balls and do the right thing. If you call me back, I'll be easier on you when we meet. And we will meet. Later."

Then I dialed the home number I'd hunted down for Julia, Hugh's office manager, since so far, no one was answering at the business number.

"Hello?" Julia responded, her voice high and quavering.

"Julia, right?" I said. "This is Ethan Masters."

"Ah...oh." A panicked pause. "How can I help you?"

"Can you tell me where to find Hugh?"

"No, I can't. I'm at home today. And I think he's out of the office, too."

"Yes, and probably halfway to Tokyo by now," I said.

"I don't know what you mean." Her voice was squeaky and thin.

"Listen, Julia. Bad things happened yesterday, after the receptionist and I got into that elevator. Hugh knew something was going to happen. I think you knew it, too."

"No! No, that is not true! I absolutely did not know anything about it! I was told to facilitate the meeting, and monitor the temp, and that is all!"

"What temp agency did you use?" I asked.

"Keystroke Temps. Please believe me. I had no idea—"

"Is Hugh in some kind of trouble?"

"I wouldn't know," she said primly. "Mr. Clemens and I have only a professional relationship."

"Fine. But if I get a sense that you were involved, I'll make sure you go to prison right along with him. I have dozens of lawyers working for me. A whole floor of them. Like an army of sharks."

"I told him I was uncomfortable with having that girl come in, and pretending there was a functioning company in that vacant space! But Hugh said to do it, or find another job! I didn't know anything bad would happen to you! I swear to God!"

I let out a silent sigh. Bullying a stressed-out woman was depressing, whether she deserved it or not. "We'll see," I told her. "You have my number. If you think of any way to identify who got Hugh to organize yesterday's hit, you would demonstrate goodwill by sharing it with me, which would be very wise on your part. Understand?"

"God, I wish I did know." Her voice burbled with tears. "I

would tell you in a heartbeat. I should have quit that job
months ago."

"Yeah, probably. Live and learn. Have a nice day, Julia."

I hung up on her, searched the number for Keystroke
Temps, and called them.

A perky young female voice answered. "Keystroke Temps,
good morning! How can we help you today?"

"Good morning. May I speak to whoever of your staff sent a
woman by the name of Katrin Banner out on a job to Clemens
and Associates yesterday, please?"

My question was met with dead silence, and then, a choked
whisper. "Cynthia! It's another one of those guys, calling about
that girl from yesterday! Will you take it?"

There was an unintelligible high-pitched ranting voice in
the background, and the call transferred to another phone with
a click. "Who is this?" asked an older female voice, sharp and
aggrieved.

"My name is Ethan Masters," I said. "I was looking for information on—"

"I have absolutely nothing to say about that person! We
never want to see her again, if she makes this kind of an
impression on our clients! We were told to send somebody
good-looking. Now the whole damn world is looking for her!
Demanding her address, her social! It reflects very badly
on us!"

"Did you give the address and social security number to
them when they asked?"

"They threatened me!" the woman shrilled. "Don't call us
again. We've thrown that girl's file away. We do not have her
data. We never want to hear from her again, or from Clemens
and Associates. We never heard of any of them. Goodbye!"

The connection broke. I let out a sigh. Nicole had all of Kat's
data. Of course.

I ignored Jenn's sour face on the way to Canlis. Too much to think about. When we got to the restaurant, I trotted out my autopilot default persona, the one that covered for me in the public sphere while my private life was falling apart. That persona had gotten a lot of practice since the disaster at Ready Line, with Shane abducted, and three Unredeemables, all good friends for over a decade, killed. Jed's apparent betrayal, too. For months, I'd been convinced that one of my best friends had sold us out.

Thankfully, that turned out not to be true, but I paid for that, too, with those horrible days in which I thought I'd lost my little sister. But Freya got through it.

It occurred to me that Freya was going to like Kat. They had a lot in common. Both were no-bullshit, regal warrior queens.

I psyched myself up for being charming and impressive with the senator. I had set this up weeks before. I wanted to persuade Senator Eleanor Brickell to vote yes on a bill regarding carbon capture tax credits that was about to come before the Senate, but I had to cudgel my brain to remember why I cared so much.

Oh…yeah. The fate of humanity, biodiversity, safeguarding the future, the oceans, all that good stuff. The continuation of life as we knew it. Right. Of course.

Fortunately, my default persona always performed. It said all the right things at the right time, even while the rest of me was howling in the dark. And the hefty sums which I'd contributed in the past to her House of Representatives and Senate campaigns definitely helped.

But the disconnect made my teeth grind. I had no business being here, doing this. I had other things to focus on. This would be my last professional engagement until I fixed this problem that was stalking my family.

I smiled and joked and charmed and cajoled Senator Brickell, but I walked out of the restaurant with my brain on fire, heightened senses cataloguing every detail around me. I had to start carrying a gun again. I felt naked without one. I had felt this way back in Afghanistan, on combat missions. Buzzing at a high frequency at all times.

Jenn slid into the car, smiling. "Thank God, we salvaged that one," she said. "Senator Brickell loves you. Now on to the ribbon cutting at that new STEM Academy, and we can—"

"Not today. I'm canceling all public appointments and appearances for the foreseeable future."

Jenn's jaw dropped, horrified. "You're...no! You're joking!"

"I have security issues, Jenn," I said. "They're not getting better. My presence does not make the people around me safer. It did not make the senator safer, either."

"But we have the launch of the Fire Glass coming up in two weeks!"

"We'll delay the launch," I said.

Jenn looked as if I had blasphemed. "But...but that would be a disaster!"

"We'll lose money, yes. Too bad. My family's safety is more important. I'm not giving the opening speech for the Emory Summit, either. It's just not happening."

"And I suppose the hot blonde you've got sequestered at the Mountain House is also important? Ethan, now is not the time to let yourself get distracted!"

I gave her a look. Jenn's face reddened. Her gaze dropped. "Shit," she whispered. "Sorry. I shouldn't have said that."

"No, you shouldn't have. Listen up, Jenn. If you heard about the hot blonde, then my loose-lipped security goons are blabbering. Did they tell you how I met her?"

"Ah...just that there was an attempt made in the elevator—"

"Yes. Eight guys with batons and stun wands got into an elevator in the Fletchley Building. With me and this blonde. Not in a dark alley at night. Not in an abandoned junkyard. Not

under a bridge. This was a shiny, high-end skyscraper in downtown Seattle during prime morning working hours. I'm only
alive because the blonde happened to be a seasoned martial
artist, so between the two of us, we got out of there with some
bruises and a nosebleed. Instead of dead."

"Ethan, I didn't mean to—"

"Suppose it had been you in that elevator with me, Jenn?
How do you think that encounter would have gone?"

"Ahh..."

"Spending time with me is not safe or healthy for you right
now," I told her bluntly. "I pay my security staff to put themselves in harm's way for me, but that's not what I pay you for. It's
not fair to put you in that position."

"Ah..." She swallowed, blinking rapidly. "Okay. Sorry. I
didn't know."

"I'm not doing this to mess with your head. I just don't want
to get anyone else killed. Manage things as if I'd been taken out
of commission for a few weeks by an illness or an injury. I don't
like looking over my shoulder for assassins while I'm having
lunch with the senator."

"Y-y-yes." Jenn's voice was unsteady.

"I really do value your work," I assured her. "I'm glad to
have someone so competent managing my affairs while I deal
with this."

"Okay." She managed a wobbly smile. "Um, so I think I'll
take a cab from here, okay? I have a couple of errands to run
before I start making all those phone calls."

"I understand," I told her.

Jenn got out, and practically ran away from the car. I realized, belatedly, that I might have just frightened away a very
competent executive assistant. Time would tell.

"Well, that's handled," I said. "Take me to Kat's martial arts
school."

Kat's school was a rundown, twenties-era ground-floor

space in Beacon Hill, big glass windows that looked out on a seedy shopping district. I walked in and looked around at the class in progress. No kimonos, just variegated, mismatched sportswear on a bunch of girls ranging from ten to thirteen. They were in a long line, running one at a time on the tatami mats, and flinging themselves into flying somersaults with varying degrees of success. I looked around. Saw and smelled water damage, old sweat. Spotted the telltale holes of termites in the aged wooden baseboards. The sports equipment was mismatched, battered, ancient. But the girls looked sweaty and determined. Like Joanna. It was the Kat Banner effect. She really brought it out in people.

A young black woman of maybe twenty-four was teaching the class, but all of them stopped and looked at Trey, Cade, and me.

"Hello," the teacher said. "Can I help you?" Her face was tense and cautious.

"I was looking for Kat," I said.

"She's not here at the moment. Leave your card with us, and I'll get it to her."

I passed the woman a business card. "And you are?"

"Danica Phelps," the girl said crisply. "And now, if you'll please excuse us. We're in the middle of a class, so I'll have to ask you to—"

"Are you one of those scary guys? Like before?" A chubby little girl with red braids bounded toward us, squinting suspiciously. "You don't look as scary as them."

"Scary guys came here?" I asked. "When did they come? Was it yesterday?"

"Charlotte, shhh! Please don't ask my students questions," Danica snapped. "If you want to ask anything about school business, talk to Kat directly. I am not comfortable sharing information with a stranger."

"They were super scary," Charlotte informed me. "They had

guns! I saw one of them! It was under a guy's jacket! He looked mean!"

"Damn it, Charlotte!" Danica hissed. "Hush up!"

"I'm a friend, I promise," I told Danica.

"Kat went to temp downtown for a while, because she wanted to get me some glasses," Charlotte confided. "That's why she's not here."

"Glasses?"

"Yeah. I'm flunking fourth grade 'cause I can't see the blackboard at school."

"Nor can she stop talking, evidently," Danica grumbled.

"Kat taught me what to say to bullies," the pigtailed girl said. "I wish I'd told those guys right where to shove it!"

"I'm very glad you didn't," I said. "Discretion is the better part of valor."

"Kat says that, too. Anyhow, you better be nice to Kat. She taught everybody here how to kick and punch. If you mess with her, we'll mess with you! All of us!"

For some reason, the kid's attitude made my spirits rise. "I'll take it under advisement," I replied, not allowing myself to smile, and turned to Danica. "I apologize for the interruption. If those guys come back, please do not engage with them."

"Nope," Danica said crisply. "We're not stupid. But I'll be glad when Kat gets back."

I analyzed what I'd learned on the way back to the helipad, but couldn't come to any clear conclusion. Other than the fact that I liked Kat Banner even more than I had before. Rescuing Joanna's cat, teaching little girls to stand their ground, temping to buy Charlotte a pair of glasses. It was strange, that her digital footprint was so light, for such a charismatic person, and her apartment was antiseptic, which suggested cold detachment. But everyone who knew her painted a picture of passionate involvement.

She was a tangle of contradictions. The one thing I knew

for sure was that I couldn't wait to see her again. Kat Banner, even spitting mad, excited me more than anyone I'd ever been with. I couldn't even call those previous experiences intimacy. Not after last night's experience.

The bar for what could be defined as intimacy had just shot up toward the stars.

CHAPTER 19

Kat

The house vibrated with the commotion. Woohoo, the master had returned.

Hmmph. I did not interrupt the long, slow tai chi form I was doing. I'd been at it for a couple of hours now on the secluded little side patio, just to keep from exploding.

Intense physical activity had always been my coping mechanism. Maybe that came from having been more or less on the run since my adolescence. I'd lived in many places after San Diego, but I always knew better than to put down roots, get attached. Not with the Petruzzi family thirsty for my blood. Besides, that murderous turd Tony Jr. was up for parole soon, so I had to be ready to jump in any direction when he walked.

I finished, pulling in my leg, crouching, rising up. Calmly concluding my form. Not flustered, nervous, blushing or babbling. Composed as could be. Unfazed. A force to be reckoned with. Zen goddess. That was the vibe I was going for.

It usually came to me naturally, but today, nothing could have stopped me from sneaking an anxious peek at myself in the mirror before I walked into the huge living room.

I saw Mick, Cade, and the guy they called Trey, walking down the breezeway. Ethan followed them. I told my heart sternly not to pound, my belly not to flutter, and my thighs not to clench, but after the events of last night, that was too much to ask of my poor bewildered body. It was totally bedazzled by him.

Look at the guy. Masters in a business suit. Like an ad for formal clothing for filthy rich European men, against a back-drop of a Tuscan vineyard or a French chateau, or a Versailles-style garden. Except he looked tougher. Big boss man.

Which had never been a turn-on for me. On the contrary. Big-boss types usually repelled me, what with my troubled history with them.

He saw me through the glass as he came in, and smiled. "Good evening," he said. "I hope you had a nice day."

I tried not stifle it, but a snort exploded out of me anyway. "As nice as can be expected, considering I'm imprisoned."

His eyebrow went up. "Were you not comfortable?"

I rolled my eyes. "Comfort's not the issue, Masters, and you know it. You're going to have to let me go. Let me assess the threat level on my own. If I decide your enemies are too much for me to deal with, I'll leave. This isn't my first rodeo."

"Hmm. I see. Can we discuss that and many other things over dinner?"

"Ohhh, gee, did I assail you with my complaints after a hard day of billionairing, Ethan?"

He gave me a devastating grin. "Not at all, but save it for our dinnertime banter. I just need to change. See you in the dining room. Assail me there."

I waved him away. "Go on, then. My rage and desperation will keep."

It was surprisingly hard to stay mad at the guy, particularly when he wined and dined and charmed me in his luxury lair. And when he touched me, well. Game over.

I spent Ethan's primping time to organize my bullet points. I'd gamed out this conversation all day, in all its possible permutations. I had to persuade him to let me go of his own accord. He was rich and powerful enough to compel me to stay, if he felt justified in doing so, which he clearly did. He was protective and bossy. He was a big brother, and a head of family, and a head of a corporation, too, It was his instinct to keep me safe and comfortable, and available. Particularly if he was fucking me.

But I couldn't allow it. Not the way I was wired up. Not after what happened with my sisters and Tony Petruzzi. If I were a normal girl with a normal past, if I'd read all the usual popular sexy romantic novels, I might even get off on being a rich man's darling for a while. It had its perks, right? Some parts of it looked like titillating fun.

But no one knew the dark side of that scenario like I did. I'd seen it devolve into control, abuse, violence, and seen it end in a lake of blood. Not that I was mixing Ethan up with Tony's ilk. By no means. I could sense that Ethan was a good guy. Principled.

But still. He was also arrogant, spoiled, and used to getting his own way. The power imbalance made it unbearable for me. Which was a goddamn shame, but there it was.

I made my way slowly through the place to the dining room, where I beheld Angela's dinner spread, which was one of the wonders of the world. Zucchini fritters, and tempura-dipped artichoke hearts, paired with a delicious dip. A platter of cheesy, sizzling stuffed mushrooms. A frilly green salad. A beautiful red wine, decanted and waiting for us. The crystal glittered, the silver gleamed, the linen glowed snow white. There was a serving dish of plump green-colored ravioli in some kind of herb and butter emulsion. It took my breath away, and made my stomach growl.

"Hey." It was Ethan's voice behind me. I turned, startled,

and my eyes were ambushed by the stunning spectacle of that guy in rich-guy-casual gear. Relaxed khaki-toned linen pants, and a soft, battered-looking ivory linen shirt that somehow managed to show off every detail of how well-made he was. Open at the throat to show a tuft of gold skin and dark chest hair, sleeves rolled up to show those big hands, those powerful wrists and forearms, the beautiful tracery of veins and tendons in his muscular forearms.

I was staring like a ninny. Embarrassing myself. *Stop it, Banner. Control.*

"Will you sit down? I hope you're hungry. Angela's going hog-wild, with you here to impress."

"I'm actually pretty hungry, yes," I said. "Only because I refused to let her cook me lunch. I had that huge breakfast, see. It looks and smells great to me."

"Good, then. You'll have an appetite." He pulled out my chair and made a courtly gesture. "Come sit down."

I did so, and he sat next to me, and poured us both wine. He lifted his glass. "To a truce," he said.

I looked at my glass, then at him. "Is this a trap?"

"You have a suspicious mind," he remarked.

"My God, yes," I agreed. "Let's drink to something else, if you want to toast. No truces unless we thrash out every last detail, one at a time."

"You should have been a lawyer."

"Actually, I might have been wicked good at that, in another lifetime," I agreed. "But we're not at war. We're just having a very lopsided disagreement."

He passed the zucchini fritters my way. "Lopsided how?"

I dipped one into the sauce, tasted it, and almost whimpered with delight. Now he was outmaneuvering me with food, the sneaky, seductive bastard. "You have all the goddamn power, Masters," I informed him, when I was done chewing.

"You have plenty of your own, Kat," he said softly. "You're

pulsing with it."

I harrumphed. "Then what am I doing in your gilded cage, buddy?"

He tilted his head to the side, silently declining to answer. "I talked to some of your friends today," he said, in a casual tone.

That gave me a rush of panic. "What? Who? Where?"

"Joanna and Ambrose, to start with. By the way, Joanna needs a call from you. She's afraid I'm a serial killer, though she concedes I don't dress like a serial killer, nor do I drive a serial killer's car. Still, you should let her know I haven't cut you up into chunks. Put her mind at ease."

"Yeah, okay," I said. "I will. Who else?"

"Danica, at the martial arts school," he said. "And Charlotte."

I blew out a shaky breath. "Oh. Did you learn anything from poking into my life?"

"I learned they all think you're Wonder Woman. And they're right."

"Oh, get out of here," I snapped. "Are you trying to butter me up?"

His eyes gleamed. "Would it work?"

"Hell, no," I told him. "Not after a long, dull day in my gilded cage."

"Here, have some mushrooms." He served me one, expertly shifting the focus of my attention away at the crucial moment. The guy was good at navigating a difficult conversation, I'd give him that.

I let the bliss of the baked mushrooms' cheesy wonderfulness wash over me, and then had at him once again. "Tell me something, Masters. Where on earth did you run into Joanna and Ambrose both?"

He let out an audible breath, looking like he was bracing himself. "At your house."

I put down my wineglass, and my fork. "My house," I said.

"You're saying you went into my house. Without the benefit of a key. Or my permission."

"Yes," he said, his eyes meeting mine. "I did. I probably would never have told you about it, given the choice, but Joanna and Ambrose busted me. I had to come clean. But I know it was wrong, and I do apologize."

"I'm not ready to accept your apology until you tell me what the fuck you were doing there," I said, dabbing at my mouth with a napkin. I was all done eating his food, no matter how delicious, until I knew what the hell he was up to.

"I have a confession to make," he said.

I crossed my arms over my chest, and waited stonily. "Let's hear it."

"I told you about Shane, the SmokeScreen algorithm, the Ready Line massacre. What happened with my sister and her husband. You saw what happened to us yesterday. The people I'm fighting are diabolical, highly skilled, highly motivated, with a bottomless budget and no scruples. And they never give up."

"And this pertains to me how?"

He let out a sharp sigh. "Until today, I was still unsure if maybe, you could be, well...bait. In a trap. Set for me."

My jaw dropped. "Me? After fucking all those guys up in that elevator? Really?"

"It was improbable, yes. But so are you," he said. "It was just too strange that the beautiful blonde secretary would leap into action out of nowhere, and defend me like a berserker warrior. Fight at my side. Earn my gratitude, spark my lust, pique my curiosity. It's as if, you were specifically designed to be irresistible to me."

I just stared at him, unable to decide between being gratified or furious. "So, what you're saying is, you weren't sure if I was a lying, murdering honeytrap whore, but you banged me anyway. Wow, Masters. That's brave of you."

"It's not that I thought you were," he corrected. "It was just a tiny percentage point of doubt. I had to put it to rest, because you're amazing, and I want to fling myself into this thing one hundred percent, not ninety-nine. So, I tried to see if your life seemed, you know. Real. Genuine. If it held up to scrutiny."

"And does it?"

"It's strange," he admitted. "You are clearly an unusual person. But your friends love you and trust you, and feel protective of you. It's plain you take care of them, and that can't be faked. So please. Accept my apology for violating your privacy."

Hmmm. I reached out for a tempura-battered artichoke heart, and studied him while I slowly savored it. He waited patiently for my verdict.

"You're throwing your weight around, big time, Masters," I told him, grabbing another artichoke chunk. They were addictive as hell.

"Yes, my sister scolds me about that. Am I forgiven?"

"Not so fast, big guy," I said. "'Forgiven' is a big word. It's too soon. But in the meantime, you might as well catch me up on everything else you learned today."

Ethan served me some ravioli. "I'll give you the short version," he said. "Clemens is nowhere to be found. He's not at his house, or his office. I talked to Julia, his office manager. My sense is she only knew enough about what was going on to feel nervous, but that's all."

"Screw Julia," I said coolly. "She used me, and threw me to the wolves, no matter what she knew or didn't know. How about the office building? Did anyone report what happened to the police?"

"Oddly enough, no. No one called them."

"No one? For a shootout?" I said, incredulously. "For real?"

"These people planned ahead," he said. "The building is new, very few tenants so far, and that day, the security staff was out sick with a violent stomach bug. The guy who staffs the place ended up unconscious in the emergency room, and he claims nobody ever called anyone to cover. The guys who attacked us just showed up and took over, smooth as silk."

"Wild," I murmured, impressed. "That is some serious organization."

"Yeah. The video disappeared, of course. The building was prepared for us. Or I suppose I should say, that building was prepared for me."

I was inclined to think he was right. This was about him, not me. It didn't feel like Tony Petruzzi's style. Tony wasn't big on guile, foresight, or planning. He wasn't smart enough. He was just a bundle of raw, screaming nerve-endings with a gun.

"Another thing," he said. "I also discovered that some people, not my people, showed up at your martial arts school looking for you. People that Danica did not like."

I winced, inwardly. Chances were, those guys were Ethan's baddies, but I wish I could be sure they weren't connected to the Petruzzis. Because if they were, I needed to pack up my stuff, take my tiny stash of money, and scram. And I didn't want to.

I would hate to leave my friends, and my girls. I'd broken rule number one and gotten attached. Then I met Ethan Masters, and proceeded to break rules two through two thousand. "That's not good news," I said.

He nodded, and we were quiet, concentrating on that incredible pasta for a few minutes while I groped around for a good starting place. I needed to say my piece.

"I hope you've concluded that I am not a whoring spy," I told him. "That's the antithesis of who I am."

"I believe you," he said. "One hundred percent."

Something deep inside me relaxed. "Thank God."

"That does not, however, explain the incredible strangeness

of finding a woman with your reflexes and abilities and training standing next to me in that elevator."

I shrugged. "Random fate. All I know about your problems is what you told me. You could keep me here for years and never get any useful info from me. I got zip."

"Okay,"' he said, as he refreshed my wine. "Tell me about your combat skills. How the hell did that happen?"

I was prepared for this question. I'd fielded it before, in other contexts, so I trotted out my standard story. "It started with a thing that happened in college," I said. "I went to this frat party, which was my first mistake. I drank a cup of fruit punch, which was my second. I woke up with a guy trying to drag my pants off. I kneed him in the teeth. He needed dental work afterward. And I was glad of it. And I decided to invest a whole lot of energy into making sure nothing like that would ever happen to me again."

"I see." I couldn't help but feel like he was unconvinced, and wanted more.

In my own defense, that story was not strictly a lie. It was just what one might call a patchwork truth. A little bit altered, a little bit out of sequence. I'd been at plenty of stupid parties during my stint in college, but I was far too cagey to drink any frat boy's punch. The pants being pulled off had not been mine. Rather, they had belonged to a clueless, passed out seventeen-year-old who had drunk too much and collapsed on a pile of coats. She may as well have had "prey" tattooed onto her forehead, but I didn't have it tattooed on mine. Not even back in college. I scared men off even then.

The knee-to-the-teeth detail was for real, and so was the guy's dental work. But that had not been my catalyst. I had already been an expert martial artist at that point.

I still wondered sometimes if that poor, drugged girl passed out on the pile of coats had learned anything from that night. One could only hope.

Ethan was giving me that look. Like he was peeling back layers and peering into the dark inside me, where he had no goddamn business looking. "Skip the creepy staring," I told him. "It bugs me."

His smile was charming and apologetic. "Sorry," he said. "It's hard not to stare. You're beautiful. And fascinating."

"There you go again, buttering me up."

"It is the literal truth," he said. "Denying it makes you look childish and silly."

I shrugged. "The thing about looks, though. It's just not that important. Or even real. It's just a trick of nature, and not particularly useful to me. I can attract some attention on a good day, so for the most part, I dress way down. Baggy clothes, a ponytail."

"You're still drop-dead beautiful," he said. "You're fooling nobody."

"And there you go again, missing my point. It isn't who I am. It's just how I look right now, and it happens to fit some current canon of desirability, which is also random. In a few years, when I've got crow's feet and a turkey neck and liver spots and a wrinkly cleavage, it won't fit that canon anymore. Seems dumb to fixate on it."

"Sorry," he said. "I see the rest of you, I swear to God I do. But I'm a mere mortal man, so you have to forgive me for loving how you look. Have mercy on me."

I held up my hand, thumb and forefinger almost touching. "This much," I said sternly. "This much mercy, and no more. But only if you stop carrying on about it."

"Okay," he promised "Just one last little thing."

I rolled my eyes. "Here you go again. What?"

"You're going to be a fucking gorgeous old lady, when you get there. Great bones, piercing eyes, amazing posture, snow-white hair. Full of power and wisdom."

I laughed, in spite of myself. "You are such an extravagant bullshitter."

Ethan smiled and lifted his wineglass. "Are you ready for that truce yet?"

I was still laughing, gaze locked with his, and my laughter melted away as his personality battered at me like a storm wind. I had such a yearning impulse to just give him what he wanted. Yield to it, relax, lean on him, just like he wanted me to, ahhhh, so sweet. To be protected, pampered, coddled, desired. But everything had its price. I wasn't quite sure what it was yet. Maybe Ethan didn't even know himself.

But the bill would come due eventually, one way or another. It always did.

"I'm sorry," I said. "But I didn't make all this effort and come all this way just to be your bed toy."

His smile faded, and he set his wine down. "It's not like that at all," he said. "I'm just so afraid of you being hurt. And knowing it was my fault would kill me. Can't we just work together to prevent that? Just until this thing is handled?"

I considered that for a minute. "Your brother has been gone for months now, and it's not handled yet. I don't see this thing wrapping up anytime soon."

"Bite your tongue," he said. "All I can do is try like hell. Please. Help me."

That was a sentiment she understood. "I have to go back to town and keep up with the classes I agreed to teach," I said. "The girls have paid for the month already."

"On sliding scales, I bet."

"What the hell is that supposed to mean?" I snapped.

"Just that you clearly need an influx of cash to get that place up to code. I could absolutely help with—"

"Hell, no. Hold it right there, buddy. Don't say one more word. Or you'll piss me off."

"How about Charlotte's glasses?" he wheedled. "Could I pay

for an appointment with a really good ophthalmologist, and get her a pair of glasses? Or actually, two pairs. She needs a pair for her regular life, and a pair of sports glasses, for her martial arts classes. Charlotte never has to know who paid for them."

I let out a frustrated sigh. That sneaky guy instinctively sensed all my weak points. "Pay for Charlotte's glasses if it makes you feel good," I snapped. "But I will not get sucked into your vortex. I worked hard to build what I have, who I am. My school, the girls. I'm not tossing that away for some guy's whim, no matter how hot he is."

Ethan's eyebrow went up. "Hot? Aww. Are you buttering me up?"

"Butter would sizzle and melt on your griddle," I told him.

He laughed. "That sounds promising."

"Take me to Seattle," I said sternly. "Tomorrow morning. First thing."

His mouth tightened. "If you insist. But I think it's stupid."

"Maybe, but it's my life," I told him. "My mission. I won't just abandon it."

For the third time, he held up his glass, with a sigh. "Truce. Okay?"

This time, I clinked mine with his. "Truce," I echoed.

"How about a kiss, to seal the bargain?"

"Why, you shameless opportunist." I smiled at the gleam in his eyes, savoring that hot clench of longing that was always there, ready to flare up into a blaze. I leaned across the table, and gave him a lingering kiss. Delicious. The man was just so yum.

"I have a suggestion," he said. "The terrace outside my bedroom has a hot tub. Let's go sip Prosecco, watch the sunset. Work out the fine details of our truce."

I smiled at him. "Okay, lover boy," I said softly. "Let's go get naked."

CHAPTER 20

Ethan

Kat Banner, naked her hair twisted up on top of her head, slowly sinking into the steaming water of my mosaic-tiled private hot tub...God. It was a peak life moment.

It was going to be tricky, not fawning and gushing over how fucking gorgeous she was, if she disliked it. I had to learn to play it cool, pretend it was no big deal.

Unfortunately, my dick had not gotten the memo. It continued to worship at her shrine. She didn't seem to hold it against me, though, as I took my place next to her in the churning water. We gazed out at the mountain sunset, a ruddy glow on the horizon. The quiet tub motor hummed, creating a mellow burbling roil of bubbles. The temperature was perfect. I tried not to stare, but when she closed her eyes and leaned her head back against the rim of the pool, I shamelessly ogled. The second she opened her eyes, my gaze would snap right back to the sunset.

Too bad she didn't like to be stared at. I could fill my eyes with her for hours. The heat had brought a rosy flush to her face. Her lashes were dark, but tipped with gold. She had small pink ears with a soft, delicate point, like an elf. I liked how her hair grew on her forehead, a mix of dark blonde and lighter streaks. And the strong angle of her determined jaw, the soft, lush swell of her lower lip, and the beautifully sculpted design of the upper one. Her mouth was stunning, with that virginal, flushed pink color. She could have modeled, but she wouldn't ever do anything so vain and frivolous.

She was a tough cookie. Severe. Uncompromising. Fascinating.

Her eyes popped open so fast, I had no time to cover, and she caught me gawking, but she just smiled indulgently, giving me a pass. "So hot," she murmured, and stood, like Venus rising from the foam, stretching her lithe body up toward the sky.

She perched on the edge of the sunken tub, so her gleaming, shapely thigh was next to my head, right at eye level. "I have to cool down," she murmured.

Oh, no. There would be no cooling down taking place tonight, not with this celestial vision right beside me. I slid off the bench, and floated around to face her, contemplating Kat's wet, naked body from below, like an eager supplicant.

"One thing I wanted to say to you," she said. "We've been using latex. But we never had the talk."

"Ah," I said. "I've had bloodwork done recently. No diseases."

"Good," she said. "Me too, since the last time I was with anyone. And you might be interested to know that I take the pill, to make my cycle more regular. I keep it with me, in my purse, fortunately. So if we wanted to, we could, ah...forget the latex."

The idea almost made me faint. I gazed up into her eyes. "Oh God, yes," I said. "You're sure?"

Her lips curved, in a mysterious smile. "I think it would be fun," she murmured.

I surged forward, half-drunk with the images in my mind. Water darkened the swirl of dark blonde hair on her mound. Drops rolled sensually down over her taut belly. Her nipples were a stiff, deep raspberry-red. That sex-goddess glow in her eyes, her soft, parted lips, the blonde wisps of hair clinging to her pink, damp face, every perfect detail made me breathless.

She seemed speechless. I decided to take it as license to put my hands on her knees, and press them, inviting them to open. An offer of passionate sexual worship.

"Let me." The plea came out in a low, rough whisper, and she allowed me to open her legs. I stroked the incredibly smooth, soft skin of her thighs, all the way up to the puff of golden hair, the tight seam of her pussy lips, and that darker, sexy frill that pouted out of it seductively, like an exotic orchid.

She let out a shaky moan as I put my mouth to her. Sliding the tip of my tongue all around the slick folds of her labia, then more, deeper, holding her legs wider, spreading her pussy open with my fingers. I lavished it with long, hungry strokes of my tongue, lapping up her delicate salt-sweet scent, her slick texture, her sweet little clit. So tight, pink, the pearly bud of exquisite sensation, too sensitive to touch directly. I had to flirt with it, seduce it, approach it sidewise, indirectly. Swirling with my tongue, sliding my finger deeper to catch the sensitive inside spots while I lapped her up...almost there...and she clutched my head, pressing me closer. Quivering and writhing and gasping in pleasure, as her first orgasm pulsed strongly against my face.

I lingered there, nuzzling her thigh. Desperate for more. That would be my natural state from now on. I'd just gotten her off, and I already craved her next climax.

I kissed the tops of her thighs, and got to my feet. My cock jutted out, prodding her as I took her hands, kissed then, draped them over my shoulders. Then I scooped her knees up onto my elbows.

Kat reached down between us and grabbed my cock, caressing herself with it, before guiding it right where I needed to be...slowly pushing my whole length into her hot, snug hole. That suckling kiss, my bare skin in scalding contact with her honeyed heat. That tight caress, the lick of her slippery lube, the pulsing thrust and glide...so good, it was killing me, scaring me. Changing me.

I waited, teeth clenched, through two more orgasms, and then I slid out, pulling her to her feet. She grabbed me to steady herself.

"Let's finish in the bed," I said.

"Ah...whatever." Her voice was breathless, soft. Not her usual brisk tone.

I liked it. Making Kat Banner breathless and dizzy, that was a life goal worthy of the name.

I scooped her up into my arms, and it was a stark testimony to how wiped-out she was that she just laughed at me under her breath. "Macho dude," she whispered.

"Oh, yeah." I deposited her on the bed, and she reached out for me, pulling me into her arms as I positioned myself. She arched and sighed as she took my cock inside herself. It felt so sweet, so hot. Caressed by her perfect body. My cock was anointed with sweet balm, hot and gleaming. Her pussy stroking me, clutching me, milking me. The lazy pump and glide, in and out. Slow, deliberate fucking. No hurry, not for a long time. Clutching, kissing, twining...we could do this for hours. Forever. No hurry.

Until suddenly, there was. The urgency grew on its own, with no help from us, and then we were bucking and heaving together, clutching, yelling, desperate. My hips drove against her. She sank her nails into my ass, demanding more. The bed shuddered, the mattress squeaked, and she convulsed beneath me, yielding to yet another deep, shivering climax, and pulling me right after her.

I was flung and tossed by it. A raging, explosive storm of emotion, sensation.

It was her stroking hand against my shoulders and hair that brought me back. I rolled off her, struggling with the bedcovers until I got Kat beneath them, and then crawled in to join her. Our damp bodies twined. I shimmered with the afterglow.

We cuddled in bed, fingers wound together. Feeling each other breathe. Night deepened, and the only light was the dim glow from the lantern I had left outside.

I couldn't stand this disconnect any longer. My feelings for her were so strong, they were uncontrollable, but we couldn't take this to the next level without honesty. I wanted her to trust me with her secrets. I had held nothing back. It was her turn now.

"Kat," I said. "What happened to you?"

She shifted against me. "What do you mean?" she asked cautiously.

"What disaster put you on this path? Who are you hiding from?"

After a moment, she pulled away from me. "I told you this topic was off limits."

"That was a whole lifetime ago," I said, "We were different people then. The boundaries have moved. The rules have changed."

"Who says?" she asked, sitting up. "When did that happen? No one told me."

"Come on, Kat," I said gently. "You know it's true. You feel it, too."

I shut up and waited. Letting silence, patience, and darkness do its work.

After a few minutes, she spoke, her voice halting. "I don't know how to talk about it. I never have. With anybody."

"No hurry," I told her. "We have plenty of time. As a matter of fact, I've cleared my schedule for a while, just so we can focus on our personal business."

She turned her head toward me in the darkness, shaking with soft, whispery laughter. "We, Masters?"

"Yes," I said resolutely. "Absolutely, we. We're in this together."

She huffed under her breath, and drew her knees up to her chin. "I don't know if I can talk about it," she said slowly. "And it's not a matter of whether I should. It's because I literally... can't. It's like grabbing a live wire. Or jumping off a cliff."

I shifted closer to her and curled my hand around her foot, and waited. It would take as long as it took.

Kat pressed her face to her knees for a minute, and then looked up, staring into the dark as if she was seeing something I couldn't see.

"My mom died of a stroke, when I was twelve," she said. "It happened in the night. I found her in the morning. I'd gone into her room to see if she would brush my hair for me, and... found her like that. Gone."

I squeezed her foot. "I'm so sorry," I said.

"Yeah. So, my sister, Raffi, was eighteen. She'd just gotten into Columbia. Full-ride scholarship. She was going to study biochemistry. She wanted to be a doctor. But there wasn't anyone to look after me and Gabri, my little sister. She was five, then. We didn't have any relatives to go to. My mom's people were all gone, my dad was out of the picture since Gabri was conceived. Gabri and I would have ended up in the system. Raffi couldn't let that happen. So she gave up the scholarship."

I flinched. "Oh, fucking ouch."

"Yeah, that was how I felt, too," Kat said. "But she told me it would be okay. That we'd all get through this hard part together, and eventually she'd figure out how to get a medical degree."

"What happened?"

"Well, she worked like a donkey. She got two jobs. She waitressed at this local Italian restaurant in the evenings, worked as a paralegal at a law firm in the morning, and she tried to take care of us. I helped with Gabri, keeping her clothed and bathed and fed, getting her to school while Raffi worked her butt off. And then..."

Kat's voice trailed off. I braced myself, my mind whirling with ugly possibilities. I stroked her foot again, a slow, soothing caress.

"Turns out this Italian restaurant was the favorite hangout of a local crime boss and his family," she went on. "Very powerful, very ruthless. They loved the Signora Sciancalepore's ragú. They went there all the time for it, and my sister always served them. They asked for her specifically. She was really pretty. I mean, insanely pretty."

"I believe it, having seen you," I said.

"She was much prettier than me," Kat said swiftly. "She was... I don't know how to describe it. Sparkly, somehow. And she spoke Italian. She'd learned it from my mom and grandma. I don't remember much anymore, but Raffi was fluent. At least in dialect."

"Your family was Italian?"

"Mom was. She said our dad was a Swede, but I have no way to corroborate that. Mom was dark, but the three of us were fair, like him. But Raffi was the real beauty. With the long curly blonde hair, and these eyes, and this incredible smile."

"Oh shit," I said. "I think I see where this is going."

"Yeah," Kat said. "I'll stop, if you'd rather not hear it. For real. No problem."

"Fuck, no," I said. "Please, go on."

"Okay. So, yeah, it was a train wreck waiting to happen. Raffi never had a chance, once Tony saw her."

"And Tony was...?"

"The crime boss's son," she said. "A real piece of work. A

total narcissistic sociopath. He saw this beautiful shiny thing, and he wanted it. And no one was around with the presence of mind to tell her to run like hell. Change her name, find another job, go to another city, do any fucking thing she had to do to get away from him."

I let out a slow, calming breath, and prepared myself. "What happened?"

Kat buried her face against her knees. "Tony was handsome, in a thick, sleazy sort of way. He was nice at first. He promised to set her up in a luxury apartment, give her a car, an allowance for clothes, jewels, etc. We couldn't go with her, of course, but the money he was promising was way more than she could earn with the waitressing and the paralegaling. She was just nineteen, with us on her back, so she did it."

She stopped again, and I sensed she was building up the nerve to push onward another step through this wall of thorns. I squeezed her ankle, patiently waiting.

"She tried to hoard money for us, but Tony got angry," she went on softly. "She'd try to sneak out to see us when he was gone, but he got angry about that, too. Then she realized that Tony got angry about everything. Because he liked being angry."

"Did he hit her?"

"Yes. Every time we saw her, she was wearing makeup to hide the bruises. Then that thing with the cat happened." She stopped, shaking her head.

"Cat?" I prompted gently.

"Penelope. Our calico cat. She adored Raffi, so Raffi took her to the new apartment, with Tony's permission. But Penelope hated Tony. Took a big dump in his Ferragamo loafers one day."

"Yay, Penelope," I said.

"I thought so, too," Kat said. "But then Tony killed her."

That made me flinch, shocked. "Fuck! He killed your sister's cat?"

"Yeah. Threw her against the wall. Broke her back. And Raffi just...snapped, that night. She tried to run. She came to our apartment, but he followed her, and...well. He had a gun."

Minutes of silence followed. I wondered if I had pushed her too hard, selfishly. Just to satisfy my curiosity. It wasn't worth it if it hurt her, stirring up old nightmares.

"So, Tony stormed in, and rants about how he hadn't signed up to pay for these fucking brats. Then he looked at me, in my underwear, and the lightbulb went on in his little reptile brain. He'd thought of the perfect way to punish Raffi."

"Oh shit," I whispered. "Oh, Jesus, Kat. I'm sorry."

"He said if I was old enough to get a man to pay my rent, I was old enough to fuck, and he went for me. Raffi freaked out and attacked him, hitting and scratching him. He shot her through the heart. Gabri couldn't stop screaming. So he shot her, too."

"And you?" I asked.

"He got me one, too," she said, rubbing the scar on her shoulder. "But I went out the window and down the fire escape. I jumped down onto a pile of garbage, barefoot, in my underwear, and took off running. I barely remember it, now. I made it all the way to the cops somehow. And I was lucky enough to talk to the right detective, a guy who wasn't on the take with Tony's dad. The detective really wanted to take those bastards down, so he protected me, for real."

"You testified against Tony?"

"Yes. Tony was convicted of second-degree murder, but he only got sixteen years. His lawyer made my sister out to be a slutty temptress who cheated on him and drove him to it. He might actually get out of prison soon. That should make life really interesting for me."

"And you've been in witness protection since?" I prompted.

"Yes, but Tony's family will never stop hunting me. That's

why falling into bed with a famous sexy billionaire who has lunch with the senator is a really shitty idea." She swatted my arm. "So please don't take it personally."

"What's Tony's surname?" I asked. "What prison is he in?"

Kat stiffened. "Uh-oh," she said. "This is where it starts, right? When you start pushing and pushing me for more info? Bound and determined to solve all my problems? Nope. Not gonna happen."

"Tell me his name, Kat," I coaxed. "This is information that I need, to help protect you."

"Listen to me, Ethan Masters, and listen good. Those scumbags already took my family from me. I will not let them take you, too. I'd rather get the hell away from you, and at least know that you continue to exist. Even if I can't enjoy you."

"Enjoy me?" I murmured. "Ooh. I like the sound of that."

"Don't make this all about you," she snapped. "Peacock."

"Right, right. Sorry."

"I will not tell you Tony's name," she said. "And I can't be your pampered concubine, either. I know you're not like Tony, but even so. I just can't."

"So," I said carefully. "Where does that leave us?"

"Nowhere," Kat said. "Which is exactly where I've been, for the past fourteen years. It's where I live, Ethan. And you can't be with me there. Nowhere is a place you can only inhabit alone."

"I can't accept that. I simply don't believe there's no solution."

"Well, tough shit. I'm not risking your life to find out. Tomorrow, I go back to my life, Ethan. I'll figure out my shit on my own, without getting anybody else killed."

I pulled her into my arms. "I can't walk away from you. Stop asking me to try."

Kat shook her head, letting out a soggy laugh. "I was thinking about how you took care of your little sister and brother when you were a kid. You weren't much younger than

Raffi was then. Shane was my age, Freya was Gabri's age. You were lucky you had a marketable skill to sell. You didn't have to sell your body to a monster."

"Yeah. But in her place, I would have done the same thing. I got lucky, with that contact in the juvenile detention center. I was walking a tightrope, back then."

"Raffi was walking one, too," she said. "But she fell off. We all did."

I tightened my arms around her and she melted against me, soft and yielding.

"I miss them so much," she whispered. "Raffi would have been, let's see, thirty-three. She'd be a doctor by now. Gabri would have been twenty-two, about to graduate from college. She wanted to be an astronaut, you know? We put those adhesive stars on her bedroom ceiling. She had star maps and posters and spaceships on her wall. Maybe aeronautical engineering, or the military. Fighter jets. She was such a bright kid."

"And you? Where would you have been?"

Kat's shoulders jerked. "Oh, I don't know. I wasn't gifted like Raffi or Gabri. And I never had a chance to dream anything up for myself. That all got shut down."

"It's not too late to dream."

"How sweet. You are a secret romantic, Mr. Masters. Truthfully, though, I don't mind what I do right now. Helping women and girls learn to stand their ground...that's enough for me. But sometimes I start to think about an alternate universe where it never happened. Raffi never had to give up her scholarship. I taught Gabi to drive. Helped her shop for a prom dress. Watched her graduate from high school. Celebrated when she got into college. It just makes me so...oh, shit, not again. Here I freaking go again."

She dissolved once more, against my chest.

I wound my arms around her, and tried to keep her all in one piece with the strength of my embrace.

CHAPTER 21

Kat

I felt so strange, when I woke up. In a good way. Floating, clean. Empty. As if a load of smothering garbage had been hauled away with a backhoe. So much open space.

Thinking about Gabri and Raffi still hurt, but the pain was different today. It wasn't like that old pain that almost made me black out. It was an ache of grief, but there was a piercing sweetness to it that swelled in my chest, and made my eyes well up with tears.

Which would get problematic, for sure. Crying every time something reminded me of my lost sisters? Please. Every damn thing reminded me of them. Ice cream, birdsongs, a cloud, a color. I'd been keeping myself armored up for fourteen years, and suddenly here I was, out there in the open, stark naked. Blasted open, no roof, no door.

I had finally cried for my sisters, for the first time since it happened, and I had done it in Ethan's arms. I'd finally dared to let myself feel just how much had been stolen from me. Not only my sisters, a family, an identity, a life embedded in other lives, but all of it, even the smaller, seemingly unimportant things. A childhood recognizable as such. A normal American girlhood, with all the moments and the milestones. I hadn't had any of those rites of passage everyone else took for granted. There wasn't a human being alive who would ever wish me a happy birthday, not on my original birth date or my fictitious one. It was just safer that way.

I didn't want to live that sterile, lonesome kind of life anymore, but neither could I pull Ethan into the danger that stalked me. He had his own family to protect.

I could take care of myself. I could take responsibility for myself, but not for him, too. That was outside my scope. And there was no way to be this man's lover without the world noticing. Everyone looked at him. Even without his genius brains and his mojo and his money, all eyes were on him just because he was so damn beautiful.

I had to pull up my big girl pants and do the painful thing that was best for everyone. Joanna, Danica, the girls. And Ethan. Even if they all felt hurt and betrayed by me leaving, they would still be alive to feel it, right? Not crumpled up on the floor in a pool of blood. Eyes empty and blank. Gone from this world forever.

Oh, lucky me. My heart had come intensely alive just in time to break into bits.

Whining didn't help, but living in the moment, enjoying every last crumb of joy I could get—well, I couldn't say it would help, per se, but why not make more sweet memories? As many as possible, to sustain me.

I'd treasure them for as long as I kept body and soul together.

The sky was lightening. I pushed the tears, the grief back in my mind. Not confined, not forgotten, but not for right now. This moment was for me. For all time.

I rolled on to my side, facing him, and placed my hand over his heart. Memorizing the sensation. Burning it into my mind so it would be part of me forever.

I slid my hand down, savoring every inch of him, every hair, the shape of his muscles and tendons, the jut of bone, the heat, the rough, the smooth. Over his belly, and then lovingly, teasingly lower. His cock was high and stiff. He opened his eyes, and looked at me. "Good morning," he croaked.

"Hey," I whispered.

"Oh, my God," he said, as I grabbed his cock, stroking and squeezing.

I lifted myself onto my knees, and clambered astride him. Holding his thick, gorgeous shaft just where I needed it as I swayed over him, stroking my pussy with his warm, broad cock-head, sliding him over and around my clit, nudging him inside my warm, slick opening...and then slowly sank down onto that beautiful, stiff cock.

He surged up and into me, and I sighed and moaned at every delicious pulsing stroke, feeling it slide and stir and caress me.

We found our rhythm quickly, the perfect dance, rising, falling. Him, thrusting up, me sinking down, squeezing him inside, sighing and panting. I splayed my hands over his chest, he dug his fingers into my hips, and we gave ourselves up to it completely. The sweetness, the wildness, the perfect, raw, live-wire intensity of it.

We exploded together, and I couldn't hide from the truth any longer. I loved this guy. I was cooked. In the middle of this hellacious shitstorm, I had fallen in love, and at the same time, concluded that I had to turn my back on him and run. Oh God, it hurt.

"What?" Ethan looked alarmed. He stroked my back. "What's wrong? Did I do something wrong?"

I wiped the tears away, and pushed myself upright. "No. You're awesome. I—"

...love you. I love you. I love you. Oh, my love.

I cut it off. It was an irresponsible thing to say, since I was leaving. "It was wonderful," I amended.

"So why are you crying?"

"I'm just feeling really emotional. I blocked it for so long. I ran away from it, buried it in a concrete bridge piling. And now it's all broken open, and I get to feel all the feelings, all at once. And you have only yourself to blame, big guy. You insisted."

"I never wanted to hurt you," he said. "I want to help. I want you to be free."

"You and me both, pal." I bent to kiss him, just for wishing it, which was a sweet sentiment, if useless. "Let's get moving. I need to get back to town. I have things to do."

His frown came right back. "Kat. It's not safe."

"Shhhh." I grabbed his hands, and squeezed them. "I know you mean well, but I am done with this song and dance. If you keep me here any longer, I will be forced to consider myself a prisoner, and you as my enemy. Neither of us want that."

"Stay with me in town, then," he urged me. "My townhouse is well located. There's a private bedroom, bathroom, and office, just for you. A king-sized bed in my room, with me in it, ready to sexually service you at a moment's notice, a domestic staff who—"

"I don't want to be a kept woman. Not here, not in your townhouse, not anywhere at all. I can pour my own cereal and fold my own laundry."

"That's not the point. It would just be so much easier to secure you there."

I shook my head. "I'm going home. I have business to attend to."

He gave me that smoldering look as I climbed off his still-erect dick and headed toward the bathroom. Under the shower,

I dissolved into laughter, or maybe it was tears, I could hardly tell anymore. It was so hard to push back against his power and charisma, but I was ready to do the right thing, the difficult thing. Even if it hurt me.

I had my unshakeable principles, too. And my mind was made up.

CHAPTER 22

Ethan

K at had been waylaid by Angela while finishing her coffee. It appeared Angela had adopted her, the way she had adopted Frey, Shane, Holly, and me, and as such, had strong opinions to share. In this case, vociferous disapproval of Kat's decision to leave the safety of the Mountain House and go back to the city.

I left her to Angela's tender mercies, since I agreed one hundred percent with Angela. Not that it earned me any points. My housekeeper had let me know in no uncertain terms that she thought I had buried my balls under a rock by capitulating to Kat's demands. That I should put my foot down. Insist on her safety. Be the boss.

But I couldn't be Kat's jailor. It was getting creepy and unsustainable. My only other option was a 24/7 security detail, which was a cumbersome, complicated, expensive solution, and Kat wasn't going to like it.

But it was that or cut her loose. And I could no more do that than I could chop off a limb.

I shamelessly took advantage of the fact that Kat was

trapped in the sunroom by my housekeeper's scolding, and went to the security room to consult with Mick.

Mick spun his chair around from the bank of security monitors. "Taking off?"

"Yes. But I need something from you," I told him. "One, find four good people for a rotating two-man security detail on Kat while she's in the city. For now, I'm calling Trey and Shelby to come down with me for today, but I need more men."

Mick looked shocked. "She's not staying here? Is she out of her mind?"

I shot him a look, and he rolled his eyes. "Right. I'll come up with more men. Anything else?"

"Yeah. You have a stash of smartphones in here, right? I want to give Kat one with our numbers in it."

Mick leaned over, opened a drawer, and pulled out a high-end smartphone with a charging cable wrapped around it. He handed it to Ethan. "There you go. Already activated and charged up. Top of the line. All standard apps pre-loaded."

I opened it up, and inserted my own number into the list. "Have you found anything else in that research I asked for?"

"No, but I'm still poking around. She's definitely hiding something."

The tragic story Kat had told me last night was still in the forefront of my mind, but I wasn't going to share it with Mick or anyone else unless I had a damn good reason to. I headed back out to the terrace, and found Arch Dorne's number on my phone.

Arch was a die-hard Unredeemable. I'd served with him in my second tour in Afghanistan. I'd been forced to retire after I took a gut wound in the course of saving his life. Just as well, in the end. I would never have started up MasterTech if I'd stayed busy with the Rangers. And MasterTech had been good for me, and my family.

Arch had gone back and done two more tours before

coming back and getting recruited by the FBI. He was now on a task force that fought organized crime. I'd tried to get him to come work for me after he mustered out, but he hadn't been interested. Too much history, he told me. I sensed the life-debt weighed on him.

Well, hell. Maybe if he helped me out today, it would weigh a little less.

The number rang, three times...four... and he picked up.

"Yo, Ethan," he said, in a sleep-addled croak. "Do you know what time it is?"

I had not, in fact, thought about how early it was on the east coast. Hell, it was early for me here on the west coast. Freya always said I was too accustomed to the whole world dancing to my tune.

"Sorry, man," I said. "I forgot about the time difference."

"The concept of time zones escapes you. With that tech genius brain of yours."

"Selective intelligence," I said. "I'm as dumb as a rock about some things."

"Good to know," Arch grumbled. "Okay, I'm awake. What do you need?"

"Got a favor to ask," I said. "I need some information."

There was a nervous pause on the other end of the line. "You know damn well I can't compromise myself professionally. Not even as a favor for a friend."

"Of course not. You don't have to. I have a woman friend, twenty-eight years old. She told me she was put into Witness Protection fourteen years ago, after testifying against a mobster. The guy killed her older sister, nineteen, and her youngest sister, seven. She called them Rafaella and Gabriella. I don't know if those are their real names. I think it happened in the Tri-State area, judging by her accent and other details, like the sister having to give up a scholarship to Columbia University, stuff like that. She currently goes by the name Katrin Banner, and claims to have been brought up in San Diego. Or she did before she confessed about the mobster and the sisters, anyway."

"So? What the hell do you need me for? She's your friend, right? She's the expert on her own life story. She can tell you whatever you need to know without compromising her career or her integrity. Unlike me."

"Don't be a tight-ass, Arch. I need to corroborate that story. I'm under pressure here to keep my family safe. You know what I'm fighting against. And you owe me."

"You lean hard on that," Arch complained.

"I try not to lean too hard on that bullet scar in my belly," I said. "It still hurts me when I bench more than two-fifty."

"Oh, for fuck's sake."

"Two things," I said. "One, is her story is true? It's a yes-or-no question. And two, if it is true, what's the name of the mobster? That's it. All I want from you."

"Shit," Arch said under his breath. "You're in love with this girl, aren't you?"

"That's none of your damn business, Arch. Can you help me?"

"Is this related to Shane's abduction?"

"It is now. She saved my life. And those fuckheads are after her now because of it. She's my responsibility now. I just need to be sure of the details."

"Wow, she saved your life? Lucky her. That means she gets to have you be her indentured servant in this life and the next, right?"

"Don't whine, Arch, it's unbecoming. I gave you the data. All I need is a confirmation. Yes, no, and the name of the killer. You can do it. I know you can."

"Send me a picture of her," Arch said sourly.

I snapped a furtive shot of Kat through the glass of the sunroom, and zoomed in to make sure it showed her whole face. She looked hunted, as one would, being scolded by Angela, but she was recognizable. I sent it, and went back to the call. "Sent."

"I'll see what I can do," Arch growled. "No promises."

"I'm trying to keep what's left of my family alive, Arch," I said. "If you can help me, great. If not, whatever."

"Fine, gotcha. Talk later."

Bad-tempered bastard. Arch was not the most amiable of the Unredeemables crowd, but he always came through.

I approached the dining room, and heard Angela's rant through the open door. I waited outside, noticing that Kat had dropped her big purse, the one she'd had with her at the office where I met her, on one of the tables outside.

"...perfectly comfortable here, with every possible luxury and entertainment! And it's not forever! It is just until the danger passes! It's insane to go back now!"

"Thank you, Angela, for caring so much, and for sharing your opinion," Kat said evenly. "You make me feel so well taken care of. I don't have a lot of that in my life, so I appreciate the hell out of it when I get it. You're very kind."

"Oh, stop it," Angela snapped. "I dislike being managed. I get enough of that from Ethan and Freya. Holly too, for that matter. Bunch of smooth manipulators, the whole pack of you."

"I'm not managing you," Kat said gently. "It's the literal truth."

But that just wound Angela up even more. "Well, I think you're being stubborn and self-destructive! Any woman with an ounce of sense would reorder her priorities!"

I tucked the phone into an inside pocket of her purse. Maybe it was sneaky and inappropriate, but it's not as if she didn't know that about me already. I'd tell her about it later, after she'd recovered from Angela's drubbing.

"Kat?" I poked my head in. "We should really get going. See you later, Angela."

Kat shot me an eloquent glance. "Goodbye, Angela. Thanks again."

"Be careful!" Angela's stern words sounded like a mandate from on high.

"Of course!" Kat fled the room, and hurried along beside me down the breezeway. "You really threw me to the wolves, back there," she grumbled.

"The wolves weren't telling you anything that wasn't true," I observed.

Kat harrumphed sharply, but didn't say another word until we got to the garage. I opened the passenger door of my black Jag, and Kat gave the car an approving look as she slid inside. "Sweet ride," she said. "Just us?"

"Trey and Shelby will be driving down on their own."

"Trey and Shelby? Why?"

"They're your guard detail," I informed her. "Whenever I'm not with you. You'll have a rotating two-man team, every hour of every day until this is all settled."

"You're joking," Kat said blankly.

"I'm not in a joking sort of mood these days. If you insist on leaving the safety of the Mountain House, you'll have bodyguards. That's not negotiable. Don't even try."

"So, the lord-and-master routine continues," she said. "No matter what I do."

"It does," I said, in steely tones.

A very silent drive to the city followed. I didn't try to start up a conversation. I sensed she felt vulnerable and shy, having revealed so much to me last night, but she was not defaulting to automatic hostility, so I decided to consider it progress.

We got to her house without incident. I parked on the street in front of the cracked sidewalk and the chain-link fence that bounded a patch of dirt which had probably never been a lawn. My Jag looked strange in that setting, but any one of my cars would have looked equally out of place.

Shelby and Trey parked behind me. I got out, strode back, and instructed Shelby to keep watch outside. I sent Trey straight out to shop for some high-quality security equipment. New door locks, window locks, alarm system.

Kat got out of the car, and I followed her into her house. She closed the door after me, looking uncomfortable. "So, you've already been through my place yesterday, so I don't have to give you the tour," she said. "I know it's a dump."

"Hell, no," I retorted. "This is anything but a dump."

Her eyes narrowed. "Oh, yeah, rich boy? How do you figure?"

"I wasn't always a rich boy. I was the head of a family when I was sixteen, and I was scrambling to feed them. I know how much energy it takes to keep things clean, and this place is immaculate. Not a speck of dust. No mold growing in the bathroom, and this is an old building in a city that's as damp as a sponge. You have ten different kinds of solvents and sprays and cleaning products under your sink. Everything's organized, nothing's out of place. It smells good. It's recently painted. I bet you did it yourself."

"Yes," she admitted.

"And you did it like a pro, with drop cloths, masking tape," he said. "There's not a drop of paint on the baseboards or the floor. The doors don't squeak, because the hinges are oiled. The sink doesn't drip."

Her eyebrow tilted up. "I hope you know how creepy it is that you noticed all these incredibly specific details," she said. "Most people notice clutter, but not the lack of it, because what's to notice? But not Ethan Masters. He's special that way."

I ignored that barb. "It's not creepy to notice a place is well kept. This is a palace compared to the places we crashed after we ran away from our uncle and aunt."

She shrugged. "I like a clean living space," she admitted. "My mom was a neatnik, and I guess I got it from her. I'd like to have a better apartment, for sure, but one of the sad things about being on the run and living under the radar is that the jobs that you can get and leave easily never pay well. To make real money, you have to commit, and I never had that luxury. But I can't tolerate squalor, no matter where I am."

"I don't like it either," I said. "But I never kept house as well as this. Not with Shane and a little sister to look after. Something always slipped through the cracks."

We froze for an instant. The thought of her lost sisters hung heavy in the air. I saw Kat push the thought away from herself by sheer force of will.

"Excuse me," she murmured, fleeing to the bedroom.

She slapped the door open again a moment later, a disapproving look on her face. "Really, Masters?" she said. "I do get that you were trying to ascertain if I was a honeypot deathtrap, so I forgive you for breaking into my house. But pawing through my clothes and my underwear and my shoes? That's just weird and pervy."

"I didn't do that," I protested, craning my neck to look into her bedroom, and her open closet. Everything looked like it was in perfect order. Shoes neatly organized on a shoe shelf, stacks of T-shirts and sweatshirts, organized by color. A bag with carefully paired socks each in its own little slot, hanging on the closet door, like something out of a fucking lifestyle blog. "Who pawed through what? Looks neat as a pin to me."

"I leave things in such a way that I know if anyone has handled them," she said.

I raised my hands in protest. "I did not handle your underwear! Not judging, but that's not my kink. Too derivative. I prefer to go straight to the source."

Kat huffed out a sharp breath and closed the bedroom door smartly in my face.

Well, shit. I couldn't get too huffy. I had literally broken in and trespassed here yesterday, so I had no moral high ground to take. I'd been pushing her boundaries and taking liberties since the first moment I'd met her.

Still and all. I had not touched her damned clothes. As fucking if.

A knock on the door jolted my lacerated nerves. "Ethan?" Shelby's voice

"What is it?" I asked.

"There's a woman here to see Kat," he said. "What do you want me to do?"

Kat marched out of her bedroom, pushed past me, and peered through the blinds. "Oh, it's just my friend Joanna," she said. "Let her in."

Shelby hesitated. "Boss?"

I met Kat's narrowed eyes. Here it came. Another scolding. "Yes. Let her in," I said, resigned.

"So," Kat said. "These bodyguards answer to you. Not to me."

"I'm the one who pays them," I pointed out, and then wished immediately that I hadn't said it. Not a detail that was going to endear me to her.

"Ah," Kat said. "Which makes them less like bodyguards, and more like, oh, I don't know. Jailors, spies, informants, babysitters? What's the right word for it?"

"Let's discuss it another time," I suggested, as Joanna burst through the door.

"Damn, Kat!" Joanna said. "What's up with the tattooed prison guard out front? What is this, the frickin' gulag?"

"Not at all," I said. "Just a security precaution."

Joanna spun around, open-mouthed. "Holy crap!" she breathed. "This is the guy who broke into your house yesterday! I caught him in the act!"

"I know," Kat said. "He's also been pawing through my underwear drawer. What the hell were you looking for, anyway?"

"I never touched your damned underwear!" I snapped back.

Joanna glared at me. "You said you'd tell Kat to call me!"

"And I did," I said. "It is not my fault she got distracted."

Kat turned back to Joanna. "Sorry, Jo," she said. "I meant to call, and I would have, eventually. But things have been intense lately."

"I was afraid he was a serial killer," Joanna confided.

"No," Kat snapped. "Just an expert at breaking and entering, evidently."

I reached deep into my soul for patience. "I'm trying to help, Kat," I said. "Stop breaking my balls."

"I'll have to think about that," she said coolly. "Probably I could think about it better without having you all up in my face. I need a break, Ethan."

Whatever. I slid my arm around her waist, pulled her tight against me, and gave her a fierce, hungry kiss. She didn't pull away. For a brief moment, she melted against me, which felt so fucking good, it made my heart thud and my eyes blur.

I pulled away, trying not to pant. "We are not done," I told her.

"Whoa!" Joanna's eyes were wide with delight. "Sexual tension! Rawr!"

Oh, for fuck's sake. That was definitely my cue. I strode out the door, and glared over at Shelby, who was leaning on my car. "I'm going to go check out some leads."

"Alone?" Shelby frowned. "Not good. You should take one of us with you."

"I'm not doing anything dangerous," I said. "I want you here, with her. Keep your eyes on her. Call me if she decides to go anywhere. Whatever it is, she has to wait until Trey is back."

"Got it." Shelby glanced at the door in trepidation.

"She's scary, but she won't hurt you," I told him. "I think."

Shelby rolled his eyes. "That's real comforting, boss. Watch yourself out there."

I set a course for the house of Jordan Meechum, the CFO of Clemens & Associates. I figured I might as well chase down another lead while she cooled off. I needed something concrete to offer her when I came back.

Right now, a peace offering would be a very prudent move.

CHAPTER 23

Kat

I stared at the door after it slammed shut, swallowing a lump in my throat.

We are not done. His words had sounded more like a threat than a promise, as pissed and frustrated as he was with me, but I still found them perversely comforting.

I was doing my usual harpy from hell routine, the one that had never failed to drive away an unwanted suitor. It gutted me to think it could actually work on the one man I'd ever really wanted.

Problem was, he was stubborn. He felt responsible for me, and I didn't have time to drive him away with my bitchiness and snark. That could take weeks. At least days.

And now I was bodyguarded, for fuck's sake. It was comical, really. I could have been a bodyguard myself. I'd been urged to be one often, but I'd always backed away. People who needed bodyguarding were all too often those people who had cameras trained on them, journalists trailing them. People like Ethan Masters himself.

It all circled back to the awful, miserable, shitty impossibility of the two of us being together. Because of what destiny had made him. Because of the demons forever on my trail. Him, a gorgeous golden boy forever in the spotlight. Me, condemned to the dark corners and the holes in the wall, like a cowering mouse in a house full of cats.

I tried hard not to be mouse-like. I had invested every last drop of my energy in learning not to act like prey. And all my efforts were for nothing. I still had to run skittering back to my dark hole in the wall whenever the light flicked on.

"Holy crap, Kat!" Joanna said, in hushed tones. "What did you *do* to that guy?"

"Oh, you know," I muttered. "I was just my usual charming, scintillating self. That's me, making friends right and left."

Joanna whistled. "That one looks like a friend worth making! Hubba hubba!"

My throat tightened, as if there was something in there that was diamond hard and aching. "Not me," I said thickly. "I can't afford friends like that."

"Who cares what you can afford? The question is, can he afford a friend like you, and the answer is unquestionably yes. The dude is stinking rich. Yesterday I looked him up. I knew I'd seen his face. And holy crap! MasterTech, for flip's sake?"

"It's not about money," I said dully.

"Okay, fine. It can be about lust, then, because he's as smoking hot as he is rich," Joanna said enthusiastically. "When I figured out who he was, I was like...nah, maybe I'm not gonna call the cops quite yet. Maybe I'll just give my friend a chance to land herself a big, big, fish. And from what I can see, you landed him hard. The guy is obsessed with you! Going through your underwear drawer? I mean, wowsa!"

"I can't do this, Jo!" I protested "I can't be with a guy like that!"

Joanna looked bewildered. "Why not? Did he do something bad to you?"

"No, no, not at all," I said. "He was fabulous. Bossy, but fabulous."

"Of course he's bossy. He's, like, American aristocracy, right? Comes with the territory. But you'll whip him right into shape."

"I can't," I said. "I have to get away from him. As quickly as possible."

"Why? Are you, like, panicking, Kat? Come on, you've got this! I mean, he's rich, he's smart, he's smoking hot, he's fascinated by your underwear drawer, and he's honest-to-God not intimidated by you, which is kind of a miracle."

"Wow, thanks, Jo."

"No snark allowed, at least until I finish talking," Joanna said crisply. "Thing is, he's not just perfect for you. You're perfect for him, too. You're, like, a warrior goddess with a magic sword, you know? You can smack a top-shelf guy like that around, keep him guessing, so he doesn't get too big for his britches. I think it works, and I'm never wrong!" She paused, embarrassed. "Except about my own boyfriends, of course, but never mind those bonehead losers. I was having a hard time imagining a guy who could work for you. Now I can see it. You need someone who's, you know. Not normal."

I snorted. "Aww. I'm touched. Me and my special needs."

"Stop being such a drama queen," Joanna said impatiently. "I mean 'not normal' in the sense of, 'larger than life.' Okay?"

I took a moment, trying to breathe down the tightness in my chest. "But I can't."

Joanna flapped her hands in frustration. "Why the fuck not?" she yelled. "Chances like this aren't just once in a lifetime! They're once in a thousand lifetimes!"

"I know that!" I yelled back. "I just don't want to get him killed!"

Joanna gaped at me. "Um...killed?" Her voice got suddenly smaller.

"Yes! Killed! Like every other person close to me. I've got problems, Joanna. I've got enemies, and they're bad ones. You should stay away from me, too. I shouldn't have gotten as close to you as I did. It's sloppy, and it puts you in danger!"

Joanna's dangling mouth closed. "Well, shitstickles," she said stubbornly. "That sucks, but I don't care. Danger, schmanger. Fuck your enemies. I got your back. And you know what? I bet that hot, rich, tough dude would have your back, too."

"I can't let you do that! Or him!" I wailed. "I can't take it again! I can't watch it. I can't be responsible for it! Not again!" To my horror, I was dissolving again. *Shit.*

Joanna was horrified to see me start to bawl. "Oh God, Kat," she said hastily. "I'm so sorry, babe. I didn't know."

"Nobody is supposed to know! But now you know, and he knows, so it's all going to hell! I'm losing my grip. And it's so fucking dangerous, Jo!"

"Well, I don't actually know anything concrete about it, except that you're upset," Jo said briskly. "And nobody should have to do it all alone. I mean, you helped me, right? You kicked Ricky's ass, and you rescued Ambrose. So I owe you, girl. Forever."

"Oh, but that was just Ricky," I said, fishing a tissue out of my pocket. "He's not a killer. He's just a no-account schmuck with anger issues."

"Oh gee, excuse my piddly problems," Joanna said, her voice ironic. "I still want to help, in my iddle-widdle-peewee sort of way, you know?"

"For real, Jo," I persisted. "I should get the hell away from everyone. From Ethan, from you, from Danica, from the girls at the school. Even your cat."

"What the hell, Kat? Did you rob a drug kingpin?"

"The less you know, the better. The one thing I can say for myself is that my own conscience is squeaky clean. I have never deliberately robbed or hurt anyone." I paused, reflecting on those words. "Aside from people's feelings, that is. And I've put the fear of God into some idiots like Ricky. But that's all."

"I never thought that you had," Joanna assured me. "Not in a million years."

"I swear to God, I do not deserve this shit," I said, exhausted.

"You most certainly do not," Joanna agreed. "You are as good as gold."

"But it doesn't matter if I'm good, or what I deserve," I said. "It doesn't matter what anyone deserves. Bad shit happens anyway. And Masters has problems of his own. He doesn't need a fresh crew of ass-faced goblins to come down on him. Plus, he's like a movie star, always in the news, all over social media. If I hung out with him for ten minutes, the paparazzi would start snapping photos, and we'd be dead meat."

"Oh, so that's why you're always the one who takes all the photos at the tournaments? So you won't appear in any of them yourself? Now I understand."

I shrugged. "Pretty much. I have to be invisible. Which means, I can't have Ethan Masters. Not even if we genuinely do have the hots for each other."

"Oh, babe. That sucks balls. I'm so sorry. And it's impossible for you to disappear in any case. You are just simply not the invisible type. Too tough, too strong, too good-looking. Too invincible. Sorry, but people notice you, whether you like it or not."

I waved that observation away. "You have to leave, Jo," I urged. "You're in danger here. And I can't even run away, now that Ethan insists on protecting me. So that big guy outside? Also in danger. All of them are. Anyone I give a shit about is in danger, even Ambrose. And I try so fucking hard not to care about anyone, Jo, so I can keep everyone safe, but I just can't do it anymore. I...just...can't."

Joanna grabbed me. I stiffened and pulled away, but she wouldn't let me go. And that, of course, made the tears flow again. "Of course you can't," she crooned. "It's not fair, and it can't go on. You deserve better. How can I help?"

I let out a sharp, bitter bark of laughter. "Walk away from me and forget I exist. That's the safest thing. Leave me to my fate. Please."

"No," Joanna said sharply. "Fuck that option. Bad idea. Forget it."

"Jo, don't make this harder," I pleaded. "You can't help. You just make me more vulnerable. It's like an evil spell. Don't get caught in it."

"I won't," she assured me. "Let's be systematic about this. Look at it step by step. What's the first step? Do you need to give the slip to your armed guard out there?"

"That'll be a tall order," I said. "He's Ethan's man, and he means business."

"I could, I dunno...try to seduce him, maybe?" Joanna cracked open my Venetian blinds and peered at Shelby, looking him up and down. "Mmm, nice. I'm not wearing makeup and I'm not in power-slut mode today, but he's kinda cute. I like 'em big and beefy and tattooed like that. Nice thick beard, too. I go for that."

"I'm sure he'd be gratified by the effort, but I'd bet you that one of Ethan's guys won't be too easily bamboozled," I told her. "I'm guessing that above average intelligence is a prerequisite for employment with that guy."

"Bummer." Joanna looked crestfallen. "Well, what else? My car's still parked in your spot in the back alley. How about I let him watch me go home...then we wait for a while to lull him into a false sense of security. Then I go out my back door, go around the block, sneak around the back, and meet you in the alley. You climb out a side window into the bushes. I hide you in the backseat, and drive you whenever you want."

"The downtown bus station," I said.

Joanna looked stricken. "You have to go? Like, go, go? Away? For good? Will you tell me where you're going?"

"I can't, Jo," I whispered. "I don't dare."

Then whoosh, I dissolved into tears once again, and she dissolved, too. Between the two of us, we were a hugging, sniffing, sobbing mess. I had an unpleasant feeling I was really in for it with the tears situation. I had so many years of backed-up, suppressed tears and snot to unload. When they all broke loose, well. God help me.

Joanna gave me a bone-cracking final squeeze to signal the end of the embrace, and a smacking kiss on my tear-wet cheek. "I'll only agree to do it if you solemnly promise to contact me somehow online after, just to let me know you're safe."

"Jo..."

"That's my one condition. You have to. Swear it, Kat."

I sighed. "Fine. I'll contact you. After a while. But I won't tell you where I am."

"We'll just see about that," Joanna said, cheering right up. "I'll give the bushes a shake to signal I'm there. Looks like Beard-and-Tattoos makes the rounds at intervals, so be sure to time it when he's out front. Just slither out the bedroom window, pop yourself into my backseat, keep your head down, and hoopla! Off we go!"

"It's risky for you to get more involved," I said miserably. "You should just stay away from the whole thing."

"Hell, no. This is exciting. And I love it that I can actually help. Let me help you like you helped me."

I bit my lip, trying not to start blubbering again.

Joanna sashayed out the front door, ogling Shelby as she left. She'd switched into full-on Mata Hari mode, in spite of not being in power-slut clothes, and was twitching her hips seductively as she walked. Shelby ogled right back as she walked away. Go, Jo.

Once Joanna was gone, I got cracking. My go-bag was always packed and ready. I didn't add much to it, just a few odds and ends of clothing. I left the rest behind.

The go-bag had my new driver's license and credit card, and a wad of cash I had saved up. I had a burner phone in there, too. Not because I had anyone to call, but only because not having one was too bleak to contemplate. Not having one meant not only did I have no one on God's green earth to call, but also that I never would.

But those were not the kind of thoughts to entertain right now. In fact, thinking at all was inadvisable. It was a time for pure action. I peeled some money from my precious stash. Left a note for the landlady, including a month's rent and an apology.

Then I lingered over the notepad with hot, wet eyes. There were so many things I wanted to say to Ethan, but what was the point, if I was just going to vanish? Why say them at all? Didn't that just make it worse, to get all sentimental on the poor guy?

Finally, I just scribbled, *Sorry. Thanks for everything. It was wonderful.*

I folded it in half, wrote his name on it, and left it on the table next to the landlady's note. I was done.

After forty minutes of nail-biting vigilance, I saw the hydrangea bushes shiver and quake. It was time. I checked on Shelby's position, waiting until I saw him come into view in the front. Then I ran to the bedroom, slid the window up, shoved out my bag, dropped my battered leather purse on top of it, and hoisted myself up onto the sill.

I forced my way through the bushes, which was a challenge. It had been years since anyone had trimmed them. I was a city girl, so gardening was not in my skillset. The branches clutched at my face and hair. I could barely pull my go-bag through them.

Jo waited in the car, wearing a dark sailor-style cap with her hair shoved up in it. I think it was supposed to be her disguise. Her face was bright with excitement. At least someone was having fun. Joanna was such a sweetheart. It was so irresponsible of me to take advantage of her, but it was too late to go back on the plan now.

I opened the car's back door, and was faced with a pile of bulky black garbage bags. They appeared to be full to bursting with old clothes, towels, and bedcovers.

"Just get down on the floor behind the seat," Joanna instructed. "Mom packed those into the car last week. She's been on me to take those bags to the Goodwill, and I've been putting it off. Looks like today's the day. I'll just pull a few down on top of you, and you'll be invisible."

I tossed my bag in, and slithered into the floor space, feeling claustrophobic as hell when Joanna rolled a couple of black-plastic wrapped bales of fabric down on top of me, blocking out the light. My face was shoved into a mess of fast-food wrappers and plastic Starbucks Venti cups.

The car lurched forward. "So, did you, like, leave a glass slipper for the guy, at least?" Joanna asked.

"Of course not," I said. "That would defeat the whole purpose."

"Well, not to throw you in a tizzy or anything, but I've been thinking. If anyone on earth could protect you from some shit-head criminal, it would be that guy. Along with his own personal army."

"I can't use him like that," I said, resolutely. "I won't put him and his family in more danger. It's the wrong thing to do, if I care about him."

"Of course," Joanna said. "'Cause you're in love with him.

It's so romantic, and sad, too, you know? Like Romeo and Juliet. Or Ladyhawke."

"Jo, dammit, if you make me cry again, I'll murder you myself," I warned her.

"Okay, okay," she soothed. "Not another word."

But it was too late. The tears were already welling up. Then they spilled over.

The damage was done.

CHAPTER 24

Nicole

Nicole sipped her green tea, and studied the mosaic of information covering the walls of her headquarters. It included every scrap of info she'd ever gleaned about the Masters and their associates, the Unredeemables. Some combination or other of those dipshit assholes had dashed every one of her plans so far.

But they were on the defensive now. She was coming for them, and they were going down.

If she'd only kept Shane Masters for herself after she had first nabbed him eight months ago, she'd been on the top of the world right now. With SmokeScreen, she would have shaken off Halliwell's yoke forever. But she'd had weak links in her team, and that shithead Vincent was one of them. Halliwell had assigned Vincent to her to babysit. She'd been cleaning up after that incompetent little prick for years.

Halliwell knew just how to get the maximum sting out of his punishments. To let Vincent strut around, lording it over her. Fucking with her just because he could.

Her jaw throbbed, in spite of the anti-inflammatories she'd taken, against Vincent's orders. She'd never forgive the look on his face while Vin watched the dentist pry out her molar and implant that poison tooth, without the benefit of anesthetic. Vin's eyes, so bright and eager. Enjoying it. He liked to see her naked and in pain. He'd always been envious. Jealous of any attention Halliwell gave her.

And Halliwell had signed off on that. He'd deliberately given Vincent permission to abuse her that way. His own daughter, his tool, his loyal servant.

Afterward, as she lay limp in the chair, naked and blood-spattered, Maynard, one of Vincent's men, assuming she was unconscious, had given her breast a squeeze. The memory still bathed her brain in killing-rage-chemicals. And the green tea was not delivering on the calming effects the online brochure had promised. The heat hurt her sore jaw. And it tasted like ass.

She needed to drain this bad energy, or she would lose control. Do something unfortunate. Which was to say, something impossible to hide from Halliwell.

That was what had gotten her into trouble before. The Masters had fucked her up twice. First, when Jed Clearwater survived the Ready Line massacre. Second, when he and Freya had survived that debacle in Oregon. Ethan and his Unredeemables had descended upon them, and she and her then-partner, Wex Boer, had gotten their asses hammered. Wex had been killed. She'd been in disgrace with her father ever since.

Father, in a manner of speaking. Vincent and Nicole had never been able to think of Halliwell as a father. None of them had. He was anything but paternal, behaving more like a capricious god. He knew perfectly well she had more brains and talent than Vincent, but he had promoted Vincent above her. Because she had fucked up.

Hence, the demotion, the tooth. She was being spanked.

She and Vincent had seen what happened when Halliwell's patience reached its end. Being his biological child was no protection. On the contrary. Halliwell hated it when his genetic offspring failed him. He took it very personally.

If she failed, the next lesson would be definitive.

Fine. The apple did not fall far from the tree. She took things personally, too. And her grand plan would change all the cards on the table in her favor.

The ideal activity to calm her inner torment would be to torture the activation codes of SmokeScreen out of that prick, Ethan Masters. Maybe breaking his dumb blonde girlfriend, right in front of his eyes. The bitch had no idea what a lying user Masters was. Most men were just as bad, but Masters bothered her more than the rest.

He'd lose interest in Kat Banner. He always did. Nicole had followed his career with the ladies, and his affairs all ended like the one she'd had with him, back when she worked at Master-Tech. That had been her first assignment after being kicked out of medical school. Halliwell had been so furious with her, but it really hadn't been her fault that time. She'd scared them, with her vision, her steely nerves. One of her med school instructors, while lying naked in bed with her, had told her she had sociopathic tendencies.

That guy had died that same night, of a heart attack. No one autopsied him, but if they had, they would have found no trace of the air bubble she'd injected between his toes. She'd dressed his body in his wife's underwear, too. Just for shits and giggles.

Pervert. Calling her a sociopath? Hah. The fucking nerve.

Masters had fucked her and then ghosted her, as if she were a dumb bunny. A toy to be used and discarded. He hadn't seen her, or sensed the power inside her. Hadn't been intrigued by it, hadn't feared it. She would never forgive him for that. She'd rather be hated, despised and feared than brushed off and forgotten.

He would fear her, before this was all over.

Banner was just a toy, as Nicole had been, which meant she might have to dig deeper for a good lever to move Masters. Little Holly, now...the guy would turn somersaults for that kid.

Nicole spat out the tea with a grimace. Fuck this stuff. It wasn't performing as promised, so it got poured down the drain. Like she would be, if she failed again.

She would not fail this time. She would never be punished again. Not by anybody. This time, she'd do the punishing. She would be top dog.

"Nicole?"

Nicole splashed tea onto her wrist as she turned, jaw throbbing at the sudden movement. Well, well, well. It was Maynard, the dick-faced tit-fondler. "What?"

"Katrin Banner's tracker is on the move." Maynard's gaze didn't meet hers. Maybe he sensed his life was forfeit for having enjoyed the dentistry show so much.

"And?" she asked. "Where's she headed?"

"She's at the bus station right now. She went there from her house."

"Already at the bus station? She got all the way from her house to downtown before you noticed? What, were you distracted, Maynard? Jerking off, maybe?"

Maynard's mouth tightened. "No," he said. "What do you want to do?"

"Isn't it obvious?"

"Yes, it is. But Egan made you team head, so it's your call."

"Aww! Maynard! You recognize chain of command. That's adorable. You and I will go and retrieve her immediately. We'll need a tranq gun and a nail gun, in addition to the usual weaponry. Get them immediately. I'll meet you at the car."

Maynard turned and left without a word.

He'd die screaming for that tit-squeeze. For that hungry,

slobbering, entitled look on his face as he'd watched her strapped into that dentist's chair.

But not quite yet. She'd keep using him until he ceased to be useful.

Nicole was nothing if not practical.

CHAPTER 25

Ethan

Pawing through her underwear drawer, my ass.

At this point, even though I didn't have an underwear fetish, I was so fixated on Kat that if I had her underwear drawer in front of me, I'd rifle through it. Hell, yeah, just to feel closer to her. And I'd be aroused by whatever I found, even simple white stretch-cotton briefs, bought six to the pack, because she was such a thrifty, practical woman.

Her fabulous ass would make those white cotton briefs look incredibly sexy.

I pulled into a coffee shop parking lot and called Arch. "Any news?" I asked.

"Sure," he said. "I can confirm the truth of your friend's story. I've matched the photos, and I'm sure it's her. I wasn't able to unseal her new identity, but I did see old pictures of Francesca Lovero, along with her older sister Rafaella Lovero, deceased, and her younger sister, Gabriella Lovero, also deceased. Definitely the same person."

Francesca. So that was Kat's old name. Pretty, but Kat suited her better now. It was short, crisp, no-nonsense, sharp. Cat-like. Perfect for her.

"It happened in Jersey City," Arch said. "The killer was a guy named Tony Petruzzi, Jr. Heir to a local boss, Tony Petruzzi, Sr. He's up for parole very soon."

"No shit. After killing his girlfriend and a little kid? Just fourteen years?"

"He wangled a reduced sentence. His defense attorneys spun the older girl, Rafaella, into a slutty femme fatale who cheated and drove Tony mad with jealousy. Boys will be boys, yada yada, the usual bullshit, in spite of Francesca's testimony. He'll be out of prison soon. Your girlfriend had better be on the lookout for him."

"Thanks, Arch. I appreciate that."

"So, are we square?" Arch asked hopefully.

I laughed. "No," I told him. "When you save my life, or the life of someone close to me, we'll be square. Until then, we're just having a conversation. Good talking to you, Arch."

Arch made a disgusted sound, and hung up.

That gave me plenty of interesting things to think about while I made my way to Jordan Meechum's place on Lake Washington. There had been no movement at Hugh Clemens' or Julia Wright's houses, so I just moved on down the company masthead while mulling on how to deal with Tony Petruzzi, Jr. I was going to deep dive into that worthless shithead's life prospects first chance I got. See who else besides Kat was still angry at him, and why. Once Tony Petruzzi walked out those gates, he was going to be so fucking sorry. He'd look back on his prison days like a dream of happiness.

A car waited outside Jordan Meechum's lavish lakefront home. It was a dusty old SUV with a tired middle-aged woman at the wheel. Neither car nor driver matched the house. A ride-share, then. Meechum was airport bound. I'd gotten here just in time.

I rang the doorbell. The door jerked open. "I told you to wait!" someone bitched.

I shoved the door wider, sending Meechum stumbling back into his foyer with a squawk, arms pinwheeling. I seized his throat. "I'm not your driver, shithead."

Jordan Meechum cringed against the wall. He was tall and skinny, with longish dark hair worn in a messy man bun. "Oh *fuck*. Ethan Masters?"

"Yeah. A visit from the crypt. Surprised to see me, Meechum?"

"Look, I had nothing to do with—"

"With what? What did they offer you? Who was your contact person? Tell me all of it, and maybe you'll survive. Maybe you'll even make it to the airport."

"I didn't have contact with them!" Meechum wailed. "I swear to Christ! That was all Hugh! I was just trying to make the business work, and we had a shortfall, and Hugh says he got this amazing opportunity, this...this chunk of money, free and clear, enough to solve our problems. Just for doing this random favor for this woman he met!"

"Which involved luring me into that building, I take it," I said grimly.

"Well, yes. But we had no idea they were going to try to hurt you! No fucking clue! We were as horrified as—"

"Shut the fuck up. You didn't speculate at all as to why they wanted me in place? You never asked yourself why they were willing to pay so much?"

"I...I swear, I didn't—"

"Think. Yeah. You were morons."

"Yes," Meechum said, his voice strangled. "A moron, sure, but not a killer. I never wanted to hurt anybody."

"Give me the contact info," I said.

His face tightened, bracing for a blow. "I don't have it." His voice was tiny. "That was Hugh's side of things. He was going to get us the money."

"Okay, then," I said. "Show me the money. Let me see where it came from."

"Um...that was supposed to come in after Hugh delivered the p-p-package," Meechum admitted. "And, uh...clearly, he never did. You got away. So...ah..."

I laughed, grimly. "They stiffed you, huh? Can't say I feel terribly sorry for you, under the circumstances."

Meechum swallowed convulsively, his Adam's apple bobbing against the unrelenting pressure of my fist. "I don't suppose you would," he said tightly.

"You're telling me you're useless to me," I said. "Very unfortunate. For you."

Meechum squeezed his eyes shut and nodded. "I'm so sorry," he whispered.

I ground my fist tighter against his throat. "Where do I find Hugh?"

"I have no idea," Meechum said shakily. "I really don't."

I ground my teeth. "Listen carefully, Meechum. I'm not the one ruining your life. But Hugh got mixed up with the people who are ruining mine. So this is the deal. If you can lead me to Hugh, maybe you'll get a free pass for your part in this shitshow."

"I genuinely don't know," Meechum said, through chattering teeth. "I haven't heard from him since the day before yesterday, right after, ah..."

"Right after you and Hugh set me up to die," I said. "Radio silence from him?"

"Yeah. Julia, too. Their phones go to voice mail. I even went to his house, but he wasn't there." Meechum began edging sideways, clawing at my hand again. "Since I can't really be of any more help to you, um, I might as well—"

I tightened my fist on his shirt collar and lifted him off his feet. "Maybe I haven't made myself clear," I said. "You fucked up. I could tear you to pieces, but I happen to be busy. Or I will be, anyway, if you help me find Hugh. If you don't, then I have nothing better to do than make you suffer the tortures of the damned."

Meechum's face was pinched and miserable. I didn't enjoy bullying people, but he deserved to be shit-scared. I'd hurt him if I had to, but I took no pleasure in it, so I put on my meanest face. The one I'd used to keep my siblings in line, back in the day.

"Fuck," Meechum quavered. "I can't be sure, but if he hasn't left the country, he's probably at his mom's house, at the lake. He goes there all the time."

"What lake?"

"Lake Sammamish, in Bellevue. I've been there, for weekends, parties."

"If you've been there, you have the GPS coordinates on your phone."

Meechum dug his phone out of the pocket of his cargo pants, and stabbed at the screen with a trembling finger. "So, this is it, for me," he quavered. "My life is over."

Oh, for fuck's sake. I snatched the phone from his hand, and memorized the coordinates. "Life as you know it, yes," I told him. "Follow the news from wherever you go. If you hear about me finding and killing the people who kidnapped my brother, then you're safe from those fuckheads who hired you guys. That'll be your all-clear."

"And, uh...what are your odds of doing that?" he asked, hopefully.

"Not great," I admitted. "But not zero. I will mow those fuckers down like grass, or die trying. But if I do succeed, and you come back to the country? Do not ever try to work in tech again. You got that?"

He blinked. "But...but...it's the only thing that I—"

"Be a high school math teacher," I said, "Open a bakery. Repair bicycles. Grow organic marijuana. I don't give a shit, as long as it's not in my face. But if I hear about you working anywhere in the tech sector, I will destroy you."

He nodded frantically. "Yeah. Got it. Absolutely. Understood."

I placed the phone back in his hand. "Is your plane ticket on that phone?"

"Y-y-yes," he faltered. "Why?"

"Your enemies will be able to track where you go with it, Meechum," I said. "Unless this is a brand-new phone, registered with brand new identity, for which you also have a valid passport."

He looked desperate. "I...I...ah..."

"Never mind." I didn't have time to educate a blithering dickhead who had almost gotten me and Kat killed. "They'll probably be too busy fucking with me to bother fucking with you. You can cling to that hope."

He looked encouraged. "You think?"

I laughed in his face. "Fuck off, Meechum. You'd better hope we never meet again." I grabbed the bag in the foyer and shoved it at him. "Now get lost."

He practically stumbled over his own feet running out the door, his wheeled suitcase bouncing in one hand, phone clutched in the other. I was glad to see him go.

It didn't take long to get to Lake Sammamish. I parked on the street, since a black Mercedes was parked in the driveway. The car door hung wide open.

The place was very fancy, lots of artful stacked glass and steel cubes. The lake was on the other side of the house. I glimpsed it through the trees, and through the transparent house, itself. The front door hung slightly open. Never a good sign.

I walked in and looked around. The place was in disarray.

Things knocked over, a glass coffee table smashed. The wind blew right into the place. A picture window had been shattered. The lot was big, so maybe the neighbors were too far away to hear it.

I drew my SIG P226 from the holster under my jacket, even though I was pretty sure whatever had happened here was long over. I stole quietly through the place. Nudged the door open with my shoe. There was blood. Not fresh. My boots crunched on broken glass as I followed the dark droplets.

I found Hugh about two thirds of the way down one path to the boat dock. Sprawled face-down. Shot in the back five times. He lay in what had been a puddle of blood, now dried and dark.

I just stood there, staring at his body, though I knew I should leave. It would look bad for me, if Meechum told the cops he had been forced to give me this address, and if any security cameras placed me near the scene. I hoped Meechum was at least smart enough to understand his best hope lay with me.

I'd find some way to give the police an anonymous tip, so Hugh's body could be properly attended to, but later for that. The living came first.

I got back into my car and sped away as if fleeing a pursuer. Clemens had been a sleazy, manipulative user, but he hadn't deserved that. Disgrace and jail time, maybe. A good, hard, ass-kicking, certainly. But not being shot in the back and left in the mud.

It triggered all my worst nightmares about Shane's fate. The ones that had haunted my waking and sleeping moments ever since they took him. I'd learned to function at a high level through them. Both Freya and I had to keep our shit together for Holly's sake. But looking at a dead man lying in the mud stripped away the hopeful masks. The keep-on-keeping-on bullshit. It exposed the bloody skeleton of raw fear beneath it.

They'd made me feel it, those filthy motherfuckers. They'd scored a point, and I fucking hated them for it.

I was back on the highway, driving well over the posted speed limit, when the call came in. It was Shelby's number on the screen. I hit "talk." "Yeah?"

"Kat's gone," Shelby blurted out. "She flew the coop. I don't know what the fuck she was thinking. What, that we were holding her hostage? Jesus!"

I was horrified. "What...fuck! How?"

"Trey came back with all the stuff he bought to secure her house, and we knocked on the door so we could start installing it. She didn't answer. We waited for a while, in case she was in the bathroom. Then we went in. She's gone. Purse gone. Bedroom window open. She left money and a note for the landlady. A note for you."

"What did it say?"

"Just 'Sorry, thanks for everything, it was wonderful.' Real touching. Real useful."

"What about Joanna? What does she say?"

"A whole hell of a lot, and it's pissing me off! She's right here, boss. Goddamn it, hold still...*shit!* That hurt!"

"Don't manhandle me, you overgrown prick!" Joanna's voice was shrill.

"I'm outside her mother's house now," Shelby said. "She told her demon cat to bite me." Bumps, thuds, raised voices, as Shelby argued with Joanna. Shelby got back on the line. "Talk sense into her, if that's even possible," he snarled. "Which I doubt."

"Screw you, too!" Joanna yelled. "Dick!"

"Joanna?" I made my voice even, soothing, "Do you know where Kat is?"

"I don't! But I wouldn't tell you even if I did!"

I let out a silent sigh. "We're not the enemy," I told her,

keeping my voice as even as I could. "We're trying to protect her."

"Guess what, buddy? She's trying to protect you, too! She said, yeah, you've got your enemies, and they suck, but she says hers are worse!"

"This is a game I really wish I could lose, Joanna, but my enemies would wipe the fucking floor with her enemies," I told her.

"Well, Kat doesn't think so! And it totally breaks her heart to leave, 'cause she's totally in love with you, but she can't stand to see more people she loves killed!"

"Joanna. If you want her to live, tell me where she went," I pleaded.

"She didn't tell me, 'cause she's protecting me, too!" Joanna's voice was froggy with tears. "Kat wants to protect everybody. That's just who she is, in spite of all the bad shit she's been through. She tries not to make friends, because she's trying to protect them, but people glom onto her anyway. But she's so freaking stressed, you know? Everything's a threat, with her. She always does these crazy rituals when she leaves her house—"

"Yeah? What rituals?"

"You know, like putting hairs over the door handles, and the drawer and closet handles. That's how she knew you'd been through her underwear drawer, dude!"

"But I wasn't," I said. "Not ever. Didn't touch them. No reason to lie."

Joanna was silent for a moment, struck by that. "Um...so who did, then?"

"Good question. Put Shelby back on," I directed.

"Yo, boss. Shelby here."

"Go back to Kat's house. Go into her closet and open the soles of her shoes. Look for trackers." I waited while Shelby jogged across the street and into Kat's place, breathing heavily into the phone. After a couple of minutes, I heard a hiss of dismay.

"Fuck me," he said. "Both pairs, the boots and the running shoes. They must have gotten her address and dusted her place that first day. Bastards are efficient, I'll give 'em that."

"Is Joanna still there with you?"

"Yeah, actually." Shelby sounded aggrieved. "She followed me back into the house, even though I did not invite her to."

"Put me on speaker with her," I said.

"Done, boss."

"Joanna, did you see what he found?" I asked.

"Yeah." Joanna's voice was small. "Jeez. So...this is like, the real deal?"

"Oh, yes," I said forcefully. "My enemies, those guys who attacked us three days ago, have a tracker planted on Kat. She has no idea, and she's all alone. So, if you know anything about where she might have gone, please tell us."

"I wish I did know!" Joanna sniffed loudly. "I took her to the bus station, is all. She wouldn't tell me where she was going. I don't think she knew herself."

Shit. "Go home," I said. "Don't get near Kat's place until we've cleaned up this mess. You don't want those bastards to take notice of you, understand? Kat wouldn't want that either. Shelby, go to the bus station with Trey, see what you can find."

"On it, boss."

I called Mick, who picked up on the first ring. "Yeah?"

I explained the situation, and Mick whistled under his breath. "Fuck," he murmured. "Ethan, I'm sorry. But you really can't protect someone who doesn't want to be protected. Maybe you should just let her—"

"Do you want to help me, or do you want to go job hunting?"

"Chill," Mick soothed. "I'll help. Did you give her that smartphone you took this morning?"

"Why?" I sat up straighter, electrified. "Is there a tracker in it?"

"Of course, there's a fucking tracker in it. Who do you think you're dealing with? I'm old school, man. Spy first, apologize later."

"It's in her purse. I forgot to tell her about it. Can you locate her with it?"

"Sure. Sending the data now. Watch it on your phone, or put it up on the car's screen. Where are Shelby and Trey?"

"I sent them to the bus station," I said.

"Where are you right now?"

"Heading east on 90, from Bellevue," I told him.

"Looks like she's moving south on I-5 toward Tacoma," Mick said.

He kept talking, but all I heard was the engine's roar as the car surged forward.

CHAPTER 26

Nicole

Traffic sucked on I-5 today. It had rained, earlier, and several idiots had spun out on the wet highway, snarling things up. Finally, after far too long a time breathing the shit-scented halitosis of Maynard the Tit-Squeezer, they had managed to dart and weave their way up behind Katrin Banner's Portland-bound bus.

Maynard put on the turn signal to move up alongside the back of the bus, but Nicole raised her hard. "Not yet."

"But I have an opening," he said. "Just use the nail gun."

"No," she said. "Wait.'"

"For what?" he demanded.

"For them to get closer to the rest area, you fucking idiot. Do you want to cuff her and muscle her into the back of the SUV in front of fifty witnesses on a slow highway? Were you dropped on your head as a baby?"

"No need to be rude," Maynard said. "If we're going to work together—"

"No, Maynard. We do not work 'together,'" she cut in. "I'm

team leader. You work for me, not with me. It's an important distinction. Are we clear?"

He looked at her swollen, bruised jaw, and then his gaze flicked down to her breasts. "Yeah, boss," he said softly. "We're real clear."

Ohhh. Death was too good for this turd.

Her phone buzzed. Nicole murmured obscenities under her breath as she pulled it out. Probably Vincent, micromanaging like the priggish, controlling little bitch that he was. Her jaw throbbed sickeningly as she squinted at the display.

Not Vincent. It was her asset in the Masters complex. A gift she'd offered to Vincent that the idiot did not appreciate. She picked up. "Mick. What have you got for me?"

"The blonde woman ran away," Mick Drummond reported, his voice low, as if he were muttering in a dark corner. "She crawled out a window and gave Ethan's guys the slip. They're all looking for her. Word is, she's headed for the downtown bus station."

"Hmmm. This news is pretty fucking stale," she replied. "We've known she was on the move for some time now. Which begs the question, Mick. How committed are you to keeping up your side of our bargain?"

"Bargain?" Mick's voice was bitter. "Hah."

Nicole clucked her tongue. "Do I detect self-pity? Looks like poor Jay will have to go without his pain meds again. It's excruciating to listen to, but we all manage so much better now that I've had him moved down to the basement level. Now no one can hear him screaming."

"No," Mick said swiftly. "Please."

"Those metastases in his spine, ouch," she said. "His bones are like chalk. The last time I kicked him, I think I broke three ribs in a single blow."

Jay was Mick Drummond's great-uncle, the man who had raised him. Drummond was pathetically attached to the old coot. After she'd had him abducted from the care home, he'd deteriorated sharply, and he was dementing fast, but he was an effective lever to manipulate Mick. With the help of some very graphic videos.

"Maybe I'll crush his kneecap," she mused. "Or I could shatter his pelvis. It wouldn't take much, at this point. Like crumpling paper."

"Please, no," Mick said hastily. "Don't. I have news that will interest you. About Kat Banner."

"Is that what they call her? Kat? That's cute. Like a little pussy-cat," Nicole tittered. "So? Let's hear your news."

"Give Jay his meds," Mick said desperately. "Don't hurt him. And I'll tell you."

"You dumb prick," she said coldly. "Do exactly as you're told, or I'll livestream a session with the meat cleaver. Don't waste my time."

Mick let out a strange sound, like air hissing out of a balloon. "I, ah...I put that software on Ethan's phone. I listened in while he called our contact in the FBI, Arch Dorne. Today, he got confirmation for the story she told him about her past."

"And this should interest me exactly why?" The traffic was still crawling along, but they'd approach the rest stop soon. There was no time for Mick's dithering.

"Kat Banner was put into the Witness Protection Program when she was fourteen," Mick said. "She testified against the mobster who murdered her sisters. An older one, nineteen, who was the mobster's mistress. The younger one was seven. Her name was Francesca Lovero. She's been flying under the radar ever since."

"Interesting," Nicole said slowly, and she wasn't even being sarcastic. That was probably why Kat had learned to fight. She knew a fight was coming, sooner or later.

"So? Is that enough? Will you give Jay his meds?"

Nicole considered it as they crawled down the roadway.

"Well, he's not completely off the hook, because you were not at all timely in updating me," she said.

"But I only just found—"

"Shut up. I won't break any more bones, but no morphine today. Be grateful."

She hung up on Mick as she saw a sign for the rest area. "Pull up now."

Maynard muscled himself in front of a car so he could pull up alongside the back of the bus. Nicole checked out the cars nearby in her mirrors. The guy driving the van behind her was busy arguing with the woman in the passenger seat. Perfect.

She rolled down the window, poised her body, and in one swift, seamless gesture, she shot the nail gun at the tire.

"Let it pull ahead," she instructed.

The bus shuddered, wavering on the road. Maynard braked slightly, and they followed the big vehicle as it lumbered forward, slowing down. The turn signal went on, which gave her a pleasant little thrill of anticipation.

This was going to be fun. By all accounts, Kat Banner was a worthy opponent. Nicole seldom had an adversary that stimulating, and particularly not a woman.

Freya had been an unwelcome surprise. No one had warned her about Freya. But oh, was she ever primed for a rousing catfight with this uppity blonde bitch.

"Maynard, just so we're clear. This should be obvious, but it's you, so I'm triple-checking. Kat Banner, Ethan Masters, Holly, Freya...when we do take them, they have to be unharmed. Not killed or maimed. We have plans for them. Is that clear?"

Maynard rolled his eyes. "Yes, I did grasp that," he said sourly.

"Good," she murmured.

They pulled into a parking spot not far from the bus, and

watched the whole scene as the driver stomped his big, swag-bellied frame to the blown-out back tire.

He kicked the good tire, and got on his phone. His conversation degenerated into shouting. Clearly, this asshole was not going to attempt changing one of those monsters himself. He needed a repair truck, a replacement bus, or both, and that would take time.

That gave her a moment to process this new information, which reverberated in her mind. That data was significant. A secret weapon of some kind. So improbable, it had to be useful. She just wasn't sure how yet.

A tragic backstory. A fake name. A fake life. Violence and trauma. She loved that stuff. She was an artist, and violence and trauma were her favorite medium.

The bus was at a standstill. She had all the time in the world to run Kat Banner down.

CHAPTER 27

Kat

For real? Come on. Too much shit luck all crowded together could not be a coincidence, at least not today. My bus, blowing a goddamn tire? What were the odds?

My body hummed with battle readiness, revving me up, but I had nothing to use the energy on, so it just cycled, making me jittery and breathless. Everything around me looked normal, dingy, tired. Nothing out of place, nothing I could beat to death.

Then again. Tony Petruzzi had looked normal, too. Just your standard rich, spoiled, good-looking guy, a little too in love with himself. You couldn't tell he was a psychopathic mafia princeling by looking at him. Raffi certainly hadn't seen it.

Monsters were good at being invisible. It was what made them so dangerous.

The bus driver was cursing outside my open window. I over-heard snippets of his conversation. "...an hour? You gotta be fucking kidding me, Paul. I got all these passengers with tight connections in Portland, and I need someone here now!...Yes! Send another bus if the repair truck is too...goddamn it, Paul! You're killing me!"

In many ways, battle mode was better than moping misery mode. I'd been torturing myself by thinking about the long, empty years that lay ahead. Years of avoiding friendship, love, sex. Years of avoiding caring about anything enough so that it could be used as a weapon to hurt me. It had put me in a dark place, and I'd defaulted to a standard Kat Banner fantasy—that of draping myself with massive firepower and taking a wild, pre-emptive run at the Petruzzis some fine day. The Angel of Justice, taking out as many as I could before they cut me down. Suicide by mobster. Bam, pow.

But my mom was still in my mind, shaking her head, and clucking her tongue.

Don't you dare take the coward's way out, Francesca. You have a job to do in this world.

Really, Mom? How could I find out what it was if I was forever cowering under a rock? And walking away from Ethan...oh, just stop, already. I was out of tissues.

The driver climbed heavily back up into the bus and seized the intercom.

"Ladies and gentleman, I am sorry to tell you this, but we have a blown tire. A crew is coming to deal with it, but they're almost an hour out. Feel free to stretch your legs and use the restroom, but pay attention to the status of our repairs, because I'll be getting this thing moving the second it's roadworthy. Again, my apologies."

At the chorus of groaning and grumbling that followed this announcement, I slid farther down in my seat and pulled the brim of my hat lower, to shade my face.

People started trickling off the bus. This was not a rest stop with gas stations or restaurants, just a low, cinder-block structure, men's and women's bathrooms on either end of the building, a sheltered open spot in the center with drinking fountains and a rack of free brochures advertising local attractions.

Through the open space, I glimpsed waving grass, a break

of trees. I waited twenty minutes, until everyone was cramped and bored and the bus was emptied out. I was close enough to the back of the bus to be enveloped in the sickly-sweet perfume of the chemical toilet, mixed with that air-freshener odor that all public passenger buses seemed to have. The air outside was looking better every second that passed.

A bus in motion was sort of bearable. A bus standing still would make me scream, and then probably cry, because tears were all backed up behind any strong emotion I dared to let myself actually feel, like water behind a dam, and the dam was cracking. Any time now, whoosh...and I would drown in a high-pressure torrent of tears. A woman on the run could not afford such powerful feelings.

I climbed out of the bus, filling my chest with fresh air. The rest of the passengers were spread out, lounging at the picnic tables, scrolling on their phones, smoking cigarettes, bitching to each other about their disrupted travel plans.

I paid the bathroom a visit. It was smelly and damp. Painted cinderblock walls, scarred and battered metal stalls, shiny metal sinks with no mirrors, floors of water-stained cement. I heard the door open when I was inside the stall, felt the whiff of outside air, and every hair on my body went on end. Chill, woman. There were six stalls. Everyone needed to use a toilet now and then. Nothing suspicious about it.

Someone was using the stall beside me, which was totally normal and to be expected. A woman in black boots and black athletic pants. I made haste, so as to get out of the stall before whoever it was exited their own, and was washing my hands at the sink nearest the door when the stall door swung open.

A young woman emerged. She looked part Asian, but not at all like Nicole had been described to me. This woman's hair was pulled back in a frowsy ponytail. Her jaw looked puffy like a chipmunk, and her eyes red and swollen. She did not have the steel-edged femme fatale vibe of the villain of Freya

Masters's wild and rip-roaring adventure. Even so, I was quick to rinse the soap off my hands, heart thudding.

"Does that soap dispenser have any soap left in it?" The woman's voice was high and girlish. "This one seems empty."

"Yeah, sure. I just used it," I said, shifting back to let her sidle up to it.

She smiled at me, lifted her arm—

Thwappp. It felt like a sharp poke in the chest. I looked down to see a dart poking out of my chest. *Fuck!* The dart fell harmlessly to the cement floor, having hit the packet inside my secret inside pocket that held my passport and my money. Pure luck. That sneaky bitch.

I attacked before she could take aim again. She swayed back, parried my kicks, then lunged at me with a shout, and we were at it.

Damn, she was fast. I was ducking and whipping back to avoid punches and kicks and slashing blows, and I did okay until I slipped in a puddle of soapy water and lost my footing for a split second. She followed up her advantage and slammed me against the cinderblocks, bonking my head. I jabbed my elbow into her throat, which should have crushed her larynx, but she jerked back just in time.

I scrambled for another opening, but I was on the defensive, and she was a powerhouse. For all my training, I'd never been in a fight to the death, other than in the elevator that day, with Ethan. Which didn't count, because that fight had been magic, more like a first date than anything else.

I'd only simulated combat. I was still untried. This woman had a distinct advantage. She'd killed before, and she loved it.

I did not want an epic showdown today, just to survive. I blocked a chop to the neck and snatched her hand, twisted it until the torque forced her to double over.

Then I shoved her down to the floor and bolted out the door, just a few steps behind her. I pounded past a couple of square-built old ladies with blue hair who shrank back in alarm, clutching their purses. "Watch out for the woman in the bathroom!" I howled over my shoulder. "She's a killer!"

I headed for the wall of foliage about thirty yards behind the rest stop building, my mind racing wildly. If they had found me here, then maybe they'd been watching long enough to notice Joanna. I'd broken the cardinal rule.

Please, please, don't notice Joanna. Don't hurt Joanna. She has no clue.

Why on earth did Ethan's enemies give a shit about me? I crashed into the wall of green, branches thwapping at my face, clutching my hair. Feet sinking and sliding, the mud sloppy soft from the recent rain as I climbed uphill, and then burst out of the thick bushes and found myself going back down a slope, heading toward what looked like a drainage ditch that was choked by a luxuriant patch of blackberry brambles.

Thorns. Perfect. I'd been in training for thorns all my life.

I dove right in.

CHAPTER 28

Ethan

The bus was parked and empty when I pulled into the rest stop. The passengers were scattered around, the driver was pacing and yelling into his phone. I didn't see Kat, though the tracker indicated she was there. Or, at least, the tracker was there, whether or not it was attached to her person.

I suppressed my panic, and kept looking, for Kat, Nicole, anything at all that pinged my what's-wrong-with-this-picture sensor.

My gaze settled on a guy who was getting out of a big black Mercedes SUV, who was notable because of his size. He was immensely muscular, tall, broad-shouldered, and looked military, in his haircut and his bearing.

And he was moving purposefully. More so than a guy who just got out of a car at a rest stop should be moving, unless he had some serious bowel problem.

And he was muttering, wearing an earpiece, and breaking into a swift lope. The lope quickly turned into a flat out run. Someone was desperate for back-up.

Then it was a sure thing Kat was involved.

The big guy sprinted around the building. I jerked to a halt, killed the engine bolted from the car, leaving the door wide open. I took off running after him.

I could read the situation better once I cleared the building. The man was running ten yards ahead of me. Thirty yards ahead of him, a dark-clad woman with a ponytail was disappearing into the trees. I couldn't see Kat at all. The branches swayed and snapped as the ponytailed woman forced her way in.

The guy was yelling into his mic. "...fast as I can, you dumb bitch! Use the tranq gun again, for fuck's sake!"

I scooped up a rock I saw ahead of me, then put on a burst of speed to make up for the ground I'd lost. I was gaining on him. He was running hard, focused on the scene ahead of him. Not worried about anyone who might be behind him.

I flung the rock. It hit him between his shoulder blades, breaking his stride. He stumbled forward onto one knee, twisting around with a shout to look behind him.

I was ready, whipping a kick right up under his chin that laid him out flat on his back. I followed up with a kick to the side of his head, to make sure he was down. Then kicked the side of his knee, feeling the popping and snapping of tendon, bone. A guttural howl of pain.

Handled. I wished I could just shoot him, but I wanted to interrogate the shit out of him. As it was, he'd live, but he was going nowhere fast.

I picked up his gun, plucked the earpiece away from him and shoved it into my own ear as I took off toward the point where I'd seen the woman disappear into the trees, pulling out my own SIG P226. I was happy to kill Nicole, as long as I still had someone still alive to question.

"Maynard, come in! Where the fuck are you? Move your ass!" It was a shrill, breathless, furious woman's voice.

Her trail wasn't hard to follow. She'd left a swathe of broken branches, trampled foliage, pocks in the mud. I followed as fast as I could with my feet slip-sliding in loose earth. I cleared the rise and hurtled down a slope into a gully choked with thorns.

And the trail ended. I stood there, afraid to call out to Kat. She might hiding, and she was probably closer to the attacker than I was.

I leaned down, peering through the trees, searching, searching...and I saw a glimpse of her jacket. Our eyes met through the waving green. My heart thudded with excitement—

A branch snapped nearby. I spun around, and saw the ponytailed woman emerge from the foliage. Black hair drawn back, wisps disarranged, an angry flush staining her cheeks, mouth open from panting. Her dark eyes were wild with rage. She held a pistol.

She glanced toward where I had been peering, and her gun swung up, aiming at Kat. *Pop. Pop. Pop.* The crack of the gun was muffled by the silencer. I shot back at her, but she flung herself into the trees, and I lost sight of her.

I looked for Kat, but no longer saw her. I flung Maynard's gun away and launched myself into the deep brambles in a panic. "Kat! Kat! Where are you?"

After a moment of wild flailing, I heard her low, careful voice. "Ethan?"

My heart stuttered to life as I thrashed through the thorns. "Kat! Are you shot?"

"I'm fine. Shhh." Her head popped up, then disappeared again. "Dude," she hissed. "Could you keep it down? We've got shooters on the loose, and we're pinned down in a hole in the ground, in case you didn't notice. So don't yell."

I started to laugh, or maybe I was crying as I waded toward her through waist high brambles. Kat was scratched and bleeding from the thorns, but she shot me a rueful grin as I approached. "I am very glad to see you, Ethan," she said, her voice hushed.

I grabbed her, hugged her, breathlessly tight. "Fuck, you scared me," I blurted.

"Aw. I'm touched by your concern." She kissed me briskly, and patted my back. "Not to kill the mood or anything, but shut your trap, buddy. That hell-bitch chased me out here, and I made this snap decision to hide in a thorn bush. Pretty thin, as strategies go. Seems more like a trap than anything. Let's get out of here. What do you say?"

I turned around and broke the biggest path I could for her with my heavy boots, kicking my way through. "Why did you run away?"

"I was just trying to protect you," she said.

"The fuck?" I said, incredulous. "Protect me? What, by running off, completely unprotected, and drawing my enemies after you? That's nuts!"

"That part was absolutely not planned," she assured me. "I didn't want to draw anything after me. I just wanted to spare you my own nasty baggage. It felt like the right thing to do at the time, I swear. It feels dumb now, but if you knew my enemies—"

"Well, you know mine, at this point," I broke in. "I hope you paid attention."

"Okay, okay," she huffed, crunching through the dead vines behind me. "When it comes to asshole enemies, you win. You get the grand prize. Happy now?"

"No! I won't be happy until you're home, wearing satin pajamas and drinking a glass of red wine! In my bed!"

"Hmm," she murmured. "Sounds nice, but save the fantasies for later."

"I want you in my corner, Kat." I cleared the brambles out of my path with savage kicks, and spun around to face her. "I want you on my team! We are stronger together, understand?" I was being stupidly loud, since we had no idea where Nicole was, but I couldn't seem to shut up.

She gave me an oddly gentle smile, reached out, and delicately patted my cheek.

"Yes," she said softly. "You've convinced me, Ethan. I'm on totally board, okay? Let's run like hell! Go!"

I turned to attack the thorn bushes again, hoping desperately that she was telling me the truth.

CHAPTER 29

Nicole

Nicole retreated, stealing very quietly, trying to keep a line of sight open so she could watch Masters thrash noisily through flesh-tearing thorns to get to his lady love. The spectacle was very entertaining. He thought she'd been shot to death. That she was bleeding out pathetically in the thorns, staring up at the sky, like the finale of some tear-jerking movie. Oh, so sad and tragic, boo-hoo.

But no. Kat Banner had been left in beautiful working condition. She had to serve as the linchpin for Nicole's huge and glorious death-and-money machine. It would have been sweet to have her in the bag now, and Nicole could have bagged them both, but not yet. Not quite yet. If she brought them in now, Vincent would fuck it up.

She was after a bigger prize now.

Mick Drummond's information had taken root, grown, and flowered. The idea was taking shape in her mind like magic. Complex, detailed, perfect in every particular. All she had to do was watch, and enjoy, and rejoice in the huge, colossal inevitability of it.

Ethan Masters would be betrayed by his lover. His heart, ripped to bloody shreds. She would settle for nothing less than that outcome. And he was so ripe for it, too. Just look at the dumb fuck, sloppy in love, howling Kat's name as he blundered across the brambles, lacerating himself. He had it bad.

And Nicole was going to make him regret it. Like he'd never regretted before.

She hoped she'd get to see the look in his eyes when he realized what a fool he'd been, how badly he'd fucked up. The moment his heart froze, his guts twisted.

Yes, Kat Banner would cut him to the bone. It was going to be beautiful.

It was going to be a challenge to sell the idea to Vincent, since he was tripping out on being the big boss right now. Tiresome, but she was already coming up with ways to spin it. Vincent wasn't hard to manipulate.

She watched through the screen of leaves as Masters and Kat Banner clutched each other in the bramble patch. Masters snatched a quick kiss, Banner stiffened, then patted him briskly on the back, saying something businesslike. Probably about the foolishness of emoting while they should be running for their lives. She wasn't wrong.

Masters looked over his shoulder, scanning the trees for Nicole. His gaze fastened right onto the spot where she huddled behind a canopy of ivy or kudzu or some botanical shit. He could feel her presence. They were connected, on a deep, primal level, and they had been ever since that night when he'd taken her to bed, in that hotel room in Vegas. He was the only man smart enough, strong enough, to be worthy of her, but he was too stupid to see it. He'd been dazzled by that snotty blonde whore.

Watching Kat Banner betray and destroy him was going to feel wonderful.

She crept back through the trees, staying out of sight until she was over the rise. Then she sprinted back down through the trees, and saw Maynard, on the ground.

Oh, for fuck's sake. The tit-squeezer was a fucking mess. That leg, bent strangely, his face streaked with blood. This was inconvenient and stupid. But not unexpected...or even all that unwelcome, now that she thought about it.

She kicked his shoulder with her foot. "Hey. Maynard. What happened to you?"

His eyes opened a slit, squinting until he focused on her.

"Fucking asshole," he croaked. "Got me from behind."

"Dumb shit. You didn't hear him coming?"

"How could I? I was listening to you, yapping in the com," he snarled.

"Ah, yes. Of course. So it's my fault."

"Yeah! It is your fault, you stupid cow! Did you get him? Are they tranqed?" He pulled out his phone. "We need emergency back-up, to get them loaded up. And me."

She bent down, twitched the phone from his hand, put it into her pocket. "No."

He gave her that thick, stupid look. "No, what? No, they're not tranqed?"

"No to all of it," she said softly. "They're not tranqed. They're gone, Maynard. In the wind. And I'll be sure to tell Vincent that outcome was a direct result of your incompetence. And Masters' team of Unredeemable commandos, of course."

Maynard looked confused. "It was just him, bitch. You could totally have taken them with the tranq gun. Why didn't you? I won't lie to Vincent for you."

"I know you won't, Maynard," she said. "You absolutely won't. But you won't deny it, either."

Maynard's eyes dilated. He saw death in her smile, and shrank away.

"He'll kill you," he said, unsteadily. "For losing them. Losing me. Not smart."

"Yes, he'll be mad at first. Then he'll get excited about my new plan, based on new intel. And he'll forget all about you, Maynard. Because you are insignificant. It'll work out fine. For me, anyway. For you, not so much."

Maynard stared up at her face, his squinted eyes glittering with hatred. He turned his head, and spat blood onto her boots. "You know what? I loved it when that dentist pulled out your tooth. When you screamed, I practically came in my pants. All that blood. The way you trembled. The way your tits jiggled. God, it was good. Peak moment for me."

Nicole did not allow her smile to waver. "Really, Maynard? I'm touched."

"You know what else? I took your tooth. Took it right out of that bloody silver pan when they weren't paying attention. I took it back to my room. I hold it in one hand while I beat off with the other. Mmmm. Sweet, sweet release."

Nicole looked down at her muddy, blood-spotted boots, and figured they were a lost cause anyhow. "All right," she said. "You chose this."

She started to kick. First the knee, making him shriek and writhe. Then his face. Maynard resisted, feebly, but the first savage blow of her foot broke his jaw. After that, it was just a matter of keeping at it until his teeth were all knocked loose.

When she accomplished that, she squatted down, reaching into the slack, bloody mess of shattered meat and bone on the bottom of his face. She flicked around, looking for the tooth she wanted. It had to be a molar. The same one they had taken from her.

Ah, yes. There it was. She plucked it out, and held it up for him to see. "This one's a beauty," she told him. "I'll treasure it, Maynard."

His eyes widened as she pointed the gun at his face. *Pop.* Right in the eye.

She stood, tucking the sticky red thing into her pocket,

along with his phone. She'd lost track of time, with this little bloody detour, and she had to hurry, before Masters and his whore made their way out of the thorn bushes. She peered through the trees, but saw no sign of them. Assholes. Taking their own sweet time. They had already forgotten her. They were in the woods, kissing, flirting, while she lurked out here with death on her mind.

She stuck her hand into her pocket, fondling Maynard's wet, hot tooth. It was disrespectful of them, not to fear her more. But she could wait.

They would learn.

CHAPTER 30

Kat

We slowed down, and stared at the corpse of the big guy lying in the mud, in horrified silence. "Um... this is the guy you said you saw?" I asked timidly.

"Yeah. He's the one running after Nicole. He was on her team."

We gazed at his mangled face. The crushed, distorted jaw. Teeth, all over the place. One eye staring up. The other socket, a bloody red hole.

"Jesus," I whispered. "Did you..." I looked at him, and shook my head hastily. "No. Sorry. Of course not. This isn't your style."

"God, no," he said, his voice sharp with frustration. "I left this fucker alive. I wanted to drag him back home and shake him down for intel. But no. Always, no."

Of course, no. Because he had to run off heroically after me, at the expense of his mission to find his brother. Yet another mark against me. Yet another price to pay.

"Whoa," I said softly. "She must have been pissed at him."

Ethan grabbed my hand and yanked me into a clumsy,

stumbling run. "Come on," he said. "We have got to get out of here. My flesh is crawling."

Well, yeah. Mine too. But my legs felt floppy and hollow as I staggered along beside him. There was the black BMV we had driven down to the city from the Mountain House, left right in the middle of the roadway, door flung wide. He'd chased after me in such a desperate hurry. Wow. Hell of a responsibility, to have someone care so much that they acted against their own interests for my sake. It freaked me out.

Ethan jerked open the passenger side door and shoved me into the seat.

"Are you carrying anything you got from your house this morning?" he asked.

"Huh?" I frowned at him, too thick and muddled to follow his train of thought.

"Shoes? A coat? A purse, a belt, anything? They found you with a trace, Kat. They went into your house, right after the elevator incident. That's why the hair you put on your closet handle was disturbed. That wasn't me. That was Nicole's team."

I gaped at him. "No shit. They broke into my house and tagged me that very first day? Damn, those people function like freaking clockwork."

"So?" he insisted. "Think, Kat! What did you collect at your house?"

"Let me see," I said, racking my brains. "My go-bag, which is still in the bus. My passport and my money, inside pocket of this jacket, but this is the jacket I had the day I met you. I've always had it with me, so Nicole's people have never touched it. I did put on these shoes this morning, though." I glanced down at my mud-slimed, thorn-torn expensive running shoes, the ones I'd elected to wear on the bus, because they were too expensive to leave, but too bulky to pack.

Ethan kneeled in front of me, prying the muddy laces loose.

He peeled off my shoes, then pulled out a knife, and attacked my shoe with it, prying off the sole.

He pulled out the tiny chip, the dangling antennae that had been somehow inserted into it. "You are deep in my shit now, whether you wanted to escape or not," he said. "There's no running away. They've zeroed in on you now. I'm sorry about that."

I leaned forward, gripping his shoulder. "I wasn't running away from your problems, Ethan. I swear. I was just trying not to pile mine on top of yours!"

"Stop trying!" he said savagely. "It's too late! You hurt me when you do that!"

I stared at him, my mouth trembling. He reached over, gripping my hand that was clutching his shoulder. Trapping it there. His hand was warm. Bloody and scratched from all the thorns, like my hands.

"I need you," he said, his voice intense. "Get it through your head. I'm better with you. Stronger. Safer. You're tough and smart as hell, and I want you at my side, helping me manage this clusterfuck so we can all survive. I don't want to do this without you, Kat. Be with me. Stay with me. I'm not asking you to be my concubine, I'm not asking you to be my bed toy. I'm asking you to be my partner."

I pulled my hand free. "I understand, but could we leave before Nicole comes back and shoots us both in the face? We can save the tender moment for later, okay?"

"Fine," he said gruffly, turning to shove my muddy shoes into the big garbage bin.

I pulled my bare, damp feet into the car and shut the door. Being barefoot made me feel vulnerable, but going out there to retrieve my bag from the bus would be worse.

Ethan floored the car, which leaped forward toward the freeway entrance. "Keep your eyes peeled for a black Mercedes

SUV," he said. "That's what the dead guy in the woods was driving, and I'm assuming they came together."

I craned my neck around, scanning the highway as far ahead and as far behind as I could see. "I'm not seeing one," I said. "But who knows. She might have come in a different vehicle. Something about crushing a guy's jaw and then shooting him through the eye really does not say 'teamwork' to me."

"Agreed, "Ethan said. "But Nicole is freaky. A stone-cold psychopath and a bitchy little girl, at the same time. This guy must have challenged her or triggered her, and she took this opportunity to put him down. Maybe she thought she could pin it on one of us. If she answers to higher authority, that is. Which I'm guessing she does."

"Maybe she made the calculation that she couldn't move him herself without attracting attention, and she would have lost her advantage," I offered. "He was huge. Everyone would have noticed her dragging him to the car. She had to resolve the problem fast, since you couldn't be allowed to question him, right? This might have been the reasoned, practical thing to do. From a psychopath's point of view, anyway."

Ethan shook his head. "I'm guessing the shattered jaw says she hated his guts. She went to some extra trouble to make him suffer. While he was still alive."

I shook my head. "Yes, that too. The whole thing is extremely weird."

"Yeah, Kat? Which part? The part where you ditched the bodyguards I assigned to you and ran off to certain death? Is that the part you were referring to?"

"Oh, come on now," I soothed. "Let's not get hung up on that, okay? I know you're pissed, but I'm very sorry. I should have listened to you. I admit it. Satisfied?"

"No," he said curtly. "You scared the living shit out of me."

"Honestly, me, too," I admitted. "That woman is terrifying. She fights like a demon. She's better than me, and that's really saying something. And she looks all sweet and normal, too. I'm a suspicious type, but she really got the jump on me."

"She let us go too easy," he said darkly.

I shifted in my seat, wincing as I looked down at myself. Everything hurts. I was slimed with mud, scratched to ribbons from the brambles, scraped, bruised, strained, and bumped from that bathroom fight. I felt like hammered shit. "You call that easy?"

"Yes, I do," he said. "She could have killed us many times over, if she wanted to. I can understand why she might hesitate to shoot me. She wants SmokeScreen, and she probably figures I'm the only one who can give her that. But why not shoot you?"

"Maybe to use me against you? Maybe she sees me as your weak point?"

He glanced over at me. "Strong," he said bluntly.

"Huh?"

"She's wrong, if she thinks you're a weak point. You make me strong, Kat."

I realized suddenly that I was smiling at him, like a simpering fool. "Um, thanks."

"But there's something we're missing here," he went on. "And it's going to bite us in the ass, if we don't figure out what it is."

"When she shot at me in the bramble patch, I think she missed on purpose," I mused. "She could have hit me if she wanted to. She wanted to make you panic. Buy some time. So she could go kill that guy, maybe? But she could have just killed me, and then used her tranq gun on you, if SmokeScreen is all she wanted."

"You think it would be that simple?" he asked. "That I'm so easily felled?"

"Sure, I do," I said. "Don't be vain, you silly man. That woman is hell on wheels. Underestimate her at your peril."

"Takes one to know one," he shot back.

I snorted. "Well, huh. Maybe that's a compliment and maybe it's not, but I'm too tired to care."

He laughed, but looked me over, frowning at my bare, muddy feet. "What size shoe do you wear?" he asked.

"Eight," I said.

"Call Trey," Ethan said, in commanding tones.

The car immediately obeyed him, which struck me as weirdly miraculous. I lived an extremely analog life, having avoided electronics and social media as hard as I could in my efforts to stay off the Petruzzis' radar. I felt like a prisoner from the past, suddenly finding herself in a futuristic fantasy. God knows, Ethan himself was the stuff of pure fantasy.

Ethan relayed the situation to Trey when the call connected, and ordered me a pair of new athletic shoes while he was at it. Just like that. I couldn't get used to it. Look at that guy, altering reality with a snap of his fingers. New shoes could just appear, if he so desired.

"You should send a message to Joanna," Ethan said. "Tell her you're alive. And to lie low for a while."

"Will do," I said. "If they were watching my place, then they might know Joanna helped me leave. It worries me. Those assholes, noticing she exists."

Ethan sighed. "You want someone to cover her, too," he said flatly. "Right?"

"Maybe for a couple of days? I mean, she stuck her neck way out there for me. She's a good friend. I hate to think of her being in any danger." I thought of what Joanna had said about liking them burly, bearded, and tattooed. "What about Shelby?"

"Well, they hate each other's guts right now, but fine by me. You better tell Joanna about this plan yourself, though. For Shelby's sake."

"Um, sure," I said. "Thanks."

Then I noticed us blowing right past an exit. "Hey, aren't we getting back on the northbound highway?" I asked. "Aren't we going back up to the city?"

"No. We're meeting the helicopter at the nearest airfield and going straight home. To lick our wounds and regroup. Silk pajamas and a glass of wine. Sound good?"

I let out a shaky little laugh. Damn. I did not like to admit it, because I was a stubborn and needlessly contrary woman, but I could not tell a lie. Not right now.

Silk pajamas and a glass of wine sounded really fabulous to me right now.

CHAPTER 31

Ethan

I was crashing when we got to the airfield. Desperately ready to get into the helicopter and let Trey take us back to the Mountain House. Maybe I could have made it home driving, but I didn't want to put it to the test. Not with Nicole running around like a scorpion under the bed.

Once again, I had failed to pin down someone to interrogate. A drama that had played out many times since Shane's abduction. I wondered if I would have succeeded in taking Nicole down if I hadn't been compromised by my fear for Kat.

But that argument made no sense. I wouldn't have gotten anywhere near Nicole to begin with, if Kat hadn't been dangling herself out there as bait.

Please, God, let that part of our weird push-and-pull be over. It felt as if we'd turned some kind of a corner, after what had happened today. Like she'd grasped something important from the day's lesson. But the woman was so damn stubborn.

Despite the huge noise of the helicopter, Kat had passed out as soon as we left the ground. She felt safe enough to let down her guard. That was heartening.

I touched her as gently as I could after we landed, but she started awake anyway, like a spooked animal. "We're here," I told her. "And we're safe."

"Okay," she muttered. "God, I can't believe I conked out in all that noise."

I undid the straps, helped her down out of the helicopter, and as soon as we were on the ground, I scooped her up into my arms.

Kat stiffened. "Oh, for God's sake. Is this a thing for you?"

"You're exhausted," I said, in soothing tones. "You've just engaged in mortal combat. I almost lost you. You scared me out of my wits. Give me this much, Kat. Indulge me. I really think I've earned it."

"You just keep pushing and pushing, you know? You just never stop!"

I couldn't really deny that assertion, but she subsided without further struggling, glaring up at me and muttering under her breath.

When we got to my apartment, Angela hurried toward us, eyes big with alarm. "Is she hurt?"

"No," we both said, in chorus.

"I'm fine. He's just being an uber-macho dude," Kat added.

"Well, so I should hope!" Angela said. "The boys told me what happened. Good God, Ethan! What were you thinking, racing off all alone?"

"I had to," I said. "I got there just in time as it was."

"Well, thank God you're both safe," Angela fussed, "I fixed you some dinner. Whenever you feel like having it, the platters are in the fridge, waiting for you."

"Thanks, Angela. I think we'll get a shower, first," I said.

"Of course. Off you go! See you in the morning."

I kept Kat in my arms, carrying her down the hall to my bedroom. She'd finally relaxed there, and now her head was cuddled against my chest. Outside the bedroom, I set her back onto her feet with great reluctance, opened the door, and ushered her in.

"Take a shower with me?" I suggested.

"Sounds great."

We stripped down without ceremony, leaving our filthy, blood-spattered clothes in a tangled pile near the bedroom door and headed for the bathroom.

I adjusted the multi-directional showerheads in my big shower for her, and then spent the next half an hour or so running my hands over every inch of her body, taking note of bump, bruise, scratch, or scrape. Keeping score. Those bastards would pay.

Then Kat boldly soaped up and returned the favor, sliding her strong hands all over my shoulders, my back, my hips, then gripping my cock. Squeezing it, twisting and stroking until I gasped for breath, on the brink of a wild explosion.

After a few minutes of that, I couldn't take anymore. I seized her, lifting her so she could wrap her thighs around my waist. The hot water stung in all my scratches and scrapes, but when she kissed me like that, I was so aroused, my skin interpreted it all as wild pleasure. Our tongues danced as she twined her leg around my waist, grabbing my cock to position it, nudging my cockhead into her slick, clinging warmth.

She made a shuddering moan of pleasure as I sank my cock slowly, deeply inside her. I gripped her ass and began pumping my cock slowly into her silken depths.

So sweet. Every pulsing surge better than the one before. We clung to each other, muscles trembling, trying to keep it slow, trying to make it last, but the intensity of the day's events overcame us, and before we knew it, I had pinned her to the wall, and we were fucking wildly. Slick, hard, slamming strokes, and she egged me on, gasping, panting. Both of us straining together toward that wild release.

Then it took us, and flung out into a timeless forever, fused.

Sometime afterward, I finally managed to release my grip. I let her slide down until her feet touched the floor. We rinsed ourselves, and I slowly dried her off with long, sensual strokes of the towel, and swathed her in a fluffy terrycloth robe.

"Hungry? Whatever Angela left in the fridge is sure to be good," I told her.

"I'm whipped, but I'm hungry, too," she admitted. "Let's check it out. A quick midnight snack, and then I think I'll crash for three days straight."

"I'll be crashed right along with you," I assured her. Sounded like pure bliss.

Angela had outdone herself. Smoked salmon, pulled pork, tender pepper-rolled roast beef, spinach pies and artichoke frittatas, feta and tomato and olive salad, sliced fruit, chocolate cake, strawberry trifle, freshly baked sourdough bread.

We fell upon it like wild animals. In fact, we were so intent on eating, we forgot all about the wine Angela had left on the counter to pair with the meal. I poured out two glasses just as we were starting to slow down a little.

"So good," she moaned, licking her fingers after savoring a bite of pulled pork. "I'm in bliss. I can't keep eating like this. It's just too damned delicious."

"Yes, you should," I told her. "You should have the best of everything in life, because that's what you always give. Your absolute best. And you ask for nothing in return. But you know what? That's all about to change."

Her eyes opened wide. "Oh yeah? Says who?"

"Says me." I looked straight into her eyes. "That's the rule, from here on out. Best of everything. No exceptions."

She let out a startled laugh. "Well, wow. I appreciate the sentiment, big guy, but we've talked about this. The pampered plaything is not my script."

"I don't want a plaything," I said. "And I'm not playing. This is dead serious."

The laughter faded from her face, and her eyes grew somber. "Ethan…"

"Like I told you earlier. I don't want a bed toy. I want a partner. I want you, in my bed, in my life, at my back. Forever. I want it all."

She held up her hand. "Slow down," she said. "I met you three days ago, under extreme circumstances. Not smart to throw down big, sweeping declarations so soon."

"I don't care how smart it is. I've played it smart all my life. I like this better."

"But it's a terrible time! Everything's upside down and backward!"

"So? If I hadn't met you that day in Clemens' office, I'd be dead now. You showed up just in time for me. I just wish I had a ring. Something really special."

"No," she said hastily. "I don't do rings. My hands are weapons, not ornaments."

I slid off the chair and to my knees in front of her, kissing the hands in question. "The most beautiful hands I've ever seen," I said. "So strong. The things they can do."

Kat sniffed aggressively, yanked a hand free, and pressed a napkin to her face.

"Not fair," she said, her voice watery. "You can't spring this on me after a day like today. Lighten up. Let me rest, chill. Then we'll see about all this romantic stuff."

I kissed the hand remaining to me, taking my time with it. Worshiping each knuckle, aware of every nick and scratch. "All right," I conceded. "I'll just keep asking. Every day until the end of time. Eventually you'll give in, out of sheer exhaustion."

She swatted me on the shoulder. "Oh, get up. You're being ridiculous."

But I could tell she was smiling under cover of darkness, as we made our way to the soft, inviting haven of my bed. And once we were there, she wrapped her lithe, warm body around me, and tucked her head under my arm.

That made me hopeful.

CHAPTER 32

Kat

T he polite tap-tap-tap on the door early in the morning sent me flying straight up into the air, nerves screaming with alarm. "What? Who?" I yelled.

"Who is it?" Ethan called out, in a sleep-roughened voice.

"It's just me, Ethan." It was Angela's voice, low and intensely apologetic. "I wanted to give you a head's-up."

"About what?" Ethan sat up." What's happening?"

"Your sister has arrived, with her husband, and Holly, and the Drakes. They are extremely curious about the new developments in your life. I just thought you two might want to know about that, before you stumbled out in your pajamas."

"Ah." Ethan robbed his face. "Jesus. Thanks, Angela. Appreciate the warning."

"Holly might come looking for you," Angela warned, pointedly. "So, you know. Make yourself decent. Chop-chop."

"Thank you, Angela, I've got it covered," he repeated. "Literally."

"Oh, and breakfast is almost ready! It'll be laid out in the sunroom. Cinnamon rolls are in the oven! Come and get 'em while they're hot!"

"We both listened to her footfalls retreating down the corridor. I looked down at my naked, disheveled self. "Holy shit, for real?" I said, bemused. "Your sister? Your niece? Oh, my freaking God. I've got to get myself together."

It hit me all at once, with a pang I couldn't quite identify. This was one of those milestones that had been missing from my life, along with all those other things people took for granted. Like a graduation ceremony, a first kiss, a senior prom, road trips with girlfriends, college adventures, being a bridesmaid. This was a specific and extremely significant milestone entitled: "Getting Introduced To Your Boyfriend's Family." The big hurdle was traditionally a mom, but moms were thin on the ground, in my world. Still, a sister and a niece—that was a momentous step. At least for me.

Then doubt clutched at me. "Ethan? They don't have to meet me today, if you're not ready," I said. "If it's too soon. It might give them the wrong impression."

His eyebrow shot up. "Are you kidding me? They'll be dying to meet you. Why do you think they came here in the first place? It's pure, in-your-face curiosity."

That was a shocker. "Wait," I said. "You mean they know about me?"

"Of course, they know about you. The Unredeemables are the worst damn gossips I ever saw. And it's not too soon. By no means. I want this, Kat. I'm excited to show you off to everyone I care about, everyone I know. I wish I had a ring, or something like that. Are you sure you won't wear a ring?"

"Nope," I said swiftly. "Not the type. Don't even try."

"Okay, so maybe some kickass earrings?" His voice was plaintive.

"Maybe I should start with some socks and underwear," I said.

"Oh, yeah, about that. I had some stuff delivered for you. Angela put your new things in the righthand closet and chest of drawers in the wardrobe."

Well, of course he did. He caught my look, grinned, holding up his hands.

"I swear, I'm not dressing you like a doll," he said. "This is just a stopgap, until we can catch our breath. Shopping takes time and energy, and you've been busy lately, you know, fighting for your life, shit like that. Please don't get huffy. I did it with profound respect, and nothing more than a desire to help."

I bit back all the ungrateful knee-jerk reactions I could have made, and probably would have, before I decided that yeah, I actually I trusted this guy. For real. He meant what he said. He was not shining me on. He was not making a fool of me.

"Thank you," I said.

His eyes narrowed. "What? Really? That's all you have to say? No cracks about concubines or bed toys?"

"Not yet," I said. "Of course, I haven't seen the clothes, so the vote's not quite in yet. Maybe I should withhold my thanks until I take a look at what's actually there."

"I had Angela pick them out," he assured me. "If it had been me choosing, it would have all been sexy lingerie."

I snorted, and took possession of his bathroom, locking him out. No time for his sexy shower shenanigans this morning. Too much was at stake. One of those precious milestones made me more nervous than anything I'd experienced in ages. Hell, I felt more vulnerable in this situation than I had when I was fighting Nicole yesterday.

It made sense, when I thought about it. While engaged in hand-to-hand mortal combat with Nicole, I wasn't wondering if she would judge me and find me wanting. I was just focused on not letting her kill me. Which was so much simpler.

Freya and Holly were a whole different thing. More fraught with doubt.

After my shower, I checked out the selection of clothes Angela had provided, and I was impressed. She had spared no expense, and she got my vibe. Nothing frilly or frothy. All classy, elegant pieces that were beautifully cut, stretchy, good colors, and it was stuff I could sprint in or fight in, if the need arose. Yay, Angela. I made a note to thank her for her good taste. She was a righteous matron for sure.

I dressed in loose-fitting flared black pants, paired with a silky blouse of deep forest-green, and cute-but-comfortable black boots. I wasted some time wondering whether or not to use makeup. If that would seem anxious. Like I was trying too hard.

In the end, I just used face lotion, swiped on a dab of mascara, and put on a little tinted lip gloss. I was too damn self-conscious to use anything else. Ethan was dressed, and waiting for me. His gaze slid up and down, admiring. "Mmm. You look great."

I rolled my eyes, nervous. "Well. Yeah. Thanks, I guess."

"You'll love my sister, and Holly. I wish they hadn't shown up today, but only because I know you needed some down time. Not for any other reason. It'll be fine."

"Sure." My smile felt sickly and unconvincing, so I let it fade.

We walked down the corridors until we heard the hum of conversation, and clink of cutlery, bursts of laughter. Just as we passed through the entryway, Ethan grabbed my hand. It took me by surprise. Too late to pull away...so there I was, facing a room of open-mouthed, suddenly silent people...holding hands with him, for God's sake.

Clatter. Someone dropped a knife.

I glanced in the direction of the sound, and saw a wide-eyed, dark-blonde girl of about eight or nine, goggling at me.

Next to her was a gorgeous woman with a halo of dark blonde curls who looked just as fascinated. They wore jeans and sweat-shirts, and had big, heaped breakfast plates. The little girl clutched a cinnamon roll. She had a smear of sugary pastry goo on her rosy cheek.

On the other side of the room were four big guys, as physi-cally imposing as Ethan, and almost as good-looking, all in different ways. They looked like guys you wouldn't want to cross, not surprisingly, being Unredeemables. I recognized them from the photo gallery. They'd been featured heavily in the pictures from Ethan's Army Rangers days. One I recognized from the engagement and wedding photos. Jed Clearwater, Freya's new husband. Hubba hubba. Extremely hot. Almost as hot as Ethan.

But the seconds were ticking by, and no one could choke out a goddamn word. They just gawked at me as if I had sprouted antlers.

I cleared my throat. "Uh...morning," I croaked.

"Morning, Frey," Ethan said. "This is Kat, everyone. Kat, this is my sister Freya, my niece Holly, my brother-in-law Jed, and these three behemoths are Amos, Remy, and Darius Drake." He looked at his sister. "Frey. You know, it's always great to see you, and you're always welcome, but we had a hell of a day yester-day, and we could've used a few more hours of rest. Did you have to descend on us at the crack of dawn?"

"Holly was anxious," Freya said crisply. "We had to make sure you were okay."

Holly bounded over to her uncle, wrapped her arms around his waist, and squeezed. "They said you got in a fight with Nicole!"

"Well, yeah, I guess I did, but I'm okay." He let go of my hand to hug the little girl, kissing the top of her head. "You don't need to worry about me. Ever."

She frowned up at him, smacking his chest. "Don't say stuff

like that," she said sternly. "It's not true, and it's just dumb. I'm not a baby, and I can worry if I want to. I know bad things happen. Ever since they took Dad, I've known it."

"I know, baby," Ethan said. "I'm sorry. I'll try to be careful. Always."

Holly squeezed him again, and looked up at me with big, curious eyes. "So, you're the lady who fights?"

"Yeah, sure," I agreed. "I guess that's a pretty good description of me."

Holly examined the angry red bramble scratches on my face and hands. "Did you get the scratches from rescuing the cat?"

I was lost. "Excuse me? What cat are you talking about?"

"She was just referring to the story we heard about you rescuing your neighbor lady's cat from her no-good ex," Freya explained.

"Oh! Ah...whoa!" I gaped at her, at Holly, at Ethan. "How on earth did you guys know about that? I did not tell anybody about that!"

Freya and Jed exchanged rueful smiles. "Well, your friend Joanna told Shelby," Freya said. "Then Shelby told Trey and Ryder, and then they told all of us. You really can't blame them. It's an awesome story. Made a big impression on Holly. Anytime you put a cat into the mix, she's all over it."

"Yeah, I love cats. I hate it when people are mean to cats," Holly confided.

"We have that in common," I said forcefully. "It's the worst."

"What did you do to the mean guy? Did you kick him in the balls? Uncle Ethan said I gotta learn to kick 'em in the balls."

"Holly!" Freya scolded "It's not your business who she kicked, or where she kicked him! Don't stick your nose in."

I shook my head with a smile. "Sorry if I disappoint you, but I actually didn't have to hurt him," I told her. "I just threatened to hurt him. I threatened really hard. And he was a big old whiny loser, so fortunately for me, that was enough. I do try to avoid ball-kicking, as a general rule. I only do it under the direst of circumstances."

"You mean, if he hadn't given you back the cat, you would have kicked him in the balls?" Holly demanded.

There was a fierce intensity in the little girl's voice. She was hungering for the bad guys who had hurt her dad to get some righteous punishment, and oh God, could I absolutely relate to that. "Yep," I said. "I sure would have. Hard as I could. Balls, boom, take that. Teeth, too. Ka-bam, pow. That'll teach the butthead."

The little girl air-punched with a big grin, one-two, and raised up her hand, to which I gave a resounding high-five. "Yeah!" she crowed. "Take that! Awesome!"

"I'm not sure if I should approve of this wanton celebration of bloodthirsty violence," Ethan said, his tone ironic.

"We didn't ask for your approval," I shot back, just because of course, I had to, it was an automatic reflex. But I immediately regretted it, because for God's sake, this was his niece. *Ease off, Kat. Take a freaking breath.*

I shot him a quick, apologetic look. "Sorry," I said. "I was just shooting off my mouth. Of course, you get to sign off on everything involving her. We were just bonding over our anger issues. It's a girl thing."

"I think we can all agree to bond over our anger issues," Freya said, in the slightly-too-long silence that followed. "We've been so excited to meet you."

"We heard lots of stories!" Holly offered. "They said you kicked a bunch of guys' butts in an elevator with Uncle Ethan!"

"Ah...well, that's not exactly how it—"

"Can confirm," Ethan said. "I was there. And I'm still here... thanks to her."

"Oh, would you please stop?'" I complained. "You're putting

me on the spot on purpose, right in front of your family, and I haven't even had my coffee yet."

I stiffened as Holly grabbed me in turn, and squeezed my waist—just like Gabri used to do. The memory blindsided me. I suddenly felt so close to Gabri, with this little girl's skinny body strangling my waist in a desperate hug, her back quivering with emotion. Gabri had been intense and over-the-top like that, too.

My arms closed around Holly and I hugged her back, my eyes prickling.

"Thanks for saving him." Her voice was choked.

"Any time, sweetheart," I told her. "But he saved me right back, you know. And he did it again, yesterday. So technically, I'm behind, pointwise."

Holly let out a soggy giggle. "Will you sit next to me?"

"How about you let her get her food first?" That was Angela chiming in, beaming all over her face and shooting meaningful glances at Freya as she marched toward the buffet with a fresh platter of bacon and sausage. "Let the poor woman get a cup of coffee and a plate, for God's sake. Grill her after she's had some sustenance!"

Soon afterward, I found myself seated next to Holly as I ate my breakfast. That put me at constant risk for another massive Gabri-nostalgia moment, but I had to barrel onward and hope for the best. No way could I armor myself against a sweet little girl who reminded me so much of my younger sister.

Holly beamed at me as I bit into a piece of sourdough toast. "Uncle Ethan never brought any of his girlfriends here before," she said. "You must be special."

I coughed on my buttery toast crumbs. "Oh, I think that was more about a last-minute security strategy than anything else."

"At first," Ethan interjected from across the table. "At first."

"Holly's right," Freya confirmed. "And we're not just talking about this house. I don't think I've ever run into his previous lady friends in any Masters' residence."

"Do you have to talk about this in front of her?" Ethan said, frowning.

Freya snorted, ignoring him. "I've run into a few of them out in the wild, maybe, but never in his private space. He's a penthouse luxury hotel suite kinda guy."

"Frey," Ethan snapped. "Don't. Holly's listening."

"Holly's the one who brought it up," Freya said. "And who invited you into this conversation, anyway?" Freya turned back to me. "Imagine our shock when word came to us about a mysterious blonde bombshell saving his ass. And then being sequestered at the Mountain House."

I rolled my eyes. "Bombshell? Oh please. Give me a break."

"True thing," Freya said solemnly. "We've been dying to check you out. And I can honestly say you have exceeded all expectations."

I felt a warm glow inside. "Well, I can't imagine why," I said, abashed. "But I appreciate the thought."

"Your blouse is pretty," Holly piped up. "I like the green. Like pine trees."

I was intensely grateful for the timely change of subject. "Thanks. I like it, too. Angela picked it out for me. I ended up coming here in such a rush, I had no time to pack my own stuff." I looked at Freya. "I had to borrow some of your things the first couple of days. I hope you don't mind."

"Good God, no. For you, anything, anytime," she said swiftly. "That elevator stunt alone earned you full access to my wardrobe for the next ten lifetimes."

"Holly, Jenn tracked down those books we were talking about," Ethan said. "They're in the library. I'll go get them for you."

Holly's eyes lit up. "The Blackthorne Key series? You got them? Oh goodie!"

"Yes, and I found a good one about the history of codes, too, like we talked about. From now on, I'll encrypt all my messages to you, and you'll have to figure out which key to use."

"Cool!" Holly crowed, clapping.

Oh, yikes. With naked alarm, I watched him get up and walk out of the room. Just leaving me here all alone with his womenfolk. Really, Masters? Criminy.

Then Holly reached out and grabbed my hand. "So, are you, like, Uncle Ethan's girlfriend now?" There was a worried crease between her dark eyebrows.

"Um, well...well..." I stammered a little. "Thing is, it's still really new. I don't want to jinx it by putting labels on it too soon, you know?"

Holly looked disapproving, but Freya nodded with perfect understanding. "I get you," she said. "Jed and I got together under intense conditions, too. It was really hard to trust my feelings under such extreme pressure. Everything was out of balance."

I was grateful for her comprehension. "That's it exactly," I said. "I just don't have any ground under my feet right now."

"Auntie Frey busted Uncle Jed out of jail," Holly confided.

Freya snorted coffee out of her nose, and dabbed her face with a napkin, giggling. "Um, not exactly," she said. "But the real story is just as strange, I promise."

My curiosity was piqued. "Tell me sometime?"

"Love to. The story is better with cocktails, though. Later on, for sure."

Ethan returned, with his arms piled with books. A stack of colorful paperback novels about an intrepid, code-cracking young hero, and a big book about codes and encryption through the ages. It looked advanced for a kid Holly's age, but evidently, she had a full measure of the Masters egghead nerdiness, because she dove right into the big book, leafing through the pages eagerly and chattering about Morse code, the Enigma

Machine, the Voynich Manuscript, Alberti's Disk. Damn. I was impressed.

After we wrapped up breakfast, Angela came out, and ruffled Holly's hair. "Folks, I am so sorry to abandon you all right when everybody finally gets home, and when so many exciting things are happening," she said. "But my niece Allegra's C-section was rescheduled for this afternoon, so I need to get back down to the city."

"Of course," Ethan said. "Do you want to use the helicopter? Is there urgency?"

"Oh, God, no. I hate those things. So far, no urgency, so I'll just drive. That way I have my car to use when I'm in town. There's tons of food you all can heat up and lay out for lunch and dinner. And I put together a platter of chicken wraps for a quick lunch for everyone tomorrow, so you're covered for a while."

"Thanks, Angela. We'll miss you," Freya said. "Let us know how it goes."

"Good luck to your niece," I said.

"Thanks! I'll get myself organized and get going." She gave Holly a hug. "Hey, sweetheart. Keep an eye on these miscreants for me, won't you?"

"Always do," Holly said promptly. "It's my job, Angela. You know that."

"That's my girl!" Angela bustled out with a wave.

The day that followed was strangely, unexpectedly wonderful. Somehow, those people had put me at my ease, no small feat. I did not feel awkward with them, or out of place, like an alien blurting out a foreign language, as I often did in social situations. Freya vibrated at a frequency that was tuned to me perfectly. Holly, too.

I ended up telling them all about my mission to empower women and girls, my martial arts schools. Then I learned all about Freya's engineering firm, and the vast array of fascinating products she designed, many of which intensely appealed to me. She'd designed a bag of disguised weaponry for her best friends, and dubbed it "the Badass Bitch Bag," and after getting me all starry-eyed about its contents, she promised to get me the latest version of it, with all its newest designs. Holly was much put upon that she couldn't have her own bag, but lethal drugs and hidden weaponry hardly seemed appropriate for a nine-year-old. I was extremely touched when they dubbed me an honorary Badass Bitch. Awww. Tender moment.

I also learned more that day than I ever wanted to know about the history of codes, and codebreaking, Holly's latest passion. The kid was definitely a future engineer.

Freya took me down to her apartment to show me her space. Holly showed me her room. Later on, it was drinks by the pool, where Holly took a swim, splashing like a dolphin, while Freya told me the outrageous tale of getting together with Jed. She was a good storyteller. Amazing that they lived through it.

And I actually relaxed. For me, anyway. Who knew what normal human stress levels actually felt like. In any case, mine were lower than they had been since I could remember, and it felt very nice. The cocktails helped, too, giving me a mellow buzz.

We cobbled together a delicious rag-bag of a dinner out of Angela's massive selection of leftovers, partaking liberally of the wine while we set stuff out and heated stuff up. By the time we sat down to eat, I was downright giggly.

After dessert, we sat together to enjoy the sunset, and when that had faded, Freya glanced at the clock on her phone. "It's bedtime, honey baby," she said to Holly. "Go get ready. I'll come tuck you in."

"Can Kat do it tonight?" Holly asked, giving me a pleading look. "She's Uncle Ethan's girlfriend, so, she's like, my new second mom, right?"

Freya shot me a nervous, questioning glance. I felt pierced by a stab of pure fear.

It was hard enough to manage all the memories of Gabri without supercharging them with a tender bedtime ritual. After Mom died and Raffi had been moved into Tony Petruzzi's apartment, I'd been the one to cuddle Gabri to sleep every night.

But the glow from that beautiful, mellow day spent with Ethan's family gave me the courage to face it. "Fine with me," I heard myself say. "I'd love to." Who could resist a little girl's pleading eyes?

My heart clutched in my chest when she took my hand and led me to her bedroom. I managed coherent responses to her cheerful, excited chatter during all the bathroom stuff. Toilet and teeth. Hair brushing and braiding. And then, the ultimate dilemma: stars, galaxies, and nebulae pajamas, or the Disney princess ones?

The princess pajamas won, but it was a near thing, because stars, galaxies, and nebulae were super-cool. She crawled into her bed, and patted the space next to her. "Come look at my star constellations on the ceiling," she invited.

I lay down next to her, hesitantly, and looked up. Oh God. The ceiling was studded with luminous stick-on stars, just like the ones Gabri and I had decorated her bedroom ceiling with, a lifetime ago.

Crap. The stars were a low blow. They were so unexpected, they slipped right past my guard. My throat closed, and my eyes filled with tears. The little greenish points of light melded into a watery blur as I blinked them away.

"Cool," I said, over the frog in my throat. "I had those when I was a kid, too."

"Uncle Ethan helped me measure out all the proportions, so we could recreate the biggest constellations," she said. "We did a map, and planned it all out."

"Yowza," I said, "I didn't do that, when I put up my stars. I just made up constellations in my head. I figured they were the stars that were visible from another planet. Planet Kat, in a galaxy far, far away."

Holly laughed and cuddled closer to me. "I like Planet Kat," she said. "I'm glad you're here. Uncle Ethan is, too. I can tell he's happy that you're here. You should stay."

Oh don't, don't, don't do it. Don't get so attached, don't hold your heart out like that, it is so freaking dangerous.

I swallowed back all my choking fears and just hugged her. "Thank you for saying that," I whispered "I'm glad to have met you."

I held her until I realized she'd drifted off to sleep, and then extricated myself very gently. I stroked my finger down the little girl's thick braid, and stole out, leaving the door a little open. Gabri had always wanted the door left open. She liked the stripe of light filtering through, and she liked to hear me puttering around in the living room, doing whatever. It made her feel safe.

Of course, there was no such thing as safe. Not for anyone. But little girls should keep their illusions for as long as possible. I hoped Holly could keep whatever was left of hers longer than I had been allowed to keep mine.

My heart felt too full to face the people still talking in the living room, so I quietly headed out onto the terrace, looking over the endless gradations of shadowy gray-blue in the twilit mountains and valleys, letting the breeze dry my wet eyes.

Freya followed me out after a few minutes. Jed was right behind her. They leaned on the railing, one on either side of me, which made me intensely self-conscious.

"Sorry about Holly putting you on the spot like that," Freya said. "She's a wonderful kid, but no nine-year-old is very big on tact. Or timing, for that matter."

"But she knows a good thing when she sees it," Jed added.

"She wants to nail all the good things into place. I can't blame her."

"She reminds me of...someone I used to know," I said. "Of course, I knew she'd be a great kid, from the way Ethan talked about her. He's crazy about her."

"Yes, he is," Freya said. "He's crazy about you, too."

"That's for sure," Jed agreed.

My stress levels jolted up about ten notches in a hot instant. "Um, guys. I think you're jumping the gun a little." I spun around, so I could look at them both at the same time. "Ease off, maybe."

Freya shrugged. "He's so different with you," she said.

"Yeah? How so?"

"Well, you may have noticed he's a my-way-or-the-highway kind of guy, right?"

I let out a bark of laughter. "Actually, so far, it's been more like, 'my-way-and-the-highway-is-not-even-an-option-so-freaking-forget-it."

Freya snickered under her breath. "Yeah, exactly. But that dominating vibe doesn't work on you. You're simply not moved by it. Which makes you perfect for him."

I held up my hand. "Hold on," I pleaded. "Let's not get ahead of ourselves."

Freya and Jed slanted each other a teasing glance.

"Getting ahead of ourselves is our specialty," Jed said. His voice had that velvety sound that made me realize I was overhearing love talk.

Freya giggled at the inside joke. They exchanged flirty, loverlike glances. Hands, arms, winding together. Madly in love. Aww. It was lovely to see.

"What are you guys talking about out here?" Ethan said as he walked outside.

"You," Freya said, with a sunny smile. "Of course. You're one of our favorite topics."

"Ouch," he said mildly. "Give it a break, Frey."

She shrugged. "Only because it's time for bed. But I'll start right back up on you tomorrow, bro. Count on it." She leaned over and kissed my cheek. "Good night," she said. "I had a great time today. I'm glad you're here. See you in the morning."

"Good night," I said, bemused. She and Jed walked away toward the stairs that led to their apartment on the lower level, holding hands, heads tilted close, murmuring to each other.

Ethan took Freya's place next to me, leaning against the railing. Close enough so I could smell his scent, feel his body heat. Without thinking about it, I leaned in and touched him. His arm went around me, pulling me close to his solid warmth.

It felt so good. It felt absolutely amazing.

"I love your family," I blurted out.

"I'm so glad." He tilted my face up, kissed me, slowly, sensually, masterfully. "What do you say? Time for bed?"

I almost laughed at how comically perfect it was. Warm sunset colors, tenderness, kisses. Strolling through this beautiful space, hand in hand. The safe, lovely house, filled with good souls who cared about each other and had each other's backs.

It was too damn perfect to believe it could actually be real... but I didn't care.

I was going to try like hell to believe it anyway.

CHAPTER 33

Nicole

"Hear me out, before you have me killed," Nicole said calmly.

Her body buzzed with adrenaline, her favorite high. Nothing like having a gun barrel digging into her cheek to focus the mind, see the world with brilliant clarity.

Vincent glared at her from his wingback chair. "Why bother?" he said. "It'll just be bullshit, anyway. Why were you even stupid enough to come back, after failing so badly, and getting yet another of our crew killed? Or was it you who killed Maynard? I know you have your little kinks, but you will have to indulge yourself on your own time, and your own dime if you work with me, you blood-drinking slut."

Nicole widened her eyes in outrage. "No! I did not! That would be counterproductive, stupid, and messy, and I am none of those things. Ethan Masters killed Maynard! He is a brutal killer. You saw what he did to Wex Boer's crew. And to me."

Vincent tilted his head to the side, studying her shrewdly. "And the crushed jaw, the broken teeth? That sounds more like your style, Nicole. One of your tantrums."

"Absolutely not," she said briskly. "I'm a skilled professional. Killing Maynard would be a waste of a valuable
resource, and would make a huge mess, too. I would never. I
admit, I miscalculated when I took only Maynard with me to
collect Kat Banner. But I thought she would be alone. I had no
clue Ethan Masters would come down on us with a six-man
crew of Unredeemables. I barely survived that experience!"

"And you've got nothing to show for it," Vincent snarled.

"Oh, no," she said. "That's not true. I have a brand-new
plan, based on brand-new information. This plan will get us
everything we need, and solve every single logistical problem
we have, all in the same stroke. You are going to love it, Vin."

Vincent crossed his legs, his mouth twisting suspiciously.
He gestured for her to go on. "You're full of shit, Nicole, but I'm
listening."

"Could you have your guy take away the gun barrel?" she
asked. "It's pressing into my jawbone, and making it kind of
hard for me to talk."

Vincent made a languid gesture toward the goon with the
pistol. "Keep it pointed at her," he said, and the cold circle of
metal painfully stabbed into the hollow of her cheek suddenly
released its pressure.

"Well, then?" Vincent asked. "Talk. Make it quick and entertaining, or Maynard's corpse will have company in the morgue
really fucking soon."

She covered up her rage with a serene smile. "I am
proposing an amendment to our original plan, which was to
compel Mick Drummond be our suicide bomber. But it's not a
perfect plan. I don't think Drummond's motivations will look
compelling or believable after the fact. Besides, I'm afraid he
might implode on us at the last minute, in a crisis of
conscience. We need someone tougher."

"Such as?"

"Well, I know we'd tossed around the idea of using Ethan

Masters himself," she said. "But his motivations are even less believable, and that works only if he gives us the functional codes to the algorithm in time, and if we're sure we can make SmokeScreen do what we need it to do without him. But time is very tight for this scenario. Too tight, in my opinion."

"We've discussed all this before, Nicole," Vincent said. "You're boring me."

"Today, while collecting Kat Banner, I discovered she has a secret double life, full of violence," she said. "And it is pure motherfucking gold for our purposes."

Vincent's foot jiggled with nervous energy. "Tell me more."

Nicole swiftly laid out the details of the grisly story, the dead mom, the older sister becoming a mafia thug's whore. The mafia thug murdering the whore and the seven-year-old sister. The lonely, wounded fourteen-year-old girl, forced to testify, subsequently tossed into the Witness Protection Program, orphaned, bereft, and traumatized.

"She's our bomber, Vin," Nicole concluded. "She's perfect. A gift from the gods. She's marked for death already, and has been since she was fourteen. She's so damaged, see? The whole world is her enemy. Who would be even the least bit surprised if she fell prey to the hateful ideology of a domestic terror group? I mean, duh!"

Vincent crossed his arms as he considered it. "And yet, you let her get away."

"There was no way to bring her in, not with Masters' whole team coming at me," she said impatiently. "And we need the little girl to control Ethan Masters anyhow, so we can just take Banner when we pick up the little girl."

"That place is heavily fortified," Vincent snapped. "We can't just waltz in. You know that."

"Of course not. But we have the perfect tool to make them jump, thanks to you," she said. "Don't you still have some of those videos you took of Shane Masters?"

He looked miffed. "I seem to recall you scrapping them because they offered too much intel," he said sourly.

God. What an idiot. He was still piqued about her criticizing his game with extortion videos. She pasted on an encouraging smile. "Well, things have changed. And now we need for Masters to follow those exact same breadcrumbs you left in your videos," she said. "You were absolutely prescient, Vincent. You sensed what we would need before we even needed it. It's your special gift."

Vincent looked suspicious, as well he should, when she gave him compliments. But his ego was so grotesquely swollen, he always fell for it like rotten fruit. "Use them if you need them," he said. "Who's your asset, again? Are you sure you can trust him?"

"Of course I'm sure," she said. God, she simply could not wait to tear the flesh from this dickface's bones. "I have the ultimate leverage."

"Ah, yes." Vincent wrinkled his nose in disgust. "The groaning old man in the basement. I can't tolerate that kind of thing in my central headquarters, Nicole. You need to move him to one of the satellite facilities. It's distasteful. And the smell. God."

"I'm almost done," she assured him. "After the Event, we can dispose of him. I think old Jay Drummond is going to make one last video tonight. A real doozy, for his great-nephew's viewing pleasure. Care to watch me make it?"

Vincent had that snotty, superior expression that had always made her want to gut him, ever since they were children. "No, thank you," he said. "I prefer to outsource that kind of thing. Too messy. And you enjoy it a little too much, in my opinion."

She shrugged. "You want something done right, do it yourself. I get results, don't I?"

Vincent harrumphed. "It's very late, to change the plan," he complained.

"I know, Vin, but trust me. This is a better plan. The psycho-analysts will eat it up with a spoon. Kat Banner has every reason to feel that the world is a shitty, dangerous place that's badly in need of punishment."

Vincent made an impatient sound. "As long as things move on schedule."

"Of course, of course," she murmured. "Let me tell you exactly what I have in mind. If you could, ah...call off your dog? So we can get to work?"

Vincent waved the guy with the gun away. She exhaled, and put her hand in her pocket, fondling Maynard's damp, sticky tooth as she laid out how the plan would work. The resources she would need, the steps to be taken. Her heart thudded with excitement.

The sweetest part of it all was going to be making Ethan Masters believe he'd been betrayed by a lying whore. Nicole had seen the way he dove into those thorn bushes for that girl. The way he'd kissed her. He had it bad. He was so whipped.

Let Ethan Masters take a turn at feeling like a fool. Taken in by a honeytrap temptress who led him by his dick...straight to his own destruction.

Perfect.

CHAPTER 34

Ethan

A scream jerked me awake. Thin, shrill, bloodcurdling. Kat and I both practically levitated off the bed, grabbing the nearest article of clothing, with Kat snagging my T-shirt, and me the bathrobe that lay on the floor. I took the gun from my nightstand before we ran out, keeping Kat behind me. We sprinted, barefoot, toward the relentless screams that came from Holly's room.

I slapped the door open. Holly sat on her bedroom rug, her head in her arms.

Kat dropped down to the floor and gathered her up. "Baby, what happened? Are you hurt?"

"V-v-v-video." Holly's normally rosy face was colorless. "Of Dad."

My stomach dropped. "What video, honey? From where?"

Holly held up her smartphone. It had a pink cover, featuring some cartoon princess or other. "From this."

Kat pried Holly's trembling fingers loose of the device. Her eyes met mine, full of dread.

"Text message," Holly said faintly. "It had a link, and I...I clicked it."

I hissed under my breath. "Oh God, baby. We talked about this. You should have brought it to me."

"I know," she whispered. "Sorry, I just...I couldn't wait. I couldn't stand it."

There it was, in the messages, all caps. I HAVE SOME-THING YOU WANT, then a link. I braced myself, hoping Holly hadn't witnessed something unspeakable.

"Is this actually your phone, honey?" I asked. "Are you sure?"

"I-I-I thought it was mine," she faltered. "It has the same cover. I guess someone could have s-s-switched it out. I just don't know when."

"Can I look at it here?" I asked gently. "Do I need to take it in the other room?"

Holly shook her head. "No, look now. I want you to see it right now."

I set the video to play. The camera first showed a beam of light coming from a high-up window, slowly panning down and showing a huge room, metal beams. A warehouse of some kind. The camera shifted lower and focused on a man who sat hunched on the ground, next to a concrete wall. He wore a filthy T-shirt and ragged sweatpants. He was extremely lean, his hair long and tangled, his beard full.

My heart started to thud. The camera bounced as the person holding it snapped his fingers. "Hey, asshole! Look alive! Say hi to the camera!"

The hunched man barely tuned his head, but he glared from under his matted hair at whoever was speaking and gave him the finger.

My heart practically stopped. Shane. Thinner, hairier, dirtier than I'd ever seen him, but I knew that look. I knew those fierce eyes. It was unquestionably my brother.

The camera holder muttered something ugly, and the camera jerked as he manipulated some device. I heard a motor hum, the rattle of metal—and the chain went tight, jerking Shane up onto his feet, and then off them.

Shane grabbed the chain that held him, holding himself up so as not to be hanged. He dangled there, spinning in midair, refusing to beg or plead or even gasp.

Then, whoever held the camera lowered him to the ground. "Okay, then, if you're so tough. Take this, you dumb fuck," the voice behind the camera muttered.

Shane's body arched, jerking uncontrollably as the collar administrated an electric shock. "Learn some fucking manners, ass-wipe." The voice sounded smug.

Holly pressed her hands over her mouth. Kat glared, saying with her eyes to take the damn phone away and watch this obscenity elsewhere. But the video ended there.

"That's all there is," I told her. "Finished."

My whole mind, body, soul, was all buzzing with rage, fear...and fresh hope, too. Which was the cruelest thing of all.

Shane could still be alive. He had been when that video was shot, which was months after I had last seen him. Long enough to lose all that weight, grow all that hair.

Don't get your hopes up. That crazy emotional rollercoaster did not serve us.

I crouched down on the rug and hugged Holly. "I'm sorry you saw them hurt him, baby."

Holly burst into tears. I met Kat's grim gaze over her head. Then Freya and Jed burst in, dressed in bathrobes. "What the hell is going on?" Jed demanded.

Kat stepped back and let Freya gather her sobbing niece into her arms.

"Someone sent her a video of Shane," I said.

Freya's eyes filled with fear. She swallowed. "And was it, ah...was he—"

"Alive," I said. "Not well, but definitely alive. At least when this was shot."

The Drakes joined us at door, along with Mick and the rest of them, a cacophony of questions, exclamations.

"Hey, listen up," I called out, over the din. "Everybody get out of Holly's room. Meet me in the war room in five. We'll watch it together on the big screen." I turned to Kat. "Could you stay with Holly? Make her hot chocolate, or something?"

Kat wrapped an arm around Holly. "Of course."

Freya shot her a grateful look and kissed the top of Holly's head. "I'll be right back with you, honey. I just have to throw on my jeans and go to this meeting."

I ran back to my bedroom to put on some clothes. A few minutes later, Freya, me, and all the Unredeemables currently in residence were gathered in the war room.

We watched the video, then watched it again, multiple times. Someone made some coffee, and we drank it as we watched it all again, just letting it sink in. Memorizing every frame. It was horrific to see him that way, but I couldn't tear my eyes off those images of my brother, starved and tortured and chained...but alive. *Alive.*

"I can't believe they sent that filth to Holly," Mick kept repeating, his voice low and furious. "Fucking sadists. They could have sent it to you, or Freya, but no. Holly, for fuck's sake."

"That's Nicole's style," Freya said. "She's saying, gotcha! Made you jump!"

"They've stripped the identifying metadata," I said. "The video is untraceable."

"He has enough guts left to flip them off," Amos reflected. "Good sign."

"Depending on how old the video is," Darius said grimly.

"The place looks familiar," Mick said. "Let's look at the video again. At the place. We can mine it for clues."

I turned to him quickly. "What clues?"

"Look at that scaffolding on the wall in the big room. Those rolls look like razor wire. Some sort of business, but the place looks defunct."

I zoomed in, enlarging the shelves. Mick was right. Razor wire, and lots of it. Maybe this was a place that had made it, or distributed it.

"Go back to the beginning, back when the camera lens is still pointed up," Mick said. "Before we see Shane. And listen."

We all waited...and heard the slow build to the roar of a plane taking off. "It's near an airport." I said slowly. "But that's not much help. There are airports everywhere."

"Yeah, but look up at that window," Mick said. "It's a ten-meter ceiling. With those distinctive arched windows, a pattern of panes missing, the clue of the razor wire, and the flight path of an airport. Those are enough data points to start a search."

"Too easy." It was Kat's voice, from the door, flat and matter-of-fact. "It's a trap. Nicole would never give you so many clues unless she wanted you to find the place. She's playing us. Throwing dirt in our eyes."

"Could be, but it's still the only lead we've had in months, so I'll take the dirt," Freya said. She glanced at her husband. "And I've done crazier things than that to scare up more leads. Shane was chained up in that place. We have to track it down and take a look at it."

"Don't let her lead you around," Kat warned. "You'll be like kittens following a laser pointer around. Herded and controlled."

"How's Holly doing?" I asked her.

"She's hanging in there," Kat said. "I heated up some of Angela's frozen waffles for breakfast, and she ate almost a whole one. She's parked in front of the TV now, watching Harry Potter. It's her comfort watch."

Darius typed furiously on his computer. "Here's a list of all industrial properties within a five-mile radius of the flight paths of SeaTac. I've filtered out buildings that appear to be currently in use. Using that criteria, I've got fourteen properties on the list."

We eliminated several of them right away, but on the eighth one, we stopped, and the room grew quiet.

"It's high enough," Mick said. "And old enough looking."

"Helmsworth Fencing," Darius said, throwing the image up on the big screen. "That fits, with the razor wire."

I stared at the dingy old buildings, trying to calm down the frantic buzz of excitement in my chest. My heart seemed to be thinking I was going to find my brother. As if those assholes would send us an embossed invitation to rescue him. It could never be so easy. Never. This was a baited trap. One they knew we could not resist.

Mange your fucking expectations, Masters. That was my brain talking.

I glanced at Kat. She didn't like this. Them, dangling bait, and us jumping for it, because that was what brokenhearted people were wired up to do.

"Don't fall for it," she said to me softly. "You're smarter than this."

That stung, and I lashed back. "You're saying if someone sent you a video like that, with one of your sisters in it, still alive, that you'd be too damn careful and smart to check it out?"

Her eyes flashed. "Fuck you." She stalked out of the room.

An uncomfortable silence followed. I didn't bother breaking it, just concentrated on clicking through the satellite photos that existed of Helmsworth.

I stopped on an image that showed us the windows along the side, and we all let out a sound. This looked right. The right height. Arched windows. The missing panes, in that particular pattern, like missing teeth. The exact reverse pattern of what we had seen in the video. "Helmsworth," Freya murmured, fingers flying on her laptop. "They specialized in barbed wire, razor wire, chain link. Went bankrupt eight years ago."

We stared at the image on the screen. I shook my head. "Holy shit," I whispered. "He was so close to us, all along. For months."

"I want to see it today," Freya said.

"No!" Jed and I said, in unison.

Freya gave us that look, the one we knew too well. "Don't even try to stop me."

"The six of us can go," Remy said, not bothering to participate in the argument. "You, Jed, Freya, and the three of us. We can send in some of Shane's drones to suss it out. Everyone else on the roster, plus Kat, holds down the fort here, to cover Holly."

"Let's get packed and ready," I told them.

I walked back to the apartment to find Kat, angry at myself for bringing up her sisters like that. That was needlessly aggressive, and I had regretted it instantly.

I found her curled on the couch next to Holly. They were watching an enormous snake slither through a gothic dungeon on the screen while the boy wizard fought for his life. Didn't seem very reassuring to me, but what did I know.

Kat did not acknowledge my existence, so I leaned over her shoulder. "Can I have a quick word in the kitchen?"

She turned blazing eyes to me. "Maybe, if the quick word includes an apology," she said. "Otherwise, I'll pass."

"It does include an apology," I said. "That's first item of business."

She studied my face for a moment and gave Holly a quick kiss on top of her head. "Be right back, honey," she murmured.

She followed me into the kitchen, and leaned against the entryway, arms crossed over her chest.

"I'm sorry I said that," I began. "I shouldn't have brought up your sisters."

"That's for sure," she said. "Don't do it again. Or I am out of here like a shot."

"Never again," I promised. "But we are going to check out that warehouse."

Her mouth tightened. "Oh, God, Ethan. Don't."

"We'll be careful," I told her. "We'll send in a drone first. Shane designed them for just this kind of thing. We won't go in ourselves unless it's perfectly safe."

Kat shook her head. "There's no such thing, and you know it. Not with these people. They just reached inside your own house and smacked your little girl, right in front of you. Now you're running right into the bag they're holding open for you. Like a chump."

I shook my head. "We'll be in and out in no time. We'll come right back to analyze any intel we gather. Don't worry. We're all of us boot-leather tough sons of bitches. We're not running into anybody's bag. I swear to God."

"You're tough sons of bitches who are not thinking clearly," Kat said grimly.

"I've got a small army of guys staying here to guard you," I assured her. "You'll look after Holly for me? You won't leave her alone?"

"Of course I won't," she grumbled. "But I hate that you're doing this."

I'm sorry, but we have to," I said. "It has to be done, and it's not as if there's ever going to be a better time to do it. What else can we do?"

"Just be really fucking careful," she said fiercely. "Promise me you will."

"Always."

I followed up with an ardent kiss, so passionate Kat swatted me away, laughing. "Save it for later, lover boy. I'm too uptight to appreciate your seductive wiles right now."

We packed up the van with all the equipment we thought

we could use, and plenty more, for just in case. I tried several times to convince Frey to stay here with Kat and Holly, using bullying, guilt, and every other tactic under the sun, all to no avail. Jed tried just as hard. We might as well not have bothered. It was like talking to the wind.

We got on the road and sped down the mountain highway. It took a tense and mostly silent hour and twenty to get to the coordinates of Helmsworth. We stopped about a mile away, and sat in the back of the van watching as Amos and Darius piloted two of Jed and Shane's designs, small Ready Line mini-drones, into the abandoned facility. The drones were as small as they could possibly be while still bearing their full load of cutting-edge sensors.

Shane's focus had always been combat robotics. He liked keeping his human personnel safer, so robot recon was his obsession. We had many of his ground-breaking designs in our arsenal.

The drones showed us a desolate, completely abandoned facility. No cars parked nearby except for a rusted-out wreck with no tires, vines twined around its axels.

The Drakes piloted the drones up and through the broken windowpanes that had allowed us to identify Helmsworth. They drifted and into the big, dim, cavernous warehouse space. There wasn't much to be seen. Shane was not there, of course, but the mechanism bolted to the metal beam to which his chain had been fastened was still there. The bucket we had seen in the video was also still there, knocked over. In the middle of the room was an old desk chair.

A telephone with a shattered screen lay on it.

We ran the drones around and around the interior. The sensors caught no discernible explosives, chemicals, toxins, though their range was limited because of their size. We saw no signs of people. The motion detectors on the drone saw nothing moving. The place seemed utterly abandoned.

"Those assholes don't have Shane," Amos said grimly. "If they did, they would have been making us jump long ago."

"Wex Boer told me his team was attacked, and that Shane was taken from him," Freya said. "Taken by a competitor, but he never said the name. He said he had no idea where Shane was, for what it's worth. He could have been lying, but why would he? Maybe this video was shot before Shane was re-stolen from them."

Wex Boer had been an ex-colleague in the Army Rangers, and with his own group of mercenaries, he had also been an occasional business partner of Shane's. Until Boer sold him out, with Nicole's help, and arranged for the total destruction of Shane and Jed's security company, Ready Line, along with the murder of their other colleagues, and Shane's abduction. Nicole's outfit had tried to pin the blame onto Jed, and stage his accidental death from a car accident, as well.

They had failed on both counts. In large part because of Freya.

"If these assholes don't have him, who the fuck does?" Jed mused. "And why aren't they making demands of us?"

The painfully obvious answer to that question burned in the air, but no one articulated it. Shane had to be dead, after all this time, after the abuse we had seen on that screen. I kept trying to swallow it, but it just wouldn't go down.

And Kat's crack about us behaving like kittens chasing a laser pointer...that analogy was bothering me more every second that passed.

"Let's go in," I said brusquely. "In and out. Film it, so we can analyze the video later, but let's not hang around here a second longer than we have to."

We made our way silently into the complex. No need for the bolt-cutters. Large sections of the rusty chain-link fence were down already, so we tramped right over them. We crept alongside buildings, darted swiftly across the open spaces, and approached what looked like a side entrance.

Someone had blocked it open with a brick. Some time ago, from the quantity of leaves and pine needles from the nearby trees that had blown inside.

I pushed the door wider and stepped inside, smelling mold, rot. Water damage stained the walls, cobwebs decked the corners. A cockroach scuttled into a crack in the floor as we walked in. The place was profoundly silent, until that silence was broken by the earsplitting roar of a plane taking off from the nearby airport—then silence again.

I saw no surveillance equipment, but that meant nothing, as it could be so easily hidden. It was safe to assume they were watching us as we did this. A flesh-creeping thought.

We moved through the place as silently as ghosts. Huge chambers where scaffolding reached the ceiling, some rolls of wire still piled on the bottom shelves. The wind whistled and moaned around the roof.

Then we walked into the huge, empty room that we all recognized from the video. We looked up to see the guide mechanism bolted to the beam on the ceiling.

The chair in the middle of the room happened to be eerily lit up by a sharp, distinct ray of light that slanted through the broken window. It was like a spotlight. I walked toward the chair, boots crunching in the dry leaves and grit that had blown through the open panes of glass. The rest of them followed me, Amos and Remy both wearing headgear with cameras that filmed everything, leaving their hands free.

We all stared down at the cell phone that lay inexplicably on the chair. It had a white winter camo cover.

"Oh, fuck me," Jed said softly.

"What?" I demanded. "What do you see?"

"That's Shane's phone," Jed said. "His private phone. The one he used only for family. I recognize that cover."

Freya reached for it.

"Don't," I said sharply. "Do not touch anything, Frey!"

She shook her head and picked it up. "I have to see."

She hit the button. Amazingly, the thing turned on. We saw the image appear behind the shattered screen. An old photo of Holly jumping rope and laughing. Her hair was in the air, lit up by sunshine.

The phone's screen went black, and a cackling shriek of canned laughter assaulted our ears. Wicked-witch-in-a-cartoon type laughter. Suddenly, a countdown appeared on the black screen. Ten...nine...eight...seven. *Fuck!*

I grabbed the phone from Freya's hand, hurled it away from us. "Get down!" I yelled, flinging myself on top of Freya.

Boom. The phone exploded, several yards away from us.

We looked up. Sickening, sulfurous fumes were heavy in the air.

Everybody looked okay. Freya was wiggling beneath me, making protesting sounds. I rolled off her, and got up, my knees weak and wobbling.

"Holy shit," I ground out, my voice shaking. "That was close."

"Yes," Amos agreed, as he got to his feet. "But they're just fucking with us."

"Meaning?" I asked.

"That wasn't a big enough explosion to kill us," Amos said thoughtfully, staring at the blackened spot on the floor, the bluish smoke cloud that hung in the beams of light from the windows. "It was just a message. They still don't want you dead."

"Scared the shit out of me," Jed said, hugging his wife.

"Kat was right," Freya whispered. "The bastards are playing with us. It was a trap. They lured us here...but for what?"

"I say, let's get the fuck out of here and ponder it elsewhere," Darius said.

Sounded like a great idea. We hauled ass without another word. I was so unnerved, I pulled out my phone for one of my check-ups with Mick. I was early, and he was going to give me shit for being paranoid and micromanaging, but hey. Indulging myself when I fucking felt like it was one of the perks of being the boss.

The phone rang...and went to voicemail.

My guts dropped straight down. Mick never missed a call. I tried Ryder, then Trey. Cade. Dale. No response.

"No one's answering their phones at the Mountain House," I announced.

Their heads all whipped around as we loped toward the downed fence.

"The fuck?" Amos asked, yanking out his own phone.

I pulled up the app that monitored the security feeds. Jed, Freya, and the Drakes were all doing the same. I shuffled through the images. They looked tranquil enough. Front view, gate view, front terrace, breezeway, just like they always were, no broken glass, no bullet holes. But I didn't see anyone there. Looking through the picture windows into the TV room, I didn't see Kat and Holly on the couch, either. Then again, they could be in the kitchen, or Holly's room—

"Oh shit," Jed muttered. "Security room. Helipad."

I flicked immediately to those images. The computers were unmanned, and I saw Cade, lying full length on the floor, unconscious. I saw the booted feet of some other man, disappearing into the other side of the camera's view. At the helipad, Mick was sprawled on his side by the stone wall. I couldn't tell if he was alive or dead.

As we took off running, I heard Nicole's mocking laughter in my mind. We were executing her plan exactly as she had wanted us to.

We were just a bunch of kittens, playing with her fucking laser pointer.

CHAPTER 35

Kat

Holly and I dove deep into Harry Potter, until Holly finally dropped off, her head in my lap. I probably could have wiggled away, tucked a pillow where my leg had been, but I couldn't bring myself to move away from her warm weight.

I stared down at the two chicken salad wraps I'd taken off the platter in the kitchen while the story continued to run on the TV. Neither I nor Holly could eat, not so much as a nibble. A brick wall blocked my appetite. Mick had asked me to take the rest of the chicken wraps to the guys in the security room, so at least they hadn't gone to waste.

The intimacy felt good. Having an innocent child trust me enough to fall asleep on me, ahhh. Like being kissed by an angel. Who knew I was so damn sentimental. I'd spent all my energy supercharging my defenses for so long, never sparing a thought for what was inside that barbed-wire perimeter. My tender, undefended heart.

I stared blankly at the TV, stroking Holly's hair and remembering Gabri and Raffi so intensely, I could practically feel them. I remembered the smell of their shampoo, the sound of their voices, the freckles on Gabri's nose, the way Raffi's mascara smeared.

My attention was caught by the sound of a helicopter approaching. My first thought was Ethan and the rest, but they had taken the van, to keep a low profile.

I had decided to tell Ethan that I was sorry for reacting as I had. Truth was, I understood what had impelled them to go look for clues about Shane, no matter the risk, no matter if they were being manipulated. Ethan's barb had been right on the money. If I had ever had even the slightest reason to think my sisters were still alive, I would steamroll anybody on earth who tried to stop me from following up on it.

So it had been pretty unfair of me to get so damned snotty about it.

Then again. He had apologized so nicely. Maybe I should leave matters as they were. After all, apologizing was a muscle men needed to exercise on a regular basis.

The helicopter was getting louder. Maybe Ethan called for one to pick them up, to save time. Rich people operated according to different rules than normal folk.

In any case, the sound was pulling me up out of my emotional reverie. I was too jazzed on stress hormones not to go and check it out. It was silly of me to rouse myself, since we were guarded by an army of Unredeemables, for God's sake. Even so. I was a nervous and suspicious woman. I might as well give in to it.

I slid a hand under Holly's head and held it tenderly as I inched myself out from under her, but Holly's stress levels were high right now, too. She woke with a start.

"What?" she asked sharply. "What's going on?"

"Nothing, I'm sure," I told her. "I just heard a helicopter, and I wanted to see who it was."

Holly leaped up eagerly. "Me, too. I'll go with you."

So I went, holding her hot little hand, which was sticky from the orange and berry flavored gummies she fallen asleep clutching in her fist. We went out onto the terrace, and I squinted up at the helicopter, which was getting closer.

"Mick would have cleared them to land," Holly said knowledgeably. "Let's go to the security room and ask him."

Seemed like a good idea, so we headed to the far side of the huge terrace. Before we got there, Holly let go of my hand and scampered ahead, into the room, calling out to them.

Her voice broke off. "Kat? Come quick!"

Her high, quavering change in tone made me leap into action. I hurried in the door, and stopped with a shocked gasp. Four men sprawled on the floor, unconscious.

"My God," I muttered, crouching down by Cade. Feeling his throat for a pulse.

There was one, thank God, and it was steady. "He's alive, honey," I assured Holly, who stared at the men on the floor. Her face had a blank, shocky look.

I knew that look. I'd felt it on my own face, back in the bad old days.

I checked the other guys, ascertaining with immense relief that they were all still alive, but I was terrified and bewildered by the implications of this. How the fuck...? Drugged, I expect. They had to be. I identified Trey, Cade, Ryder, and Dale. *How?*

"Where's Mick?" Holly's voice was squeaky with panic. "Do you think Mick is sick, too? Maybe he's all alone! We have to find him! Let's go look for him!"

She ran out the door before I could shout to stop her, so I leaped up and gave chase, a looming dread clutching at my insides. Something was terribly wrong, there was danger, and I had to get a handle on it fast. I sprinted to catch up with Holly as she pelted down the breezeway, to the stairs that led up to the helipad and the parking lot.

The helicopter's roar got louder. Then Mick came into view,

walking backward, signaling. Even over the noise, he heard Holly's shout, and turned.

Oh, shit. I knew, the instant I saw his face, even from a distance. It was that look in his eyes. Burned holes opening into the pits of hell. The man was in agony. I recognized it right away. I knew that feeling, far better than I wanted to.

Mick had done this. He had done it reluctantly, but he'd done it. The drugged men in the control room were his work. Whoever was in that helicopter was no friend of ours.

Which meant, we were fucked.

Holly waved her arm at him, jumping. I grabbed her hand and pulled her back. "Come on!" I yelled, over the helicopter's noise. "We have to go!"

"But we have to tell Mick about the—"

"No, baby. We can't talk to Mick about anything," I said.

Holly gulped as the implications of that sank in. "You think that Mick...oh no. He couldn't. Kat. He couldn't!"

"I'm afraid that he did, sweetheart," I said, miserably. "Hurry. How do we get out of the house, and into the woods where we can hide?"

"Hide?" she squeaked. "We have to hide?"

"Focus, please," I pleaded. "Help me. You know this place better than I do. We have to run right now!"

Holly's eyes welled full of tears as she glanced at Mick, but she blinked them away and grabbed my hand. "This way," she said, taking off at a dead run.

We sprinted together. The kid was holding up like a pro, after everything that had happened. I followed her off the terrace and down two flights of stairs, then out a gate that led to a wooden walkway that disappeared into the forest.

We took off down the walkway. I pushed Holly ahead of me to shield her from whatever was behind, and then saw the red dot of the laser sight on the back of her head.

"Stop." A harsh voice shouted. "Stop running, or we'll

shoot. Turn around! Hands up where we can see them! Both of you!"

I stumbled to a halt, stopping Holly, too. The strength went out of my knees.

I couldn't risk it. Couldn't go through it again, the horror of seeing a little girl shot down. I squeezed her hand. "I am so sorry, baby," I whispered.

Holly nodded, doubled over and panting. "Not your fault," she whispered.

We stood there and waited for them, those little red laser dots of instant death trained on us, as men boiled out of the gate we had recently left, swiftly overtaking us. They jerked our hands back, and put plastic cuffs onto both of us.

"Really?" I asked the guy securing Holly. "You're that insecure? You feel the need to cuff an eight-year-old girl?"

"Nine," Holly corrected.

"Shut the fuck up, or I'll gag you both," the guy snarled.

We were dragged by the arms, back up the way we had come. Up the stairs, onto the big terrace, then down the breezeway.

Nicole was waiting for us, Mick next to her, looking ashamed and miserable.

"Mick?" Holly quavered. "Did you...are you on her side? Really? Why?"

"I'm sorry, Holly," he said. "So damn sorry. They got to my Uncle Jay, and they were torturing—"

"Shut up!" Nicole rapped out. "Asshole. I didn't tell you to run your mouth."

"So sorry, sweetheart," Mick said brokenly. "So sorry."

"Don't call her that, asshole," I said icily. "You no longer have that right."

"I said shut *up*, bitch!" Whack, Nicole bashed the pistol across my face, a sharp blow that made my head ring and my vision blur.

I lost track of the conversation for a while, and finally words made sense again.

"...don't have to kill them! They've been drugged!" Mick protested. "They're still out cold, and they will be until well after you're gone. Leave me here, unconscious. Just leave them where they lie. Let them think she did this." He gestured at me. "Wasn't that the plan? Isn't she the new fall guy? She brought them the sandwiches! And I only escaped because I didn't eat any, since my ulcer was acting up. It all tracks, see?"

"Fall guy?" That zapped me back to absolute attention. "Me? What? Who?"

"I wanted to thin them out," Nicole complained. "This is the perfect time."

"But you can't. It ruins the story," Mick pleaded. "You lose me as your inside man if you do that. If you kill them, I have to come with you."

"Or I could just kill you, along with them," Nicole mused. "That would look good, too."

Mick gulped. "I can still be useful," he said thickly.

"Hmm," Nicole scoffed. "You think?"

"You still need me here to establish her as your inside man," Mick insisted. "She's your infiltrator. She drugged the guys, and screwed us all over. If you kill them, that story won't stand up. There won't be anyone to incriminate her. She'll just look like a kidnapped victim to them."

"Don't try to do my job, Drummond," Nicole said. "Are you wearing Kevlar?"

"Yes," he replied. "I had all of us put vests on today when you—"

Bam-bam-bam-bam. She shot him in the chest. "You talk too much," she said.

Mick stumbled against the wall, gasping for air.

"Did that break some ribs? I certainly hope so. It helps your story," Nicole said.

Mick slid down to the ground on his ass, still wheezing for breath.

"I suggest you just collapse," Nicole said brightly. "Take a nap. Wait for your people to get back. I want a report, as soon as they're here, got it?"

He didn't answer, still fighting for air, so she kicked him in the side, making him yelp. "Understand?" she repeated.

"Y-y-yes," he forced out, coughing.

"Don't go into shock and die," she directed sternly. "That would be weak and stupid. If we don't have you working here, there's no reason not to put Jay into the incinerator." Her arm flashed out. A hollow *thunk*, as she whacked him on the side of the head, and Mick toppled to the side, unconscious. Blood matted his hair. "That's better," she said. "That looks good."

Nicole turned, her gaze flicking over us. "Get those two strapped in," she said.

I wished for the whole hellish ride that I could reach out and grab Holly's hand, but they had kept my cuffs on. I tried to do it with my eyes, but poor Holly was staring blankly into space.

I couldn't gauge how long the trip lasted. Not a lot more than an hour, maybe. Cloth bags were jerked down over our heads before we landed, so there was no way to check out the environment there, either.

When we were dragged off the helicopter, we were bundled into the back of a van. Holly was tossed on top of me, which made it possible to curl one of my hands around her fingers. Hers tightened on mine, holding on for dear life.

After some other unmeasurable unit of time driving, the van stopped and we were hauled out. I struggled to keep my balance. I kept staggering and swaying.

I could hear Nicole's crisp, click-click footsteps, and the squeak and scuffle of Holly's athletic shoes, stumbling next to her.

"You turned Mick by hurting his uncle?" I said. "You're a real piece of work."

"Oh, but I am," Nicole replied. "Smelly old geezer doesn't give much satisfaction, though. He's a stoic, and he's too used to pain. I like them nice and fresh and juicy, with so much more to lose. Like you two, for instance. You two will be fun."

That shut me up. I didn't want her to spout any more of her shit to terrify Holly.

Another set of footsteps approached. "You have them here? Wait, don't take them downstairs yet. I want a look at them." A man's voice, youngish.

Nicole ripped the bags off our heads. "Be my guest," she said. "If you must."

We stood there, hair tousled over our faces, blinking and swaying as a slim, well-dressed man with short hair and glasses approached, and looked us over.

"So this is your Payback Bitch, eh?" he said, lifting up a lock of hair that had fallen over my face. "I feel a little let down. She doesn't look as feral and ferocious as I expected."

"Watch out, Vin," Nicole said. "She'll bite off your hand."

"Who the hell are you?" I demanded.

His eyes widened, as if taken aback that I possessed the faculty of speech, and then laughed at me. "I am Vincent Egan, the head of this operation."

"You?" I looked over at Nicole, startled. "This guy is the boss? Then what are the hell are you? His errand girl? His nasty little bitch? His rabid dog?"

"Watch your mouth, Kat," Nicole said, through her teeth. "Or Holly pays."

Vincent laughed delightedly. "Oh, yes. Feisty, bloodthirsty. This is going to be fun, Nicole. You've done well. You're an excellent nasty little bitch. Good girl."

Nicole's smile was frozen stiff. "You're pushing it, Vin. Get out of my way and let me put them to bed. I've got things to do."

We were dragged down a few flights of stairs, into an area that smelled of moisture, mold, cement dust, and worse things that I did not try to identify. A door opened, and a square-built, muscular guy wheeled a gurney out of a small, dark room that looked like a broom closet.

A thin, still figure lay on it, eyes open, his livid body covered with bruises and lesions.

"Don't look," I whispered swiftly to Holly, but she had seen it. Her eyes were huge, bruised-looking, and her lips trembled.

"What the hell is this?" Nicole shrilled. "What happened? Is he dead? Who killed him?"

"Nobody killed him," the man pushing the gurney said sullenly. "Except for you. You're the one's been messing with him. He just croaked, is all. He was sick. And older'n shit."

I put it together. "Oh God. That's Uncle Jay, right? Mick's uncle. You really have been sending Mick nasty videos of you torturing that poor old guy? Oh, Nicole. You just *suck*."

Nicole swung around, backhanding me so that I crashed against the wall. "Put them in Jay's room," she spat out, her voice vindictive. "Since he no longer needs it."

"It's a stinking mess," the guy said. "There's blood every-where, and it—"

"Good. Let them look at it and consider what their future holds."

We were herded into a gray-painted cinderblock room that looked like it had been a broom closet before. It had a narrow, bloodstained cot. Old, brownish blood was spattered on the floor. There was a bloodstained, prison-style toilet and sink.

It smelled unspeakably bad in there.

Nicole hesitated for a moment. She pulled out a blade, and slashed through Holly's cuffs. Then she cut mine, shoving me sharply forward so I was still stumbling when the door slammed shut. When the lock engaged, Holly's mouth began to shake.

I held out my numb, aching arms, and she came right into them.

We found the least bloodstained corner of the room and huddled together on the cold, clammy floor. I cradled Holly in my lap, her head under my chin.

It was so ironic. I could almost laugh, if it wasn't so awful. This whole shitty scenario—being captured, imprisoned, threatened with torture and an early death—all that was old hat for me. I was familiar with that nightmare, because I had always known perfectly well it would end like this for me, sooner or later, once the Petruzzis caught up with me. It was just a matter of time.

But I had clung to the notion that at least this time, I would be alone. That they wouldn't be able to hurt me by hurting my family. They had already done their worst, so I had nothing left to lose, right?

Hah-hah-hah. The joke was on me.

CHAPTER 36

Ethan

I ran down the stairs from the helipad and found Mick sprawled on the ground, the side of his head sticky with drying blood. Jed and Freya sprinted toward the house, calling for Holly as I crouched down and checked his pulse. "He's alive," I told Remy and Darius. "You two. Get him into the house."

I got to my feet, leaving the others to tend to Mick as I ran down the breezeway, I didn't know toward what. Or what I thought I could do now.

The worst had happened. They had neutralized my defenses, which I had trusted implicitly. I had invested so much time and thought in making this place a fortress, in hand-picking the people worthy to defend it. But I'd fucked up, and I had left the people I loved most vulnerable.

Now, I had to pay for my mistake. The ultimate price.

Jed came charging back from the security room, meeting me halfway down the breezeway. Freya followed more slowly, eyes horror-stricken.

"The guys are all unconscious," Jed said grimly. "Alive, but out cold, every last one. Drugged or poisoned. The ambulances are on their way up. No sign of Kat or Holly."

"Oh, God," Freya whispered. "Oh my God. My sweet baby."

Jed pulled Frey into his arms, and I was glad he was there to do it, because I was in no position to give comfort. How the fuck…? How was this possible, that I had left five tough, seasoned, battle-hardened men, tested in the field, men I had trusted my life to multiple times, and Nicole had sliced through them like they were nothing?

There was something terribly wrong here. Not even any signs of a struggle, other than the blood on Mick's head. How the *fuck*…?

We moved forward somehow with caring for our injured. Got Mick inside, carefully worked his jacket off, and then the Kevlar vest which had evidently saved his life, judging from the bruises beneath it.

Mick's eyelids had begun to quiver. They opened a slit, squinting against the light of the lamp.

"Mick," I said. "What the fuck? What happened?"

He coughed, wincing. "She shot me," he whispered. "I had the vest."

"She, who?"

"Nicole, I assume. She didn't introduce herself. Asian woman, or part-Asian. Long haired, fit. Good-looking, I guess. I don't know how she was able to land. I was down on the bottom floor, and I heard the chopper, so I came running up. When I got there, they'd already landed."

"Where are Kat and Holly?"

"They're with her," he croaked out. "I'm so sorry. They're gone."

"Did she say anything?" I demanded.

"Just that she'd be in touch," Mick said, his face tight with agony. "And Kat…"

"What? What about Kat?" I couldn't stop myself from yelling.

"She's with them," Mick said, his voice shaking. "She's... she's one of them. On Nicole's team. I'm so sorry, Ethan. I don't know how it—"

"I don't believe that," I said harshly. "That's not possible."

Mick's face contracted. "I'm so fucking sorry, man," he croaked out. Tears were leaking from his eyes.

The ambulance came, a welcome distraction from what Mick had just said, which was impossible to process. I put it all aside and helped load up Trey, Cade, Dale, and Ryder. Mick refused to go to the hospital with them, in spite of the pain, the broken ribs, his possible concussion. His face was dead pale, lips tight and bluish. He'd always been good buddies with Holly.

When the ambulance was gone, I poured Mick a glass of Scotch and started grilling him, pain or no pain. "What the fuck happened, Mick?"

"Kat must have dosed the sandwiches," Mick said wearily. "We should have what's left of the sandwiches tested. It couldn't have been the coffee, because I was drinking that, and I wasn't affected. But I skipped those chicken wraps. My ulcer was acting up."

"Who made them?" Jed asked.

"Angela," Freya said. "I remember her saying that she'd leave a cold lunch for us before she left. Chicken wraps. But we can certainly rule out Angela."

"Kat brought the sandwiches into the security room," Mick said. "She could have put something in them right before that."

My brain just stopped. Refused to even entertain the thought. No. Fucking. Way.

"Ethan," Mick began, hesitantly. "You have to face the fact—"

"No," I said. "It's not possible. Don't even say it. I'm warning you."

"I have to say it," Mick persisted. "I was the only one who didn't eat one of those chicken wraps. This was an inside job. I saw her leave with Nicole, talking with her, on good terms with her. I'm sorry, Ethan."

"But she ran away yesterday," I said. "To protect us. Why would she do that?"

"To make it look good, I expect," Mick said. "She knew damn well you'd chase her. They probably timed Nicole's attack to coincide with the moment you showed up. We were all wondering how you two got away so easily yesterday, and this explains it. Nicole wanted Kat to go back with you for a tender reconciliation. To consolidate your bond. It's not your fault it worked so well. Any one of us would have been fooled."

I sat there, my mind blank, while they hashed it out, voices raised, arguing with Mick. Freya, like me, wasn't ready to accept it yet. Jed just looked miserable and unsure. I just sat there, watching my whole world go to shit, trying to imagine how I could have been that wrong. That gullible.

For God's sake. I had been begging that woman to marry me. Laying my fortunes at her feet. And if this impossible thing was true, then she had preferred to hurt and terrify an innocent little girl rather than accept my love.

Fuck. The cognitive dissonance was shaking my mind to pieces.

Then Holly's princess phone rang. A single buzz. I grabbed it, and found a text message like this morning's. It read HAVING FUN YET? It was followed by a link.

Freya, Jed, and Mick hung over my shoulder as I hit "play." I couldn't even breathe, I was so terrified at what she might make us watch.

The video began with a smiling cartoon pig mask which filled the entire screen. Sharp dark eyes glittered through the eyeholes, which had exaggerated fake lashes glued on, and the mouth was an exaggerated, pouting pink cupid's bow. The effect was grotesque, especially when the pig began to speak in a mechanically distorted voice. But there was no question of who it was who was speaking. Her vibe was unmistakeable.

"Hello, Ethan, Freya, Jed!" the pig said. "I'm enjoying our stimulating game so much. I was impressed by how quickly you got to the warehouse. And kudos to you all, for not losing a hand to my fun little surprise! I suppose you're wondering if your niece and your girlfriend are still in one piece, and the answer is yes...for now. But you may or may not be surprised to know that your new bed toy is actually one of mine. That's how we got in and out so smoothly. She's a real find, I must say. So talented, so intense! If it's any consolation, she found it no chore to service you sexually. In fact, she told me all about your heroic exploits!"

I stared at the screen, seeing it and everything else tinted red from the rage that permeated my entire being.

"Your blonde fuckbunny made the whole thing possible. So many things you don't know about your new little friend! Like her connection to domestic terror groups, for instance. Go ahead, do some research on her while you're waiting for your marching orders. She's been spewing hate in online forums ever since it was a thing. Her handle is Payback Bitch 898. Amuse yourself by exploring her hidden depths! But you really should have known, Ethan. I mean, all that blood and trauma? What did you expect?"

"Blood and trauma?" Jed asked. "What's she talking about?"

"Later," I snarled. "Shhh."

"...anyway, never mind the traitorous bitch, right?" Nicole went on. "Let's talk about little Holly." The camera panned over, landing on Holly, who sat in a straight-backed chain and stared straight at the camera. She appeared to be unharmed, her hands unbound and clasped on her lap, but her face was dead pale. She was frowning, blinking back tears. Squeezing her eyes shut, then blinking, then closing, looking straight at the camera. Probably trying not to cry. Such a tough kid.

"Say hello to your Uncle Ethan, Holly," Nicole directed.

"Hello," Holly said woodenly.

Nicole's pig mask appeared again in the camera's view next to Holly, this time brandishing a sharp knife. "Oh, no, no, no," Freya whimpered. "Don't, don't, don't."

Nicole yanked up a lock of Holly's rumpled dark blonde hair, but Holly didn't wince, just kept staring and blinking. Maybe she was in a fugue state.

Nicole hacked it off, and flung it at the camera. "Do as I tell you, understand? Instructions will arrive soon. No police, or Holly will pay. I'll be in touch."

The video ended.

"What did she mean?" Jed asked. "About the blood and trauma? Should you have suspected something? Why, Ethan?"

I shook my head, still unable to speak.

Mick stepped into the breach. "Kat had some trouble in her past," he explained. "Her older and younger sisters were both whacked by the mob right in front of her when she was only fourteen. She testified against the killer and got him put in jail, but the crime family's been after her ever since. She went into Witness Protection."

"Oh, my God." Freya said. "That's terrible. And even so, I don't see how the woman I met could have done this. I just don't buy it."

Mick shook his head, his eyes full of raw pain. "I am so sorry," he muttered.

"It's not your fault," I said dully. "I'm the one who rolled out the red carpet for a honeytrap spy, not you."

"Don't call her that," Freya said sharply. "I'm not ready to accept Nicole's word about fucking anything, Ethan."

"But how else can we possibly explain what happened?" Amos asked. "The drugged sandwiches, and all that?"

"Honestly? Even the sandwiches seem out of character for Nicole," Freya said. "If Nicole were doing this, she wouldn't have had our people drugged. She would have used something horrible that causes an agonizing death, preferably with lots of blood. That's more her speed." She turned to Mick. "And you," she said. "I don't mean to be cold or heartless, but I confess, I'm puzzled that she didn't pump bullets into your head. She left you alive. Was that just sloppy? Or was it on purpose?"

"Don't know," Mick said, his voice colorless. "Might have been better if she killed me."

"Do not mope, Mick," Freya snapped. "Not useful. We have enough problems."

"Can you imagine what Shane would say, if he knew?" I asked. "I completely failed. I did not protect his little girl."

"This is not your fault!" Freya said furiously. "Don't blame yourself! You have been doing everything possible to keep us safe! Even when we make it almost impossible, like I did. You never stop trying. You go to outrageous lengths!"

"Maybe, but even so," I said. "That bitch has our baby girl. I fucked up."

"And why is that on you, rather me, or Jed, or any of us?" Freya was crying angry tears. "Damn you, Ethan. You always think you have to be the big man. The smartest one, the one who is in charge, the one who carries us all and takes all the responsibility. But it's too much. You can't ever make a goddamn mistake. If Kat really is a mistake, and I will tell you from the heart, I am not convinced of that yet."

"I don't see any reason to deny reality when it's being shoved down my throat," I said. "I was thinking with the little head. That's all."

"There's no way you could have known, if it was Kat who

betrayed us. We all loved her. All of us bonded with her. Holly loved her, Angela loved her, you loved…"

Her voice trailed off. I got up, waving her back, and walked outside, going over to the railing to look down into the mountain valley, letting the breeze cool my hot face.

Yeah, I had loved her.

I couldn't connect the two realities in my mind. The Kat who I loved, and the Kat who had betrayed Holly to torture and terror. They couldn't be the same person.

I had spent the last eight months trying not to picture my brother being tortured, and I had thought there couldn't be anything worse.

This wasn't worse. It was just more of the same, multiplied by infinity.

Freya followed and leaned on the railing next to me. I couldn't look at her.

"I just hate it," she said. "It's so wrong. The minute you finally let down your guard, the very first goddamn time in my life that I ever see you do it, you get stabbed to the heart. That just hurts me."

I nodded. "Yeah," I whispered. "Me, too."

CHAPTER 37

Kat

I drifted in and out of a nightmare-studded haze of exhaustion that couldn't really be called sleep. Not when every time I dozed off, I was jerked awake by the image of my sisters. Gabri, curled up on the floor in the fetal position, a pool of blood spreading fast. Raffi, with the bullet wound in her chest. Blood sprayed all over the kitchen tiles.

Holly was sitting in my lap, also fitfully asleep. We couldn't use the bed, since it was in a grisly state, so we had opted for the cold concrete floor in the corner. Holly's weight had put my ass to sleep, but that was a small price to pay. I wasn't shifting her limp, warm weight for anything.

Holly had come to represent everything that was good in the world. Everything worth fighting for...or even dying for. I would have made that sacrifice for Gabri, or Raffi if I had been given the chance. Who knew, maybe I'd get another shot. Real soon.

So, yeah. These were the things I aspired to. A glorious death, traded for the life of someone I loved. What a weirdo I was. Almost funny, if you thought about it.

Well, on second thought, not really.

Holly stirred, and looked up at me. I smiled at her, and she tried to smile back.

"Hey," I said, "You were too stressed out before to tell me what happened when Nicole took you away. Did you send that message, like we talked about?"

"I tried, for sure. Hope I got it right." Holly sighed, snuggling closer. "But everything she did was super creepy and gross."

"That doesn't surprise me one bit," I said.

"She put on a pig mask for the video," Holly said. "Which is super insulting to pigs. Pigs are nice. She's horrible."

"I couldn't agree more," I said. "And? What did she tell them?"

"She said you were the one who drugged the guys. That you worked for her, and that you'd tricked Uncle Ethan. She said a whole lot of mean things. Like, that you were a terrorist, and stuff."

"Well, I'm not," I said. "She's a big liar."

"I know that," Holly said. She gazed over in the direction of the blood-spattered cot. "I was thinking about Mick."

Hah. She wasn't the only one. "What about him?" I asked.

"I think I understand why he did it," Holly said softly. "If they were hurting his poor uncle. That old guy we saw. I wouldn't be able to stand it if someone was hurting Uncle Ethan or Auntie Frey. Or you. So, like...I get it."

I harrumphed. "Thanks, honey. That's very charitable of you, but you'll have to excuse me for still being mad as hell at him. Especially since they're pinning it on me right now. Everyone back at the Mountain House thinks I'm the villain. Not fun."

"Well, I don't think you are," Holly assured me. "I know you're good. And when they save us, I'll tell them the truth, so it'll all be okay in the end."

I gave her a tight hug, wishing I could share her innocent faith.

I was under no illusion that I'd be able to protect her from anything here, and she was used to her uncle's strength and agency. God knows, the kid could be forgiven for thinking Ethan was superhuman. He seemed like one to me, too. Disillusioned, prickly, cynical scold that I was, he still seemed like a goddamn superhero.

At that moment, the lock rattled. We jerked upright, cringing back to the wall.

Nicole walked in, followed by a huge, shaven-bald guy with a thick, heavy face and vacant eyes. He held a gun on us, his expression utterly blank.

Nicole sat on the edge of the bloodstained mattress, heedless of the gore, and crossed her legs.

"We have things to discuss," she said.

"I have nothing to say to you," I said.

"That's convenient, since I'm the one talking, and you're the one listening," Nicole said. "All you need to do is say, 'yes, I understand.'"

"I won't do anything for you," I announced.

Her lips curved in a pitying smile at the false bravado in my tone. "Of course you will, Kat. You can forget about your reputation. It's gone. Permanently trashed. It's been documented now, on many forums, that you are a bloodthirsty psychopath, steeped in hatred. You want nothing for the world but pain and destruction and fiery death."

I snorted before I could stop myself. "So, essentially, I'm you?"

Nicole tittered. "Oh, no. I want much more than that. I also want power, money, and absolute control. But Kat Banner, aka the Payback Bitch 898, doesn't have that kind of vision. She just wants to burn and kill. And tomorrow, she finally gets her wish.

She gets to end her miserable life, in a blaze of self-immolating glory. Ka-boom!"

My jaw ached from clenching my teeth so hard, and my lungs just wouldn't expand. I wished Holly was not hearing this. Her body was rigid in my arms.

"No one who knows me would believe that," I said.

"Well, not all that many people really know you at all, do they, Francesca? Ever since that awful thing that happened in Jersey City all those years ago, you've kept yourself so aloof from the world. Except online, of course. That was your only emotional outlet, and you have been so prolific! You've been posting in hate groups daily for years now, spewing toxic rage like a fire hose. It's all there, ready and waiting for the forensic psychologists to pore over and write bestselling books about afterward. There will be a miniseries for sure. Multiple documentaries. The whole enchilada."

"I don't have an online presence at all," I said stiffly. "On purpose."

"Well, great!" she said brightly. "That plays right into my hands. Because Payback Bitch 898 sure does. I'm very good at setting a scene."

"How could you set this scene up so fast? You only just found out I exist!"

"I've been cultivating Payback Bitch for years," Nicole said. "Keeping her in my back pocket, just waiting for you to turn up and embody her. She was a real person once. I took notice of her, and thought all that psychotic rage would have to prove useful somehow. But the real woman was a big letdown, when I tracked her down. Dull, boring, tediously self-absorbed, with bad hair and an overbite and some sort of bacterial overgrowth that gave her terrible body odor. Her online persona was the valuable asset, far more interesting than her physical self. So, I took the asset, and scrapped the rest."

I blew out a sharp breath. "You...you killed her? For her online *handle?*"

"Oh, stop. I did the poor woman a favor," Nicole said lightly. "God knows she wasn't enjoying her wretched little life. I took over Payback Bitch myself. I've been cultivating her ever since. I pruned her, expanded her, cleaned her up, and now, she can become you, seamlessly, like slipping on a coat. It's worked out so perfectly. The original Payback Bitch's grammar was a bit iffy, but not many people have heard you speak, so I'm not worried. And I've been improving her grammar slowly, over time."

I stared at her. Wow. And I had thought the Petruzzis were evil. They were small potatoes compared to this terrifying, inhuman thing, smiling at me.

"You are vile," I said.

Nicole bowed, as if I had given her a compliment. "So," she said briskly. "Your itinerary. Pay attention. The Emory Summit, a gathering of leaders in the world of banking, investments, trade, is being held at the brand-new Willamette Convention Center right now, not far from here. It's in full swing today, over a thousand attendees, and tomorrow at noon, Owen Halliwell will give the keynote address. Tomorrow morning, your job is to drive a caterer's van full of explosives into the Conference Center's parking garage. It will detonate during Halliwell's speech, on live TV. The explosion will kill everyone in the radius of an entire city block."

"I can't do that," I whispered. "I can't."

Nicole did not seem to hear me. "The whole country will hate and revile you, but it won't matter, because you'll be dead. We'll have your boyfriend running his magic algo for us, if he wants to keep his little niece in one piece. He'll manage the financial chaos post-bombing, and we'll come out vastly rich. Rulers of the new world order."

"I won't do it," I told her.

"Of course you will," Nicole said briskly. "Your van will have a screen with an open video call. It will show you everything I'm doing to your little friend. In real time."

The icy hole inside me got bigger, deeper. Impossibly deep. Nicole saw it, and started to laugh. Nicole was absolutely right, and we both knew it.

She had me by the throat.

CHAPTER 38

Ethan

Freya came into the room, holding a steaming cup of tea, and looked over my shoulder at the computer screen in front of me. Mick was sprawled in a chair with his hand over his eyes. Jed lay on the couch. The air in the room was heavy with despair.

The video Nicole had sent kept looping on the screen. I had turned off the sound, since I had already processed every word the woman had said, as well as how she said it. But something compelled me to keep studying it. I kept feeling as if I was missing something. Like a phantom flicker in the corner of my eye. Driving me nuts.

"Some tea?" she asked.

I shook my head.

"Maybe take a break?" Freya suggested gently. "You've been looking at that awful thing for hours. Give your mind a rest. It'll work better for you later. You used to lecture me about that yourself, when I was cramming in high school. Remember?"

"Soon," I said stonily. "Not yet."

Holly appeared on the screen next to cartoon-pig-Nicole,

staring. Said hello. Nicole yanked her hair. Holly did not flinch. She never took her eyes off the camera, except to blink. Her eyes seemed so strangely blank and faraway, opening and closing as if she were drugged. She had a deep frown line between her eyebrows.

She looked ferociously concentrated. Strange, considering the stress she was under. I would have expected to see terror, confusion.

I had seen that look on Holly's face while she was trying to solve a puzzle, or doing some math calculation in her head, or playing mental chess with me in the car. We did that a lot, visualizing the chessboard as we sped down the highway. I'd done it with Shane and Freya, too, back in the day. Good exercise for the brain.

Holly was thinking too hard to be as frightened as she should be of that woman. What was she thinking? Was the frown just an effort to be tough? That blinding light in her face was making her eyes blink and water. She kept squeezing them shut, then staring at the camera, then blink-blink-blink. Short blinks, a long squeeze...wait. Wait.

Oh...holy...fucking...*fuck.*

A pattern. There was a pattern to her blinking! I jerked up in my chair, knocking the keyboard askew on the table and making everyone in the room jump to attention. God, what an idiot, not to have seen it sooner. Not to have expected it from Holly.

"Morse code," I said. "Holly is talking to us. With the blinking."

"Holy God," Freya spilled her hot tea over herself in her excitement, hissing with pain and flapping her hand as she hastened to get nearer the screen. "Run it back, run it back, to when we first see her. Do you remember Morse code?"

"Yes." I dragged the message bar back to where Holly first

appeared on the screen as Jed appeared behind me, and Mick on the other side.

"That kid," Jed said, in a low, wondering tone. "She's going to rule the world someday, and the world will be lucky to have her do it."

"Hold on to that thought," I said tersely, grabbing paper and a pen. "But don't distract me. Dah-dah-dah, space, dit-dah, space, dah-dit-dah-dah, space, dit-dit, space, dit-dit-dit, space, dah-dit-dit, space, dit, space, dit-dah, space, dah-dit-dit, space, dit-dah-dah-dah space, dit-dah—and that's it. That's all. Then it ends."

The video ended. I stared down at what I had written. It was incomprehensible.

I cursed under my breath, ran the video back, and went through it again to make sure there were no mistakes from my end.

Jed leaned over my shoulder, staring at the paper. "OAYIS-DEADJA," he said softly. "Means nothing to me. Maybe the video cut her off before she could finish."

"Wait," Freya said sharply. "The first letter, that O. O is three dahs, right? But what if we missed the first dit because she started blinking before the camera landed on her, and that letter was actually a J? Maybe she started repeating the message with those last two letters. Change the O to a J, lose the last two repeating letters, and it's JAYISDEAD. Jay is dead."

"Yeah," I said. "And those are words, in English. But it still means nothing to us."

"Could she be getting a letter wrong, or more than one? God, the kid just learned Morse code yesterday, when you gave her that book! Could she be telling us a place name? A town, a building, a business? Suppose the D were actually an H? The dah-dit-dit becoming four dits? Oayisthead, Jayishead? Shit, we are so close! I can feel it!"

"Me too," I said. "I'll write a program that can run through every possible permutation she might be getting wrong, and we can—"

"No," Mick's low voice said, behind us. "Holly didn't get any letters wrong."

I spun around in the chair, startled. "Why do you say that? Do you recognize it?"

"Yes." Mick's face was stiff, as if he was braced for a blow. "The reason you don't understand this message is because it's not for you. It's for me."

The room was deathly quiet. We all stared at Mick. I felt like the ground was about to open beneath my feet. I took a deep breath, flexed my hands. "Explain that statement," I said. "And don't make us wait."

"It's about my great-uncle,'" Mick said, his voice bleak. "Jay Drummond. He took me in when my dad threw me out, when I was fifteen years old. He was tough, but fair. He pulled me into shape. Helped me get through school, pushed me toward the military. He was a good man. My real father, in every way that counted."

"Okay. Now tell me how Holly knows he's dead," I said, although the obvious answer to that was unfolding in my mind. Along with a world-splitting anger.

"They took him." Mick's voice thickened and broke. "A couple of months ago. They've been sending me videos. Hurting him, to keep me in line. To make me inform. Jay has cancer. Had cancer, I mean," he corrected himself. "It had gone into his spine. Extremely painful. She liked to film him, in agony, no pain meds, and show it to me. Then she started beating him. Cutting him. She always had to escalate it. Every time."

"You're the mole." Jed's voice hard. "You, Mick. You've known us for ten years. You threw Kat under the bus, and handed Holly over to that hell-bitch."

"I am so sorry," Mick said. "I love her. Holly is like my own—"

His voice choked off as I seized his throat and slammed him against the wall.

"You put our little girl on the block," I said. "I don't care what reason you had. You hurt my baby girl, and I will kill you for it."

From far away, I was vaguely conscious of Mick clawing at my hands, mouth open, eyes bulging. Through the roaring in my ears, I heard Freya and Jed, on either side of me, yelling in my ear.

Amos and Darius and Remy pried my hands loose from his throat and dragged me back, as Mick slid heavily to the ground. "You fucking traitor!"

Mick clutched his throat, gasping for breath, his eyes wet. "I know," he ground out, wheezing desperately. "It's true. I'm sorry. But I had to. They were hurting my—"

"She's nine years old!" I yelled, lunging against the Drake brothers' iron grip. "She trusted you! And Kat? You despicable, lying asshole, pinning your shit on her!"

"Yes, he's a spy," Freya blocked me, her hands flat against my chest. "Yes, he was their mole, and yes, he's an asshole who deserves everything coming to him, but right now, he's our only hope, Ethan! So don't you dare kill him! We *need* him!"

I struggled to pull it back, to breathe. My whole body shook with rage.

Freya stepped back, and looked down at Mick. "Get up, Mick," she said crisply. "You're no use to us cowering on the floor. It bugs me."

Mick did as she directed, stumbling to his feet. He couldn't look us in the eyes.

"You are a traitor and a shithead, but I'm sorry for your loss," she said, her voice oddly formal. "Holly set you free, at great cost to herself. I hope you're grateful."

Mick nodded, his eyes downcast. "I am," he muttered. "I wish I could make you understand how sorry I am."

"We really don't care, Mick," Freya said. "We have more important things to think about than your feelings. And so far, you've definitely put yourself first."

His face contracted. "I know. And I'm so fucking sorry. It's been torture."

"Hmm. Really." Freya put her hands on her hips, and swept her gaze over all of us, like the teacher about to give a tough assignment. His sister, taking charge, as she was born to do. "Thanks to Holly, we know they have lost their leverage over Mick. But they do not know that he knows. That's the only small advantage we have. Our job now is to exploit it. So, everybody? You all need to get really fucking smart, right now." She glanced at Mick. "If you're still with us, of course."

"Fuck, yes," Mick said fervently. "Please, let me help make this right. If I can help save Holly—mmmfff!"

I slammed him against the wall by the throat again. "Get her name out of your lying traitor's mouth," I hissed.

Mick grunted and mewled, mouthing the word *please*.

"If at any time you need to refer to her, you can call her 'Miss Masters,' or 'your niece.'" I growled. "Is that perfectly clear?"

Yes, Mick mouthed.

"Let go, Ethan," Freya said sternly. "We don't have time to emote. Let's work."

I let go and stepped back, convulsively flexing and fisting my hands. I was going to have to try not to look at him, or I would lose my shit, and tear him to shreds.

"Why the fuck didn't you tell us?" Jed asked him. "We would have done anything to help you."

Mick rubbed his reddened eyes. "I almost did," he said hoarsely. "More times than I could count. But it was almost like Nicole could smell it on me, in the air. Just as I was working up my nerve, another video-call would come in. Jay, screaming. Every new one worse than the last. Every time, I kept thinking, I'll just keep pretending to be compliant, keep gathering more intel until I can save Jay, and that just stretched on and on. I swear, I'm not trying to excuse myself."

I just stared at him. "You're not holding anything back now, right?"

"No reason to," he said dully. "I'm all yours."

That made me flinch. "Don't say that, because I don't want you, asshole. Hey. Are you wearing a listening device? Did they put anything on you? Inside your body?"

"No," Mick said. "So far, all contact has been on the phone."

"And how about that phone? Have they put anything in it? Do they listen to us? Have you planted anything here?"

"No. Just your phone. I have been listening to your calls, for the last few days."

That stung. I gritted my teeth. "You asshole. This whole time."

"Yes. I'm sorry. But I was able to persuade Nicole that you would be sure to find any bugs or cameras with your obsessive bug-sweeping protocol, so she didn't make me plant anything here," he said. "I haven't found anything running on my phone, but I leave it in a drawer by my bed, just in case." Mick pulled out another phone. "I've got another one. With a sensor that alerts me if her ringtone sounds, so I won't miss her calls."

Amos stepped forward. "Okay, Mick," he said. "What have you got for us that you can trade for your worthless, miserable life?"

"It better be fucking good," Remy said, his arms folded over his brawny chest.

"I'll give you all of it." Mick sat at a computer and inserted a flash drive. "First off, their plan is to explode a huge mother-fucking bomb at some financial summit in Portland." He glanced at me. "The one you were supposed to go to."

"The Emory Summit," I said. "Right. I bailed, after the elevator incident."

"They needed a suicide bomber," Mick said, his voice flat and lifeless. "I was sure they were planning to force me to do it, by threatening to do some horrible thing to Jay. But they probably decided they liked Kat better, after I told them about the mob hit on her sisters. All the violence in her past tracks better with the—"

"You told Nicole about Kat's past? For real? You *volunteered* that information?"

"I...I had to," Mick admitted, miserably.

"The summit has already started," I said. "It's in full swing now. I was supposed to give the opening statements this morning."

"Yes," Mick said. "She decided to wait to nab you, until closer to the summit. They made their play in the elevator, but that went to hell, so they moved on to this."

"If the summit has begun, the bomb could go off anytime," Jed mused.

"They'll reel me in first," I said thoughtfully. "They'll want me right on hand, to do their dirty work afterward. In all the chaos."

"I bet she would wait to detonate the bomb until the moment when the most people possible are looking," Freya said. "She's a grandstanding bitch. She wants it to be seen by everyone."

"So, the keynote address?" Darius mused.

Freya paged through something on her phone, frowning at the screen. "That's tomorrow—no, it's midnight thirty, so it's today," she said. "At noon. Jesus, it's all happening right now. We've got no time."

All eyes turned to Mick. He looked around, throat bobbing.

"So?" I prompted. "Where the fuck are they? How many? Give us everything."

"I don't have a lot," he admitted. "Today was only the second time they made any physical contact with me, aside from the very beginning."

"Which was what? Spit it out," I prompted, through my teeth. I was going to have to drag this shit out of that dickhead.

"I met Nicole in a bar," Mick admitted. "She chatted me up. Then she took me out into the parking lot and invited me into her car. I got in thinking I was going to get lucky. Then she showed me the first video of Jay, and my whole world went to shit."

We all looked away from him. The conflict, being so murderously angry and also feeling his shock, horror, and despair—it made my flesh creep. "What did you do?"

"I was so blown away, I didn't get anything more than her license plate that night," he said. "When I followed it up, it was just a long-term rental from the Seattle airport. Reported stolen six months ago. When they told me they were coming today, I prepared as best I could. I still hoped I could save Jay, so I—"

"We don't give a fuck what you were hoping," Darius snarled. "We would have, if you'd come to us for help. We would have done any fucking thing in the world for you. But you didn't, so fuck you. Stick to the point. What have you got for us now?"

Mick pulled up a city map. I came closer, recognizing the rivers and bridges of Portland, Oregon, a few hours' drive from us. "I needed to find out where they were headquartered," he said. "When she said she was coming, I rolled up about two hundred of the round mini traces in sand-colored putty and scattered them all over the helipad. I figured someone was bound to step on one of them, and take it back in his boot treads."

"Did they?"

"Yes. Six of them made it into the helicopter. And they all

went...here." He pointed. "A defunct hydraulics factory in northwest Portland. It's called Braithwaite."

Darius nodded, slowly. "And you chose to let hours go by before telling us."

"I was waiting to see if they contacted—"

"Shut the fuck up, Mick. We're not interested," Remy said curtly. "Let's go to Portland."

"Wait." Mick held up his hand. "We can't just up and leave—"

"Watch me," Remy retorted.

"Really. Listen," Mick pleaded. "She'll have specific instructions for Ethan. She'll expect him to follow them exactly, in real time, and if he doesn't, she'll punish Holly and make you watch. Trust me, I know. She does not bluff. On the contrary. She gets off on it. We have to at least seem compliant. Both of us do."

"Don't ask me to trust you," I said. "You were pretty fucking compliant, Mick."

Mick let out a slow breath, lifting his hands. "Yes," he said softly. "Yes, I was. I hate myself for it. I'm so sorry. I'll do anything I can to fix this."

"Let me tell you how this works," I said. "If we pull off a miracle, and Holly and Kat all live through this, you can leave. Go as far away on this earth as it is possible to go. I never want to see or hear from you again. But if anyone I care about gets hurt, then nothing can save you. I will hunt you down, and I will tear you to pieces."

Mick gave me a jerky nod. "Fair enough," he said. "I'm willing to die, if it comes to that. Grateful, even."

"I don't give a fuck if you're willing or grateful," I told him.

Mick nodded. "So, back to being compliant. When she calls, she's going to order you to go straight to her. Alone and unarmed. What are you going to do?"

I shrugged. "I'll go," I said. "What the fuck else can I do?"

Freya made a sound under her breath. "Oh, God, Ethan."

"You're a fine one to talk," I told her. "You pulled the exact same stunt yourself when they got Jed. I don't want to hear a single fucking word about it out of you."

"Aside from that," Amos said. "You and Mick have to look compliant, but the rest of us don't, right? That is, if Mick is telling the truth."

"I am telling the truth," Mick said, through his teeth.

Amos's eyebrows tilted up. "If he's telling the truth about the surveillance situation," he repeated, his voice stony. "...then she doesn't have eyes on us at the moment. Darius and Remy and I could go on down to Portland right now, and start gathering intel on Braithwaite. There's no time to lose."

"It's safest to assume Nicole monitors our outside gate," I said.

"Then we'll go out the tunnel," Amos said. He turned to Mick. "Unless you told Nicole about the tunnel, of course."

"Of course not," Mick muttered.

The tunnel was an escape hatch I'd designed when I built the place. It was a short tunnel blasted through the rock that led from the garage to a longer, hidden natural passage through the thick woods. It opened out onto an old logging road a couple of miles away that connected with the highway farther on. If they didn't use headlights, no one would ever see them leave.

"Sounds great," I said. "Thanks. Make it happen. Please."

"Okay. Darius and Remy and I will blast out of here right now. We'll set up shop as close to Braithwaite as possible. Send in a fleet of micro-drones, check the place out, start getting hard intel right now. Preferably before she reels you in. Keep us posted as to what she says and does."

I nodded, grateful for their loyalty and their competence. "Excellent."

"Then let's load up and go." Amos got to his feet, and Remy

SHANNON MCKENNA

and Darius followed suit. They hesitated, near the door, looking uncomfortable.

"Good luck," Darius said.

"Watch yourself," Remy said.

I nodded. After the Drakes filed out, the room took on a suffocating, breathless silence, like we were all waiting for an ax to fall. In a way, we were.

I made an inpatient gesture at Mick. "So? What are you waiting for? Give it all to us. Blow by blow. Every interaction you ever had with her."

For the next couple of hours, we grilled Mick mercilessly, and combed through every data point he could give us. The trackers, five of the six, were still clustered in the Braithwaite facility. One wandered off for a while, but soon came back. Maybe someone going out to fill a vehicle with gas, or going to pick up take-out.

We studied satellite photos of the place, we hacked blueprints, we searched out sales records. It had been bought by a shell company, and there wasn't either the time or the headspace tonight to do the kind of nitpicky forensic accounting work necessary to track down who owned what. Chances were, they'd covered their tracks well, in any case.

At some point, I got up to stretch my legs, and went to the kitchen. I turned on the water in the sink, splashed my head and face. Grabbed one of Angela's neatly ironed tea towels to rub my hot face, my aching head. My jaw hurt from grinding my teeth.

Freya followed me, and leaned on the kitchen entryway, studying me.

"Try not to punish Mick right now," she said quietly. "Do it later, if you want. When Holly and Kat are safe. We need him as functional as possible right now."

I shrugged. "I'm being more than fair. He made his choice,

and he didn't choose Holly. I'm being as civil as it is humanly possible to be, under the circumstances."

She nodded. "I feel the same. It's a fucking nightmare. And even so. I can already think of three things to be grateful for right now."

"Tonight? Really?" I let out a harsh laugh. "Three?"

"True thing," she said, her face solemn.

"I know you want to tell me what they are, so go on. Put me out of my misery."

"That, big brother, is beyond my power right now. But here they are. One, I'm so incredibly glad Angela wasn't here when all this came down."

I hissed in a sharp breath, imagining it. "Fuck, yeah," I muttered. "That's lucky."

"Two, our niece is brilliant," Frey went on. "She broke the spell Nicole had on Mick, which left us an opening. Not much of one, but still. What a kid."

"Okay, I'll concede that one, too," I said. "Holly rocks. And the third?"

Freya gave me a gentle smile. "Kat," she said softly. "She was for real, from the very start. No matter what happens, you don't have to swallow that bitter pill. Your heart steered you true. You were right to trust it. That's something to celebrate."

I have no idea what look must have come over my face, but she made a low sound in her throat, grabbed me, and held on tight.

I hid my face in her curly hair and just kept on trying to breathe.

CHAPTER 39

Ethan

Holly's phone buzzed again. The sound worked on me like an electric shock.

One single ring, and the phone lay silent. I picked it up. A new text message was highlighted. The subject line was HUP HUP BETTER GET MOVING!

Like the other time, there was a video link in the message. I set it to play.

Nicole was wearing the hideous pig mask again. She gave them a finger-fluttering wave. "Good morning, Mr. Masters!" Somehow, the electronic voice modifier did not remove the toxic, sickly sweetness from her tone. "Welcome to your new identity, as our humble, hardworking little bitch!"

"Go fuck yourself," Freya snapped. "Snotty hag."

"Shhh," I hissed. "Listen."

"I know you're eager to hear your first instructions. First of all, all the plotting and planning you're doing to rescue Holly? Forget it. Not going to happen. Accept it, and everything will be easier. Especially for Holly, if you get my drift."

I clenched both my hands as she spoke, trying to breathe

down the anger. I needed to be cold for this. Distant, detached, sharp as a razor blade.

"It's time for you to get into your car, and drive at the legal speed limit to this address in downtown Portland...alone." She held up a small whiteboard, with a street address scrawled on it in pen. "Leave your car outside, right on the street, keys inside. We'll take care of it for you. It's not like you'll ever need it again, God knows."

"God, I hate her so much," Jed muttered.

"When you go inside, tell the security guard you need to talk to Franco," she went on. "He'll tell you what to do. And another thing, very important. Come with no cell phone, no trackers or traces, no electronic devices of any kind. You'll be going through a portal that can sense everything, even items that are hidden inside your body, so don't even try to get sneaky. Or Holly will pay. Do not doubt it."

The pig fell silent for a moment, waiting as if waiting for a response from him. Then she made an impatient shooing gesture with her hand. "So? Get moving! Don't just sit there trying to think of a way to trick me. There isn't one. I have thought of everything. And remember. No one follows you. And I mean no one."

The video ended. I looked around at all of them. "So," I said. "Time to go."

"You're just throwing yourself into her mouth," Freya said. "Just like that."

"I'll go out the main gate," I said. "You three go out through the tunnel." I turned to Mick. "If she contacts you, tell her that Freya and Jed have taken off, and are following me against my orders."

Mick looked shocked. "But...but she specifically said that no one—"

"She knows Jed and Freya. She knows perfectly well those two would die before they willingly stayed behind, certainly if family's involved. If you try to convince her they're doing as they're told, she'll get suspicious."

"But what am I supposed to tell her, for fuck's sake? That I stayed behind, that I'm with them? She'll want me to bring them in! I won't know what to tell her!"

I shrugged. "Tell her they're hard to manage. She knows that already. Tell her you're struggling, that you can't control them. Maintain what trust she has in you. Figure it out. Play dumb. Stall. Play for time. I can't do it for you. Your part's out of my hands, so step up, for fuck's sake!"

Mick nodded slowly. "Okay," he said. "Okay, I'll do what I can."

Freya hugged me. I was in frozen mode, and I felt as if she were hugging another person, and I was watching remotely, from someplace far away. Jed gave me a fierce hug as well. I wished I felt present for it. Who knew if this was the last time.

I went out and up the breezeway, out onto the helipad. Got into the first car I came across in the garage. Freya and Jed trailed after me. Her face was shiny with tears.

"Stay sharp, for Holly," I told her. "And keep an eye on Mick."

She nodded. I activated the gate opener, and found myself reflecting bitterly upon how much money, effort, design, and thought had gone into the security of this place, and how little it all meant in the end.

Aw, fuck it. We all had our weak spots. It was just a matter of who was more ruthless at exploiting them. I would never regret loving my family.

It was hypocritical to be so furious at Mick. I was exactly as compromised as he had been. Obediently doing as I was told, just as he had done, and I hadn't even gotten myself spanked yet, not like he had. Over and over. Brutally.

I didn't dare let myself think about that. My soul recoiled from it.

Master of Secrets 325

And our plan wasn't even a plan yet. There wasn't enough info plugged into it to decide upon any course of action. There was nothing to do but wait for more. Go in there, blind, no plan. Fingers crossed that the Drakes could pull something out of their asses that might help us. Please, God.

It took three hours and twenty minutes to drive into downtown Portland. My mind was racing the whole way, grinding through all the info I did have. It was still too early for the real morning traffic crunch, so I got to the shiny, high-budget new office park on the riverfront that Nicole had designated without getting stuck in morning gridlock. The place wasn't far from the new convention center. I could see it from where I was parked. I could smell the river when I got out of the car.

I left the car in front of the main entrance, exactly as I had been instructed, in spite of the no-parking zone. Inside the building, it was quiet and empty. Just a bald, heavyset security guy seated at the desk.

His gaze fastened on me as I approached. "Can I help you?"

"I need to speak to Franco," I said.

The man scribbled something on a stick-on badge, and handed it to me. "Go to the first elevator bank," he said, his voice expressionless.

"What floor?" I asked.

"Don't worry about that," the guy said, without looking up at me. "It'll take you where you need to go."

I exhaled slowly as I walked to the elevator. I felt like a condemned man walking to the gallows. These were my last moments of freedom. Not that I could call this freedom, while they held the people I loved hostage.

At least Freya was still free, and thank God she had Jed, who would defend her like a junkyard dog. I was fiercely glad of that.

The elevator went down, down, down, without me asking

anything of it. I smiled grimly to myself, at how oddly appropriate that was. I'd gone full circle.

The door opened into the parking garage. Five big guys stood there, pointing guns at me. Pretty much what I'd expected. Banal, even.

One stepped forward with a businesslike air, holding up zip ties and a hood.

"Turn around," he said. "Hands behind your back."

I complied. My hands were fastened. The hood was jerked over my head. It smelled bitter and faintly chemical. I saw very faintly through the weave.

I heard the sound of a car trunk opening, and then I got roughly shoved and stuffed into it. The lid slammed down, and it was absolute darkness. The motor roared to life, and the car started to move.

Into the mouth of the wolf.

CHAPTER 40

Jed

They parked the van a few blocks away, and all three of them peered through the binoculars as they watched Ethan get out of his car, look around, look up at the sky...and walk into the building.

And that was that. No going back. Visual contact lost.

Freya made a low sound in the back of her throat. She had that waxy gray look he disliked. Her lips were bluish. Her face a mask of tension.

The cell phone on the seat of the van Mick was driving buzzed, and he grabbed it, grateful for anything that might distract him from the thought of Holly in that woman's hands. Both he and Freya had experienced her psychotic sadism firsthand.

It was Amos. Freya leaned in to listen as he answered. "Yeah."

"Where are you guys? You nearby?"

"In Northwest Portland," Jed told him. "Ethan just followed Nicole's directions into an office building near the river, on Front Avenue. He's gone now."

"We're not far," Amos said. "Braithwaite is only a few miles away from that. I'm sending our position. We're a half a mile away from Braithwaite, in a parking lot of an asphalt factory. We have eyes in there. When they bring him in, we'll see."

"You took the drones inside?"

"Yes, each one of us piloted a Bumblebee69. Saw some interesting stuff. The place has about twenty armed men. Darius's bee sniffed explosives. I'm sending the image now. We think the ordnance is stored inside a catering van that's parked inside. The logo on the outside says, *Orgoglio & Delizia Fine Catering*. I checked online. Same company that's catering the food for the summit."

"Interesting," Freya murmured.

"Just to have more options, we paid the catering company a visit. We slapped a trace on the undercarriage of every one of their vans parked near their headquarters. If we should need to get one of them, we'll know whichever one is closest."

"Excellent thought," Jed said. "How about Kat and Holly?"

"No sign of them yet," Amos said. "I'm thinking, if they send Kat out to drive that van, they'll probably want to be in constant contact with her visually. Our signal jammer could scramble that connection."

"Good idea. See you at the rendezvous point. It's still early, but we'd better preemptively snag one of those catering vans. If they send Kat to the convention center, Mick and I need to be ready to follow, and you three have to go in for Ethan and Holly."

"Gotcha. On it. Later."

He felt the weight of Freya's eyes, and carefully avoided looking at her.

"Jed," she said.

"What?" he snapped.

"You and Mick will go after the explosives van, the Drakes

are going into the Braithwaite facility for Ethan and Holly...and me? What do I do?"

"You stay at the rendezvous point," he said flatly.

"Ah," she said. "Right. For this, I've been training like crazy in small arms and hand-to-hand combat. To sit alone in a car, and listen to the wind in the trees while literally all the people I love most in the world are fighting desperately for their lives."

"Frey, for fuck's sake—"

"We've been lovers for months, Jed. We've saved each other's lives. We've exchanged rings and deathless vows. But sometimes, I have a feeling you still have no fucking idea what you're dealing with."

He let out a sigh. "That is the God's own truth."

CHAPTER 41

Ethan

They didn't drive me very far, or very fast. The car slowed down after only a few minutes, which made me think we were probably at the Braithwaite facility. I was very close to Kat and Holly right now. Not that I was of any use to them at all, alone, unarmed, hooded, cuffed. In this state, I was just a weapon to hurt them with.

Though I was the one, of the three of us, with the goods these assholes wanted. Chances were good that I was the one who would have to watch someone I loved be hurt.

Don't think about that. No point in it. Moment by moment. Just breathe. Wait. Be alert for openings, opportunity, change. It was all I could do.

They left me in the trunk for what felt like a long time, but my sense of time was skewed. Right now, time was marked only by panting breaths, frantic heartbeats, terrified imaginings. I tried to slow those down, insofar as I could, but I clenched up in wild panic when heavy footsteps came near, and the trunk finally popped open.

I saw light, behind the mesh of the black fabric. Air, at least on my skin. My lungs were still crying out for it, inside that smothering bag.

They grabbed me under the armpits and hauled me out of the trunk and onto my feet, more or less. I was yanked along so swiftly I kept stumbling.

From the feel and sound of the place, I got a sense of wide-open space. Just from the vague outlines I could see through the bag, the way it echoed. It seemed like the machine room of a factory. Massive mechanisms, hoses and tubes and pulleys and panels. My brain kept on in its frantic and probably useless efforts to process information. As if any detail I could glean at this point could help our cause.

It couldn't. I had no cards to play. All I could do was hope for rescue. They had Holly. They had Kat. They had me in a fucking vise, ever since that helicopter left my house.

They shoved me through some kind of big portal, like an airport scanner. I could barely see the outline. Must be the thing that checked for electronic signals. I passed, evidently. Then rough hands put some kind of heavy metal collar around my neck, like a horseshoe shape, snapping it into place. It was painfully small, pinching the side of my neck. When they closed it, I felt a thin wire, cutting across the front of my throat.

Hands groped at the back of my neck. I heard a loud *snick* as a big lock snapped to, connecting me to a chain. I could tell from the rattle, and the slither of the heavy metal links on my back. I let out a gasp as the chain went suddenly taut, jerking me up onto my toes. The wire cut deep. Fuck, that stung. Maybe it was the same device Shane had worn in that video.

The chain stopped short before my toes left the ground, or my own body weight would have slit my throat then and there.

"Cut off his cuffs. And take off his hood. He's harmless, now, and he'll need to use the keyboard for us." It was a man's voice, not one I recognized. Smug, preening.

The hood was wrenched off. I sucked in a deep breath of air, blinking in the light, and taking it all in.

Yes, it was a warehouse. Brightly lit. I saw the machine room I had been dragged through beyond a big open door. The place was huge, with high ceilings, like the warehouse in Tacoma. It took a while for my eyes to adjust enough to see the two people standing in front of me. One was Nicole, and the other was a man, slightly taller than her, and about the same age, early to mid-thirties. He was slim, unremarkable-looking, and wore rimless glasses, and elegant casual clothing. Both were smiling. Their smiles seemed weirdly similar. Maybe it was the madness in their eyes.

"At last," the guy said. "I suppose I should introduce myself. I'm Vincent Egan. And of course, you're acquainted with my sister, Nicole Volange."

I was visibly bewildered. "Sister? Her?"

"Half-sister," Nicole corrected. "His mother was German, and mine was Japanese. Our father really got around. He begat many children."

"But why should I introduce you?" Vincent said, his voice taunting. "I'm sure you remember her. After all, you fucked her, right? Or don't you remember?" He studied my bewilderment, and slanted Nicole a mocking look. "He looks puzzled, Nicole. I would have thought you would be a more interesting lay."

"Get stuffed, Vin," she said, expressionless.

I stared at Nicole, trying in vain to remember any sort of sexual encounter with a woman who looked like her, but felt no spark of recognition. Admittedly, there had been a lot of them over the years, but damn. Not so many that I forgot them completely.

Nicole saw me struggle to remember, and snorted. "I worked for MasterTech for a while, five years ago," she said impatiently. "It was a temporary contract. We hooked up at a tech conference in Vegas. You left my room while I was in the shower."

"Oh." Brief erotic adventures with strangers in conference hotels were a common enough occurrence in my former life, but damn. "So, is that why you're doing this? Because I was a dick the morning after in a Vegas hotel?"

"Not at all," she said. "The experience was unmemorable for me, too. It was your approach to writing algorithms that really turned me on, during my time at MasterTech. So when I heard about SmokeScreen, I had to have it."

"*We* have to have it," Vincent corrected. "We, Nicole. I'm the head of this team. Remember that."

She gave him a brilliant smile. "Oh, yes! Of course, Vin! We. Never doubt it."

Vincent held up a small white remote control. "That collar you're wearing? I designed it. One wrong move, and I push a button that winds you right up to the ceiling, so we can enjoy watching you hang. Or I can push this other button, which tightens the tension of the wire until your throat is cut."

I felt it with my fingers. It exerted a painful, knife-edged pressure.

"Let me show you how it works," Vincent went on briskly. "I'm quite proud of it. Grab the chain, though, and hang on to it tightly, or that wire will garotte you! Up, up, up you go!"

I grabbed the chain over my head just in time to take the pressure off my throat as it jerked me up off my feet. I dangled and swayed six feet off the ground, arms shaking with the effort of keeping the wire on the collar from cutting my throat.

"You put Shane in this thing," I said, my voice breathless and choked. "In that warehouse in Tacoma."

Vincent looked smugly pleased with himself. "Yes, his device was similar. I have a whole line of different collars, actually. I'm a bit of an engineer myself."

I had the sense he was waiting for polite acknowledgement

of his ingenuity, but I was too busy keeping the pressure of that lethal wire from severing my carotid artery. After a while, he huffed, petulantly, and pushed the button, reeling me down. I landed hard, and felt the rush of hot blood down my throat as the wire sliced deeper.

"Vincent gets off on making implements of torture," Nicole remarked. "I'm more practical about that, myself. I always felt like anything can be an implement of torture, with a little creativity. But what do you expect of a guy who pulled worms and bugs apart as a child?"

"I don't care what he did as a child," I said. "Where are Holly, Kat, and Shane?"

Vincent's mouth tightened. He held up the remote and hit the button, and the wire tightened. Fresh blood welled from the cut.

It loosened, and I could breathe again. But the bleeding was constant now.

"Be polite," Vincent said coldly. "You don't ask the questions. You don't make the demands. You do as you're told. No more, no less. Say you're sorry."

I pressed my hand on the bleeding slice. Unable to swallow. "Sorry," I croaked.

Vincent smiled. "That's much better. The chain is just long enough to allow you to sit down in that chair." He pointed to a desk, with a computer on it. "Access SmokeScreen. The real one, not any of that dummy shit like your sister pulled on Nicole the last time. Play any tricks like that, and Holly loses a hand. Are we clear?"

"What do you want me to do with it?" I asked.

"I want you to run a simulation," Vincent said, with a smile that looked almost lascivious. "Tell me how the market will react if a massive bomb takes out the CEOs and CFOs of these forty companies, all at once." He handed me a sheet of paper with a printed list of names. CEOs and CFOs of the biggest companies in the world. Corporations worth tens of billions, or hundreds. "Of course, I've spent the past several months running my own simulations, and making my own projections. That's my personal specialty. But I would be extremely interested in seeing how SmokeScreen's projections match up to them. Nicole's been talking them up for a long time."

Holy shit. He was killing all those people at the summit just to make money? I shook my head, stung by the utter pointlessness of it. "Seriously?" I said. "That's what this fucking psychodrama is all about? A little bit of money?"

Vincent frowned. "Don't judge," he said coldly. "It's a fuckton of money. I am logging every keystroke you make. If you try to pull any dirty tricks, my system will detect it, and Holly will pay. I know how sneaky you Masters can be. Speaking of Holly, Nicole, bring her in. Let her witness these historic events with us."

"Let her go," I said. "I'll do anything you want with Smoke-Screen. I can use it to generate trillions of dollars for you. Or to manipulate any situation to your advantage."

"Of course you'll do that for us," Nicola purred. "But letting Holly go? Just give up all our leverage? Ethan. Seriously? That's an insulting suggestion. Do you think we're stupid?"

I shook my head diplomatically.

"My favorite idea is to lock Holly up all alone in an empty, windowless room, with a camera watching her at all times," Nicole said. "Pass food to her through a drawer in the wall. You can watch her fade away like a flower while you work for us.'"

Her words made my stomach drop. Endless, icy depths.

"Sounds boring," Vincent said. "I would prefer something a little more exciting, dynamic. But there's no rush. We'll work out the perfect motivation for you, and keep you eager and obedient for a long, long time. So? Run the scenario. Now."

The two of them gazed at me, with identical expectant looks on their faces.

What were the odds? Two sadistic psychopaths, same generation, same family? I wondered if they'd been warped into that state on purpose. Chilling thought, but I had no energy to speculate about their family while they were trying to destroy my own.

I put my hands on the keyboard and got to work.

CHAPTER 42

Kat

We were rousted out of the wretched little cell after a few hours. The door burst open, and four big, burly, gun-toting dudes rushed in. Two for Holly. Two for me.

Four? Fuck a duck. Did they not remember the elevator episode? My skills rated at least six of these brainless turds, if not more. If it weren't for Holly being there, held up like a knife to my throat, I could have wiped the floor with these mouth-breathing dipshits with the greatest of ease, and looked around for more.

But that was the whole point, I supposed. Holly was there. Ergo, nothing. All my hard, ceaseless training was totally useless.

Yeah, that was the price of love. Which was to say, ruinously high.

The guys hauled us briskly over to a white van that was parked in a busy loading dock. It was a catering van, I saw, with *Orgoglio & Delizia Fine Catering* in fancy lettering on the side. Nicole stood next to the open door with a wide, self-satisfied smile on her face, beckoning us to look into the open door. Inside was a huge metal box, bolted to the bottom of the van. The top of the box was open. I could see the bundles of explosive material beneath the tangle of wires and circuitry on top.

"Isn't it impressive?" she said brightly. "I built it myself. It'll take out the entire city block, if all goes well, and probably damage all the surrounding buildings, too. Every window in the neighborhood will be broken for miles around. It's epic."

Wow. I stared at her, marveling. The woman was so far out in orbit, she was actually proud of herself.

"I'm just showing it to you to demonstrate that the bomb can't be removed from the vehicle without detonating it. See?" She gestured at the bolts welded to the bottom of the van. "I bolted the box down, and designed the wiring just so. If you detach the box from the van, or if you pull the bomb out of the box, you will trigger it to blow instantly. Just in case you have a misplaced crisis of conscience."

I glanced at Holly, wishing I could cover her eyes and ears. No child should be exposed to this much toxic evil. But Holly looked back at me with eyes that were all too aware. She knew exactly what was happening. No stress fog, no trauma disassociation. The kid's mind was as clear as a bell. I almost regretted it, but I still admired her for it.

"Look at me, not her, Kat," Nicole said sharply. "We don't have much time, so you have to listen carefully. I have designated a very specific route for you to drive on your way to the convention center. I will be watching your progress every second of the way. We will be in constant contact with a videocall. I have a router, a phone, and your tracker, all attached to the dash, so we can watch you being a good girl and doing what you're told, and so you can watch what's going on with your little friend back here. Just in case you need some motivation, at any point in the process."

"What happens to..." I stopped, my voice trailing off. I realized I didn't want Holly to hear the answer to my question. I was afraid to hear it, too.

Too late. Nicole let out a manic titter. "What happens to your precious Holly? Oh, sweetie, that depends entirely on you. First, Holly functions as a lever to control you. And once we've used you up, we'll recycle her, and she'll be used to control her uncle. I'm afraid her life as an extortion tool won't be much fun. Boo-hoo for her!"

"You are super mean," Holly said coldly. "You are the worst."

"Oh, you have no idea," Nicole crooned. "I have not even begun to be mean."

Holly stared back at her stonily. Not giving an inch.

Nicole turned back to me. "Don't deviate from the instructions I give you," she said. "I need for you to be seen in that van by a series of public security cameras. Any funny stuff on the route, and your little friend will pay."

I had no words harsh enough to express my disgust for that, at least not words I would use in front of a nine-year-old, so I swallowed down the hot lump of rage in my throat. "Ethan is going to make you pay," I told her.

"I think not," she said triumphantly. "He's here right now." She gestured to the large main building behind her. "Chained up. Helpless. Completely under our control."

Holly let out a gasp of despair, and a black hole of misery opened up inside me, like a chasm that reached straight down to hell.

Holly's eyes welled full of tears. "Can we see him?"

"Well, you can," Nicole said briskly. "I want him to see you. That's the whole point. But not her." She jerked her chin at me. "She has a job to do. And she should get to it. Right now."

"Can I hug her goodbye?" Holly asked.

"No. We have no time to be sentimental." She gestured imperiously at the van. "Get in. The call is already live. I'll direct you every step of the way."

The look in Holly's eyes made my heart hurt. Nicole saw the glance we exchanged, and chuckled. "Look at you," she said. "I just knew that if we used Holly, you'd be putty in my hands. It's because of your little sister, am I right? Watching her die? Awww. You thought you were so tough. News flash, cookie. Love makes you weak."

I shook my head, not breaking eye contact with Holly. "No," I said, pitching my words just for the little girl. "Love makes you strong. And it's worth any price."

"I'm not actually interested in your prattling bullshit, so get your ass into the van and go," Nicole directed, her voice hardening.

"Goodbye, sweetheart." My voice cracked. "I love you."

"I love you, too." Holly's eyes were streaming.

I got into the van. There was a tablet clamped on to the dash, and the call was already open. I saw movement on the screen.

I turned the key in the ignition, and the image on the tablet jerked, spun, and resolved into Nicole's smirking face, arm wrapped around Holly, hand resting menacingly over the little girl's throat. She waved, and made a fluttering shooing gesture with her fingers. *Run along, now. Be a good little terrorist. Blow up a thousand innocent people. Chop-chop!*

I put the van in gear and pulled out of the building. "You see that gate, straight ahead of you?" Nicole asked. "Go out, and turn right."

The gate was opening. I saw cars passing outside, going about their normal business, with no idea this deadly drama was taking place. I felt disoriented as I drove the van toward the gate. As if it wasn't me driving at all, but some animated doll.

In a sense, I was. My will, hijacked. My heart, used as a weapon against me.

I had a weird moment as I pulled out, turning right onto the street as directed. Here I was, alone in a vehicle with an armed bomb, free to drive any direction I chose—if I had the stomach to pay the price. This dilemma was so fucking cruel.

"I know what you're thinking, Kat." Nicole's voice, from the little speaker on the tablet. The image of her smirking face bounced as she walked. "You're thinking, is it my civic duty to drive this bomb somewhere else, no matter the terrible cost to Holly? And of course, the answer is yes. But just look at this." The camera's eye shifted until it was looking at Holly, her pale face confused and frightened. Nicole's hand whipped out, slapping the little girl so hard, she stumbled and fell.

Nicole grabbed her arm and yanked her back up, making her yelp. There was a red splotch on her cheek, but Holly's wet eyes burned with righteous anger.

"That's a taste, Kat," Nicole said. "Just the tiniest taste of what would follow if you disobeyed me. I'm sure you can imagine how bad things can get, having watched your sisters die. Am I right?" She waited. "Answer me, bitch! I need to know if the audio is working!"

I swallowed, but my mouth was dry. "Yes," I croaked.

"Yes, what?" Nicole shrilled. "Speak up!"

"Yes, I understand. Yes, you are correct. Yes, I can imagine how bad things can get. Yes, you are in control, I promise. Just stop hurting her."

Nicole let out a sharp laugh and kept walking, dragging Holly along.

I tried not to look at the screen. Tried to keep my eyes on the road. Nicole's instructions were constant and detailed. Turn here, change lanes there, pull over here and wait twenty seconds, and on and on. I realized after about fifteen minutes that I was retracing my steps for the third time, going in a big loop through the neighborhood.

"Where am I going?" I asked. "Anywhere in particular?"

"At the moment, you're just being registered by all the security cameras in the area," Nicole said. "You are demonstrating a

SHANNON MCKENNA

final agonizing convulsion of doubt about what you're about to do, which you will be overcoming in just a few minutes. Now pick up some speed here on the straight stretch, and—"

The connection flickered, and broke.

Shit! Pure panic exploded inside me. Nicole was going to think that was me, fighting back. She would think that I'd been the one to break the connection.

I was so horrified at what she might do to Holly, what she might already be doing, I barely braked in time to avoid rear-ending a van that had slewed right into the lane ahead of me and jerked to a stop, forcing me to stop in turn. Fortunately, we were at a red light. Maybe Nicole would assume that I was still being compliant despite the connection failing. I could make a case for having stopped for the light, I hoped.

Huh? The van blocking me was white…and identical to mine. Same logo on the side. I didn't know what it meant. But the way my day was going, it could not be good.

I gasped as Mick and Jed jumped out, running to my van. Mick was holding up some kind of electronic device, like a handheld radio.

I buzzed down the window. "Get that fucking traitor away from me!" I yelled. "That lying son of a bitch sold us out!"

"We know," Jed said. "He confessed. He offered his help, and we needed all the help we could get with these assholes. But we don't have time for that now. What's the status of your surveillance? Is Nicole's team watching you right now? And how?"

"We had a video call going on the tablet, so she can hurt Holly and make me watch in real time," I babbled. "She's following the trace on the dash, but the connection broke, and I know she'll think I did it. I have to do what she says, Jed! She has Holly, and she will hurt her. She's not bluffing. They have Ethan, too."

"He went in of his own accord," Jed said. "The Drakes and

Frey are at the facility, doing what they can. Cross your fingers for them. Go on, get the hell out of that van. We'll take it. Mick is using a signal jammer, but she won't buy it for long."

"But...but I—"

"Now, Kat!" Jed jerked open the door, grabbing my arm, and pulling me out. He reached inside, prying the tablet and router and the trace off the dash. The light turned green and cars began to honk and blare behind us.

Mick followed, continuing to hold the jammer near the router as Jed swiftly situated it onto the dashboard of the van they had been driving, and an understanding of the switcheroo they had planned finally sank into my mind. Along with a thousand horrible images of what would happen to Holly and Ethan if the Drakes and Freya failed. If I proved to have failed them, too.

I stared into Mick's eyes. "You are a piece-of-shit traitor," I told him.

"I know," he said. "I'm sorry. I'm trying to fix it. That's all I can do now."

"The gum on the bottom of the trace won't stick to the dash, but it was next to the screen, so Nicole shouldn't notice," Jed said. "It's lying on the seat next to you. There's also a security badge that we found in the van when we took it. I hope it'll get you inside the conference center garage without any trouble."

"But...but what do I—"

"Buy us time," Jed said urgently. "Drive this to the conference center, park where she tells you, look beaten, look scared, make her feel like she's in control. Buy us all the time you can. We need every fucking second. Go!" He shoved me toward the van.

I got in, and took off. The cars had continued to beep and blare angrily, and by now they were veering around us, giving us glares and middle fingers.

I gave the car gas and lurched forward. In the rearview, I

saw the other van pull a fast, illegal, extremely hazardous U-turn, causing still more braking, still more beeping and general consternation.

I speeded up. The phone flickered on just as I saw the dangling rabbit's foot and religious medals dangling from the mirror. I snatched them up just in time, looped them over the mirror so that they wouldn't bounce and sway in front of the video camera.

Nicole looked furious. "What the fuck happened to you? Your connection broke! You're fucking late now, you lying bitch! What are you trying to pull?"

"Nothing!" I wailed "I didn't do a fucking thing to it myself, I swear!" That assertion had the advantage of being literally true, so I hoped she felt my sincerity.

"You braked!" Nicole said, her voice accusing.

"Well, yeah! I braked to avoid rear-ending a car that slowed down in front of me, and the engine stalled," I explained, slowing to a stop at the red light.

"So why the fuck are you stopping again now?" she demanded shrilly.

"The light's red, Nicole!"

"Just run the fucking light, you dumb cow! You need to get to the conference center right now! It's not like you'll ever have to pay the traffic ticket!"

Huh. Whatever. I accelerated, right out into the stream of ongoing traffic, weaving back and forth. Brakes screeching, cars skidding, horns blaring. I heard the crunch of at least one accident behind me. They'd be cursing my name back there, if only they knew it, and I was sorry, but hey. Extenuating circumstances and all.

When I reached a straight stretch and edged my way back into my lane, I floored it and drove like a bat out of hell, leaving the noisy mess far behind me.

The shiny new conference center loomed in the distance. I

had a bad moment at the entrance to the parking garage. Every-thing depended on whether the most recent theft committed by Jed and Mick of the *Orgoglio & Delizia Fine Catering* van had been noticed and remarked upon yet. But the guy just looked at me, the van, glanced at the security badge I held up, and waved me through.

"I'm inside," I said to Nicole.

"I can see that," Nicole snapped. "Listen carefully. Park in the E Section. Next to the inner wall."

I followed the signs, found a parking spot in the area Nicole had directed me to, and pulled the van to a halt. My heart raced, my head spun, and I wanted to vomit.

On the screen, Nicole had flung her arm around Holly. She was smiling triumphantly. The moment of truth was fast approaching. My own personal version of hell. Any second now, my ability to play for time would end. Everything was completely outside of my control now. Then again, it probably always had been.

Tears ran down my face. Ugly-crying on camera for Nicole's entertainment was the last thing I wanted, but I couldn't stop. I wanted to stay strong for Holly, but I couldn't nail down my feelings anymore. I'd lost the ability. I was just one big naked beating heart, now, shrinking away from all the fresh pain that was about to be inflicted.

Vincent appeared on the screen. He also looked excited, bright red spots on his cheeks. "Nicole, show Kat her lover one last time, so she can say goodbye," he said, his voice affable, as if doing me a favor. "It's the least we can do!"

The camera image swirled and spun in a dizzying arc, and then centered on Ethan. I gazed at him hungrily. He was harnessed, chained, wearing some kind of diabolical collar. It stretched a tiny wire across his throat that had already sliced into his skin. His neck and chest were red with blood, but he was alive. And he didn't look frightened or defeated.

He looked pissed.

Ethan's eyes burned into mine. No tender goodbyes from that quarter. He was looking at nothing but pain, slavery, torture in his future, but he hadn't given in.

The rage in his eyes heartened me. After all, this guy was wicked smart. Smarter than those pinheaded assholes could even imagine. Ethan Masters' engine ran on pure rocket fuel. Theirs ran on pond scum and festering shit. If he could just stay alive somehow, he would eventually outsmart them, and save Holly. I was dead sure of it.

"Well, Kat?" Nicole prompted sweetly. "Say goodbye, Kat. It's time!"

I looked straight into his eyes. "I love you," I told him. "Holly, too."

Ethan didn't respond. I couldn't look away from him. The eye contact was like an electrical connection, and it was all rushing through my brain, the brilliant aliveness I'd felt these past few days since I met the guy. Since my life blew up.

No regrets. Even if he thought I was a demented terrorist, I was glad I knew how it felt to feel again. To love again. It was all worth it. "Goodbye," I whispered.

Vincent held out a flip phone. "He's started the keynote speech," he said to Nicole. "And he sounds very pleased with himself. Want to do the honors?"

"I'd be delighted," Nicole purred. She started punching in numbers, sparing me a triumphant grin. "Bye-bye, Payback Bitch! Let's get this party started!"

CHAPTER 43

Jed

oly fuck. What have we done? A panicked voice in his mind kept asking that burning question, over and over again with increasing intensity.

The right thing. So don't whine. Only response he could offer. Cold comfort.

Goddamn. Yes, he would do his duty, no matter the cost. But something inside him screamed out loud for what he was sacrificing. This precious thing he'd found with Freya. The shining miracle of it. The adventures, the laughter, the fights. Passionate nights and lazy mornings. Long years, to pass with her. Winters and summers, growing old together. Kids, maybe. And Holly. Already, she was like his own child.

His friends, too. They had been his salvation, back when he was young and dumb and monumentally fucked up. Ethan, Shane, all of the Unredeemables. Even Mick, for fuck's sake. Mick hadn't redeemed himself for what he'd done, not by a long shot, but here he was, voluntarily driving the car bomb from hell, so he was definitely making an effort. Call it a down payment on redemption. A guy had to start somewhere.

Mick was bug-eyed, sweating, breathing hard. His hands were white-knuckled, clamped down hard on the wheel as they sped past factories, warehouses, parking lots, containers, water towers, mountains of crushed rock. Finally, they had reached an area that was emptier, more wide open. Good for the rest of the world, but it still sucked for them. Lots of green, various parking lots. He saw tugboat docks at the shore of the river, boats docked alongside them. The clock had ticked over. It was now after twelve.

"What time is that keynote speech supposed to start?" he asked.

"It's well underway," Mick said grimly. "Make your peace with Jesus, buddy. Those fuckheads will blow this thing sky high any time now, so live every moment."

Jed processed a fresh jolt of panic as Mick directed the van suddenly off the main road and onto a smaller, older one, that was ill-kept, full of potholes and cracks and broken cement. Every bouncing jolt made him intensely aware of the massive quantity of ordnance packed into the van behind them.

"We were so focused on getting Kat out of her rolling bomb, we never planned what we were going to do with this thing," he said. "So, ah..."

"I'm open to suggestions." Mick's voice was curt. "But if you don't have any brilliant ideas, don't distract me."

Thump. We veered off cracked, bleached asphalt and accelerated onto a dirt road that paralleled the river. There was a chain-link fence between us and the water.

The van rattled and bumped as we sped along in grim silence. The river was visible through a fringe of trees, about a hundred yards away. There were buildings all around them. Maybe far enough away to be out of the immediate blast range, maybe not. They hadn't had a chance to study the bomb itself, so who the fuck knew.

The road choked off abruptly at another chain-link fence,

delineating a big lot full of containers and trucks. Mick skidded to a sudden halt at the big metal traffic barrier that blocked the road. "Move that thing out of my way," he said. "Quick!"

"Mick—"

"Fucking move it, Jed!" he bellowed. "We don't have time to argue!"

He jumped out, dragged the heavy thing out of the roadway, but when he reached for the car door, it *thunked* shut. The door lock was engaged.

Jed grabbed the handle. Rattled it. "What the fuck?" he yelled. "Mick!"

The window rolled, just an inch. "This job doesn't require two people," Mick said. "Get behind one of those containers. Tell Holly I love her. That I'm sorry."

"Mick!" he yelled. "Don't! We'll just leave the van here, and run like hell!"

"Too late." The van surged forward, bumping and rattling over the uneven track through the dirt toward the river. Mick was heading for one of the docks. It looked deserted. It stretched way out into the water. No tugboats were docked there.

Jed sprinted for the nearest container, his sense of impending disaster getting sharper with every step. He dove behind it for whatever shelter it could give. Maybe the blast wave would knock it down over him and crush him where he lay. Who knew. Who could possibly know any goddamn thing for sure, ever. God, what a clusterfuck.

He crawled to the edge, peering around it. The van was on the dock. He faintly heard the rattle of the weathered, water-swollen wooden planks as Mick drove faster, and faster...and then pitched off the end.

He was too far away to hear the splash, the gurgle.

The van went down fast. Mick must have opened the windows so it wouldn't float. There was nothing else to look at after the van had disappeared, so he put his arms over his head, eyes squeezed shut.

Memories rushed through his mind. Those tours in Afghanistan with Mick. They had trusted each other. Had each other's backs, time and time again. His throat hurt, like someone was squeezing it in an iron claw. Maybe Mick could swim free of the van. If he got out of the water in time, he could be on land before the blast wave could—

Boom.

The explosion shook very the earth. He looked up, saw water fountaining into the air. The dock was blown up, pieces of wood rising up, up, up...and then arching back down again to the ground, *thud, thud, thud.*

A huge piece of some wooden structure landed heavily, and bounced just a few feet from him, knocking dirt into his face.

His chest heaved with sobs as the river water pounded down around him.

CHAPTER 44

Freya

The Drakes didn't want her to come along but goddammit, it wasn't up to them. Her brother and niece were trapped inside that hellhole. No way was she hanging back when the people she loved most in the world were in mortal danger. The options of the Drakes brothers at this point were to let her come, or else tie her up and leave her helpless and trussed, a sitting duck for Nicole's goons. They couldn't do that to her, but they were furiously angry and unhappy about it.

Too fucking bad.

The plan was the best they could do, with so little intel, and under such time pressure. Using the info Darius's drones had gleaned, they would creep inside the place, thin their enemies' ranks until the element of surprise was lost, and then, it was anything goes. They did whatever they could to create mayhem and disruption, with pistols, flash bangs, grenades, stun batons. No retreat, no delay, or Ethan and Holly would vanish into the same black hole that had swallowed Shane.

She was desperately glad to have something challenging to

do. The love of her life was stealing a van with a massive bomb in it, driving it off to who the fuck knew where. Her brother and niece were in the hands of sadistic psychopaths.

It was too much. It was driving her wild. Doing something about it was preferable to thinking about it. Preferably something risky and ill-advised.

They were hoping the security of Braithwaite would not be too high. After all, this site was chosen only for its proximity to the convention center. Those assholes wouldn't want to leave evidence behind, so they would be packing light. As soon as they executed their plan, they would blast out of there, leaving as little trace as possible. There would be no time to dismantle a complicated security apparatus.

Darius was piloting one of his smaller drones, armed with a soft disc of sticky putty clutched in its tiny mechanical grip. The disc was no bigger than a quarter, but the tiny machine struggled to carry even that much weight to the height of the video camera. They watched the monitor, not breathing as he maneuvered it into place in front of the camera...*yes!* The disc draped over the security camera's lens and stuck there, creating a blind spot. They could only hope no one had been watching while the drone did its work. That with things all coming together, their enemies would be too distracted to be watching the monitors.

They moved fast into the blind spot that the Drakes had carefully chosen, the one that had the most cover once they got through the fence. There were various cars and machines and containers to weave around, and dart behind. They hoped the spot was not surveilled by another camera they had not seen.

Hope, hope, hope. That was a crap-ton of hope to rely upon. Hope was a shitty substitute for intel, but they had no choice. Love demanded what it demanded.

Amos worked the bolt cutters on the chain-link, and peeled

back a chunk of the fencing. Darius first, then Remy, then her, and Amos taking up the rear.

The Drakes darted ahead of her. She saw a flash of movement to her right, as Darius dragged a man around the corner of a container. A choked grunt as he bashed the guy's head with a baton, dropped him to the ground, and kept moving. A flurry of movement, to her left. Remy had his arm clamped around a guy's neck. A squeeze, a jerk, a thud as he hit the ground, and Remy moved smoothly on, like a shadow.

They crept closer, darting around corners, crouching behind barriers. A man turned a corner in front of her, eyes widening in shock. He opened his mouth to yell.

She stabbed her stun baton right into his throat, zapping him.

Down he went, gurgling and twitching. Someone behind her shouted.

Bam. The bullet hit the back of her vest, knocking out her wind. *Bam*, again, and she stumbled down onto one knee. She spun around, swung up the gun, pulled the trigger.

Bam. The guy running at her went down, clutching his neck, like a tree crashing down. Blood spurted, spattering her face. She struggled out from under his weight, and ran, soaked. Bullets zinged and popped. Men were shouting, cursing—

Boom.

The bomb. Oh, fuck. Jed. Oh, my darling. Please don't be dead. Please.

Whatever had happened was done, for better or for worse. That knowledge broke something loose in her. She ran full tilt toward the main building, shooting wildly. A harrowing battle shriek tore out of her throat. Bullets whizzed past her ears. Another thumped hard against the Kevlar vest that covered her back, making her stumble forward. *Bam*, a streak of hot fire sliced across her thigh.

She just kept on running.

CHAPTER 45

Kat

Boom.

Whoa. The bomb had gone off...somewhere. Not too near, but not too far, either. The sound had been muffled by all the layers of concrete, but the vibration shook the whole building. I thought of Jed and Mick. Hoped they were okay.

What the hell was happening over at Braithwaite? The webcam had been knocked askew, and all I could see in the video-call was the high metal beams of the room's ceiling, and a piece of paper that had fallen partway across the camera's view. I heard noise. Yelling, shouting, men's and women's voices. Thuds, crashes, gunshots. Shit was going down, this minute, and I was stuck in this damned hotel, useless to them.

And through it all, I heard Holly's shrill, constant screaming.

Keep screaming like a teakettle, baby. That way I know you're still alive.

I had to scream too. I would explode if I didn't let off some steam. People walking past my van from their car shrank back at my banshee howl, and took off in a nervous, shuffling run to put distance between us. I revved the van and sped past them, tires squealing as I took the turns on my way up to the exit.

When I got there, the bar was down, and the security guy had a look on his face that I recognized instantly. I was busted. He gestured imperiously for me to stop. He'd heard from his boss, or the caterers, or the cops, or maybe all of them. The jig was up.

"Stop!" he yelled. "You're not supposed to be in that van! That van is stolen, and you are not authorized to be in here! Get out of the vehicle right now!"

Fuck that. I mouthed "*sorry*" at him as I gunned the engine, and crashed through the bar, crumpling the hood, cracking the windshield. I bounced up and veered out onto the street, taking the turn on two wheels. Cars braked to avoid me, honking furiously.

I floored it, going as fast as I knew how to drive. At this point, the more cops they sent after me, the happier I would be.

We needed all the help we could get.

CHAPTER 46

Ethan

B*oom.*
   Kat. Oh no, no, no. Kat.
   Wait. Wait. It took a shocked, timeless second to realize what had not happened.

Huh? The man up on the screen who was giving the keynote address at that conference was still talking. The speaker had reacted to the sound of the bomb, had made a comment about it. He looked worried. There had been a nervous murmuring from the crowd. They had all heard the explosion, but from afar.

Kat had been in the hotel garage. They had shown her to me there. But the hotel was not reduced to rubble. Owen Halliwell, CEO of Halliwell Enterprises, was talking, smiling. If Halliwell was alive, Kat was, too. Terrified joy almost overcame me.

Nicole and Vincent exchanged horrified glances. "What the hell?" Vincent sputtered. "What happened?"

Nicole walked over to me, and slapped me hard, making the wire bite even deeper. "What the fuck did you assholes do?"

she yelled. *Slap, slap.* "How did you do that? You fuckers! Fuck you!"

Gunfire, outside. Then muffled pops of a silenced pistol, and then return fire, not silenced. "Holly, get down!" I yelled.

I did not have that option. The length of the chain didn't give me that kind of range.

The first through the door was Freya, screaming bloody murder, her face spattered with blood. Nicole shot at her, but she just stumbled and came on. Holly leaped up, flinging random objects at Nicole and Vincent, screaming like a tin whistle.

I grabbed my chain and leaped up onto the desk, aiming a kick at Vincent's head. I was too far to land it, the chain held me back, so it was just a glancing blow, but he yelled in outrage, and lunged for the remote. He hit the button that started to reel me up into the rafters, and I grabbed the chain, in an effort to keep the pressure of that wire from cutting my throat as it yanked me up—and up, my feet dangling...

Bam. Bam.

I crashed right back down among the scattered office furniture. Frey had shot through the chain. My little sister was a crack shot. Who the fuck knew.

Vincent realized I was loose, and pounced on Holly, putting her in a chokehold. She wiggled, struggled, and he howled in fury as she bit him, startling him. She broke free and ran. He gave chase, and I leaped up and followed, chain trailing and rattling behind me. No way was that shithead troll going to touch my little girl.

Holly darted into the machine room, slithering into some opening between two big metal vats, where Vincent couldn't fit, cowering behind them.

The turd lifted a gun, aiming at Holly. I leaped for him, knocking the gun out of his hand, wrapping the broken end of the chain around his throat. Wrenching it tight.

SHANNON MCKENNA

He made coughing, gurgling sounds. His eyes bulged. He clawed at my hands.

I wanted to kill this bastard so badly, but he knew where Shane was, goddammit, so I flung him down to the ground.

"You and I are going to talk," I said. "About my brother."

Vincent pulled his hand out of his pocket, his bloody teeth showing in a big, grin. "You won't be talking to anyone ever again, idiot." He pushed the button, just as I realized he was holding the small white remote. Oh *fuck*.

The wire tightened...and tightened. Blood started to flow. Shit. I was done.

Bam. Vincent went limp, but I was down, crumpled to the floor now, barely able to breathe. Freya skidded up to me sideways, on her knees. She'd shot him.

"Jesus, Ethan," she babbled. "Your throat. That thing is cutting your throat. How do I get it off?"

"Remote," I whispered. "Vincent...holding it."

She leaped for Vincent, scrabbling around his motionless body. I was weak from blood loss, but the wire hadn't severed an artery yet, or I'd be dead already.

Freya dropped to her knees beside me again. "Fuck!" she wailed. "There are three buttons, and nothing is written on them! It's like, the lady and the fucking tiger! How do we know which one tightens and which one loosens?"

"We don't," I whispered, taking it from her hand. It was smeared with blood. Hers, mine, Vincent's.

"What are you doing?" she shrilled.

"I'll push it," I mouthed. "So, if I fuck it up and die, it's not you. It was me."

"Goddammit, Ethan!" She was crying, her face distorted.

"Love you, baby sis," I whispered. "Proud of you." I pushed a button for the thirty-three percent odds. Nothing. Time for fifty-fifty odds. I pushed the second button...

...and the pressure eased. I sagged against her, panting. And alive.

"Oh, dear God," she whispered. "Dear God, Ethan." She grabbed the front of my shirt, yanking it up, wadding a handful of cloth and pressing it to my neck. "Hold that on your throat. I've got to call an ambulance. Get you to a vascular surgeon. Right fucking now."

"Hey," I whispered, trying to press the cloth to my throat. "Holly. Where's Holly?"

We both looked around, frantically. I opened my mouth, trying to call, but my throat stung from the slash.

"Holly!" Freya howled. "Holly! Where are you?"

I tried to get to my feet, but they buckled, dumping me onto the floor again. "Go after her," I said. "I don't see Nicole, either. Run!"

"Press that shirt against your throat!" Freya yelled back, as she took off at a dead sprint.

CHAPTER 47

Kat

As luck would have it, the gate was grinding open the moment I arrived, so I bounced right through it, accelerating when I saw the black Mercedes sedan on the road in front of me. Nicole was driving, her face wild-eyed and blood-streaked.

My mind spun, trying to think of what to do now. *Wipe her off the face of the earth, idiot, what else? Floor the accelerator. End that bitch. At all costs.*

Yes. Nicole Volange was stopping all of her evil shit right... fucking...*now.*

Nicole's eyes widened in panic as I sped toward her. Then Holly's face popped up from behind her, from the backseat. Holly's face was streaked with blood.

Shit! I braked, wrenching the van sharply to the left, skid-ding into their car sideways.

A huge *crunch.* Glass shattering. *Oh Holly, baby. Please be okay.*

I stumbled out of the van, blinking the blood out of my

eyes. I'd bonked my head. Nicole staggered out of her Mercedes, and came at me, wild-eyed, her hair in blood-stiffened elf-locks.

She had me on the defensive from the start, forcing me to block rapid-fire kicks and punches. I got in a few good ones, but she got in more. I was slowed down, clumsy. I risked getting in close, stabbed my fingers into her eye. Was rewarded by a shriek of rage, but she recovered fast, snatching my hand and torquing it until I was bent over, dragged off balance. Fuck. I was exhausted, concussed, seeing double, and she knocked me against her car and forced me down to the ground, pounding me.

Then she was on top of me, squeezing my throat with brutal strength. I fought her, clawing at her hands, but I felt everything start to get dimmer, quieter, farther away.

But even from that faraway place, I heard the wet *crunch*. Then sudden silence.

Something landed on me heavily. Hot, wet, inert. I struggled, gasping for air, until it slid off me to one side, thudding to the ground.

As air came back, and awareness, I saw Nicole, lying unconscious. Our bodies were touching. I shrank away from the contact as if she were toxic waste.

Then I saw Holly standing over us, swaying. Her face was blank and shocked. She held a rusty piece of rebar, bloody on one end. She'd hit Nicole on the head.

I dragged myself to my feet, nudging gingerly at Nicole with my foot to see just how genuinely down for the count she was. I wanted no more surprises, thank you.

She showed no signs of movement, so I dared to turn away and gently pry the length of rebar from Holly's cold, shaking hands. She couldn't let go, so I had to peel her rigid, claw-like fingers off the thing one at a time.

When she dropped the rebar, I pulled her into my arms. I heard sirens in the distance. Saw the strobe of police lights.

Good. Bring them on. The more the merrier.

Then Holly started to cry, and damned if she didn't get me sniffling right along with her. Tears were contagious.

Then Nicole made a sound, that jerked our heads around, sucking in a panicky breath. She was choking, panting, and then convulsing, her feet drumming, body arching. She started to foam at the mouth. I left her to it, pulling Holly's face against my chest. "Don't look at her," I said, backing away. Letting karma take its course.

Nicole went still, her face turned toward us, eyes wide and blank and red-rimmed. She had been weeping blood. She looked monstrous.

"It's over," I whispered to Holly. "She's done."

And just like that, so were we. We sagged down together onto the ground and just rocked, hugging. We were oh, so done. Too done for questions, or to even notice or care about the flashing lights, the yelling, the people running around in a dither.

I roused myself only when I saw Ethan being wheeled by on a gurney. His neck and chest were blood-soaked, but his eyes were open and sharp. Thank God.

He saw me and Holly, and lifted his hand as he went by, with a ghost of a smile. I wanted to run after him, but Holly was wrapped around me, and I couldn't toss her off.

Then Freya appeared. She was battered and bloody, but ambulatory. She grabbed us both, hugging us so tightly poor little Holly was practically squished.

Predictably, that hug devolved into yet another sob-fest, this time a three-way, and even more intense. Freya kept thanking me weepily for saving Holly, which made no sense to me. I'd done it purely for myself, and Holly. It would have killed me if they'd gotten her. I couldn't go through that again. I'd rather be fried by a bolt of lightning. I was a protector of girls, at the core of my being, because of my sisters. Life had forged me into that by fire and blood, and I had no other choice.

Nor did I want one, I realized, as I rocked in Freya's and Holly's tight embraces.

CHAPTER 48

Kat

I opened my eyes to a dim, unfamiliar room. Not a hospital room. Or not exactly. Some kind of hybrid room. I was having that weird sensation where you forget everything; not just where you are, but who you are. Or maybe that was just my jacked-up, stress-rattled brain. Me, running away from myself. Who knew.

Then I felt the warm weight on my shoulder. It was Holly, fast asleep. Her tousled head was cradled in the crook of my arm. That explained how numb it was, but it was worth it, for the soft rush of tenderness that rose up in me.

It all rushed back, in a torrent. That brave, tough little sweetheart. Looking at her made the truth of who I was spring to the front of my consciousness with a vengeance. I was Kat Banner, formerly Francesca Lovero, and I would go to any lengths to punish and destroy slime-sucking assholes who preyed on women and kids. For Gabri's and Raffi's sakes.

That was who I was. It was good to know it, and embrace it. It steadied me.

The flood of emotion practically drowned me as I looked at

her. The tenderness, the anger, the wonder. That kid was a freaking miracle, and she had been so badly used, I wanted to kill someone to compensate for it. But I had absolutely failed to do so. Holly had been forced to take matters into her own hands. Damn, what a brave, excellent kid.

I hated how she looked so pinched and ashy pale. The scrapes and bruises on her little face stood out in sharp relief. Her forehead was bandaged, from when Nicole had hit her head before shoving her into the escape car. But that could not keep Holly down.

None of the wounds I saw were serious, but no one knew better than me about damage on the inside. Wounds no one could see, that never really healed. They just ended up making people impatient and frustrated with you. Wounds that left you lonely and bewildered. Nightmares, stress flashbacks, permanently hiked up stress levels. Anxiety, depression, and God knows what all else. It hurt to think of it.

I wished I could suffer it for her. I was already an expert. I could take it.

A hurt, terrified nine-year-old girl had found the nerve to bash that monstrous harpy on the head with a chunk of rebar. She was a freaking boss, and yet, it was so wrong that Holly had been the one forced to deal that blow.

I looked around the room, struggling to remember what had happened, and in what sequence. The recent past was a blur, after the painkilling drugs, but the time before that was disordered and fragmented too. Like a pile of broken glass shards.

I wondered, in a detached way, if I would have problems with the law, after all the awful stuff Nicole had pinned on me when she made me her fall guy. But whatever. My conscience was clear, and I didn't have the energy to worry about it. Later for that.

The room had some hospital equipment, but it had more

the air of a luxury hotel. Probably some high-end clinic for the super-rich. They got sick, too, I supposed.

That thought reminded me of Ethan, and that bleeding cut across his throat. Someone had given me a shot that scrambled my brains before I could follow up on his status. I couldn't bully info out of anybody in that soft, floating state.

But I was awake now, and I had to see how he was doing. The man had walked into that hellhole for Holly and me, without hesitation, alone, unarmed. Which was ass-for-brains stupid of him, but full of heart. And I loved him for it.

No, I just loved him, period. Every minute that passed, I was more aware of this new state of being. So unshielded. Like my heart was just running around buck naked outside my body, uncontrolled, unprotected. It felt so risky, so dangerous, but it wasn't as if I had any choice. I was destined to love him. Help-less to stop.

Same went for Holly. I'd be stuck to that kid like glue from here on out.

I took exquisite care in extricating my arm from under Holly's head. I nestled her up in the pillows, tucking the blanket tight around her. I'd just check on Ethan and hurry right back. I did not want my girl to wake up all alone in a strange place after this shitshow. I had on a knee length, soft jersey night shirt, thank God, not an ass-baring hospital gown, but I had no memory of putting it on, or having it put on me.

I crept down the hall, silent on my bare feet, and opened up the first door. It was Amos, his shoulder and arm heavily bandaged, with an IV drip next to him. I was grateful to see him alive. I was grateful to the cavalry, for charging in and saving us, against all hope. Even Mick had come through in the end. Amazingly.

Oh, shit. *Jed.* What had he and Mick done with the bomb? Where had they taken it? The fear that Jed had been in that van when it blew shook me to the bone. He and Mick had been so valiant, sweeping in to take that terrible burden from me. Jed was a good guy, brave and selfless, and I did not want Freya to be a widow. She'd just now found love.

In the next room I found Ethan, and my heart swelled and thudded with joyful excitement to see him. I crept forward and gazed down, drinking him in. He was alive. His throat was bandaged, and he showed some general superficial damage, but he looked intact, thank God. He was gorgeous to me, even all fucked up.

His beautiful, strong hand lay on the blanket. I had to make sure he was real, so I laid my own over his. It was icy cold, so I slid my other hand underneath to warm it.

His dark eyes opened, startling me.

"Oh crap," I said softly. "I'm sorry I woke you. I know you need to rest. I just had to make sure you were okay. That you were actually here."

He formed words with his mouth, but made no sound. I leaned down and put my ear to his mouth. "Can't talk out loud right now," he whispered. "But I'm fine. Or I will be, when this heals up."

"I woke up with Holly in my bed." I dragged a chair over next to the bed.

He smiled at Holly's name. "You're her idol," he mouthed.

"The feeling is mutual," I said fervently. "That kid is unstoppable."

He gestured for me to lean closer again. "You okay?" he asked.

"Fine," I assured him. "Perfectly fine. Sore, and tired, that's all. Hey, I hate to make you talk, but what about Jed?"

"Good," Ethan whispered. "Fine."

I let out a heaving sigh of relief. "Oh, thank God."

"Mick locked Jed out of the van and drove it off a tugboat dock, into the Willamette River," Ethan whispered. "Blew the shit out of the dock. Tons of water, blown up into the air.

Pure dumb luck nobody else was there. No casualties but one."

"Ah." I was silent for a moment. "So...that means Mick ..."

"Yes," he said. "Gone."

"Oh." I tried, without much success, to process that. "I was so angry at him for setting me up. And sacrificing Holly in favor of his uncle. But I'm sorry he had to go that way. Maybe... maybe he made up for it. Partly. With that gesture."

"I say maybe he did," Ethan murmured. "Almost, anyway. No other losses. Some injuries, nothing life-threatening. Vincent, dead. Nicole, dead."

"Good," I said, with grim satisfaction. "Excellent. Wiped out of existence. You don't even have to worry about putting them in jail. Or keeping them there."

"Nope," he mouthed. "No one to question, either. We're no closer to Shane. The goons they hired don't know anything. The ones left alive, anyhow."

Ouch. "Shit," I said. "I'm so sorry about that. Hey, Nicole had convulsions, after Holly hit her in the head. She was actually foaming at the mouth. I wonder what that was all about. It wasn't anything Holly did."

He gestured for me to lean closer again. "Poison tooth," he murmured into my ear. "Vincent wore something that monitored his vitals. When he died, it sent a signal to her tooth. Burst it open."

"Holy cow." I was genuinely shocked. "That is some twisted shit."

I read his fervent agreement in his eyes.

"Well, then," I said. "I expect we have our work cut out for us now. Explaining this convoluted crap to the Man will not be fun. They won't like the way you took action on your own. Though I will always maintain that you had no choice."

"That's for sure." Ethan's lips twitched. "Yes, the police will disapprove of my choices. But I can face anything if you're with me."

My hand tightened on his. "Wait," I said. "About that. Are you still sure you still want to take on all my problems, after what just happened? Once the press comes down on us, my enemies will spot me. It's a mathematical certainty. There's no way to hide from the media blitz about to hit. Haven't you had a belly full of this shit? Aren't you afraid of your family being in danger? I'd understand it, if you were. For real."

His eyes burned with intensity. "It's my problems that put you in danger, Kat. Not the other way around." His whisper was intense. "You crushed them. You're a goddess. We'd be dead without you. Holly would be gone. We'd still be in hell."

"Oh, get real," I said. "All I did was get my ass captured and stuck in a cage."

"No. You had Holly's back. You stayed at her side. You drove that van to the hotel for her. You came back to save her. You always put her first. Thank you for that."

"You don't have to thank me," I said. "I did it for Holly's sake. That kid is my hero. She saved me, too. You all did. This isn't the first time I've been in a fiery-pits-of-hell kind of situation, but the last time, no one came to my rescue, and the devil won that round. I survived, but only just. This time, a whole army of brave, strong, excellent people swooped down and kicked the devil's ass. And that is so, so much better."

His hand tugged, and I leaned to listen. "This thing on my neck is really cramping my style," he whispered. "I want to sweep you off your feet. Kiss you madly. Fuck you all night long. But they told me I can't move yet. Told me very sternly."

I leaned down and dropped a feather-light kiss on his scratched, bruised cheekbone. "I'll wait," I said simply. "That scenario is worth sticking around for."

We just gazed at each other, our eyes doing all the talking. I wanted to leap on him and cover him with kisses, but I wasn't messing with that oh-so-carefully patched up wound, so I kissed his hand, pressing it to my cheek. My sopping-wet cheek. Damn it. Enough with the tears, already. I spotted a box of tissues, and grabbed a few. "Sorry," I muttered, sniffling. "I billed myself as a real tough broad, but I've gone sappy lately. Everything makes me cry. That's your fault, you know. You made me all emotional."

"Lay it on me. I'm emotional, too. I love when you're a tough broad, and I love the sappy emotional stuff, too. I love all of you, Kat. So you'll stick with me? Forever?"

"Hell, yeah," I told him, sniffling. "Buckle up, buddy. You're in for a wild ride."

His smile spread into a grin. "Sounds like pure heaven to me."

WANT to know how Kat and Ethan deal with the Petruzzi family? Join my newsletter to find out! You'll find many juicy bonus stories featuring beloved characters, available only to my newsletter subscribers! Click here to join, at: http://shannonm ckenna.com/connect.php.

...and see what happens next to Kat and Ethan!

MEET SHANNON MCKENNA

Shannon McKenna is the NYT and USA TODAY bestselling author of over thirty novels, ranging from sexy contemporary romance to action packed, turbocharged romantic thrillers. She loves tough and heroic alpha males, heroines with the brains and guts to match them, terrifying villains who challenge them to their utmost, adventure, blazing sensuality, and most of all, the redemptive power of true love.

Since she was small she has loved abandoning herself to the magic of a good book, and her fond childhood fantasy was that writing would be just like that but with the added benefit of being able to take credit for the story at the end. The alchemy of writing turned out to be messier than she'd ever dreamed, but whatever, she loves it anyway and hopes that readers enjoy the results of her experiments. She loves to hear from her readers. Contact her by email at her website, shannon mckenna.com, or find her on Facebook to keep up with all her news! Follow her on Bookbub to get new release and discount alerts!

If you'd like to know when new books will come out, and hear about discounts, giveaways and promos, join Shannon's newsletter. She has special goodies waiting for you there... exclusive bonus stories that are just for her subscribers, and a free Obsidian Files novella! She hopes to see you there!

ALSO BY SHANNON MCKENNA

The Unredeemables

Master of Lies

Master Of Secrets

Master Of Chaos

The Hellbound Brotherhood Series

Hellion

Headlong

Hellbent

Heedless

Havoc

The Obsidian Files Series

Right Through Me

My Next Breath

In My Skin

Light Me Up

The McClouds & Friends Series

Behind Closed Doors

Standing In The Shadows

Out Of Control

Edge Of Midnight

Extreme Danger

ALSO BY SHANNON MCKENNA

The Unredeemables

Master of Lies

Master Of Secrets

Master Of Chaos

The Hellbound Brotherhood Series

Hellion

Headlong

Hellbent

Heedless

Havoc

The Obsidian Files Series

Right Through Me

My Next Breath

In My Skin

Light Me Up

The McClouds & Friends Series

Behind Closed Doors

Standing In The Shadows

Out Of Control

Edge Of Midnight

Extreme Danger